Heavenly Romance

by Jeffrey T. Bristol

Trilogy Christian Publishers

A Wholly Owned Subsidiary of Trinity Broadcasting Network

2442 Michelle Drive

Tustin, CA 92780

For information, address Trilogy Christian Publishing

Rights Department, 2442 Michelle Drive, Tustin, Ca 92780.

For information about special discounts for bulk purchases, please contact Trilogy Christian Publishing.

Cover designed with assets from Freepik and Unsplash

10 9 8 7 6 5 4 3 2 1

Library of Congress Cataloging-in-Publication Data is available.

B-ISBN#: 979-8-89333-071-7

E-ISBN#: 979-8-89333-072-4

DEDICATION

I first and foremost dedicate this novel to God. He was the person who inspired me and downloaded the idea into my mind and spirit to write this novel in the first place. I wouldn't have written this novel if it weren't for God. He gets all of the glory. I secondly want to dedicate this novel to my mother. She has had such a tremendous and life-giving influence on me throughout all of the years of my life. My mother is the most godly, tenacious, tender, compassionate, hard-working, and loving person I know, even with the numerous hardships that she has endured. She has been the person second to God who has helped me improve in learning how to walk again. My mother has also greatly helped me in several other areas of my life.

TABLE OF CONTENTS

INTRODUCTION

Meet Ben Lawson and his family. Ben was born in 1984. His parents, Dave and Leslie, in addition to Ben and his younger brother, Josh, are devout Christians and live a godly family lifestyle in the present year of 2001. They live in a suburb in Evart, Michigan. Ben starts out as a sixteen, almost seventeen-year-old teen who enjoys life and eagerly anticipates all of what God has in store for him in his life. Josh has had some difficulties fitting in in high school and finding his purpose in life. All the while the two teens' parents care for and teach them how to live godly lives, the two of them make time to connect and grow in their marriage in addition to working at their jobs. This family is put to the test after Ben has a life-altering incident in his life that takes away his ability to walk while enjoying a thrilling seventeenth birthday celebration. In addition, the teen had been accepted to Evart University the day before. Dave, Leslie, Ben, and Josh are thrust into a completely different way of life after this incident, which none of them could have predicted or imagined.

Now, Ben Lawson is a mechanical engineering student at Evart University, but he is deeply struggling to adjust to his new life with not being able to walk. The teen is intent on creating a way for him to walk again, even though his zest for life has dwindled a bit. Even more so, Ben yearns to find a young Christian woman to marry and have the amazing marriage with her like his mother and father have. Will Ben receive help from a student at Evart University or somewhere else to help him navigate this very difficult phase of his life? How will the teen be able to walk again and find the right young Christian woman to marry? Only time will tell as a couple of years go by. More importantly, God knows everything that happened to Ben, and He knows the desires of his heart. There will be another tragic incident, but God will have Ben in the palm of His hand. Then, God will prosper the teen in all of what he does.

PROLOGUE:
The Gift of Life

Dave and Leslie Lawson were on the way to the main hospital in Evart, Michigan, on a rainy afternoon in their red minivan that they just purchased four months ago. It was Thursday, January 5th, 1984, and Dave and Leslie were going to the main hospital in Evart to deliver their firstborn son. The hospital was ten miles from their house, and at an average speed of fifty miles per hour, they would make it to the hospital in twelve minutes. This was the calculation that Dave thought of in his head for the first two minutes after leaving the house, all the while calming and comforting his wife and driving.

"It's all going to be okay, Leslie," Dave said in a reassuring tone and a medium-deep voice. "We're only ten minutes from the hospital, and we're going to have our son there."

Right as her husband said the second part of his reassuring words, Leslie made a face at him that was contorted a bit out of a little aggravation but mostly pain after her water broke two minutes ago.

"You think that some words can soften the pain that I'm feeling in the lower part of my stomach, hmmm?" she said in a slightly higher tone and a somewhat high-pitched voice that was laced with sarcasm that Dave knew all too much for the year and a half that they had been married for.

He knew that Leslie was having a bit of fun with this even though she was in pain.

"Have you ever had something the size of a melon come out of a smaller area? I don't think so," Leslie said, as she always knew that Dave would pick up on the fun that she was having with him even though she felt like she was being kicked and punched from the inside of her lower stomach area, which was nearly a foot in length, sticking out from her with her light blue T-shirt and red jacket covering it. The red jacket was from the private college that she went to, which was called Evart University, and it spelled out the name of the college in dark blue letters.

"No, I haven't," Dave said as he began to laugh a little bit. "But, I'm sure that the closest thing that could ever come close to that would be having to move a kidney stone out of me." He looked at Leslie for several seconds as he drove on a straight, paved road. There wasn't anything that he wouldn't go through together with his wife. Her faith and belief in God, her blue eyes, and her perfect wavy blond hair that was just a few inches longer than shoulder length reminded him of why he married her. She could withstand anything that life threw at her and her husband. Plus, she had the most beautiful body and a good sense of humor. Leslie was in good shape for her age of twenty-six. She was White, five feet six, and very attractive. Leslie now worked as a biology teacher at a private high school a few miles from her and her husband's house. She received two weeks of maternal leave with some payments that she got started yesterday. Dave had always thought and felt he was the luckiest Christian man in the world.

"That's definitely close," Leslie said as she began to laugh a bit. "But, really, thanks for your comforting words." Leslie's tone was now smooth and sincere. She always liked to have fun and be humorous with Dave in their year and a half of marriage and even before that when they dated for four months. It took Dave about a month to get used to and have fun with her sense of humor. He was a Christian, like her, and she always admired his faith and belief in God. In addition, Leslie always loved his abilities to sympathize and empathize as best as he could in the appropriate situations, his sense of humor that he uses at the right times, and his patience, tenderness, kindness, and perseverance in every situation. Dave always managed to come out on top in every bad situation and circumstance after praying to and talking with God and coming up with some personal techniques to get back in the game and thrive. In addition, Leslie always thought he was the most handsome man she had ever seen with his blue eyes and short black hair. Dave was White, had on a dark blue short-sleeved shirt that just about matched his eyes, and black jeans that fit him really well. He was also strong and well-built at the height of six feet because he worked out at a little gym a couple of miles away from their house several times a week after work. Dave worked at a local food market as a financial bookkeeper. He was twenty-seven years old.

He called the manager of his department a couple of minutes ago and let him know that he wasn't going to be able to work today because of the arrival of Leslie and his baby. The manager was totally fine with that and said that Dave could have the rest of the week off but expected him to be fully back to work on Monday of the next week. Dave was kind of surprised by his manager's kindness and generosity but thanked him profoundly and said that he would be back to work at a 100 percent on Monday. The manager luckily had one other employee who had more time on her hands and was qualified to do Dave's work in addition to her own work for the rest of the current week. Dave was relieved to hear that as he had started driving away from his and Leslie's house.

By this time, Dave and Leslie were halfway to the hospital. The couple rode the rest of the way in silence, with only the somewhat cracked cement making the only sound as they drove over it. It was more of a straight path to the hospital now after making a couple of turns since leaving the house. Dave and Leslie came upon the final street called Turtle Drive and then turned right and into the main Evart Hospital parking lot. The parking lot was about half full, and there were plenty of parking spaces right next to the front entrance to the hospital. Leslie was now having more pain, so Dave quickly parked in one of the spots near the front entrance.

Once they had parked, Dave got out of the driver's seat, shut the door, and came around from the front of the car to the other side and gently but firmly picked up Leslie. He closed the door and went on his way to and through the main entrance doors to the hospital. Right as Dave entered the hospital, he said to the lady in the check-in area with a calm, firm, and commanding voice that had urgency in it, "Please, help me! My wife is close to giving birth." She was an African-American young woman of about twenty-nine years of age with long black hair in braids. Her name was Debrah Welsh, as it read on her white name tag with black letters on her red shirt. She looked to be in good shape. Luckily, there was nobody in line to the check-in area. All the people there were waiting for their appointments, looking anxious and somewhat curious about the current situation. There were about a dozen people in the main waiting area just opposite the check-in desk a few feet away. They all looked to be middle-aged people and young adults except for one older man who looked to be about sixty years old and was wearing a yellow shirt and light blue jeans. He briefly stared at Dave and Leslie in a way as if he understood and knew everything that they were about to go through. The man in the yellow shirt was white, with short gray hair and blue eyes.

There were almost an equal number of men to women in the main waiting area. Most of the other people in the other adjacent waiting areas were getting their stuff and leaving. Debrah looked up at Dave and called out in a loud voice, "Get the emergency room team here!" The team came into the check-in room almost immediately with their light turquoise green hospital attire, pushing a movable bed, and quickly recognized the situation. They took Leslie and put her on the movable bed and welcomed Dave into the birthing room if he wanted to. Leslie nodded, indicating that she wanted him to go with them. Dave noticed and followed, and the process began.

It took a long and painful twenty-four hours of labor to have the baby. Well, the first ten hours were not as painful as the next fourteen hours, which seemed to drag on for an eternity for Leslie. Dave was right next to her on the right side of the bed. It was three o'clock by the time that the two had gone into the birthing room, and the night was filled with a few checkups to give Leslie pain medicine. Dave ate some dinner that a nurse gave him at nine o'clock and then just held his wife's hand for the rest of the night. He got just five hours of sleep, mainly just dozing off several times when Leslie was a bit more comfortable, but he didn't mind sleeping less. Dave was slightly jolted awake when his wife felt more pain and in correspondence to the checkups. Another two checkups came in the morning and afternoon the next day at nine o'clock and one o'clock to give her more pain medicine.

Once the next two hours were up, everything changed forever. The midwife gave Leslie her and Dave's baby boy. All the while the little well-shaped baby cried, Leslie felt an amazing wave of love for her and Dave's newborn child, whom they had named Benjamin, as she held their baby. It was as if Benjamin and she were instantly connected in a deep and intimate way. Dave felt the same way as his wife handed him their baby after he asked if he could hold him. The married couple immediately felt at the same time that there wasn't anything that they wouldn't do for their baby boy. They didn't know that the beginning of a very unique, emotional, trying, and interesting story was yet to come down the road.

CHAPTER 1:

LIFE'S JOYS AND PAINS

It was almost seventeen years later. The day was Thursday, January 4th, 2001. Dave and Leslie had another baby boy a little over four and a half years after Benjamin's birth. They called him Josh. All four of them lived in a house with a master bedroom built for two, two other smaller bedrooms, a family room, a living room, and two bathrooms with showers that totaled about 1,800 square inches. The outside of the house was painted turquoise blue, and all of the rooms and walls were royal blue. There were a few paintings with silver and gold colored frames and several framed pictures of the same colors, which were of the family and varying family members at different events. Plus, there were several decorations in each room that each person in the family liked. Dave, Leslie, Ben (as Benjamin called himself now), and Josh attended their local church, Light of the World, every Sunday, which was about two miles from their house. Everyone in the suburb and in the other areas in Evart was in the middle class, except for a few selfish millionaires in central Evart.

Ben's seventeenth birthday was the next day, and his parents had a big surprise for their oldest son. Very early on in Benjamin's life, at the age of four, Dave and Leslie soon realized that Benjamin was really interested in cars. This was especially the case when Dave and Leslie bought their son two medium-sized sports cars with a corresponding, downward-curved double race track. It was Christmas 1988, and Benjamin was almost five years old. He was absolutely fixated on the cars and double race track. Benjamin and his parents always used to race the cars several times every day for a few months. The only thing that rivaled Benjamin's love for cars was his love for his parents, his zest for life, and all that God had for him and his family. In saying that, Dave and Leslie had the idea a few months before Ben's seventeenth birthday that they would drive their son to a professional race track near the outskirts of Evart, where a couple of professional NASCAR racers and a supportive team were hosting a charity event. In addition, Dave and Leslie had saved up enough money to buy their firstborn son an electric blue truck that was always of interest to Benjamin.

There was another specific reason why today was also special. Ben had just graduated from high school in the fall of 2000, and he applied to Evart University about two weeks after his graduation. His acceptance or denial letter was supposed to arrive today or tomorrow. It was almost 3:00 p.m. on a cloudy Thursday afternoon that seemed to indicate it was going to rain within an hour and last for a few hours. That was the typical rainy and snowy weather in and around Evart in the winter season.

Ben was in the living room, perusing around on his laptop that he bought for himself for the upcoming freshman semester at Evart University. He was also a well-fit and built young man for his age. Ben went to the small, local gym with his dad every day since he graduated high school. He was almost exactly like his father in structure, except that the teenager's facial cheeks had a bit more skin on them, like his mother's. Dave had more bony cheeks with less skin than his wife, Leslie. In addition, Ben's black hair reached down to the middle of his neck.

Dave came into the living room, his short black hair now having streaks of gray on both sides of his head at the age of forty-four, almost forty-five. Leslie was in her and Dave's master bedroom, watching TV. Dave was walking with an excited expression on his face. Ben noticed that and the envelope in his father's right hand, on the left side of which were the letters "Evart University," where the sender's information was. The teenager moved his chair back from the living room table and stood up with that same expression of excitement, plus a bit of curiosity, on his face.

"Son, this is for you," Dave said as he gave Ben the envelope. "I believe that there is good news inside. You were always a straight A student in high school and very active in your chess and tennis clubs as a leader and player. In addition, you're a really great and God-fearing individual who does his best in every area of your life. I'm very proud of you, Ben. Nothing will change that."

"Thanks, Dad," Ben said in a thankful tone and a somewhat deep voice as he started opening the envelope.

"Leslie, Josh, come in quickly," Dave said with a moderate tone of insistency and urgency, mixed with some excitement.

"What is it now, Dad?" Josh asked with some sarcasm in his tone and his somewhat high-pitched twelve-year-old voice. He came out of his room, where he was listening to rock music on his dark green MP3 player. "Did Ben get the golden ticket to Willy Wonka land or some mental institution?" Josh asked with the same tone. Josh had been struggling with his individual identity and trying to fit in with other people his age since the beginning of seventh grade, which was why he was a B and C student at that time. The twelve-year-old was now going to begin high school this semester because he managed to jump one year ahead in his schooling. He had short blonde hair and greenish-blue eyes, which were parts of a recessive gene—Leslie's father had green eyes. Josh was in good shape because he ran a lot a few days a week and did chores like his older brother every day, but Josh wasn't as fit and built as him.

"Come on, Josh," Dave said with some insistency and firmness in his tone. "Be happy for your brother. This is a big step forward into his future."

"Yeah, take it easy on your older brother," Leslie said as she emerged from the master bedroom. She now had several gray hairs at the age of forty-three. "You'll have your time of success, and you'll have great friends and other company soon."

"Mom's right; you'll have your time, Bro," Ben said as he finished opening the envelope and began to pull the letter out. "Just do your best, put yourself out there, and trust God that He has the best for you in every part of your life, even when things don't work out the way that you expect."

"Very true, Leslie and Ben," Dave said in a calm and confirming voice. "I couldn't have said it better. For now, let's see the letter that Ben got."

By this time, Ben had taken out the letter. Dave and Leslie were both eagerly awaiting the good news, which they believed that it was. Josh was just standing to Leslie's left, staring somewhat blankly at his brother and the letter in his hand. There was still something in Josh that was egging him on to transform himself into more of what he saw in his brother. Little did Josh know, his time was also coming and beginning to fan into flame in an unexpected way, but he didn't know when, how, and if it would happen.

Dave and Leslie were eagerly and expectantly waiting as their firstborn son read the letter. Josh was a couple of feet next to his mother, just waiting for the news.

"I got accepted into Evart University!" Ben exclaimed with excitement in his voice.

"That's great news, Ben!" Leslie said with equally as much excitement as she came forward and hugged her son.

"I'm very proud of you, Son," Dave said as he also came in for a hug. "Your mom and I knew that you would be accepted."

"Good job, Bro," Josh said as he came up and patted his older brother's back with his left hand. "Thanks for always being there for and encouraging me even when I don't necessarily show that I'm thankful for it."

"Thanks, Bro," Ben said as he returned the pat on his younger brother's back with his left hand after their mother and father noticed the moment and drew back several feet. "I'll always be there for you and do my best to help you in any way that I can, no matter what happens to us. We're brothers, and that's what we do."

"For sure," Josh said as he drew back to where Dave and Leslie were.

"Well, then, let's celebrate this great news by playing one of our favorite board games, Monopoly!" Dave said. "Then we can make and have one of our favorite dishes for dinner, chicken parmigiana!"

"Yes!" Leslie, Ben, and Josh exclaimed almost simultaneously.

It was almost 3:15, and the expected rain had already begun to fall as the Lawson family began setting up Monopoly. They spent the next two and a half hours playing the board game, laughing, and having fun. Once Leslie had won and the time approached five forty-five, she and the rest of the family began preparing and making the chicken parmigiana. They ate dinner when it was ready, shared recent stories about things that had happened at school and work, and continued laughing.

The day had finally arrived, Friday, January 5th. It was Ben's seventeenth birthday, and nothing was going to get in the way with his NASCAR experience at the charity event. The time was eight in the morning. Ben usually got up at that time during school breaks and vacation times. However, he chose to sleep in a bit more until 8:30 a.m. after setting his alarm clock to half an hour later the previous night. It would be the best extra sleep he would have for several months. As it would turn out, Ben did have a great and restorative night's sleep, and the extra half an hour did help.

Ben woke up at 8:30 a.m., got up, and took a refreshing ten-minute shower in his and Josh's bathroom. It was a quarter to nine in the morning when he got into the living room where the kitchen was. Dave had already made Ben's favorite breakfast: three medium-sized chocolate chip pancakes, four slices of bacon, and five spicy sausages that looked like full brown tubular capsules that were about five inches long. Ben could hardly wait to eat it all. He usually eats meals in ten minutes, but he decided that he would take twenty minutes to fully enjoy his favorite breakfast. Leslie and Josh had already arrived at the living room/kitchen table about fifteen minutes ago, but Dave and his wife insisted that they and Josh wait to eat breakfast until Ben got there.

"Good morning, Ben," Dave said. "Happy birthday! Here's to another great and God-blessed year ahead of you!"

"Thanks, Dad," Ben said with a smile on his face that lasted for about four seconds.

"Happy birthday, my wonderful boy!" Leslie said as she came up to hug her son right after Dave came up for the hug for Ben.

"Happy Birthday, Bro," Josh said as he also came up and congratulated his brother with a few pats on Ben's upper back and then a quick hug. Ben said thank you to his brother as the two of them were separating.

"You deserved the extra sleep that you got," Ben's mom said with a growing smile. "Don't think I didn't notice the change in your get-up time. You look really refreshed. I'm glad that you slept in a bit, especially on your special day."

"Thanks, Mom," Ben said as he smiled and then pulled a dark blue wooden chair out from underneath the family's brown wooden table.

"You know what, today is going to be even more special for you, my son," Dave said as he took the pancakes, bacon, and sausages off from their heating sources, put them on a green plate, and slid it over to Ben. "Your mother and I have a big surprise for you later today in the afternoon at one. We are not going to tell you anything about it except that it's on the outskirts of our town and that you will greatly enjoy it."

"I'm sure that I will love it," Ben said in an excited and appreciative tone. "Thank you, Mom and Dad, for this. I'm truly blessed by God that I have you two and my brother, Josh. I will always remember that no matter what happens in the future."

"We are so proud of you for the young man you are becoming," Leslie said as she came over to hug her son a second time. Ben's dad and brother followed suit after responding with good remarks about Ben's comments. Josh said only a few words to his brother because he was still going through his personal issues with himself. It will only be a matter of time before things rapidly change and growth occurs in all of the family members. For now, the four of them had planned to play card games and watch TV in their living room after breakfast.

Two hours had passed, and the Lawson family was ready to leave their house and go to the NASCAR charity event on the outskirts of Evart. They were not terribly far away from the charity event, just an easy twenty minutes. Their house was relatively close to the outskirts of the suburb that they lived in in Evart. Josh was moderately interested in where they all were going, but he didn't know what they were going to do. This was because his and Ben's parents didn't tell him as well as Ben. It was eleven o'clock in the morning when all four family members were in the silver Toyota that Dave and Leslie had bought after selling the red minivan seven years ago and saving up extra money for it.

"Here we go," Dave said as he revved up the engine after putting the keys in the ignition compartment. Not even ten seconds had passed before the Lawson family was on the road that was perpendicular to the drive-in to their house.

Ben and Josh just sat in the back two seats behind the driver's and passenger's seats in complete silence for the whole twenty-minute drive to the event, but even so, their facial expressions couldn't have been any different. The birthday boy had two facial expressions that he went back and forth from, one of curiosity and the other of reflection. He was genuinely looking forward to the surprise that his mom and dad had in store for him. Plus, Ben was reflecting on how his life was and the adventures that lay in front of him. Little did he know that those future adventures would be beyond his wildest imaginations, but they would come after hefty tests in his life mentally, emotionally, personally, and spiritually. Josh was just tilting and leaning his head back on the back corner and door of the car in a sort of boredom. The youngest brother was interested in where his parents were taking him and Ben, but definitely not as much as his brother. He was mostly just going through the motions, waiting for the exciting things to begin and looking for opportunities to lend his help to fellow victims of boredom and seemingly aimless life journeys. Josh was yet to find out that those opportunities to help others were just about to start.

The built-in clock in the silver Toyota blipped to 11:20, and the Lawson family had arrived at the NASCAR charity event. They had twenty-five minutes to scope out and roam around the site, excluding the race track, until the hour and fifteen-minute preparation and safety class started in the main building. Dave and Leslie let out more of the surprise and the excitement that they bottled up on the way to the event as they exited the car.

"Now, this is cool!" Josh exclaimed excitedly after he opened the door to where he sat.

"Thank you so much, Mom and Dad!" Ben said with a more excited tone in his voice than his brother. "You know how much I like racing, race cars, and cars in general!" he added as he hugged them after they came out of the car and came around to where Josh was.

"Hello," a young man in his mid-thirties said to the Lawson family as he approached them from halfway to the main building. "It is a pleasure to meet you all. My name is Dan Reece; I'm a guide for this charity event. May I show you all around the site before the safety and prep class starts? I was told by the event coordinator, John Wess, that we would be expecting you four for your son's seventeenth birthday."

"That's right, John and I spoke on the phone about a week ago," Dave said as he firmly shook Dan's hand. "It's also a pleasure to meet you, and yes, we would appreciate a look-see around the site before the class." The father then went to introduce his family. "This is my wife, Leslie. Here is Ben, the birthday boy, and here is our other son, Josh."

"It's great to meet you all," Dan said after Leslie, Ben, and Josh waved to him. "Now, let's move on to a quick tour of the site. Follow me." Dan then motioned the family to follow him with his right hand.

Dan had medium-long blonde hair and brown eyes. A person could tell that he was strong by his muscular appearance, but not like a bodybuilder. Dan wore a white volunteer collared shirt with a silver name tag that had his name on it in black letters. The white collared shirt was paired with dark blue jeans. He began the tour by showing the race track from afar and pointing out the twists, turns, and straightaways. He then showed the family the hangar where the NASCAR driver volunteers and the charity event volunteers put the race cars and sports cars, which was about a seven-minute walk away from the race track. The sports cars at the event were Corvettes, painted in shades of blue, red, and green. The race cars had the famous black and white checkered flag logo on each, painted with bright colors and little red, orange, yellow, silver, and purple patterns.

Fifteen minutes had passed since Dan had begun the quick tour around the NASCAR charity event site. It was 11:35 when all five people started back towards the main building, where the safety and prep class was being held. Five minutes had flown by when Dan and the Lawson family got into the room where the class was. There were about two dozen other people in there, young to middle-aged men and women, waiting excitedly and expectantly for the main event to begin in an hour and twenty minutes.

"All right, here is where we stop," Dan said. He then positioned himself in the back left corner of the room, only about fourteen feet away from the family.

Two other men, who looked to be in their early forties, came up to the front of the silver-gray-colored room. The first one was almost bald, with hazel-green eyes and a thin layer of brown hair that had streaks of gray, similar to that of Dave. He was a Hispanic man, wearing a dark blue NASCAR charity event shirt with light blue jeans. The other man was a few inches shorter, about six feet even. He was a Black African-American with black hair that was styled like a crew cut. The man had on a red sports car shirt with light blue jeans.

"Hello, everyone!" the man in the dark blue charity event shirt said. "My name is John Wess, and I am the coordinator of this NASCAR charity event that a few of the NASCAR competitors, like James here to my left, were more than happy enough to do for all of you. There are a couple of other competitors here in the top and back right corners of this room, Blake and Hal." Blake and Hal waved and said hi to the crowd of people. They were wearing sports and race car attire similar to that of James. Blake and Hal were brothers, and they looked very similar with their white skin, medium-long dark brown hair, and brown eyes. The only difference was that Hal was several inches taller and leaner than his brother, who had a bit more muscle on him.

"Without a further ado, welcome to the NASCAR charity event!" John excitedly said. "However, before the safety and prep class that James here is going to teach, let us recognize and celebrate the seventeenth birthday of one of our attendees, Ben Lawson!" he exclaimed as he looked at Ben and the rest of his family. Another male volunteer with short light brown hair, hazel-green eyes, white skin, and similar attire to that of Dan entered the room from another door in the middle of Blake and Hal. He was holding a round gold plate with a chocolate cake made from vanilla frosting and dark chocolate squares that had the race car flag logo on it.

Ben and the rest of the Lawson family blushed as the second volunteer came up to them with the plate and cake in hand and as all of the attendees, volunteers, competitors, and even

John erupted in chorus: "Happy birthday to you, happy birthday to you, happy birthday, dear Ben, happy birthday to you!"

"Thank you all for doing this," Ben said with excitement and surprise in his tone. "This means a lot to me."

"You are very welcome, young man," John responded gladly. "There is also another surprise here for you at this event. You get to go first and ride and drive with the competitor and car of your choice."

"Fantastic!" Ben replied excitedly.

"All right," John said. "Let's start the safety and prep class. James, take it away."

"Thank you, John," James said as John went to sit down in a chair in the front left corner of the room. James pulled a silver laptop out of his black briefcase and put it on a wooden desk in front of him. "Let us start out with the basics of safety rules, and then we will progress to the descriptions of the sports cars and the race cars that we have here. We will have a short quiz after the class just to make sure that everyone is prepared. In saying all of this, let us begin." James started the class, and everyone sat down in the chairs that were next to them. Ben had yet to find out that the grand adventures in his life had just begun, and he was going to be tested by challenges soon after the beginning of those adventures.

The beginning of any series of great and God-breathed life adventures usually starts out in one of two ways. They can start out on a high note, then go through low notes of varying time lengths, and then finally pan out to be the absolute best life adventures that God planned out. However, the second starting point can begin with those difficult low notes of differing time lengths and then end up being grand adventures and, therefore, the ultimate life that God has in store for every person. Both points wind up leading them to the best life that a person can only dream of until it becomes their reality. The key is to not lose hope and to keep on loving God and people. The first of the two starting points was what Ben was going to find out as the safety and prep class for the NASCAR charity event/birthday celebration for him wrapped up.

The excitement in Ben's facial expression said it all as he, his family, and Blake went over to the hangar to pick out which car he and Blake were going to take turns driving. Ben chose a sleek orange and yellow painted race car with the flag logo on it. Dave, Leslie, and Josh stood a few feet to the left of the sports car after Blake motioned for them to do so with his right hand.

"You three can feel free to take turns riding and driving with me after Ben and I are done," Blake offered in his smooth, medium-deep voice.

"Very cool, thanks!" Josh said to Blake. "Can I ride in the race car with you after you and my brother are done?"

"For sure, kid," Blake replied. "The pleasure is all mine. You'll have a great time. You remember that you are not allowed to drive since you are only twelve, right?"

"Yeah, I know," Josh said with a disappointed tone. "I remember hearing that in the class. At least I'll be able to ride along."

"Hey, cheer up," Blake responded with a reassuring tone. "You can always come back here after you turn sixteen, and then you'll be able to drive."

"Okay, sounds good," Josh said with a bit more hopeful sound in his voice.

"All right, then," Blake said. "Who wants to go next after Josh?"

"I think I'll be fine just watching everyone have fun," Leslie said. "Next time, I might take you up on the offer. Thanks, though."

"No problem," Blake replied.

"In that case, I will go after Josh," Dave said with a bit of excitement in his tone. "Thank you for your most generous offer."

"As I said to your second son, Josh, the pleasure is all mine," Blake responded with sincerity. "I enjoy doing these things and participating in charity events, more so especially when it's someone's birthday, like your son Ben, here."

"Do you mind if you drive first?" Ben asked. "I want to save the best for last with me driving. Plus, I probably need you to show me how to drive even after the safety and prep class."

"For sure, young man," Blake said. "I was going to suggest that I drive first just to show you how it all works with driving this beauty of a race car."

"Sounds good," Ben replied as he opened the car door next to the passenger's seat and put on his seat belt and helmet that Blake handed him. Blake quickly followed suit with the door to the driver's seat, his seat belt, and his helmet.

"All right, here we go!" Blake said a bit louder, with excitement in his tone as he revved up the engine. "Make sure you're seated in well and that your helmet is on mostly tight. This race car goes up to 140 miles per hour.

"Okay, sounds like a plan," Ben replied in an equally louder voice. "I'll probably only go up to one hundred miles per hour if I think I can do it when I drive."

"Have fun!" Dave, Leslie, and Josh somewhat shouted almost simultaneously as Blake slowly drove the orange and yellow race car out of the silver-painted hangar.

"Let the birthday celebration begin!" Blake shouted as he and Ben approached the five-mile-long race track that seemed to be mostly in two figure-eight shapes, according to what Ben could see.

The experience was like nothing that Ben had ever experienced before. First off, he heard his family excitedly shouting and screaming for him as he and Blake went on the race track. There was a sudden jolt as Blake increased the speed of the car from five to thirty miles per hour. Blake then steadily increased the race car speed by a cautious ten miles per hour every five seconds until he stopped at a fast 140 miles per hour. Ben could only see the parking hangar as a silver speck as the exhilarating drive continued. The two figure eights of the five-mile race track that Ben initially thought that he saw became two bigger figure eights. It would make sense that the two figure eights of the race track would be bigger so that the driver could maintain maximum speed without any difficulties, but Ben wasn't thinking of that as he and Blake zoomed past their surroundings. The trees, bushes, patches of grass, dirt, and nearby houses went by in a blur that mixed together with the sky and clouds. Ben was having a blast as Blake was driving the race car, with him turning the steering wheel at several points and as Ben was leaning into the curves.

The newly minted seventeen-year-old couldn't be any happier and thought that this was the second-best moment of his life besides coming into a relationship with Jesus Christ and the Holy Trinity at nine years old. Ben had yet to learn that there were even greater and more joyous moments and adventures ahead of him than riding and driving in a race car. However, those moments and adventures would have to wait until after the teenager went through a season of personal trials that would test his relationship with God. Anyway, it was truthfully only several minutes of riding in the race car until it was time for Ben to drive. He didn't care about how much time passed. Ben was enjoying every second of it. They were once again back inside the parking hangar, waiting for the teenager to take the steering wheel.

"How was the ride?" Ben's mom asked him as if asking for the rest of the family due to their curious facial expressions. Even Blake turned to face Ben with that same look as the professional race car driver stopped the car several feet from the Lawson family.

"It was like nothing I've experienced before," Ben replied. "The adrenaline rush was great. However, I do think I'll just drive up to one hundred miles per hour at the most."

"It's your birthday, kid; do whatever you want," Blake chimed in as he and Ben got out of the car with their helmets still on and switched seats. "Here we go again! Remember to use a little more caution when driving."

"Sounds like a plan," Ben said as he got into the driver's seat, clicked in his seat belt, and revved up the engine. Blake had already fastened himself in safely and comfortably in the passenger's seat.

"Have fun! Be safe!" Dave and Leslie shouted as their son cautiously pulled out of the hangar.

This was it—another dream came true. Ben was about to drive a race car. The thought was in the forefront of his mind as he eased onto the race track. He had already made up in his mind that he was going to gradually increase the speed of the metallic beast by five miles per hour every seven seconds until he was at eighty miles per hour. The teenager was only going to drive at one hundred miles per hour on more straightaways. A few beads of sweat were already beginning to perspire on his forehead underneath the helmet as he pressed his right foot down on the gas pedal with excitement in his facial expression. Then, he and Blake were off!

Ben found out that it is more difficult to drive a race car than the gray Ford truck that he practiced driving with when he turned sixteen. He didn't want to start driving all the time on his own until he was seventeen. Ben didn't feel he was ready at that time. Now, in the current moment, he felt that he was ready. The newly minted seventeen-year-old was determined to drive and drive fast, as you could say at the moment. Ben went up to eighty miles per hour in one minute and fifty-two seconds. He remained at that speed when driving around the first figure eight. Then, at the end of the first circle of the second figure eight that signaled a straighter path for about five miles, Ben stepped down on the gas pedal even more and steadily increased the speed to one hundred miles per hour. The rush at driving at that speed, and even at eighty miles per hour, was all the more thrilling and purely exhilarating than simply riding at top speed. The teenager quickly learned how to drive and maneuver a low-rising car after figuring out that steering a race car requires more precision than steering a truck.

Meanwhile, there was a long line of people forming behind the Lawson family in the parking hangar. The people were gazing and awing at the vast assortment of race cars and sports cars. John, the NASCAR charity event coordinator, and Hal and James, the other two race car professionals, were standing in front of the line of attendees who couldn't wait to have their own experiences as Ben Lawson was currently having his. All of a sudden, Dave Lawson's navy blue flip phone buzzed inside his pant pocket. The call was from Ben's doctor, Shiela Blisk, carrying news that would change Ben's life and certainly the lives of his entire family forever. Dave, of course, was too busy excitedly and proudly looking for and watching his firstborn son drive a race car. That was the same for Leslie as she attentively watched the orange and yellow spec, which was the race car that Ben was driving. It was only until the end of the buzzing of his phone that Dave looked down towards his pant pocket and stared at it for a second as if it was something foreign to him. He had his left arm around his wife as he was looking down. Leslie noticed the change in her husband's posture as his left arm became slightly more firm around her.

"What is it, Dave?" Leslie asked curiously.

"Somebody is calling me," Dave replied.

"Are you going to answer your phone?"

"It can wait until after we're done here. This is a special occasion. I'm not going to miss a second of it."

"That is definitely a good reason."

As Dave was finishing saying that last sentence, the buzzing ended, and the call went straight to saved calls. Then, there was also a voicemail waiting for him. Immediately following their exchange of words, Dave and Leslie went back to looking for and watching Ben as he was driving. Josh was also watching for his older brother, but not as much as his parents. Little did Josh know that his time for coming into his true helpful self and personality was at hand. Many more good things were attached to that, but they would come in time. Nobody had any idea of what was to come.

Ben was finishing up his second lap of the five-mile race track with Blake in the passenger's seat. The seventeen-year-old repeated what he had done in his first lap, but instead of going at a speed of one hundred miles per hour on the more straightaways, he sped up to 120 miles per hour. Ben's confidence had shot up quite a bit after doing what he did during the first lap. He had made sure to adequately slow down to the comfortable speed of eighty miles per hour due to a lack of confidence in going one hundred miles per hour around turns at that time. However, Ben had memorized the turns after completing his first lap. This had allowed him a few degrees of freedom and relaxation to go up to the incredible speed of 120 miles per hour for his second lap. The second lap felt exponentially more amazing than the first lap. Now, as Ben was starting to complete the last quarter of his birthday celebration race car drive, he gradually slowed down. The teenager had slowed down to two miles an hour as he easily drove the orange and yellow race car back into the parking hangar and parked the metallic beast. Ben noticed that the only difference in the hangar now was that the charity event attendees, including his family, were all in there. They were about twenty-four feet from him, safely away from potential danger. Ben's family watched his whole race car driving dream and journey unfold from beginning to end. They came up to him as he exited the race car and took off his helmet. Blake was not far behind him in doing the same process.

"I do have to say, kid," Blake began, "you did surprisingly well."

"Thanks," Ben replied. "Must have been that one year that I practiced driving with the gray truck."

"Is that so?"

"Yeah. I didn't feel completely ready to drive until today. Today was a blast!"

"I'm glad that you enjoyed it! Happy birthday!"

"Thanks!"

"So, you thought that our son did good?" Leslie excitedly asked Blake as she and Dave came closer to the professional race car driver.

"For sure!" Blake replied. "He is a fast learner. However, he did have a few issues with what speed to drive at during the first lap and taking turns at that time. All in all, your son did pretty well. He sure surprised me a bit."

"That's great to hear!"

Leslie then turned a few degrees to face her son and embrace him. Dave was not far behind her. Blake and Josh stepped back and let Ben and his parents have a moment together. Blake and Josh briefly talked about how fast Josh could go when he was able to drive and come back for another NASCAR charity event. All the while, Dave and Leslie were embracing their son and talking with him.

"I'm so glad that you had a great time!" Ben's mom began. "Did you feel safe while driving?"

"For the most part, yes," Ben replied with certainty. "The experience was incredible!"

"That's probably one of your many experiences that you'll remember for the rest of your life," Ben's dad chimed in as he went in to embrace his son as well. "Your mother and I are very proud and happy for you."

"Thanks," Ben said as he was hugging his mom and dad. "And thank you, Mom and Dad, for this memorable birthday present!"

"You are very welcome, our handsome young man!" Leslie replied for both her and Dave as she kissed Ben on his forehead. The three of them separated from each other, and Blake and Josh rejoined the group.

"Now, the question is," Blake started out with, "who wants to go next, Josh or Dave?"

"I want to go next!" Josh exclaimed.

"All right, I'll go last," Dave responded.

"Perfect, it's settled then," Blake said. "You two will have a great time."

The next eleven minutes were the last minutes that Ben Lawson and his family would have before their lives were thrust onto paths that would change their lives forever. Five minutes went by, and Josh was already in the orange and yellow race car with Blake behind the wheel. Ben thought he heard his brother tell the professional race car driver to go at the maximum speed. Blake was totally cool with doing that; it was the same thing that he did when Ben rode with him. The five minutes ended with Blake and Josh beginning their first high-speed lap as they went onto the race track. Suddenly, Ben felt a little twinge in his lower right leg. He shrugged it off as if it were nothing, thinking that it must have been triggered from pushing down excitedly on the gas pedal of the race car before flying to 120 miles per hour. However, the same thing happened again, but this time, it was in his lower left leg. This occurred just as Blake and Josh were finishing up their second lap. Ben then thought that that was a little odd.

"Hey, Mom," Ben began, "I've had these two little twinges in both my lower right and left legs. They happened about five minutes apart from each other."

"That's weird," Leslie said. "Do you think they are from pushing down on the gas and brake pedals when you were driving?"

"That's what I thought. It was odd to me that would cause it..."

Ben had felt something else happen after he trailed off at the end of his last sentence. He was going to tell his mom and dad what was happening, but it was too late. Ben collapsed and fell backward onto the smooth but hard hangar floor after feeling intense pain in both his lower right and left legs. Ben had enough recognition of all of what was happening to keep his head forward as he collapsed and fell so as to not fracture his skull. Blake and Josh were barely getting out of the race car when this happened. Dave, Leslie, and Blake immediately saw and watched in worry and horror as the situation unfolded before their very eyes. It took Josh a couple of seconds to realize what was happening, but then he raced over to his older brother. Josh was standing and leaning over Ben as if Ben was a wounded soldier. It was also as if Josh was a fellow soldier, attending to and caring for his brother-in-arms. This was the time that something began bursting through Josh on the inside, but Josh had yet to fully figure that out. It would come in time.

"What happened?" Blake asked in total shock as he went over to Ben's parents for answers.

"I don't know!" Leslie started out with tears starting to well up in her eyes. "Ben just told me about a minute ago that he felt a twinge in each of his lower legs, which happened five minutes apart from each other. I think my son had felt the first twinge about ten minutes ago but didn't say anything about it for five minutes. I don't know. Now he is like this. I can't believe this is happening!"

Dave was already there to hold and comfort his wife, all the while in a state of shock of his own. A lot of the charity event attendees saw what had happened, and they started to gather around the Lawson family, asking them how Ben was and if there was anything that they could do. The event coordinator and the other two professional race car drivers were also doing the same. Blake and Josh were already ready to try to help Ben to his feet.

"All right, kid, let's try to get you to your feet," Blake said as he and Josh went to pick up Ben, Josh on Ben's right and Blake on Ben's left.

Ben grunted in pain as he was hoisted up onto his feet. Blake and Josh switched tactics a bit, put one arm each under Ben's arms, and took off a lot of the weight that was previously held under Ben's feet. This move greatly alleviated the pain that the seventeen-year-old once had.

"Someone should call a doctor," Josh chimed in, mostly unaware of the character growth that was taking place inside him. Somehow, he was starting to feel a little bit of that growth, but he still had a ways to go until it came to complete fruition.

"Good call, Son," Dave said with a sudden urge of pride in his son. "Let me check my phone and see who called me, just to see if it's Ben's doctor or someone in the main hospital in Evart." Dave fumbled in, trying to get and hold his phone. He checked his saved calls and voicemails, and to his astonishment, it was indeed Ben's doctor who had called him and left him a voicemail. A sudden prick of disappointment in himself rose up inside him as if he was responsible for not noticing the twinges in his oldest son's lower legs in the first place. This was going through his mind as he started calling back Dr. Blisk, Ben's doctor. Nobody except Leslie knew what was going through Dave's mind with his slight change in demeanor and attitude.

"Blake and Josh, help get Ben into our car," Leslie said. "Make sure that he is laying down along the horizontal floor line between the car's front and back seats. You might have to prop up his head and core a bit against the inside of the right door to the back seats."

"Will do, Mom," Josh responded.

"Will do, ma'am," Blake said almost at the same time as Josh's response. "I hope that your son gets better quickly. I'm sure that he will be all right; he seems like a strong kid."

"Thank you, and thanks for all your help," Leslie said as she did her best to hold back her emotions and tears, even though that didn't completely work.

"I'm always happy to help whenever a situation arises," Blake replied as he and Josh started carrying Ben to the Lawsons' car. Josh showed Blake where the car was, and in a couple of minutes, they arrived at it. Blake then took Ben by himself and put him in the car in the position that Leslie described after Josh opened the door.

"You're going to be all right, kid," Blake said to Ben as he finished comfortably positioning the teenager into the car. "Just stay calm and keep yourself in a positive state of mind."

"Thanks. I'll do my best." Ben replied with a bit heavier voice as he experienced another surge of pain in his lower legs. Blake then leaned forward to fist bump the seventeen-year-old, leaned back outside of the car, and then closed the door.

Josh had already sat himself inside the car, but just inside the parking hangar, Dave told his wife the urgency of the situation, according to what he heard from Dr. Blisk. Dave and Leslie immediately had to get to their family's car and drive to the main hospital in Evart. Dr. Blisk had told Dave what probably triggered the twinges in Ben's lower legs and that she would explain the whole situation to them and the rest of the Lawson family when they got to the hospital. Dave and Leslie quickly urged the NASCAR charity event coordinator, the other professional race car drivers, and the attendees to remain calm and thanked them for their kind-heartedness and offerings to help. They also told the crowd to go along with the rest of the event and have fun, all the while keeping Ben and the rest of the family in their prayers. Dave thanked Blake for his help and told him he would take him up on the race car ride and drive another time. Ben's parents then immediately ran to their family's car and started off towards the hospital, completely unaware of the events that were to come.

Believe it or not, the trip to the main hospital was the least crazy of the current events and the many future events that were yet to unfold. There were several incidents during the trip when Ben felt more intense pain and discomfort in his lower legs because of the small potholes and concrete road cracks that they had to drive over. Fortunately, the hospital was just twenty minutes from the NASCAR charity event. Even so, Josh was there for and comforted his brother when the pain and discomfort arose. Both Leslie and Josh told Ben to hold on and that they were close to the hospital. All of these things happened just five or so minutes before the Lawson family reached the hospital. It was a great relief for Ben as Dave parked close to the hospital entrance. Dave and Josh quickly picked up Ben in the same way that Blake and Josh did at the charity event. Leslie was also there to hold her firstborn son's upper legs, just above his knees.

"Someone help us!" Dave said with urgency as the four family members entered the waiting room. "We need Dr. Blisk!"

"I'm on it right now," Debra Welsh said as she immediately saw the situation and then called Dr. Blisk. There were just a half dozen people in the waiting room and three more people in line for appointments. They seemed to not mind that much that the current situation had changed. Debra told them to wait a minute and that she'd be right with them. The Lawson family demanded her full attention at the moment. Fortunately, the family of four could quickly get an urgent appointment with Dr. Blisk. They arrived in her office in a couple of minutes after navigating the hallway corridors to Dr. Blisk's office. Dave, Leslie, and Josh laid Ben down on a smooth plastic foam table opposite Dr. Blisk's desk. She arrived just a minute later.

"Sorry, I was with a patient when Debra called me up about Ben," Dr. Blisk said in a little exasperated voice. "I came as soon as I could after telling my patient that I would be back with her soon."

"No problem. Sorry to barge in unannounced," Leslie said with shock still in her voice.

"No need to be sorry. Did you all get my phone call? And you four can call me Shiela. We have known each other for ten years. I'm always glad to help any one of you. We're like family. By the way, Happy birthday, Ben! I'm deeply sorry that your day has been ruined by this turn of events."

"Thank you, Shiela," Ben said while grunting a little bit in pain and discomfort.

"Thanks, Shiela. It's been a pleasure getting to know you over these ten years. Anyway, I got the call, but my wife, Josh, and I were watching Ben ride and drive in a race car with a professional race car driver at a NASCAR charity event for his seventeenth birthday," Dave chimed in. "I just wish that I would have quickly listened to your voicemail."

"It's totally understandable that you and the rest of your family would just want to enjoy and celebrate Ben's seventeenth birthday, especially with that special activity," Shiela replied. "I'm just glad that you all got here as soon as you did. I'm afraid that we will have to take action today based on what you told me, Dave."

"What do you mean by taking action today?" Dave asked.

"What's going to happen to my brother?" Josh asked a second later.

"Is Ben going to be all right?" Leslie asked with a bit of concern in her voice.

"I will answer all of your questions," Shiela began. "I first want to briefly describe what is happening to Ben. I have been looking at his genetics recently, and something very bizarre occurred. A rare disease appeared in Ben's lower legs. I assume that the race car riding and driving triggered a reaction. Also, I think the disease just recently came to the surface because it was recessed in his genes. I'm afraid that we will have to amputate his legs at just above his knees. That is because I don't want the disease to spread upward anymore. I am deeply and profoundly sorry to inform you all of this horrible news."

"What?" Dave, Leslie, Ben, and Josh exclaimed and questioned with horror in their voices.

"Oh, God!" Leslie said while bursting into tears and leaning onto Dave. Ben and Josh just stayed where they were, in shock and disbelief. Dave also began to tear up and cry.

"I can not imagine the pain and shock you all are in now. Again, I send my deepest condolences. We have to act now so that the disease doesn't spread," Shiela said as she went to call Debra from her office phone. "Debra, get me an OR team and do it fast."

The year of 2001 began as such a great year with Ben Lawson's seventeenth birthday and college at Evart University starting for him on January 10th, five days after he had experienced both a big high and a big low in his life. Ben just wanted to get the procedure done and over with after learning about the life-changing news from Dr. Blisk. He just wanted to stay in the state of unconsciousness during the procedure. However, change must happen, whether it be good or bad, but "...we know that in all things God works for the good of those who love him, who have been called according to his purpose" (Romans 8:28).

In the meantime, the entire Lawson family was thrown into a year-long state of denial, frustration, confusion, and anger. Ben did his best to do well in his freshmen year of college, but the loss of his legs and his now current use of a manual wheelchair threw a huge curveball at him. He averaged C's in all of his first-year mechanical engineering classes. Ben was determined to know more about mechanical engineering, given what had happened to him, and therefore, he chose that major. Dave, Leslie, and Josh dealt with themselves harshly and played the blame game of how Ben's situation happened. However, Dave and Leslie were determined to eventually resolve the mess in a healthy way with God's help. Josh was becoming more aware of what he was supposed to do in life, but he first had to work his way through a wave of confusion. Everything was going to work out for everyone, but it was going to take time.

CHAPTER 2:

Missed Love

Hardships of all shapes, sizes, and variations come to everyone on earth, no matter how good people try to be. There are bound to be problems and issues sometimes in a person's life. Jesus said, "[...] In this world you will have trouble. But take heart! I have overcome the world" (John 16:33b). Ben Lawson was currently going through his own struggles with fully adjusting to his new life. It was 7:30 a.m. on Wednesday, January 9th, and he had been awake since 7:15 a.m., thinking about the tasks and responsibilities that he had with his classes as he was starting his sophomore year of college at Evart University. The now eighteen-year-old didn't think about the fact that God had a grand plan for his life. He was more preoccupied with just getting through college to get his mechanical engineering degree in order to be able to make himself a pair of prosthetic legs. His parents were not able to save enough money to get their son prosthetic legs. Anything that was prosthetic was ridiculously expensive. It costs $180,000 to get prosthetic legs. Dave and Leslie were barely getting by and providing for their family with a combined yearly salary of $40,000. Ben's situation and the fact that Josh was starting his sophomore year of high school didn't help things.

Ben didn't really think about having a great future as he hoisted himself into his manual wheelchair as his alarm clock approached 7:30. However, he kept leaning on and praying to God that he would get back to where he was before the life-changing incident and then just have a good future. He was thinking about having a good life after making himself a pair of prosthetic legs as he casually wheeled himself to his bathroom to give himself a quick sponge bath and brush his teeth. Ben would then get himself dressed before eating breakfast and having his dad drive him to the university. Dave and Leslie bought a dark blue van for their son's transportation to and from Evart University and wherever Ben needed to go. Little did the Lawson family know that things were going to get even worse before they got so much better.

Diego Sanchez was one of the brightest students in one of Ben Lawson's core mechanical engineering classes. He was a tall six-feet-four-inch Hispanic/Latino foreign exchange student from Chile with dark brown hair that was styled in a crew cut, brown eyes, and no facial hair. He was wearing a dark green polo shirt with dark blue jeans. Diego transferred to Evart University from a smaller college in a city in the southern part of his home country. He felt that God led him to Evart University. In saying this, this young nineteen-year-old from Chile was a true God-fearing person in addition to the rest of his family. He had a great relationship with Jesus/God. The thing was that Diego had not known the reason God had led him to Evart University other than the fact that that university had one of the highest-ranked mechanical engineering majors. However, Diego was starting to see the true reason why God had led him to this university. Ben Lawson had a look of discontentment and disappointment on his face and in his body language. He needed someone to encourage and guide him through the next several years, and God planned on using Diego to do just that.

Ben was sitting two rows and one chair ahead and to the right of Diego Sanchez in a stadium-like auditorium for their first mechanical engineering course of the day. It was 10:00 a.m., one hour into the hour-and-a-half class. Ben and Diego hadn't met each other, but that was about to change a few minutes after the lecture was over for the class.

Diego decided to casually introduce himself after both he and Ben exited the auditorium-like classroom. He wanted to start things somewhat slowly on the first day and figure out the root cause of Ben's look of discontentment and disappointment that he saw in the classroom. Diego wanted to get to the root of his fellow sophomore's problem within the next day or the next few days.

"Hey, man, what did you think of the lecture today?" Diego asked in a curious tone and a medium-deep voice as he came up next to Ben on his right.

"It was fine," Ben replied with a kind of deflated voice as he wheeled down a corridor leading to an elevator to get to the ground floor. Diego followed along with him. "The lecture gave me more information on what I want to do for a personal project."

"Interesting. Do you want to hang out and get some lunch during one of your breaks tomorrow?"

"For sure. Sounds good. I have a break from 11:30 a.m. until 1:00 p.m. We can meet up at noon."

"Perfect. Does Chick-fil-A sound good at the student union?"

"Yes. They have the best sauce for their sandwiches."

"Sure do. By the way, my name is Diego. Nice to meet you."

"My name is Ben. Nice to meet you too."

"For sure, Ben. See you tomorrow for lunch," Diego said as he and Ben parted ways, Ben going in the elevator and Diego going down the stairs.

That day when Ben and Diego first met went by in a hurry. Ben had two other mechanical engineering classes and two gen eds. The two gen eds were sports philosophy and Latin American history. They were amusing to him, but he still was on track to only get B's in both of the gen eds. Something was lost after Ben lost his legs. His zest for everything in every area of his life had been diminished a lot. Little did he know that two occurrences in his life journey would help bring him back to his normal self. They would come with their own big challenges as well. Ben would just have to wait until the next day and the second semester of his sophomore year in a Christian religion gen ed class, which he was excited for to find out what they were.

It was now the next day. "Hey, Ben," Diego said with a bit of excitement in his voice as Ben wheeled into the cafeteria in the student union. There were several fast-food restaurants in the cafeteria, including Taco Bell, Subway, Burger King, and Chick-fil-A. Ben said hi to Diego, and then they ordered and got their sandwiches. The two college sophomores finally sat down at a little silver and square table next to Chick-fil-A.

"You like the spicy chicken sandwiches, huh?" Ben asked curiously as he looked at Diego's sandwich. Ben had heard what his fellow college sophomore ordered.

"Yeah. I like spicy food. It's the spice of life that makes everything interesting. Some of the things in life are bad, and some other things are good. You just have to trust God in everything in life, and He will take care of you. What about you? I heard that you ordered a regular chicken sandwich?" Diego replied.

"I like to keep things plain and simple nowadays, knowing what I want and getting those things, including Chick-fil-A sandwiches. I do agree that we should trust God in everything that comes our way in life. Why are you talking like this to me?" Ben was halfway through eating his sandwich and then transitioned to eating some waffle fries.

"I noticed during class yesterday that you were in a negative mood."

"Wow, somebody noticed me being in a negative mood. Big deal. What do you care about me?"

"I believe God sent me to Evart University for a reason. I'm originally from southern Chile. I transferred to this university from a smaller university in my hometown. At first, I thought that God led me to Evart university because this university had one of the highest-ranked mechanical engineering programs. I then thought that there must be more to it than that. That's when I noticed that you were not doing so well. I believe I'm supposed to help you during this part of your life. You can feel free to share your story if you want." Diego then finished his sandwich and the rest of his waffle fries after saying this. Ben was not too far behind in doing so as well.

"Well, your story sure was a good story. I am glad that you felt led by God to come to and attend Evart University; truly, I am. I don't feel like sharing my story. Just stop trying to help me. I don't need help, and I certainly don't need saving from myself from you." Ben didn't mean it on the inside, but he was still feeling so at the moment. It had been like that for the whole of the eighteen-year-old's freshman year of college. Diego noticed and had a sense that his fellow college sophomore didn't mean it.

"All right, then. I can see that you are hurting, and I want to be there for you and help you. I'll be here when you feel like opening up. Here is my number." Diego slid a piece of paper with his number on it. Ben begrudgingly took the piece of paper and stuffed it into one of the little pockets in his backpack.

"I think I should be heading over to my next class. It's a ways away, and it's 12:40. I also want to be early."

"You can be like that, Ben. Just remember that I'm here to talk to you when you are ready." Diego said this as he was getting up to throw his wrappers from lunch away and head over to his next class as well. "I hope to see you soon. Take care."

Ben went on with his day after Diego talked to him. The classes and information seemed to fly by for Ben. Maybe it was because he was interested in anything that would take his mind off of what Diego had said to him. He thought about what his fellow college sophomore had said. Ben was hurt, disappointed, and dissatisfied with his current situation with being in a wheelchair and not fully being able to to what he normally did before the incident and procedure. He chewed on in his mind what Diego had said to him during lunch when his dad went to pick him up from Evart University. Ben said to Diego that he didn't want help, but there was something deep inside him that wanted help. However, he didn't feel the need to seek help. That would change by the early morning of the next day. It was 5:15 in the late afternoon/early evening when Ben's dad picked him up after his college classes.

"How were your classes today, Son?" Dave asked as he and Ben were halfway home. "Did anything interesting happen in between them?"

"My classes were fine. Pretty much nothing happened in between them," Ben replied with little to no enthusiasm. "Other than this guy and I had lunch, and he talked to me about my less than positive attitude and offered to help me."

"Hey, at least you had lunch with someone, Son. I had been hearing from your mom that you were eating lunch alone before today. You should accept your fellow college sophomore's help during this part of your life; I mean it. Your mother and I are getting concerned about your change in attitude and outlook on life."

"The person at college doesn't know what I've been through. He just believes that God sent him to Evart University to help me. He just views me as someone that he needs to help."

"Nobody knows what you have been through, Ben, except people with disabilities and men who have come back from war with injuries. As for the person at college, I think it is great that he felt led by God to go to Evart University and help you. You have to let this guy and other people into your life who you can trust. I think that you should become friends with this fellow sophomore and truly accept his help. I believe this is the start of great things in your life, including a wife and possibly a family. I know you had been looking for a girlfriend last year during your freshman year. I could see in your eyes that you wanted to grow personally in that area of your life in addition to getting prosthetic legs to help you walk again. Just trust God with what and who you want and trust that His plan is better than yours and better than what you are going through now. Maybe your mother can help you more with what you're dealing with. Promise me that you will consider letting this guy from college help you and that you will keep an open eye for God's goodness in your life. I believe God will cause everything to work out for your good soon."

"I promise," Ben said a bit reluctantly. "I have one question, though. Did you just come up with that out of thin air?"

"I've been thinking about what I could say to you to help you," Dave replied before he let out a little comical sniffle. The father and son rode the rest of the five minutes home in silence. Then Dave got out of the van when the two of them got home and electronically opened the door to where his son was with a little silver remote control. Ben wheeled himself onto the ramp once it was down, and then Dave lowered his son down to ground level. The college sophomore then navigated himself through the garage and then up a little wooden ramp that led to the back of the inside of the house.

"Welcome home, Ben," Leslie said as she got up from the living room table to meet and hug her son near his room, halfway between where he entered the house and where his mom was. "How was your day?"

"It was all right. I'm just glad to be home now," Ben replied as he was still in his mom's embrace.

"That's good. Do you want to talk about it?"

"Maybe later tonight. What's for dinner?"

"Hamburger rice bowls with fresh onions and bell peppers."

"I'd take that any night," Dave said as he came up and kissed and hugged his wife. Ben detached from Leslie a few seconds before his dad came in and then looked away from his parents while they shared their affection for each other. Dave's words about Ben wanting a girlfriend/wife seemed to ring true as his son looked away from him and Leslie. Ben looked away out of hurt and loneliness because he had lost opportunities to get a girlfriend during his freshman year. Most young women simply don't go for a guy in a wheelchair without most of his legs. However, that didn't stop Ben from trying, albeit in a little of a nonchalant way sometimes. The eighteen-year-old wasn't looking for a young woman in his first semester of sophomore year. He was just going through the motions of going to his college classes this semester.

"I will help with making dinner," Dave started again after gently pulling away from his wife's mouth. "I can thaw out and break apart the hamburger into bitesize pieces, and then you can mix in the onions and peppers with the rice. How does that sound?"

Dave and Leslie often made it a fun activity to make dinner together. They really loved doing that. One of them would individually make dinner several times every couple of months too. It was a special event or celebration when Dave, Leslie, and their sons would make dinner. That happened when Ben got the letter of acceptance into Evart University. It still happened recently with birthdays and holidays, but it wasn't the same since Ben's incident just before he went to college. However, all four of the Lawson family members still did all of their best to participate and have fun making those dinners.

"That sounds great," Leslie replied and then leaned forward to kiss her husband again. Dave warmly, kindly, and greatly accepted that kiss.

"I'm looking forward to dinner," Ben started after his parents gently pulled away from each other and headed towards the kitchen to make dinner. "Let me know when it is ready. I'll be in my room doing homework."

"For sure, Ben," Leslie replied as she got out the bowls for the hamburger rice bowls when they were ready. The last thing Ben saw before he wheeled to his room to do homework was his parents smiling at and laughing with each other as his dad started thawing out the hamburger while his wife watched him do it. He hoped to have what his parents had someday.

Dinner was very tasty and satisfying. There was some small talk around the dinner table in the dining room where the Lawson family usually had dinner. It was mostly Dave, Leslie, and Josh doing the small talk with Ben listening to them. Ben enjoyed eating dinner for the most part and then went into the living room to wind down and relax before getting ready for bed. It was now 7:00 p.m., and the teen switched on the family TV with the remote and turned it to one of his favorite movies, *Star Wars: A New Hope*. The movie was about halfway over. The whole family then flocked to the living room to watch it. Dave talked with the family for a little bit about when he and several of his friends went to see the movie when it first came out in theaters, and he talked about how it was an incredible experience. The whole family then proceeded to watch the rest of the movie, thoroughly enjoying it. A few of the main thoughts that Ben had when watching the remaining portion of the *Star Wars* film were as follows: *Where is the new hope for me and my life? And where do I go from this part of my life?*

It was eight thirty at night, and the movie had just ended. Everybody went to their own rooms to be by themselves. Dave and Leslie went into their room and fully enjoyed each other's company. Ben and Josh got ready for bed at ten after hanging around in their own rooms. The oldest son was just finishing up getting ready for bed and then transferred himself by his usual arm strength onto his bed when his mom knocked on his door and asked to come in. Ben called out that it was fine for her to come in, and then she sat down next to him on his bed.

"Do you mind if we talk a bit about what happened today with you at the university?" Leslie politely asked her son.

"Sure, we can do that," Ben replied somewhat reluctantly. He could feel a bit that he now wanted to talk about what happened earlier in the day even though he didn't fully want to.

"Okay. Well, as you have probably heard from your dad, he and I are worried about your mental and emotional well-being."

"That's another way of saying it," Ben replied in somewhat of a nonchalant way as he pulled his bed covers onto his chest.

"I'm sure that your dad had his way of talking to you. He told me in the middle of making dinner about what you said happened today at college. He and I both agree that you should accept this help offer from your fellow college sophomore and become friends. You need to have friends and other people in your life besides me, your dad, and Josh. You have been going to church with me, your dad, and Josh every Sunday ever since your incident. However, you had deflated and depressed expressions on your face. I can see now that it has changed a bit. Start by praying and talking to God about how you're really feeling, and I'm 100 percent confident that He will guide and help you in what you do. I'm always there for you, in addition to your dad, when you need to talk to someone."

"Thanks, Mom," Ben said sincerely. "I'll do that."

"You're very welcome, my handsome young man," Leslie replied warmly before kissing her son on his forehead and then leaving his room. "Get some good sleep. Good night."

Leslie closed the door after saying good night, and then Ben was left with his thoughts swirling around in his head. He prayed and talked to God for several minutes, going into detail about how he was feeling in his current situation with being in a wheelchair and not being able to do what he wanted to do. In addition, he described to God what he fully wanted, including to be able to walk again with the use of prosthetic legs and to have a girlfriend/wife to spend the rest of his life with. Ben finished praying and talking to God by asking for His help and guidance, knowing what to do with accepting Diego's help offer. The teenager then gradually began to fall asleep, getting lost in his thoughts again for a couple of minutes. One of the thoughts that raced through Ben's mind was what the NASCAR driver, Blake, said to him as he put him into his family's car. *"It's going to be all right, kid,"* Blake had first said. *"Just stay calm and keep yourself in a positive state of mind."* Those were Blake's last words to him before Ben went to the hospital with his family, only to hear the life-changing news. Ben thought about how deflated, depressed, and disappointed he had been this past year and then about how he had failed to heed Blake's final words. Everything about how the teen was feeling was going to change by the early morning the next day. Ben was going to make sure that he wasn't going to let Blake down again. He then drifted off into a good sleep with that thought.

The next day came, and it was now seven thirty in the morning. Ben woke up closer to that time instead of seven fifteen. He felt more refreshed after having a good night's sleep. The teen quickly took a shower in his shower chair, which he left to the right of his bed. He then put on a red and blue *Star Wars: A New Hope* T-shirt and blue shorts for the day. Ben figured that he would start off the new day on a good note. He then ate breakfast before his dad started to drive him to Evart University.

"I can see that you are doing better, Son," Dave started as he and his son got onto the main road away from their driveway. "Nice T-shirt choice."

"Thanks, Dad," Ben replied in a good, normal tone. "I thought that I would start this new day with a good reminder of hope."

"For sure," Dave replied a bit excitedly at the sound of his son's change in tone and attitude. "I like how you sound, Ben. What did your mom tell you?" This question was a bit rhetorical.

"Mom helped me a bit, but I thought it was time for a change."

"I'm glad to hear that, Son. I'm proud of you. I love you no matter what state of mind you're in."

"Thanks, Dad. I know that the ultimate source of hope is in God."

"Amen to that. I'm sure you'll have a great day today with your classes and accepting the help offered by your fellow college sophomore. What's his name, by the way?"

"For sure. His name is Diego."

"Cool. I'm sure you and Diego will become good friends through this process."

"Definitely."

Ben and his dad rode the rest of the way to Evart University in silence. Once the teen got down to the university grounds after arriving there, he was more prepared to do better in all of his classes than he was a week ago. You could say that Ben's college day went by in a blur in a good way. Ben was more so invested in and paid attention to what the lecturers were teaching. Above it all, he was ready to give Diego a call at night to accept his help. The teen's dad saw more of that desire for help in his son as he picked him up at five fifteen from college.

"How was your day, Ben?" Dave asked as he was starting to drive his son home.

"Pretty good," Ben replied with a bit of enthusiasm in his voice.

"I'm glad to hear that, Son. Did you talk to Diego today?"

"No. I didn't see him today in any of my classes. I will and want to call him tonight, though. He gave me his number yesterday after getting lunch with him."

"Sounds good. I'm sure you will go a long way with his help in this part of your life."

"For sure."

Dinner came and went after Ben and his dad came home. Dave and Leslie made Salisbury steak with egg shell noodles and asparagus. Ben, Josh, and their parents fully enjoyed eating it. It was now seven fifteen at night, and Ben decided to finish his engineering and vector math homework before calling Diego. The teen did really well in completing his homework for the next day and was very confident in doing so. He then took out the slightly crumbled piece of paper from the little pouch in his navy blue backpack and flattened it on his dresser. Ben then called the number that Diego had given him.

"Hello," Diego said with a hint of a questioning tone in his voice as he picked up Ben's call. "Who is this?"

"Hey, Diego," Ben replied. "This is Ben from our engineering class at Evart University. We had lunch yesterday, and you gave me your number."

"Hey, Ben! I'm happy to hear from you. How are you doing?"

"I'm doing pretty good, actually. By the way, sorry about the way I acted yesterday. I've been through a lot in the past year."

"No worries, man. We all go through multiple hard times at one point or another. What do you want to talk about?"

"I'm ready for your help. We can talk more in person tomorrow over lunch during my break at eleven thirty."

"Sounds good, Ben. See and talk to ya tomorrow."

"Okay. See and talk to ya tomorrow. Bye."

"Bye."

It was now nine thirty, and Leslie had slightly overheard her son's conversation with Diego as she was heading from the living room to her and her husband's room. Ben's door was closed, so his mom knocked on it. The teen wheeled on over to the door and let his mom in.

"Hey, Mom, what's up?" Ben asked.

"I overheard a little bit of your conversation with the person that you said you were ready to get help from, but I didn't hear his name."

"His name is Diego."

"Nice. I am extremely confident that you will gain much help from him and that you two will become good friends."

"Those are the goals. Thanks, Mom."

"Anytime, my son," Leslie said as she and her son hugged.

"I think I will get a bit extra rest for tomorrow's classes."

"Sounds good. I love you. Have a great night's sleep. Good night."

"Love you, too, Mom. Good night."

Leslie then exited her son's room and went into her and Dave's room. She relayed what she and Ben talked about to her husband. He was excited for and proud of his firstborn son. Dave and Leslie enjoyed each other's company before getting ready and going to bed. Ben had gotten ready and went to bed twenty minutes before his parents.

The next day and the rest of Ben's first semester of sophomore year at Evart University went by in a flash. Diego taught him a lot about ways to strengthen his relationship with God and to know God's will. In addition, the Southern Chilean helped Ben with knowing and fine-tuning what God's heart was for him in terms of reading God's Word and what He had for his life in terms of different feelings, insights, and revelations that come into play. Ben opened up to Diego about his incident that happened early in 2001 and the personal and spiritual struggles that he dealt with after getting his legs amputated. Diego was also really helpful in helping Ben with the lingering issues he had with what happened to him.

Ben and his fellow college sophomore became really good friends during the rest of the first semester of his second year at the university. The two of them would regularly hang out with each other on the weekends. They talked about things that guys talked about, which included young women, in addition to talking about God. Ben and Diego went to and played baseball events, went to movies, and played several *Star Wars* plug-and-play video games while hanging out at each other's houses. That summer was the first time that Ben met Diego's parents, who ended up moving to Evart with their son. They were very nice and God-fearing people who went to a different church several miles away from the church that

Ben and his family went to. Diego turned twenty years old on June 16th, and he planned to move out of his parent's house at the end of the next college semester and settle in an apartment for the rest of his college career.

The teen from Evart did incredibly well in all of his mechanical engineering classes and gen eds as well. Ben ended up getting A's in all of his classes by the end of the first semester of sophomore year. He and Diego had a lot of fun hanging out with each other during the summer, even with going to their jobs. Ben had gotten a job as a dishwasher at a burger joint called American Burgers just off of campus in the middle of that first semester. Ben eagerly waited for the Christian religion gen ed class that he was going to take next semester. He was once again for all of what God had for him in every area of his life.

It was now the fall semester of 2002, and Ben was ready to tackle the schoolwork and work that was ahead of him. He had three mechanical engineering classes, one math class that ties into mechanical engineering at a higher level, and two general education classes, including the Christian religion class he was super excited about. Diego had also signed up for the Christian religion gen ed. He and Ben were now in more mechanical engineering courses together as well. Ben's first day of his second semester of sophomore year started on a Monday with two of his and Diego's engineering courses. Then, it ended with the Christian religion gen ed. That was Ben's class schedule for Mondays and Wednesdays. The teen from Evart had his other three classes on Tuesdays and Thursdays. He only worked at American Burgers on Fridays and Saturdays from 11:00 a.m. to 6:00 p.m. for each Friday and Saturday.

There was one young woman in particular who caught Ben's attention as the lecturer was in the middle of teaching the class that day in yet another auditorium-shaped room. Her name was Sophia O'Donnell, and she was gorgeous. She was five feet four inches tall and had beautiful white skin, flowing natural red hair that almost came down to the middle of her back, and hazel-green eyes. Sophia was wearing light blue jeans that fit her well with her normal body form. She also had on a light purple short-sleeved shirt that had some light blue patterns on it. She was also a fellow second-semester sophomore and lived with four other female students in a dorm. A unique feeling stirred up in Ben, and he wondered if perhaps it was a feeling from God that Diego had talked to him about at the end of the previous semester. Ben could also feel that he was really attracted to her.

All of a sudden, two weeks had already gone by in Ben's second semester of sophomore year. He was doing really well in all of his courses, classes, and homework. It was an extra bonus and motivation having Sophia O'Donnell in his Christian religion gen ed. Diego had already noticed a week ago that his good friend's attention was on the beautiful redhead in addition to his courses and classes. He planned on confronting and asking Ben about her and what he was feeling. The general education was about to end for the day.

"Hey, Ben," Diego started as he and Ben headed out of the college classroom. "I've noticed that you have been looking at that young redheaded woman for a while. You should ask her out. Have you felt anything for her?"

"First of all," Ben replied in a good, comical tone, "congrats for figuring that out. I'm still a bit surprised at how fast you figure things out. Second, I'm thinking about asking her out. It's been difficult getting and going on a date because of my situation. So, I'm a little hesitant. Finally, I felt the feeling you taught me during the summer about the feelings that God gives you about things in terms of knowing God's heart for those things."

"What can I say? I'm a keen observer. It's one of my gifts from God. Don't be hesitant about asking her out. When you get a feeling that was given to you by God in the form of an insight and revelation, you should trust Him that He has you. I'm very glad that you have received my teaching well. I'm just doing what God told me to do to help you."

"Huh, insight and revelation. I'll pray about the situation tonight. Thank you for your help. I greatly appreciate it."

"No problem, man. I'm always happy to help. I'll see you tomorrow. Later." Diego said this while starting to branch off from Ben towards the place where he parked his car.

"See you tomorrow. Later." Ben replied as he wheeled out of the building that housed the Christian religion class. Diego heard his friend as he was turning around and waved goodbye to him as he approached his car. The distance from where the gen ed class was to where Diego's car was was fairly short. The Southern Chilean native had a sleek dark blue Honda with black door handles.

The time came for Ben's dad to pick him up just a few minutes after Diego had driven off. The teen got on the electronic ramp with a smile on his face, which his dad noticed as he got his son up into the van and tied him down.

"Do you want to tell me who has gotten you this excited?" Dave curiously asked after fully looking at and taking in his son's smile.

"I want to tell everyone during dinner," Ben replied.

"Sounds great, Son," Dave said as he started heading up to sit in the driver's seat to begin their way home. "I look forward to hearing the story."

"Perfect," Ben said as Dave pulled out of the parking spot and began driving home. The father and son sat in total silence as they were making their way home. The teen thought about the endless possibilities that he and the young redheaded woman could have, all of which were good. He was all the more excited to pray to and talk with God about the situation in terms of asking out the young woman and being in a relationship with her. Ben was beginning to feel a good amount of peace about all of it.

The time for dinner came about forty-five minutes after Ben and his dad had arrived at the house. Dave and Leslie made hamburger helper, which consisted of diced hamburger and egg shell noodles. Ben was ready to tell everyone the good news after everyone started eating.

"Excuse me, I would like to tell everyone some fun news about what has happened to me in one of my classes for the past two weeks, if I may share."

"Fun news, that sounds very interesting. Please share," Leslie chimed in after hearing what her son said.

"For sure, Bro; tell us what has happened," Josh said with genuine curiosity in his tone of voice. That was still a little surprising to Ben. Ever since his incident, Josh had been better, kinder, and more interested in how he talked to and interacted with him.

"Come on, Son, tell us the story," Dave prodded encouragingly with great interest in his tone.

"All right," Ben started with that same smile and level of excitement that his dad saw in him when he went to pick him up from the university about an hour ago. "It all started for me at the beginning of this college semester. I saw this young redheaded student in my Christian religion gen ed class...

"Ooh, a redhead. This is getting interesting indeed," Leslie interrupted as her son paused for a second.

"I like where this is headed," Josh chimed in. "Go on."

"Yes, please go on; sorry for interrupting," Leslie apologized.

"It's all good, Mom," Ben kindly replied with a smile. "Diego's teachings to me about knowing the heart and will of God for our lives that I told you all several weeks ago relates to me seeing this redhead. I believe that there is more to be had for her and me in addition to fellow classmates. Something deeper. I have had these feelings of peace and other positive feelings and little insights for the past couple of weeks since the Christian religion gen ed began. They have led me to believe what I just told you. In saying all of that, I'm going to ask her out on Wednesday to have Starbucks drinks on Saturday. I was a bit hesitant at first to ask her out because of my past difficulties in going on dates with young women. However,

Diego pushed me a bit to ask this young woman out. That's it. I'm going to pray about the situation tonight and see how it goes. I would appreciate all of your prayers for this. Thank you for listening."

"We are always happy to listen, Ben," Dave started. "And wow! That's absolutely great news to hear! I'm glad that you're going to put yourself out there and ask out this redheaded young woman from your Christian religion gen ed class! You have made me very proud with the amount of growth of character that you have had. I'm very glad that Diego has taught you really valuable teachings about God and that you two are good friends. I'll definitely be praying for you and this young woman."

"Congrats, Bro," Josh said with equal excitement as Dave. "I'm sure it will all work out for you and your new girlfriend. Shall I call her that? And how deep of a connection are we talking about?" Ben's younger brother said and asked these things with a bit of sarcasm in a genuine way.

"Josh, don't make fun of your brother," Leslie said in a slightly stern tone. "We all know that you were genuine in saying those things, though."

"Of course, I didn't mean it in a bad way; I was just poking at him," Josh replied in a good tone.

"Thanks, Bro," Ben replied while laughing a bit. I appreciate that you are not too sarcastic anymore but still have a sense of humor. I'm proud of you."

"Thanks," Josh said.

"As for the whole girlfriend thing, I have a feeling that it might go there with her and hope so."

"Now, let's not get too carried away, Ben," Dave chimed in. "Definitely pray about this situation with her, see if you're still feeling what you're feeling from God, and see where it goes."

"For sure. I would also say that you should trust your gut and what it says after praying to God and seeing if you still have those insight feelings, as your dad said," Leslie responded.

"Thanks, Mom and Dad," Ben replied with gratitude in his voice. "I will definitely do all of those things."

"You're very welcome," Ben's parents said about a couple of seconds apart. The family then fully resumed in eating the rest of their dinner. Next, the college teen went to his room and did his homework for the day before playing a *Star Wars* plug-and-play game with his brother for a while. It was 10:00 p.m. when the two brothers were done with the game and then got ready for bed. Ben wanted to talk with his mom about something, so he asked her if she would talk with him in his room. She kindly obliged to his request.

"What do you want to talk about?" Leslie asked. "What's on my little boy's mind? You know you will always be my little boy."

"I know, Mom," Ben replied warmly with a little smile on his face as he and his mom hugged each other. Leslie then kissed her son on his forehead before the two of them let go of each other. "Do you mind if I ask a question about you and Dad?"

"Not at all. What is it?"

"How have you and Dad stayed really close with each other and gotten along great recently, even with my incident?"

"That's a more complex question. First of all, when your dad and I knew what was going to happen to you after Dr. Blisk told us the news, we were deeply in shock. It took us a few months after that to recover from the shock. Your dad and I then played this blame game with each other and Josh as to whose responsibility it was for what happened to you. It got pretty ugly, and there were many nights that we had bad arguments, as you probably heard some. Nonetheless, we were determined to get through all of it with God at the center and to lean into His help to move forward from this nasty little blame game and to grow closer together as a married couple. In saying that, God did help us do those things and so much more. Your dad and I got to know and connect with each other in a deeper way. We knew how to listen to each other better and knew what each of us wanted and needed at all times in every way. Plus, we knew how to make each other laugh more. I hope that answered your question."

"It did. That's a great story and an incredible testimony! I hope to have what you and Dad have someday."

"Thanks. I'm sure that you will have what your dad and I have someday. Maybe it will be with this young redheaded woman in your Christian religion class or another young woman. Just trust God no matter what happens, trust your gut, as I said earlier, and keep your eyes open."

"Thanks, Mom. You're the best."

"You're welcome, my young man," Leslie said as she and her son hugged each other again before starting to head out of the room. "Get some great sleep. Good night."

"Good night," Ben replied as he began to get himself in his bed. He then pulled the covers onto his chest and flicked off the light switch that was just a little bit to his left on the wall behind him. Ben prayed and talked to God about asking out the young redheaded woman and about the potential for there to be more for him and her relationally. The teen still felt the peace and the other feelings about the situation. He believed that there was something starting to form in his gut that said to go ahead with asking out this young woman and that there was more to him and her in terms of a relationship.

Tuesday went as fast as it came. Now it was 7:30 a.m. on Wednesday. Ben still had those feelings in his heart and gut. In addition, he believed that God gave him a little go-ahead message on Tuesday night in a dream. It was simple. There was a green hand in the position of an "okay" gesture with a thumbs up. Ben now proceeded to get up and go through his morning routine before his dad drove him to the university.

"All the best in asking out this young redheaded woman," Dave said as he and his son drove into the main university parking lot and found a parking spot. "God go before and be with you."

"Amen. Thanks, Dad," Ben replied as his heart was beginning to pound inside his chest in expectation, excitement, and a bit of nervousness with a dose of anxiety all at the same time. Dave unclipped his son's wheelchair to the spot inside the van and dropped him down on the electronic ramp to send him off on his adventure.

The next several hours of Ben's mechanical engineering classes and his break seemed to go as slow as a tortoise. It was like the two professors' voices were slowly droning on as they were teaching their students. However, it was valuable information that Ben would use later on in his senior year to build his own pair of prosthetic legs. He would do the building by himself, but he just needed the parts, which he would buy. It will definitely be cheaper than buying a brand-new or slightly used pair of legs. The total amount for Ben to purchase all of the parts was about eighty thousand dollars plus an extra five thousand dollars for a more experienced engineer to fix the mistakes that he could make. These were some of the thoughts swimming around in the teen's head during his classes and break, which helped the time go by faster. His heart rate began to go up a few more intense beats as he was halfway over with his Christian religion gen ed for the day. The intensity was so great that he wanted to ask the young redhead out right after the class was over. However, Ben knew that he had to keep calm and composed. In addition, he had not met her before, so he planned on and wanted to talk with her a bit before asking her out. The introductory conversation would suffice as a means to lower the intensity that he was feeling and keep him calm.

Ben immediately began texting Diego a few minutes before the class ended, saying that he wasn't able to talk and hang out with him after class. He told Diego in the text that the reason for doing so was that he was going to talk with the young redhead and ask her out. Diego shot back a thumbs-up emoji, wished him all the best, and said that God has him and the situation in His hands and that he would talk to him later in the evening to see how everything went. The time now came for the gen ed to end for the day, and Ben took a much-needed deep breath before wheeling up to the young redheaded woman.

"Hey, how did you like the lecture today?" Ben asked her as he went up beside her to make sure that she noticed him. Sure enough, she did.

"I liked it," she said in a gentle and smooth voice with a little concealed surprise as she looked at Ben. "It was cool how the professor tied the boundaries that God sets for us to live good and godly lives to what is happening in the world. It is quite a shame that not many people heed to those boundaries. God put those in place to keep us safe, not to tell us what to do and what not to do. What do you think about the whole thing?"

"I absolutely agree with you. If everyone started thinking and acting like boundaries are good and necessary things for us instead of rules of what to do and what not to do, the world and its people would be in a better place."

"Well said," the young redhead responded as she and Ben reached the door of the building. She was kind enough to open it for him.

"Thank you," Ben said with gratitude in his voice as he wheeled out of the building.

"You're welcome. I'm Sophia. What's your name?"

"My name is Ben. Nice to meet you, Sophia."

"It's nice to meet you, too, Ben. Do you live in a dorm on campus or somewhere else?"

"Somewhere else. I actually live with my parents about twenty minutes from campus. You?"

"I live in a dorm on campus with four other young women like myself."

"Cool. What is your major?"

"Psychology. You?"

"Psychology is a great major. Mine is mechanical engineering."

"Very cool. What do you like to do in your free time when you're not doing homework or going to your classes?"

"I like to go to and play in baseball events with a good friend of mine in my free time in addition to hanging out with him and other friends and family, going to see movies, and playing video games. You?"

"Nice activities. I also like hanging out with friends and family, going to see movies, and playing video games. I also like to play volleyball with a few friends of mine on Saturdays."

"Very cool. Speaking of Saturdays, I was wondering if you would like to meet up this Saturday for Starbucks drinks sometime during the day before or after you play volleyball with your friends." Ben was confident that he had done well thus far. He and Sophia were at the spot where his dad usually picked him up. It was about five minutes before his dad would arrive. Ben suddenly had a bit of a sick feeling in his stomach as Sophia looked at him before she replied. He knew that Sophia was doing her best to not look at the foot-long stubs that he had that used to have legs attached to them. However, Ben knew that she was looking at them and that she was not that interested in meeting up/going out with him. A wave of a new level of disappointment began to creep into his heart and mind.

"I'm sorry, but I'm going to be busy this weekend with homework. Speaking of which, I want to head home to get a little head start on it. I'll see you on Monday for class, though. Bye," Sophia replied.

"Bye," Ben said before Sophia went to her car and drove off. She had a red Lexus, but Ben did not pay attention to that. There were still two minutes left before Ben's dad arrived to pick him up. Fortunately, the two minutes went by really fast. Ben did not want to stay on campus for any longer than he needed to.

"Hey, Ben," Dave started as he lowered down the ramp for his son to wheel on. "How did everything go with asking out the young redhead?"

"We can talk about what happened later. I just want to go home. It was a long day," Ben replied with enough tiredness to bypass his dad's question and let the situation with Sophia remain a mystery.

"All right, Son, let's go home. However, I do want to hear about what happened with her sometime before Saturday, as I'm sure your mom and brother would love to hear about it as well."

As soon as Ben and his dad got home, Ben went to his room and buried himself in his homework before coming out for dinner. Leslie and Josh were very curious as to how Ben's day went with asking out Sophia. They did not know her name, and they wouldn't know it until the start of Ben's junior year of college. Ben was skilled in dodging the topic of Sophia and topics in general. In saying that, the teen easily dodged the topic of Sophia and asking her out by saying to his family that he choked and didn't end up asking her out. It was a lie that was carefully concealed with such made-up sincerity that it seemed real. This convoluted lie even fooled Diego when Ben called him on the night that he said he would.

As for the rest of the second semester of Ben's sophomore year, it seemed to hurry on by, and at the same time, it seemed to drag on a bit. The teen did heavily invest himself in his mechanical engineering courses and the two gen eds. He ended up doing better in his mechanical engineering courses than in the other classes. Ben managed to pull off A's and B's, respectively. He was still interested in the Christian religion class but not as interested as before he talked with Sophia. That was why he got a B in that class. Ben still worked at his job at American Burgers as an excellent dishwasher, which also helped take his mind off of Sophia in addition to college. However, the heart sickness was still there. He was sure there was more to him and Sophia, but he was duped again. Only time would tell if that was true or not.

CHAPTER 3:

Just Another Day

Everyone experiences sadness and disappointment at varying levels and at different stages of life, depending on what happened. The thing is that people have to come to a point of trust and faith in something or someone to help them through the sadness and disappointment. Christians have the ultimate benefit of surrendering all of that emotion to God and trusting Him that He will get us through them and the corresponding situations to the best place of joy and contentment on the other side. The Bible says that you have to "trust in the Lord with all your heart and lean not on your own understanding" (Proverbs 3:5).

The lesson of fully trusting God was a lesson that Ben Lawson was currently learning. Ben believed, had a relationship with, and trusted God, but there were still the two areas of his life that he had not yet come to fully trust God in. Those two areas were, of course, getting a pair of prosthetic legs made and being able to walk again in them and finding a young woman to have a serious relationship with and marry. The latter area was the area where Ben had more trust issues with God in light of the situation with Sophia opting not to go out with him.

Today was the first Saturday of Ben's first semester of his junior year at Evart University. It was 7:00 a.m. on January 11th, 2003, and Ben was just waking up from a decent night of sleep. He couldn't and didn't want to force himself to get a refreshing half an hour's rest before getting up to start his weekend. The teen had already made plans with Diego to come over to his apartment and just watch TV and play a *Star Wars* plug-and-play game for a few hours. Ben wanted to do as much as he could to keep his mind off of Sophia. His crafty lie that he told everyone he choked when asking her out had been successful so far. However, Ben's dad had just figured out a few days ago that his son lied to him and planned on confronting him after breakfast. Dave had wanted his son to come clean when he figured it out, but that didn't happen. As for how Ben's dad figured out that his son was lying, Dave knew his son's expressions and could read right through them. Dave knew how genuinely happy Ben was when he had those insight feelings about Sophia. In addition, Ben's dad had been studying his son's expressions ever since that happy moment. However, it took Dave quite a while to sift through the lie. Anyway, Ben came into the kitchen at 7:30 a.m. for the Saturday breakfast of sausages, bacon, and chocolate chip pancakes after taking a shower in his shower chair and getting dressed for the day in a plain white T-shirt and royal blue shorts.

"Thank you for breakfast, Dad," Ben said as he wheeled up to the kitchen counter.

"You're welcome," Dave started as he placed his son's plate with breakfast in front of him. "By the way, Ben, do you mind if we talk for a bit after breakfast?"

"For sure, Dad, we can do that." The teen said this before delving into his breakfast. Dave did the same as he took his own plate with the same breakfast to the sectional couch in the family room several feet from the kitchen table. Ben's dad turned on the TV about seven feet from the sectional and scrolled to one of the channels with one of the family's other favorite shows on, *The Princess Bride*. It was nearly one-third into the movie. Ben watched adjacently from a distance of about ten feet, distracting his mind with the movie and eating breakfast. He wondered what his dad wanted to talk about. The teen really hoped that his dad hadn't found out that he lied about the situation with asking out Sophia. The time seemed to drag on as Ben awaited the time until Dave and he talked. Ben was glad that time seemed to extend itself as he enjoyed his sausages, bacon, and pancakes. However, the inevitable of having the unknown conversation was bound to happen. Then, just like that, Ben finished eating after fifteen minutes. His dad was already done with his breakfast and turned off the TV.

"Ben," Dave began in a serious tone, "what really happened on the day that you asked out the young redheaded woman from your Christian religion class last semester? I know that what you said after that time was a lie. I find the fact that you lied to me, your mom, and your brother disappointing. Your mom and I raised you to be better than that, and we taught you to come to us whenever something was bothering you. Now, come closer to me and tell me the truth. Don't lie again."

It was just what Ben dreaded of talking to his dad about. He let out a sigh of frustration and hesitantly wheeled closer to him. Neither Leslie nor Josh could hear Ben and Dave because they went out to breakfast and a movie together.

"I don't know what to say," Ben responded with some frustration in his voice. "I didn't want to tell any of you because it hurt too much. You're right to say that you and Mom raised me better and taught me to come to you two whenever anything was bugging me. The truth is that this young redhead, Sophia, didn't want to go out with me for the obvious reason that I don't have my legs."

"Son, I'm really sorry that happened to you. It hurts me as well to see you frustrated and disappointed. It really does. I know that you were feeling very strongly from God and yourself that this Sophia and you were more than just classmates and that you were hoping that you and she would have a relationship sometime down the road. Maybe Sophia isn't the one for you. Only God and time will tell if that's true or not. Again, I'm really sorry that she rejected you and your offer to go out with her. Now, I encourage you to always come to me, your mom, or both of us if you want to talk about anything about Sophia. No more lies or secrets."

"Thanks, Dad. I will not lie to or keep secrets from you or anyone ever again," Ben replied with a little sad sniffle. Suddenly, a huge weight was lifted off of him about the whole deal, and he mentally vowed to himself to never lie or keep secrets ever again. "What do you say about watching the rest of *The Princess Bride* together?"

"I would love to do that with you," Dave said as he turned the TV back onto the channel where the movie was.

Ben could only dream of having an adventure and love story like that of *The Princess Bride* as he watched the rest of the movie with his dad. The nineteen-year-old would be Wesley, and some young woman would be Princess Buttercup. However, the teen would prefer not to die at the hands of a real-life Humperdinck person. It would be cool to be brought back to life, though. The ending was great and all to Ben, but he was always left with a sense of longing for just a bit more of the storyline with Wesley and Princess Buttercup. Ben wanted the storyline to continue just one more day or so with the two characters as they began to live out the rest of their lives.

"Hey, Dad," Ben began as the end credits finished rolling.

"Yeah, Ben," Dave replied.

"Is it okay if you drive me to Diego's apartment after dinner at seven? I want to be there at seven fifteen."

"I can do that. However, I think it's only fair to your mom and Josh if you tell them what truly happened with Sophia sometime before I drop you off at Diego's apartment. I imagine that you kept the truth from Diego as well, and I encourage you to tell him that too. Does that sound good?"

"Yes. I want to tell all of them the truth and then just do my best not to think about Sophia for a long while."

"Good. What are you and Diego planning on doing at his apartment in addition to telling him the truth about Sophia?"

"We are just going to hang out and play a *Star Wars* plug-and-play game that I'm going to take over."

"Would you be up for playing the game for a bit with me as a warmup for tonight with you and Diego?"

"Totally, sounds fun," Ben replied enthusiastically as he wheeled over to the game shelves that were under the TV. He brought out a square-like game console that had a couple of illustrated pictures on it, including a lightsaber game and a *Star Fighter* game. The nineteen-year-old put the two blue and black game console plugs into the corresponding insert holes in the TV. His dad turned the input to video game mode on the remote, and then, suddenly, a flashing picture of the *Star Wars* game appeared on the screen with the blinking word "continue." Ben pressed the red "start" button, and then the two lightsaber and *Star Fighter* games appeared. He toggled the joystick to the left and chose the *Star Fighter* game.

"Do you remember how to play?" Ben asked as he paused the game with the pause button.

"Of course I do," Dave replied confidently. "It's been a few months since I played this with you and Josh, but I remember how to play."

"Cool. Do you want to go first?"

"Sure, thanks," Dave said while Ben handed over the console to him. Ben's dad then unpaused and started the game. A person played as Luke Skywalker in his X-wing star fighter, fighting off and shooting down TIE fighters before going into the trench of the Death Star and eventually blowing it up. The degree of difficulty increased as more TIE fighters appeared and as you got closer to blowing up the Death Star. Ben's dad had come close to getting halfway through the Death Star part of the game a few months ago before getting shot down and consequently losing. Ben and Josh both blew up the Death Star the last time they each played it. Dave and Leslie had gotten the game for their sons for Christmas in 2001. Leslie had played the *Star Fighter* game a few times when she and her husband got it for Ben and Josh. She blew up the Death Star once when they all first had the game console and then came close to blowing up the station the other two times before losing. The other two times came when Leslie first played the game and then after the successful second attempt. As for the current moment, Dave is doing quite well for not playing the *Star Fighter* game for the past few months. Unfortunately, his run abruptly ended right before entering the Death Star trench as three TIE fighters surrounded and shot him down.

"Aaaggh," Dave annoyingly grunted a bit. "Well, that was fun and a good attempt for not playing for three months. Anyway, here you go, Ben. Have at it," Ben's dad said these last two parts while handing the game console to his son.

Ben gladly received the game console from his dad. Dave wanted to stay on the sectional next to his son to see how he did. The nineteen-year-old began a new attempt in the *Star Fighter* game. He started out like he knew every flight pattern of every TIE fighter that came up behind and aside him. The stars whirred by as Ben strategically flew Luke Skywalker's X-wing starfighter, shooting down all of the TIEs in his path towards the Death Star. It was like Ben was completely, thoroughly, and vigorously invested in this attempt in the *Star Fighter Battle of Yavin-4* game. That was exactly what Ben was doing. He channeled his frustration and sadness about the situation with Sophia rejecting him and the offer to go out with him and easily got into the Death Star trench. He then looked even more intense as he fought and navigated his way to the reactor shaft. Ben finally shot out the proton torpedoes into the shaft and then flew out of the trench several seconds before the space station was blown up and destroyed. He let out a little shout of victory as the actual word "victory" came up on the TV screen in gold letters.

"Show off," Ben's dad said as his son went to the main screen where the pictures of the starfighter and lightsaber games were. "How do you do it? You looked pretty intense while shooting down those TIE fighters and the Death Star."

"I guess I have figured out the patterns and then just busted right through the game," Ben confidently replied.

"Patterns? All right, I can believe that. You must also had help from how you feel about 'the Sophia situation.' Am I right?"

"You are correct. It's a good and constructive way to deal with what I'm feeling. It's also very rewarding when I accomplish the mission of blowing up the Death Star."

"That must be very rewarding. The Force is strong with you," Dave said in his best Darth Vader voice impression.

"That's real funny, Dad." Ben chuckled a bit. "I bet you won't get as far as me in the lightsaber game."

"Bring it on, Son. At least the lightsaber game is the one that I can get really far in, as I remember correctly. It could be a little tough for you to keep up. I remember how to play that game completely."

"We'll see about that. Enough trash talk. I go first this time."

"All right, let's do it."

Ben selected the lightsaber game, and the two of them started it. This game was a bit different from the *Star Fighter* game in terms of being slightly freestyle. It's a game in which the player can choose various Jedi or Sith, depending on how high of a level the player gets to. You start out with Luke Skywalker from *The Empire Strikes Back*. The player then fights through several levels that have three parts in each level, which include the Death Star from *A New Hope*, in which you unlock and get old Obi-Wan Kenobi after defeating that character, and Bespin, in which you finally unlock and get Darth Vader. The last new part of each level is in Emperor Palpatine's throne room, in which you collect him after beating him. The levels repeat in order but get even more difficult to pass. All of the characters have different Force abilities, which the player can use by pressing a blue B button. Luke only has Force push, Obi-Wan has Luke's ability plus Force repulse, Darth Vader has both of those abilities plus Force choke, and Emperor Palpatine has all three abilities plus Force Lightning. Each character has varying lightsaber moves, and you can use them by pressing red A, C, or

D buttons. The red joystick was used for moving and blocking attacks with the character's lightsaber. Ben and his dad were equally as good in the lightsaber game, both of them getting to the third level in the third Emperor Palpatine throne room part.

Ben started strong in his turn, as if the first level with the three parts was a piece of cake. He was saving his mental strength and special combos a little bit for the end of the second level but mostly for the third and, possibly, fourth levels. The second level came and went, with it being slightly tougher to defeat Emperor Palpatine again, but it was easy enough for Ben to pass. Ben had some trouble getting through Darth Vader in the Bespin part of level three, but he finally defeated him with a final flurry of lightsaber strike combos and the signature Luke Skywalker Force push. Now, it was going to be extremely difficult getting past the Emperor for a third time. The nineteen-year-old threw almost every possible lightsaber and Force push combo he had at the Sith, blocking and countering a lot of his opponent's lightsaber and Force lightning attacks with his character's blue lightsaber. Ben did his best to defend his Luke Skywalker avatar from the Sith's other Force abilities and to counterattack. The nineteen-year-old also pulled out the same emotions that he channeled to beat the *Star Fighter* game again. It worked equally as well as he finished off Emperor Palpatine for the third time with only a quarter of his green life bar left in the game.

The bar completely replenished itself as Ben headed towards the beginning of the fourth level. Ben had quite a bit of trouble defeating Obi-Wan for the fourth time, and he barely escaped the first part of the fourth level with a sixth of his green life bar. It proved very efficient to use all of what Ben was feeling about "the Sophia situation" to get past Obi-Wan again, in addition to his wide array of lightsaber and Force push combos. Ben used all of his tricks to squeak by the Bespin part of the fourth level, just edging a super-tough Darth Vader in combat. However, all of that was not enough, as Ben's Luke Skywalker character was barely defeated by the Emperor in the final part of the fourth level.

"Impressive. Most impressive," Ben's dad comically said in his Darth Vader voice.

"That's how it's done," Ben began confidently. "Let's see how you do now."

"Oh, you'll see how I do," Dave replied equally as confidently as his son handed him the game console.

Dave began as quickly as his son had, blasting through the first level with the three parts after he chose to play as Emperor Palpatine. He cut through and zapped Luke Skywalker, Obi-Wan, and Darth Vader in the Death Star, Bespin, and the throne room parts, respectively. The second level was almost as easy as the first level. Ben's dad had a bit more trouble with getting past Darth Vader at the end of the second level. Dave consistently had all kinds of trouble defeating Luke, Obi-Wan, and Darth Vader in the third level, going down to a fifth of his green life bar each time. Ben's dad finally came to the first part of the fourth level, in which he had extreme difficulty defeating Luke for a fourth time. Dave used all of the lightsaber and Force push, repulse, choke, and lightning attacks that he knew to finally beat his opponent, going down to a sixth of his life bar. His run came to an end in the Bespin part of level four, in which he was defeated by Obi-Wan, who cut down Dave's Emperor Palpatine character with vicious lightsaber strikes at the end of his turn.

"That was actually quite good, Dad," Ben said before he continued. "Considering that you hadn't played this game in a couple of months."

"Yeah, I guess that I am just better at the lightsaber game than the *Star Fighter* game. I do have to hand it to you, Ben; you have bested me in both games."

"Thanks. Good games," Ben said while shaking his father's left hand.

"Good games. Well, it's almost 11:30, and I'm sure your mom and brother are just about to head home from seeing the movie they went to see."

"Cool," Ben started as he unplugged the game console from the TV and put it back in the place he got it from under the TV. "I do have to comment about Josh. It's still a bit too surprising about the way he has opened up to and interacted better with the family."

"Definitely. I'm thinking that your incident began to switch on something in him. I began noticing it when Josh suggested to the family and Blake at your NASCAR birthday present that someone should call a doctor. I'm very proud of the young man that I see emerging from inside him. I think we should just enjoy and celebrate that fact about him. That's probably why your mom wanted to go to breakfast and a movie with him."

"For sure. I'm definitely proud of Josh as well. It's fun getting to spend more quality time with him, like when he and I rented and watched the new *Star Wars: Attack of the Clones* movie last week."

"Wasn't that the second time that you two watched it together other than when all four of us went to see it in theaters last year when it first came out?"

"Yes. Josh and I wanted to watch it again. So, we asked Mom to get it, and she went and rented it from the Blockbuster store about ten minutes from our house."

"Cool. I ended up watching it with your mom near the expiration date. I thought the movie was better than *The Phantom Menace*. The best part of *Attack of the Clones* for me was when all of the Jedi fought against Dooku's Separatist droid army on Geonosis. However, your mom and I were not big fans of how Anakin creepily interacted with Padmé. Go figure that he would become Darth Vader in the original trilogy."

"I totally agree with you about all of that. I think the Jedi versus Separatist droid army scene has been the best in the prequel trilogy so far."

"Yeah. I'm looking forward to the last movie in this prequel trilogy. It's coming out in 2005, right?"

"Yes. I can't wait to see how George Lucas ends the trilogy. It'll be cool to see how Anakin becomes Darth Vader. The redemption storyline of Darth Vader at the end of *Return of the Jedi* is the best, though."

"For sure, Son. That storyline is surely the best in terms of a good analogy of how God can turn bad people into good people, just like He turned Saul into Paul in the New Testament."

"Absolutely."

"Anyway, how is your job at American Burgers going?"

"It's going well. I'm still a great dishwasher. However, I'm looking to get the cashier position in a couple of months after Alberto leaves that position and goes on to work at a Walmart next to where he lives."

"I'm glad to hear that, Ben. I hope you get the position. All the best to Alberto for the job at Walmart. Are you confident you can perform to the fullest as a cashier?"

"Definitely. It will be a good challenge. I'm up for it."

"That's great! I love your confidence about working in that position! You'll be a really good cashier. I'll be praying that you will get the position even though you'll only be able to work on Mondays, Wednesdays, and Saturdays because of your Tuesday, Thursday, and Friday college class schedule. Why are you off today?"

"Thanks, Dad. I'll also be praying that I will get the cashier position. I'm going to talk to Claire, the manager of American Burgers, on Monday as well when I head into work. As for today, I'm off because there was another person coming in who is filling in for my position. I'm looking to be a server during the couple of months that Alberto will remain at American Burgers in the cashier position."

"Sounds like you have a good plan. All the best for talking to her. Sounds like quite a few people are coming to, switching positions, and leaving American Burgers."

"Thanks. Yeah, but I think the restaurant will become more stable in terms of holding positions a little bit into the college semester because we will need to do that. We will have more customers during that time. Anyway, I think I hear Mom's car driving into the garage in the back of the house."

Sure enough, Leslie was just about to park in the garage at the back of the house. Josh was sitting in the passenger seat to the right of his mom. Leslie had gotten a sleek silver Honda about a year ago. Dave was more than happy enough to pay for half of the car's cost. Leslie paid for the other half.

"Hello," Leslie said as she and Josh made their way into the house from the garage.

"Hello, you two," Dave responded as he went over to greet his wife and son. Ben shortly followed his dad. "How was breakfast? Where did you go?" Dave continued with the two curious questions.

"It was pretty good," Leslie responded. "We went to Denny's."

"Denny's is always good. What movie did you two see?"

"We saw a hilarious comedy movie," Josh chimed in.

"Yeah, it was quite funny," Leslie sad.

"Cool," Ben began. "I'm actually looking forward to two other comedy movies that come out later this year. *Secondhand Lions* and *Bruce Almighty*."

"I've heard that *Bruce Almighty* will be really good and funny," Leslie responded as she lead the way with her husband back to the family room sectional couch where all four of the family members sat down and relaxed. "*Secondhand Lions* sounds like an intriguing movie."

"Yeah," Dave jumped into the conversation. "*Bruce Almighty* is going to have some Christian themes to it, from what I have seen on the internet. It's bound to be really funny. Jim Carrey seems like a pretty good guy."

"Definitely," Josh responded. "I'm looking forward to both *Bruce Almighty* and *Secondhand Lions*."

"For sure," Ben responded. There were a few seconds of silence after he spoke.

"Well," Dave began, talking to his wife, "I think Ben has something to share with you and Josh."

"Really, what is it?" Leslie asked.

"Yeah, Bro, what's on your mind?" Josh asked curiously

"Nice setup, Dad," Ben said before continuing on. "Well, I wanted to come clean and share with you two some clarifying information about my past encounter with the young redhead I told you all about. I lied to you two and Dad. Her name is Sophia. I didn't choke when asking her out; she didn't accept the offer because of my disability. I could sense her looking at where my legs should have been, even though she was doing her best not to look at that area. I've told Dad all of this, and I'm really sorry that I lied to you and Josh," Ben finished saying to his mom and brother.

"Oh, Ben, I'm so sorry that happened to you. I wish you would have told your dad and us the truth when it happened. I'm there for you if you need to talk," Leslie responded genuinely with sadness in her voice.

"Yeah, Bro," Josh began before continuing. "Why did you lie to us? You should have told us the truth sooner. If you ever need to go to the gym to let loose and beat up a punching bag, I'll be there alongside you. Plus, we can immerse ourselves into playing the *Star Wars* game."

"Thanks, Mom. I'll be happy to talk when I want to talk with you," Ben said as he addressed his mom before turning to Josh. "We can definitely do some damage in the *Star Wars* lightsaber game, Bro. And I think I'll take you up on going to the gym sometime."

"Sounds great," Josh replied.

"Yeah," Leslie began as she addressed Ben before continuing. "I think it will be good for you and your brother to go to the gym sometime. We, as a family, should also go see *Bruce Almighty* when it comes out in theaters."

"All of these plans sound good," Dave responded. "They are good ways to get over disappointments. What do you say about going to see the movie as a family, Ben?"

"That sounds like a blast and another good way for me to take my mind off of Sophia. The thing is that I still feel that there is more to be had with her and me despite what happened last semester."

"That sure is interesting," Dave began in a curious yet pondering voice. "I think only God and time will tell what happens with you and Sophia."

"Your dad is right, Ben," Leslie responded while thinking about what her son said about there still being more to be had with him and Sophia. "You never know where things may lead. Maybe Sophia will change her mind about going out with you someday. For now, just do your best to take your mind off of her and let God fully handle the situation."

"Sounds good, Mom," Ben replied. "I want to do my best to not think about her, and I will only have God handle the situation from now on, no matter what happens."

"That's the spirit, Son!"Dave said before continuing. "Both of these hardships, with you losing your legs and Sophia not accepting you for who you are, will be worked out for your good by God."

"Amen," Leslie agreed.

"Amen," Ben joined in agreement.

"Yes, amen," Josh said in agreement as well before continuing on a humorous note. "I think that we should do a fun but safe prank on Sophia, like stringing her dorm door or door at wherever she lives with a silly string can or something like that so that she gets sprayed when she opens the door."

"No, Josh, we are not going to do that," Dave responded while chuckling a bit in laughter. "But that would be a bit funny."

"Agreed," Leslie said with an equal amount of laughter in her voice as her husband.

"That would definitely be funny, Bro," Ben said while cracking up a bit more in laughter than both of his parents. "I will settle for just not thinking about her for a while, playing the *Star Wars* game several times with you, going to the gym, and going to see both *Bruce Almighty* and *Secondhand Lions*, though."

"Oh, all right," Josh replied in a faked voice that sounded disappointed. "I'm glad that I can make everyone laugh, though."

"We are very appreciative, Josh," Dave responded a little bit before he was done laughing.

"Definitely," Leslie agreed after her laughter trailed off.

"For sure, Bro. Thank you," Ben said while still laughing a bit.

"You all are very welcome," Josh replied

"Now, how does a game of Monopoly sound with all of us before we get some snacks?" Ben asked after he was done laughing. "I'm determined to overthrow your reign, Mom."

"Oh, that's how it's going to be," Leslie replied with sarcastic curiosity in her voice. "It's on, Ben!"

"Yeah, all the best to you, babe," Dave replied before continuing. "Ben has been in a really competitive mood today."

"I see," Leslie said with more curiosity in her voice with the same sarcastic tone.

"Sounds fun," Josh responded as he and the rest of his family began to set up the Monopoly board and went by their usual rules. Those rules included handing out a certain amount of money and dealing out properties based on how high of a number each person got after rolling the two dice that came with the game. Each of the family members chose their moving pieces before beginning the game.

All the while the Lawson family was playing Monopoly and then making lunch snacks, a sneaky plan was being concocted by two brothers. Their plan would throw the Lawson family through an even bigger and more chaotic event. The two of them were known as the Dragano brothers. Yennik Dragano was the older brother, and Erik Dragano was the younger brother. Erik was twenty-three years old, and Yennik was twenty-six years old. They were Russian-American and had come to extreme poverty in Evart in 1999, when they and their parents, Ivan and Rena, moved to the American city from Moscow, Russia. Ivan and Rena were doing their best to provide for their sons, but they eventually were unable to keep up with the bills because Yennik had an asthma issue in eighth grade that lasted for five years and gradually worsened as the years went on. In addition, Erik had anger issues in high school due to his being bullied by other schoolmates. Erik damaged several of the school buildings. Ivan and Rena spent a lot of money paying back the school for the damage and then spent a small fortune on counseling for their young son. Yennik's asthma issue cleared up by the end of his high school years, and Erik got mostly better mentally after counseling several weeks after he graduated high school.

The parents then turned to drug dealing towards the spring of 1999 to provide for Yennik and Erik. Ivan and Rena enjoyed quite a bit of success selling heroin and cocaine. They were beginning to get back to the wealth that their family once had. Unfortunately, one of their heroin deals at the end of July 1999 went south, and they were arrested by the local police on the southern border of Michigan. Ivan and Rena had left Yennik and Erik at their modest home in Evart because they wanted to keep their sons safe. However, after Ivan and Rena were sent to a secure prison near the southern border of Michigan, the police found out where the two parents had been living in the middle of Evart. Ivan and Rena were never heard from again. One might assume that some other prisoners killed them. The police arrived at the house and took away all of the hidden money from the drug deals. They started the process of foreclosing the house and tried to put Yennik and Erik into a local foster parent home. The brothers became angry with the police because they had been denied permission to go see their parents after demanding to do so. Yennik and Erik figured out a way to kill the several policemen who were at the house and then started living life on the streets because it wasn't safe at the house. The two brothers would have been found out and thrown into prison as well. Thus, Yennik and Erik began stealing valuable items and reselling them to criminals. They bought a small house half an hour away from the Lawson family, on the opposite side of Evart, after they had made enough money to buy it. Yennik and Erik bought a small house in the area because they didn't want to draw attention to themselves. Plus, nobody in their neighborhood knew that they killed several policemen.

Now, at noon on January 11th, 2003, in their house, Yennik and Erik were plotting their next robbery. Erik was standing next to his brother, who was sitting in a comfortable couch chair with a little wooden coffee table in front of him. Displayed on the table was a colored map of the area that they were in in Evart. Yennik was deep in thought as he perused the map with his dark brown eyes that had a cold and calculating feel to them. The older brother had short, tight blond hair and was wearing a dark brown jacket over a plain white shirt, just like his brother. Yennik and Erik both had on dark brown trousers that had pockets for each of their pistols. The only few differences between the two Dragano brothers were that Erik had medium-length light brown hair and light blue eyes and was a bit less fit than his brother.

"What are you thinking, Yennik?" Erik asked in a perfect Russian accent, wanting to know which places they were going to hit next.

"I'm thinking that we hit the Evart University Art Museum and this apartment complex," Yennik began in an equally perfect Russian accent before continuing. "The Art Museum is bound to have some valuable works of art that we can take. Plus, I did some research on this apartment complex, and it looks like they have several expensive items that we can take as well. I gathered from my research that it is a very nice apartment."

"Sounds great. I think it will be easier for us to steal these items at night. I'm thinking that we can start heading over at a quarter to 10:00 p.m. The Art Museum and the apartment complex are close to us. I would think that it is about a ten-minute drive to the museum, and the complex is probably a five-minute walk from the museum. I can go to the apartment complex after you drop me off, and I can pick an apartment and get the expensive items, and you can walk over to the museum and get the works of art and other valuable sculptures. We will have to pretend to be students who are enjoying the nightlife, which shouldn't be too hard because of our age. How does all of that sound, Bro?"

"That sounds like a solid plan. I was thinking the same thing. It's smart to split up. Are you sure that you want to hit the apartment complex?"

"Yeah, I can hit it."

"Good. We will need to change our outfits a bit to blend in. We go at nine forty-five. As for now, let's make ourselves some lunch. I'm starving."

"Let's do it. I'm pretty hungry myself."

It was now four thirty in the afternoon, and the Lawson family was finishing up their late lunch hamburger, cheese, and A1 sauce bite snacks at their kitchen counter after a highly competitive game of Monopoly. Ben finally won and ended his mom's three-time winning streak.

"I still can't believe that you finally beat me, Ben," Leslie said in somewhat of an incredulous voice that was more incredulous immediately after her son beat her.

"Yeah, I'm a bit shocked that I won," Ben replied in a shocked voice before continuing. "You and I were placing hotels on all of our properties and getting mostly lucky with not landing on each other's and Dad and Josh's properties. There were a couple of times that I was scared because I landed on your, Dad's, and Josh's hotel-laden properties two to three times each. I was doing my best to strategically place hotels on my properties."

"It sure seemed that way," Leslie said before continuing. "You were really focused and intense in that game."

"For sure," Josh jumped into the conversation. "I thought I had a chance at beating you all when I had a lot of money and several hotels, but I ended up in third place.

"Well, you did better than me," Dave replied to his younger son. "I ended up in last place. We got smoked by Ben and Leslie. Anyway, what does everyone think about watching some TV before dinner?"

"Sounds fun," Leslie responded.

"Sure, let's do it," Ben said as his brother nodded in agreement.

Dave went to the sectional couch along with the rest of the family and turned on the TV. He scrolled through the channels, and something caught all of the family members' eyes. It was an episode of a show called *Smallville*. The episode was a few minutes more than halfway over. Josh was the first one to get totally enraptured in it, then the rest of the family followed like falling dominos. The episode was a repeat from season two the year before. Ben and the rest of his family remained glued to the TV for the remainder of the current episode and the next episode. The Lawson family quickly became fascinated with the early adventures of Clark Kent, who would later on become superman. Dave and Leslie got up at 6:00 p.m. to start making dinner after the second episode was done.

"Gosh, that was the most fun I have had watching a TV show in a long time."

"Absolutely," Leslie agreed excitedly.

"Same here," Ben chimed in. "I want to know more about Clark Kent's early adventures before he became superman. We should get the first season and then the second season when it comes to Blockbuster."

"You can count me in on that as well," Josh responded enthusiastically.

"Okay, sounds like a fun plan," Leslie said before continuing. "Your dad and I will get the first season on Friday of next week, and we all can watch some episodes after we all get back from work and school. How does that sound?"

"Sounds great; I'm looking forward to it," Ben responded enthusiastically.

"Same here," Josh agreed.

"Same for me as well," Dave responded. "Now, your mom and I are going to make shredded beef burritos for dinner. It is a faster dinner to eat, and Ben is going over to Diego's apartment to hang out with him. I believe that you forgot to mention your plan for tonight, Ben."

"Sorry, I got too wrapped up in watching *Smallville*," Ben replied in a genuinely sorry voice.

"That's fine, Ben, just be safe," Leslie responded cautiously.

"I will be safe, Mom, don't worry."

"All right."

"I'm going to drive Ben to Diego's apartment at seven, and he will be there by seven fifteen. I will pick him up at ten. He will be safe. I will look out for suspicious people. Does all of that sound good, Ben?"

"Sounds good to me," Ben said in agreement.

"That sounds good to me as well," Leslie responded as she went to kiss Dave. Dave accepted the kiss and kissed her back. The two of them then went into the kitchen to make dinner.

"Okay," Dave said warmly before continuing. "Dinner will be ready in about twenty-five minutes." Ben and Josh stayed next to and on the sectional couch and found a movie to watch while they waited for dinner.

Dinner came and went in a blur. Ben really enjoyed the shredded beef burritos, as did the rest of the family. It was now a few minutes before 7:00 p.m., and Dave was going out to the garage to drive the van out and get it ready for his son.

"Have fun at Diego's apartment," Leslie said.

"I will, Mom," Ben replied.

"Have a great time, Bro," Josh responded before continuing. "Have a blast playing the *Star Wars* game with Diego."

"Thanks, Bro. I'll see you later."

"Later," Josh replied as he went to hug his brother. Ben then wheeled out of the house through the garage and got in the van with the *Star Wars* game in his lap.

It was a fifteen-minute drive to Diego's apartment. Ben felt a deeper sense of peace about "the Sophia situation" and the incident that cost him his legs. He felt that sense of peace all the way to the apartment complex. Dave was looking out for suspicious people as he and his son arrived at the apartment complex. Once Dave and Ben got out of the van, Ben noticed how nice it was, even though everything was a little darkened by the cool night sky. There were two beautiful water fountains in the middle of the complex. All of the apartments that Ben could see were made of sleek teal green stone, which probably was pretty expensive to use, Ben thought. They each were three stories high. The doors to the apartments were made of wood of great quality and texture, as far as Ben could tell by looking at them. The wooden doors were completely smooth and had a round, silver-colored door handle on each one of them. Ben knew Diego's apartment number: 8001. It was one of the first apartments that he and his dad saw as they got out of the van. All of the apartment numbers were to the right of the apartment doors. Dave did some more scouting for suspicious people on the way to Diego's apartment but found nobody who fit that description. Ben knocked on his friend's apartment door once he and his dad got to it.

"Hey, Ben and Mr. Lawson," Diego said after he opened the door.

"Hey, Diego, how is it going?" Dave asked.

"Pretty good, Mr. Lawson, thanks for asking. I'm glad that you could bring Ben here."

"For sure. I know Ben has been looking forward to coming to your apartment. I have to say, this is really nice."

"Definitely," Ben agreed. "It's a great place."

"Thanks, you two. Come inside, Ben."

"All right," Ben replied to Diego before switching his attention to his dad. "I will see you at ten."

"Sounds like a plan," Dave said before continuing. "You are safe here, from what I have seen. See you later. Nice to see you again, Diego. Bye."

"You too. Bye, Mr. Lawson," Diego replied just as Dave was walking away from his apartment. Ben then went inside the apartment, and Diego closed the door. "I see that you brought the *Star Wars* game from your house. That will be fun to play."

"For sure," Ben replied excitedly before continuing on a more serious note. "Can I talk to you about something first?"

"You can talk to me about anything," Diego said as he sat down on his small dark brown couch behind the TV.

"Well, you remember when I told you about how it went with me asking out the young redhead from the Christian religion general education class last semester?"

"Yeah, I remember. You called me that night and told me that you choked when asking her out. Did you attempt to ask her out again a little bit down the road? I'm sensing that there is more to this story. You would have told me what else happened."

"I definitely would have told you what else had happened. The thing is that I lied. The young redhead's name is Sophia. I didn't choke. Sophia rejected my offer because she saw that I have no legs. I didn't want to tell you because it was too painful to talk about that situation at that time. I'm sorry for lying to you, and I promise that I won't lie to you again."

"Hey, man, I'm deeply sorry that Sophia rejected you just because you have no legs. Life is more than having legs to walk. Disabled people like you can adapt and make things work out with where you are at. Sophia should have looked past you, having no legs, but I guess she must have been scared and turned off by the idea of going out with you. You should have felt comfortable telling me what really happened, but I completely understand why you didn't tell me. My ex-girlfriend and I broke up a year before God called me to come to Evart. It took me a few months to get over the experience of breaking up with her and to open up to my parents about the whole situation. I appreciate that you just told me what really happened and that you will not lie to me again. Again, I'm sorry about Sophia rejecting you."

"Thanks, man. We're good, right?"

"Totally. Just know that you can talk to me about anything, no matter how big or small that thing is."

"I will definitely do that. Can I share something else with you?"

"Sure, go on ahead."

"I have still been feeling that there is more to me and Sophia even after the incident with her last semester."

"Well, my advice to you, as always, is that you should pray about the situation and see where God leads you and Sophia. I hope that it works out for you two somehow."

"Sounds good, thanks. I will do that as well. Sorry to hear about your ex-girlfriend. You should have told me about her. We have talked about young women in addition to our conversations about God, video games, and baseball, but I guess not that specifically. Are you seeing any young woman now?"

"You're right; I didn't want to talk about my ex-girlfriend for the same reason that you didn't want to tell me about Sophia rejecting you and your offer to go out with you. I haven't been as good as a friend as I should have been in terms of talking about my personal life. My ex-girlfriend's name was Claire, and we started well in our relationship, which lasted for two years. We had fun interacting with each other and going to events within the boundaries of an appropriate relationship in the sight of God. However, as I later found out, she wasn't that spiritual and didn't have that great of a relationship with God because of past personal trauma. We eventually broke up because of that the year before I came to Evart. It was still painful to break up with Claire because it was the only relationship that I had and because I thought God intended for us to get married. I ended up not telling my parents about the breakup for a few months, as I said before, and it took me several months to sort things out with God. As a positive during that time, I grew stronger in my relationship with God. Then God sent me to you. To answer your question, I'm currently talking with a young woman whose name is Vanessa, and our conversations are going pretty well. I'm having God handle our future together, and it looks bright so far. I promise to be more open with you about my personal life from now on, same as you with me. Anyway, on a different note, are you ready to do some damage in the *Star Wars* game?"

"We can definitely play the *Star Wars* game now. I appreciate you being open to me about your past relationship with Claire. I pray that everything goes great with you and Vanessa."

"Thanks, Ben, that means a lot. Let's play the *Battle of Yavin-4 Star Fighter* game first."

"You got it," Ben replied as he handed Diego the game for him to plug into the TV. It was now about seven forty, and the two friends played games for the next two hours. Diego really found another gear when he triumphantly defeated the *Star Fighter* game, as if it were as easy as a knife going through butter. Ben emerged as victoriously as his friend did. Both Ben and Diego shouted a bit in victory after they completed the game. Then Ben started playing the lightsaber game. He used all of his tricks, skills, and emotions to get to the first part of level five with Luke Skywalker as his character. Ben lost to old Obi-Wan in the first part of level five, and then Diego took his turn playing the lightsaber game. Diego got to the final part of level four with old Obi-Wan as his character, but he lost in that part to Emperor Palpatine. The two friends played the lightsaber game again, and both of them got to the first part of level six before losing. Ben and Diego then began to wrap up their night at nine forty. It was just another day for Ben Lawson and Diego Sanchez, who had fun hanging out with each other.

It was also just another day, or night in this case, for Yennik and Erik Dragano as they prepared to begin their robberies at the Evart Art Museum and the apartment complex that they were targeting. Little did they know that Diego Sanchez lived in one of the apartments in that complex and that Ben Lawson was with him. Ben and Diego were directly in the crosshairs, and Diego was going to experience a chaotic and life-altering moment that was going to happen to his friend.

CHAPTER 4:

TIME OF DEATH AND NEW LIFE

Yennik Dragano dropped off his younger brother, Erik, at the apartment complex that Diego Sanchez lived in at 9:53 p.m. The two brothers got lucky in getting two out of four green traffic lights on the way to the apartment complex. It was an eight-minute drive instead of a ten-minute drive, so they thought that was good. There were only a few parking spaces left in the parking area about twenty-four footsteps away from the apartments, and Yennik had parked in one of them. Most of the students were out partying and de-stressing from the past school week. The other students who were at the apartment complex were just relaxing in their apartments. Those students had parked their cars in the parking spots right up against the edge of the apartment complex. None of them were close to the apartment that Erik was going to steal from. The two Dragano brothers were rehearsing their plan in their heads as Yennik turned off his and Erik's red Ford truck. They would meet back at the truck and drive off after they accomplished their tasks. Yennik began his five-minute walking journey towards the Evart Art Museum in black sneakers, light blue jeans, a white Beatles shirt, and a black jacket that concealed a pistol that had a silencer on it.

Erik began his short journey towards the apartments in black and gray sneakers, dark blue jeans, a red shirt with a few dark blue horizontal stripes, and a black jacket like his brother's that concealed a pistol with a silencer on it. The younger brother took his time walking towards the apartments, acting like a student casually going to his apartment. Erik already had chosen an apartment to break into and take valuable items from. Two minutes had passed since Yennik started towards the museum. Erik was using the two minutes to calm himself down in addition to acting like a student. He wanted to get one or two things as quickly as he could. Erik finally arrived at Diego Sanchez's apartment. It was now 9:55 p.m. Erik knocked on the door.

Dave Lawson decided to go to pick up his son a few minutes earlier than ten. He still wanted to be careful with Ben being at Diego's apartment complex, especially with things that could happen after ten at night. Leslie talked to her husband about that safety issue, and he completely agreed with her. However, Dave was going to be a couple of minutes too late.

"I think my dad is here," Ben said to Diego after they heard the knocks on the door. Ben was talking to Diego about the *Smallville* TV show before the knocking started. "He is sometimes two to five minutes early when picking me up from my college classes and work. I'm going to see."

"All right, I will head over to the door with you," Diego replied before continuing. "By the way, you will have to invite me over to your house to watch *Smallville* when you and your family get the first season. It sounds like a really interesting show."

"For sure, that will be fun!"

Erik Dragano knocked a couple more times before Ben and Diego got to the door. It was too dark for the two friends to see who the person was in the window. Plus, they couldn't see the person anyway because of the angle of the window's view to the door. The window was not that big, and it was further away from the door to the right. Ben opened the door a few inches, but by the time he did that, it was already too late. It all happened immediately. Erik pushed the door open just enough so that he could squeeze halfway through the doorway. Then he quickly withdrew the silenced pistol that was concealed in his black jacket and shot Ben two times in the chest, a few inches to the right of his heart.

"No, Ben!" Diego shouted as Erik pulled up his silver-gray pistol to aim at Diego. Erik simultaneously pushed the door open the rest of the way, sending Ben reeling back and slightly to the left. Diego quickly dodged and moved to the right just before Erik fired off another shot. The Southern Chilean dived to the right into the kitchen area. Erik was closing in on him and preparing to take a fourth shot. Diego ducked down after instantly grabbing a big thirty-ounce glass cup and then waited after the fourth shot from Erik came and missed. Erik was standing right next to a crouched-down Diego. Diego instantly used the counter to immediately get himself up and slapped aside the pistol to the right with his free right hand. That gave Diego just enough time to slam the glass cup on Erik's temple on the left side of his head, smashing the cup into about a dozen pieces. Erik then fell backwards onto his back with a thud on the smooth wooden floor, completely unconscious. Several pieces of the glass cup lay around Erik's body. Diego hurried over to Ben, who was leaning a bit to the right with blood coming out of the right side of his chest. Ben was at the far left corner of the kitchen area, near the hallway that led to Diego's bedroom and the bathroom. The Southern Chilean heard a larger car engine and guessed that Ben's dad had actually arrived or that it was someone coming to help. Diego immediately went to Ben instead of finding out who else came to the apartment complex. Ben's dad had indeed arrived, but Diego wasn't focused on that at the moment.

"This is a reason why I didn't end up having any roommates," Diego said to himself. He was able to afford the monthly rent and other expenses with his IT job that he did on several days after school. The other reason for Diego not having any roommates was because he just wanted to live by himself in his apartment.

"Oh, God," Dave Lawson said in horror as he pulled up in front of Diego's apartment and saw Diego leaning over Ben. The thing that horrified Dave the most was not the unconscious body near the kitchen of the apartment. It was seeing his son bleeding out that made him deeply horrified and scared to death. "Ben!" Dave shouted as he instantly got out of the van and hurried over to his son and Diego, not paying any attention to the unconscious body.

"Hold on, Ben. Your dad is here," Diego said in a shaky but reaffirming voice. It was now 9:57 p.m. Ben felt like everything in his body was stopping and that life was gradually being drained out of him.

"Dad," Ben managed to say in a bit of a distorted whisper as his dad got to him and Diego.

"Don't talk, Son, just stay calm," Dave said before turning his attention to Diego. "What happened?"

"This guy, who's unconscious now, knocked on my door, and Ben thought that he was you. Ben said that you sometimes arrive a few minutes early to pick him up from his college classes and work. I had no freaking idea that this would happen."

"Okay, stop freaking out, Diego, it wasn't your fault," Dave replied reassuringly.

"Really? It doesn't feel that way. I let my friend open my apartment door, thinking that the person outside was you. Ben got shot as a result. It sure feels like my fault. At least I knocked out that son of a gun. He deserved to have had more done to him."

"All right, just cool down. You didn't know this was going to happen. By the way, I'm glad that you knocked out that good-for-nothing guy. At least nobody else got hurt."

"Thanks, but that doesn't make me feel better at the moment."

"I know. Me too," Dave said, still with horror in his voice and on his face. He then switched his attention back to his son. "All right, Ben, just hold on. I'm going to tie my jacket around the spots where you got shot in order to stop the bleeding as much as I can. I'm going to call your mom, and she and Josh will meet us and Diego at the hospital." Dave called Leslie before Ben could say anything. Then Ben spoke again as Dave's phone was searching for an answer from Leslie's phone.

"Dad," Ben started in that distorted whisper, "I don't think I'm going to make it to the hospital. I feel cold." Some blood was coming out of the right side of Ben's mouth.

"Just hold on, Son!" Dave said in a louder but slightly trembling voice before speaking to Diego. "Diego, help me get Ben out of his chair and get him into the van. We need to get him to the hospital now."

"Definitely," Diego replied, still in a shaky and now a more shocked voice. "Here we go." Diego carefully unbuckled Ben's seat belt as Leslie picked up her phone."

"Hello, babe," Leslie said before continuing. "Did you pick up Ben?"

"Um, that's the thing," Dave replied, trying to calm down. "Ben got shot. We need you and Josh to meet us at the hospital as soon as you can..." The next thing that Dave heard was going to haunt him for the rest of his life, but it would get a bit better.

"What?" Leslie shouted before going into a mixture of a loud scream and a cry. Josh heard his mom and came running to her and asked his father what was going on. Dave tried his best to remain somewhat calm while retelling the abbreviated story that he said to his wife. Josh then slammed his fist on the living room table in anger.

"Diego, don't try to pick me up," Ben said to Diego in the same voice that he was currently using. "I want to speak to my mom and Josh."

"No, Ben," Diego was now pleading with Ben in a trembling voice. "We are going to get you to the hospital, and you are going to be okay!"

"I'm not going to make it, and you know it. I don't want you and my dad to pick me up and get me in the van to go to the hospital," Ben replied as he put his right hand over Diego's right hand before Diego was going to attempt to help pick him up.

"Listen to him, Diego," Dave said in a defeated voice. "Put my phone next to his right ear." Dave switched his attention to his phone before Diego was allowed to grab it. "Hey, Lez and Josh, Ben wants to talk to you two. We are not going to make it to the hospital. Get to Diego's apartment as soon as you can."

"Hey, Mom and Josh," Ben began in that all too familiar distorted whisper after Diego put Dave's phone up to his right ear and mouth and held Ben's core and the rest of himself up straight. Ben could hear his mom and brother rushing to the garage to get into Leslie's Honda. He waited until the two of them were in the car. Josh immediately got in the passenger seat. "I just want to let you two know that I love you both so much. Mom, thanks for always driving me to my sports activities, helping me with school and my homework, cheering me up when I was down, and giving me wise advice. I want you to do your best to stay calm and get to where I am as quickly as you can. Josh, thanks for always being a good brother, even with your past difficulties. I have loved playing sports and the *Star Wars* video game with you. I know God has great plans for you in every area of your life."

Diego took away the phone after Ben gave him a thumbs-up. Diego gave the phone back to Dave. After two minutes, Leslie and Josh had now driven a good amount of distance. They were going as fast as they could.

"Tell Mom and Josh that I'm sorry," Ben said to his dad as he was feeling the life being drained mostly out of him. "I'm going to hold out for as long as I can, but I think I only have a couple more minutes. I'm sorry, Dad. Thank you for helping me through 'the Sophia situation' and for helping me be a better man."

"You're so welcome, my son," Dave said as he was beginning to tear up. "That's what I'm here for. I will make sure to tell your mom and Josh that you were sorry that you couldn't hold out long enough for them to get here. I truly love you so much, Ben." Dave began to weep a little bit after he kissed his son's forehead, which was becoming colder.

"Diego," Ben began before continuing, "thank you for helping me when I most needed it, even though I didn't accept your help at first. You have been the best friend that I have ever had. I know that things will work out with you and Vanessa."

"Thanks, Ben, that means a lot," Diego started while he, like Dave, was breaking down and tearing up a little bit. "You are so welcome for the help, man. It doesn't matter that you didn't accept it at first. The thing that matters is that you accepted the help that I gave you in the end. Say hi to God for me. We all will miss you so much. It has been an honor to be your best friend."

Ben gave his friend a thumbs-up with his right hand and then saw the light of Diego's apartment disappear from his eyes as they closed. Then Ben Lawson died. The time of death was 10:03 p.m. on that cool night on Saturday, January 11th, 2003, inside Diego Sanchez's apartment. Dave's light, white fabric jacket that he tied around Ben's chest now had large circles of blood on the areas where he got shot. Diego then broke down into more of a light sob. Dave wept a bit more loudly, almost at the same time.

"I'm going to call the local police so that they put away that lunatic of a guy for the rest of his life," Diego said while somewhat recomposing himself. He called the local police so that they would take Erik Dragano away. Dave could only give Diego a thumbs-up while he was mourning the death of his firstborn son. It took the police a few minutes to arrive after Diego described what happened to his best friend. Leslie and Josh arrived at Diego's apartment just after the police had arrived. The two of them quickly hurried over to where Dave and Diego were inside Diego's apartment. Leslie and Josh then began to sob intensely, leaning over Ben's lifeless body. Diego had let go of Ben's body after he died, and it went back to leaning to the right. The policemen took away Erik Dragano's still unconscious body and hauled him into a police car. Erik would later wake up on his way to a prison, where he would remain for the rest of his life. The Lawson family and Diego didn't want the police to take Ben's body to the mortuary at the hospital. The four of them wanted to do that and then have the funeral when they were ready.

A few events happened after Ben died. The first event was that Ben went to heaven. The experience was so amazing to Ben. He was closing his eyes one moment when he died, and then the next moment he was in heaven. The nineteen-year-old was caught up in a cloud-like atmosphere. Ben looked down, and he saw that he had his legs back. In addition, Ben saw that he was dressed in all-white clothing. He didn't feel sad or mad, but he felt truly content and fulfilled. Ben looked straight out again and saw an open pearly gate and streets of gold behind it. The streets of gold were like transparent glass. An angel stood at the pearly gate. Ben waved to him, and he waved back. There was also a high wall on both sides of the gate. It had twelve foundations that were made of twelve precious stones. Ben knew all of the names of the stones even though he had only known three of them before he died and went to heaven. He guessed that believers/Christians knew everything and every other believer/ Christian when they went to heaven. There were a couple of other pearly gates and more of the high, twelve-stone wall that Ben could see on his left and right. Two more angels stood at those gates. There were also three more gates on each of the other three sides of heaven, which was also where the New Jerusalem was. He saw a majestic, crystal-clear river that flowed all the way to God's throne. The tree of life stood on each side of the river of the water of life, as it is called. Ben remembered reading about this in the Bible's book of Revelation.

There was someone walking towards and through the open pearly gate. He was also dressed in all white, and there was a unique glow all over His skin. The man had straight but somewhat curly and wavy shoulder-length brown hair. He also had a similar colored beard that was about one and a half inches long and stretched from ear to ear, where His sideburns were. His eyes were hazel green. Ben guessed that the man was Jewish because of what Ben had learned about Him in Sunday school. The man stopped a few feet in front of him. Ben immediately knew that the man was Jesus/God/the Holy Spirit, also known as the three-in-one Godhead/Trinity. Jesus had a compassionate and loving look on His face, and His voice matched that facial look. There was also a little bit of a sad look on His face, but it only lasted for a second.

"Welcome, Benjamin Lawson," Jesus said just before He hugged Ben in a loving embrace. Jesus was thinking of the John 10:10 Scripture verse, which said that "the thief comes only to steal and kill and destroy; I have come that they may have life, and have it to the full." The thief, also known as the devil, who had used Yennik and Erik Dragano to kill Ben and to attempt to steal valuable items from Diego's apartment and the Evart University Art Museum, had done exactly what the beginning of the Scripture verse said. Jesus had the second part of the verse in mind as He let go of Ben. Jesus also had something in mind for Yennik Dragano after Erik was hauled away in the police car. It was another incident that would happen to Sophia O'Donnell at that same time that greatly saddened Jesus, as well as what happened to Ben.

"Am I in heaven?" Ben asked Jesus before continuing. "It is completely amazing here. I'm in awe."

"Yes, you are in heaven," Jesus replied in His loving and compassionate voice before continuing as well. "I'm glad that you love it here. It is quite an unfortunate reason why you are here now. I knew this would happen, and it broke my heart to see you get shot by Erik Dragano. I'm so sorry that happened to you. I have something that I want to do for you."

"Thank You for Your condolences, Jesus. I don't feel mad or sad about what happened. I just feel fully content and fulfilled being with You in heaven. The memory of how I died and came here is gone, which is great. I'm glad for that. Plus, I have my legs back. What do You want to do for me? Can I stay here with You, every other Christian, and the angels? I want to see them."

"That's the beauty of heaven. No more tears, which My Father will wipe away, just like it says in the book of Revelation. There will be no more pain, death, and sorrow as well. I'm very joyful and happy that you want to stay and that you will get the chance to be with Me and everyone else, but I want to give you more of a taste of what I can give you in life on earth. I know you had a zest for wanting to experience everything that I could offer you in life, and I am prepared to give you exactly that. I also want you to tell every Christian you meet one of two very important messages from Me. They are more important than anything else that I have said. The first message I want you to tell them is that I will always love, protect, and provide for them, especially Anthony Markus and Hannah Rine at Evart University. They have been going through some tough times in terms of loneliness. They each want to be in serious and godly relationships with members of the opposite sex. Plus, both Anthony and Hannah are going through a rough time just after each set of their parents got divorced. As you know, divorces greatly grieve me. Anthony and Hannah both feel a sense of abandonment because of the divorces. You should also tell your family and your best friend, Diego, about My message of love, provision, and protection. They are greatly saddened about what happened to you."

Jesus continued by saying, "I also want you to tell My first message to the nonbelievers you meet, including the nonbelievers you interact with at your job at American Burgers. You will not be able to tell all of your co-workers about My message, so I will also lead the co-workers to whom you tell My message to share it with the rest of them. I will ignite all of the nonbelievers' minds and hearts with a hunger for Me and to have personal relationships with Me after they have repented of their sins and are saved. I forgave all of their sins, in addition to all of the sins of the Christians, when I sacrificed Myself for them over 2,000 years ago. Plus, I will forgive the sins of the nonbelievers again when they repent of them and ask Me into their hearts. They will receive My message and follow Me, as well as the Christians. Secondly, I want you to tell both the Christians and the nonbelievers that the kingdom of heaven and all of its goodness is in every born-again Christian who has a relationship with Me and obediently does the will of My Father."

"I'm good with all of that, even though I want to stay here. I believe that I will experience everything that You want me to experience. I will tell everyone I meet what You want to say to them, especially my family, Diego, Anthony, and Hannah. When can I come back to heaven?"

"That's also another thing that I want to talk with you about. Sorry for not telling you that a minute ago. I thought it would be better if I told you now because there are other things attached to your request. It will not end well for you on May 13th of 2005. I want to spare you from that unfortunate event. Once you get back to your family's house tonight, write down what I'm going to say to you now and keep it in a safe place. Take the longer route to your and your future wife's favorite restaurant on North Waterfront Avenue instead of the fastest route. I also want to spare you and her from the many hardships of marriage, which I told My servant Paul to write down under the inspiration of the Holy Spirit. The first two years of marriage for you and your wife will not have big challenges.

"Also, I want to spare you and your wife from the times ahead on Earth that will be very troubling for the two of you and both of your families. Some of the troubles include a stock market crash, robberies, viruses, and diseases. Finally, no matter what you do and ask of Me, your town will present life-threatening events to you and your wife for just over a year after May 13th, 2005. It would be several times each month that you and your wife would die a few times until June 4th, 2006. The first life-threatening event with the drunk driver on May 13th, 2005, which I've told you how to avoid, is totally preventable. The second life-threatening event is on May 14th, 2005, but you and your wife cannot prevent it. Someone else will prevent the second life-threatening event for you and her. I won't tell you who that person is, but I can tell you that it will make sense with what that person chooses to do for a short time in his or her life. There is nothing that I can do to stop the violent people from killing you and your wife during the time period from May 14th, 2005, to June 4th, 2006. It is somewhat like a plot line from a 2002 movie called *The Time Machine*. I cannot change the free will of those violent people who would kill you and your wife. I don't want you two to experience death again, though.

"Therefore, you and she will come back to heaven on May 14th, 2005, at 2:00 p.m.," Jesus said this, and the thought of what would happen to Ben towards the middle of 2005 began to appear in his mind. Ben and his wife would be on their way to a dinner date at one of their favorite restaurants, but a drunk driver would T-bone them at full speed, killing both of them. Jesus immediately put that thought aside and never thought about it again. The stock market crash of 2008, viruses and diseases, and other horrible disasters in every way tried to pry their way into Jesus's mind, but He batted them away as easily as the thought of Ben and his wife's car crash. That potential second death and numerous hardships would not happen to Ben and his wife because of what Jesus had instructed and told Ben to do about what would happen when the time came.

"Thank you. I really appreciate that. I will write down and remember what You said and keep it safe. Wait, hold on. Will I have a wife? Who is she? Will my family and Diego be okay after I come back to heaven?" Ben knew and felt that the things that Jesus said were right and true, even the hardships and deaths that he and his wife would have to experience. Fortunately, Ben and his wife would not experience death again.

"I'm not going to tell you. You will have to find out by yourself. As for your family and Diego, they will be good after you come back to heaven, but they will wrestle with the fact that they won't have you anymore for some time."

"Okay. Yeah, it will take time for them to digest that."

"For sure. Well, Ben, this is where we part for now. Remember, I will always love you, your family, Diego, Anthony, Hannah, and everyone else, and I will always provide for and protect all of you. I love you, Ben, My dear child."

"Sounds good, Jesus. I love you too. All of my hope and trust is in You for everything from now on."

"I'm very happy to hear that. See you later. Tell Diego that I said hi back."

"Oh, I forgot to say that he wanted to say hi. I will tell him that You said hi back. See You later, Jesus."

Then Jesus sent Ben back down to earth in the exact place in Diego's apartment after Ben said that. Ben's family and Diego were just about to pick up Ben and put him into the van. Dave said to everyone that they should stop when he saw an incredible and miraculous sight. Ben started to breathe again. Ben's dad quickly removed his bloodied jacket and found that the bullet holes in his son had healed up to only scars. However, there were still holes in Ben's T-shirt. Plus, there was still blood around the T-shirt holes, and Ben still had some blood on his mouth. Dave, Leslie, Josh, and Diego became immensely excited when Ben finally opened his eyes again. Everyone embraced Ben and didn't let go for a couple of minutes. Ben's family and Diego praised God for this absolute miracle.

"My beautiful son, I'm so overjoyed that you are back with us!" Leslie said in the middle of crying tears of joy.

"Yeah, Ben, you scared us to death," Dave responded after mostly recomposing himself. "We're extremely grateful that we have you back."

"Yeah, Bro, I was so worried about you. I'm sorry I didn't go with you to protect you," Josh said in kind of a regretful voice towards the end.

"Yeah, man, that was super scary to have to experience. I, too, am very thankful that you are back with us," Diego responded.

"Yeah, guys, I'm excited to be back with you all as well!" Ben said in his usual strong and firm voice, full of complete health, as he started hugging his family and Diego. He then continued, "You all should hear the amazing story that I have! I went to heaven and saw Jesus and talked with Him for a little bit!"

"What?" Everyone exclaimed simultaneously.

"How was it like in heaven?" Diego asked first.

"It was like nothing you have experienced," Ben replied in kind of an awestruck voice. "I felt completely content and fulfilled, and I honestly wanted to stay in heaven."

"That's awesome, man! I could imagine that you would want to stay in heaven. We all would have missed you a lot, though. Why did Jesus send you back to us? Did you say hi to God for me? I still can't wrap my head around the Trinity."

"For sure. Jesus said that He wanted to give me another chance to experience all that He has for me in this life on earth and to tell everyone that He will always love, provide for, and protect them. I actually forgot to tell Him that you said hi to Him. However, He knew that you had asked me to tell Him that, and He said hi back to you."

"Sweet, dude!" Diego exclaimed. It's awesome that Jesus gave you a second chance at life to experience all He has for you and to tell everyone that He will always love, provide for, and protect them. Plus, it's amazing that He said hi back to me."

"Yeah, Son," Dave said in total amazement. Leslie and Josh were speechless and could only smile at the moment. "All of this is just so amazing and overwhelming at the same time! I think we all should just go back to our family's house, and we can talk for a while more before finally deciding to go to bed. I don't know if any of us will get any sleep, though. Diego, you are welcome to come with us and sleep on the sectional couch for the night if you want."

"For sure, Mr. Lawson, I would absolutely be down for that. Thank you for the offer," Diego replied with gratitude in his voice.

"You're welcome. You're always welcome at our family's house."

"Okay, I think it is time for all of us to head to the house. Diego, you can follow us in your car."

"Sounds like a plan."

"I just want to say that I have some other things to tell everybody when we get home," Ben added.

"I bet you do, Ben," Dave replied with great understanding and interest in his voice before he started to head over to the van.

"Yeah, Bro," Josh responded with amazement in his voice before continuing. "I can't wait to hear about all that you experienced." Josh then walked over to Leslie's Honda and hopped in the passenger seat, and Leslie followed after him and got in the driver's seat.

"I, too, look forward to hearing about your incredible experience in heaven," Diego said before he went over to his own car.

Ben was the last one to leave Diego's apartment and head into the van after Dave dropped down the powered ramp. The nineteen-year-old deeply thought about all that happened to him that day and night. He had seen that he still had no legs, but he knew and believed that everything was going to work out, just like Jesus said. Ben thought of a perfect place in his backpack where he would put the piece of paper that would have the life-saving information. He pondered all of these things while he and his dad were on their way home. It was now 10:18 p.m., and Ben still had his experience in heaven to share with his family and Diego.

The second event that happened, which was actually five minutes before Jesus brought Ben back to life on earth, was that Yennik Dragano came out of the Evart University Art Museum at 10:10 p.m. after looking around at the wonderful and expensive works of art. He had taken his time, not wanting to draw attention from the few other visitors who were there. Yennik did a great job acting like a student looking at the works of art before the museum closed at ten thirty. He made his move after the few visitors had left. The Russian-American stole a medium-sized Picasso painting with several little diamonds around the gold-colored frame. Yennik also took a small silver sculpture of a famous Native American warrior. He quickly put the sculpture underneath the left lower flap area of his jacket and supported it with his left forearm and hand. Yennik placed the Picasso painting underneath the lower right flap area of his jacket and supported it with his right forearm and hand. His silenced pistol was underneath the painting.

The final event that happened was that Sophia O'Donnell was walking towards the museum, heading towards her dorm after a light late-night jog. Sophia also arrived at the wrong place at the wrong time. Her dorm was in the middle of the apartment complex where Ben Lawson had just died and the museum. She saw Yennik and noticed he was holding two objects underneath his black jacket. Sophia asked him what he was holding, especially since he had just exited the museum. Yennik didn't waste any time because the police were driving towards the museum from Diego Sanchez's apartment. He put the Picasso painting underneath the sculpture. Sophia didn't have time to shout to the cops to come to grab Yennik. He drew out his pistol and shot Sophia two times in the chest, a couple of inches to the right of her heart. Sophia fell backwards onto the concrete sidewalk in front of the museum. Yennik then put his pistol back where he got it and started running in the direction that Sophia had come from. The police had seen him shoot Sophia and immediately called an ambulance. Then they sped up their police cars, doing their best to catch Yennik. Yennik tried to cross a street in front of him, but the police got in front of him and turned on that street, knocking Yennik down.

The police arrested Yennik and put him next to his brother, who was starting to wake up. Both of them had metal cuffs on that put their hands together in front of their bodies. The Picasso painting cracked in several places after the police knocked down the Russian-American. The sculpture was partially to blame for cracking the Picasso painting because the sculpture hit the painting hard enough for it to crack. Yennik suffered moderate to high bruising both from the police knocking him down and the sculpture and painting hitting his left side when he went down. The sculpture broke into a few pieces when it hit the ground. Aside from the works of art being damaged, the police thought that it was their lucky night to catch the two Dragano brothers. Yennik and Erik would share the same prison cell for the rest of their lives. The police returned the cracked Picasso painting and sculpture to the museum for it to be repaired, if possible. The workers at the museum threw away the sculpture after the police also returned it to them. It was too broken. However, the workers were able to repair most of the Picasso painting. Then, the police sped off with the two criminals at 10:15 p.m.

An ambulance arrived a couple of minutes after the police had left, and the medical team picked up Sophia, put her on a stretcher cart, and wheeled her inside the ambulance. The medical team then zipped away in the ambulance with Sophia inside it. They turned on their lights and sirens and desperately tried to get to the hospital as fast as they could. It was usually a ten-minute drive to the hospital from the Evart University Art Museum, but the medical team was on track to make it there in five minutes. There weren't too many people driving on the road at this time of night. The people who were driving at that time pulled over to the right when the ambulance came by. The medical team had put an oxygen mask on Sophia's face and mouth and put a bandage on her shot wounds to help stop the bleeding as much as they could. Unfortunately, it would be too late.

"She's not breathing," one of the medical team members said in a medium-deep voice after he noticed and felt with his right hand that Sophia wasn't breathing. He was a mostly fit African-American man in his early forties with short black hair and brown eyes. His name was Carl Wendleson, and he was wearing a traditional white and red medical team outfit like everyone else on the team. The driver pulled into a parking spot right next to the hospital doors just as Carl said that Sophia wasn't breathing. The five minutes had already passed by.

"That's not good," another medical team member said in a smooth and somewhat deep voice. She was a younger African-American woman in her mid-thirties. Her name was Tess Debor. She had shoulder-length black hair and hazel-green eyes and was in good physical shape. "Get her to the ER! Let's move it!" Tess shouted this right before the rest of the medical team opened the ambulance doors and wheeled Sophia out on the stretcher.

It was already too late as the medical team hurriedly busted through the hospital doors and told Debra Welsh that they were taking Sophia to the emergency room. Tess was shouting "code blue" as she and the rest of the medical team rushed her into the ER. Sophia O'Donnell died at 10:22 p.m. Her spirit, the same as Ben's, was immediately taken up into heaven. Sophia and her family were devout Christians just like the Lawson and Sanchez families. They lived for God every day, going to church on Sundays and loving God and people. As for the present moment, it was all so weird but incredible for Sophia. She breathed her last breath at 10:22 at one moment, and then the next moment, she was in heaven, dressed in white clothing and standing in the same cloud-like atmosphere. She saw everything that Ben saw when he went to heaven. In addition, Jesus was standing several feet in front of her, waiting for her. He looked greatly saddened for a second, just as He looked right as Ben went to heaven, but then Jesus instantly went back to looking loving and compassionate.

"Welcome, Sophia O'Donnell," Jesus said.

Sophia immediately recognized who Jesus was and quickly and excitedly walked up to Him. Jesus was standing where He was with His arms open wide to embrace Sophia. The two of them remained in each other's arms for a minute, and then they let go of each other. Jesus wanted to do the same thing for Sophia as He did for Ben.

"I'm so happy to meet and see You, Jesus," Sophia said with excitement and enthusiasm in her voice. "Can I stay here with You and everyone else in heaven? I would really love that even though I didn't exactly do all of what I wanted to do on earth."

"It brings Me a lot of joy that you are happy to meet and see Me. Your last sentence is one of the reasons why I want to send you back down to earth. I know that you have wanted to love a man and, in return, be loved by him like I love the church. You yearned to marry him. You had only one boyfriend in high school, and your relationship with him was good in the sight of Me, My Father, and the Holy Spirit, but you and your boyfriend were too different, and you two were on different paths. I believe his name was Nate."

"How do You know all of that?" Sophia asked somewhat rhetorically before continuing. "I know that You know all things, but it's taking me a minute to wrap my head around that concept," Sophia said with amazement in her voice, knowing that all of what Jesus said was true.

"Yeah, it can take a little bit for that to sink in. Anyway, what do you think about My offer?"

"That sounds wonderful. I accept. Who am I going to meet? When can I come back to heaven, though? It's perfect here."

"I think that you should try Ben Lawson again. He is a good servant of Mine even though he has been through some rough times. He also has a great heart and a passionate love for life."

"Jesus, I love and respect You, but I don't think Ben Lawson is the right guy for me."

"I have a question for you. Is the body more than its legs? I know that Ben currently doesn't have legs from just above his knees and down."

"Of course, the body is more than its legs. I just don't think that he and I are a right fit because of his disability."

"I think you should try again. You will be pleasantly surprised. The human mind and heart can make up for any physical loss when that person's mind and heart are completely surrendered to Me and set on accomplishing and attaining all that I have for that person. Just start by going on a date to Starbucks with Ben, and I assure you that you will never regret it. Ben is better than any other guy that you will meet in Evart. Just trust Me."

"Okay, Jesus, I trust You, and I will do what You say and go on a date to Starbucks with Ben. I believe all of what You said is true and good. What rough times has Ben been through?"

"I think it's best if you ask Ben that question."

"Okay, I will do that."

"Good. As for your other question about coming back to heaven, you will come back here on May 14th, 2005, at 2:00 p.m. There are several other details, but I think that it's best if you figure them out by yourself with the help of your future husband on Earth, who already knows the details besides Me. I also want you to do a very important thing for Me that is more important than anything else. I want you to tell two messages from Me to every nonbeliever that you meet. The first message is that I will always love, protect, and provide for them, especially Carl Wendleson and Tess Debor, who were a part of the medical team that picked you up in the ambulance and took you to the ER at the hospital after you got shot. The other nonbelievers that you will meet will want to know more about Me and have personal relationships with Me because of this message, so I want you to first tell the medical team. I will ignite their minds and hearts with a hunger for Me, and they will receive My message and follow Me after they have repented from their sins and are saved. I forgave all of the sins of the Christians and nonbelievers when I sacrificed Myself for them over 2,000 years ago. Plus, I will forgive all of the sins of the nonbelievers again when they repent of them and ask Me into their hearts. Carl is trying to completely immerse himself in his medical team job after losing his older brother, Frank, to lung cancer. Tess is doing her best to do the same thing as Carl after her husband cheated on her with another woman and did not repent from that sin. Both Tess's condition and the fact that her husband cheated on her really grieve Me. I also want you to tell My first message to every Christian that you meet as well. Secondly, I want you to tell both the Christians and nonbelievers that the kingdom of heaven and all of its goodness is in every born-again Christian who has a relationship with Me and obediently does the will of My Father."

"Absolutely, I will do that. I also trust that You will reveal the other few details about me coming back to heaven from the person that You have shared the details with. All of my hope and trust is in You, Jesus. I believe that You only have good things for me. Will my family and friends be good after I come back here?"

"I'm very happy and joyful that you said that. Your family and friends will be good after you come back to heaven, but it will take some time for them to let that sink in. All right, here is the part where we must say goodbye for now. Remember that I will always love, protect, and provide for you and everyone else. Make sure to tell your family and friends My messages as well. I love you, Sophia, My dear child. See you later."

"I will make sure to tell everyone Your messages, including my family and friends. I love You, too, Jesus. See You later."

Then Jesus brought Sophia back to life and sent her back to earth. She immediately opened her eyes and found herself in the emergency room at the hospital that she was sent to. The doctors had declared that she was dead and had asked the medical team to take her to get an autopsy. That was not going to happen. The medical team was utterly and profoundly stunned to see that Sophia was alive and breathing again. It was nearly two minutes before the other doctors were going to take Sophia's once-dead body and perform an autopsy on her. Sophia now had the mission and messages that she was tasked with by Jesus to carry out and tell everyone that she met.

Ben Lawson told his family and Diego about all of the things Jesus talked to him about and instructed him to do when everyone got to the house. They were distressed, baffled, amazed, and a bit anxious. The part when Ben told everyone about the fact that he was going back to heaven on May 14th of 2005 made them a bit anxious, but they were good with it. Diego and Ben's family were good with Ben and his wife going back to heaven because that was way better than having the two of them experience death again when the life-ending events started. The four people were obviously concerned about the car crash that could happen to Ben and his wife, but Ben assured them that he and his wife would be safe. The fact that Ben would have a wife was great news to Ben's family and Diego. They all wondered who she would be.

Ben told everyone that he would write down the instruction that Jesus told him to avoid the car crash. He also told everyone that he was going to write down everything else that Jesus had said to him and put the paper in a safe place in his backpack. Ben's family and Diego were good with Ben writing down everything and keeping the information safe. They were overjoyed when they heard the encouraging and helpful messages that Jesus said to Ben to tell them and everyone else that he met. The Lawson family and Diego got ready and went to bed after Ben was finished telling them everything and writing all of it down. They and Ben couldn't get any great sleep after hearing what Ben had told them. However, they were happy that all of what Ben had told them was good news.

CHAPTER 5:

A Different Perspective

"Oh my God, this is a miracle!" one of the medical team members exclaimed in a somewhat high-pitched voice right after Sophia O'Donnell suddenly opened her eyes. It was 10:29 p.m. on that cool Saturday night on January 11th, 2003. The medical team member's name was Sabrina Chaldez. She was a fit thirty-five-year-old Hispanic woman with really long dark brown hair and brown eyes. She came from a family that didn't believe in God, except her aunt and uncle on her dad's side of the family. This sudden event with Sophia would spark great interest in God and would reach her entire family. The fourth and final medical team member's name was Chad Wilson, a slightly overweight thirty-eight-year-old White man with short light brown hair and hazel-green eyes. He was speechless and couldn't say anything at the moment. He was totally stunned. The medical team was about to hand over Sophia to the autopsy doctors before she came back to life. They all were in a corridor with a silver door three yards in front of them that led to where the other doctors performed autopsies. Sophia and the four medical team members were completely alone.

"How can this be?" Carl Wendleson asked in amazement before continuing. "It was confirmed that she was dead."

"I'm just as shocked as you are, Carl," Tess Debor said in amazement as well.

"I remember something about my family," Sabrina said in total astonishment. "My aunt and uncle on my dad's side of my family believe in this one God. Could this possibly be this God's work?"

"I have the answer that you are seeking," Sophia responded after finding her newfound strength and listening to all of the medical team members. She sat up on the stretcher and continued. "This God that your aunt and uncle on your dad's side of your family know is real, Sabrina."

"How can that be?" Sabrina replied with that same astonishment in her voice. She couldn't believe that Sophia was now sitting up and speaking as well as what and who Sophia was talking about. "How is He real?"

"He is the one who created all things and people. He knows all things. God is in heaven, and He cares for everyone and everything."

"I can see by the fact that you are alive again that God cares for you. What about the rest of us? Why are there still hardships for everyone?"

"I know that Jesus/God cares for everyone because He said to me to tell everyone that I meet that He will always love, protect, and provide for all of us. Plus, God also told me to tell everyone that the kingdom of heaven and all of its goodness is in every born-again Christian who has a relationship with Him and obediently does His will. God's will is that every person will repent of their sins, live for God, and help other people do the same things. This world is imperfect, and that means that there will always be hardships here. I'm sorry to say that. I really am. However, God promises that He will always get us through hardships because He has overcome the world. Also, God came to us on earth two thousand years ago and is still with us so that we can have life and life more abundantly. Sabrina, I think you should talk more with your aunt and uncle on your dad's side of your family. I believe that they can help you know more about God if you want to do so. I hope I have helped and encouraged you."

"You did, thank you. I want to and will talk to my aunt and uncle about God."

"I'm glad that I can help. Are you Carl?" Sophia asked this while looking at him.

"Yes, I'm Carl," Carl said before continuing. "I attentively listened to all of what you said to Sabrina. I didn't believe in and know that God was real. I'm greatly interested to know more about God. How can I do that?"

"You can look up and reach out to a local church, and you can actually have a relationship with God after saying a simple prayer and believing in Him," Sophia replied.

"Wow. That is amazing. I will definitely do those things. How does it feel like to be in a relationship with God?"

"It feels like you don't have to worry about anything anymore because God will always be there for you."

"All right, all right," Tess interjected before continuing. "All of what you're saying is nice and good, and I respect Sabrina and Carl's opinions and what they think and want, but how do we really know what you are saying is true?"

"Yeah," Chad finally chimed in after listening to all of what everyone had said. The thirty-eight-year-old man had a somewhat high-pitched and smooth voice when he spoke. He couldn't believe what and who Sophia was talking about. Then he continued on, still really stunned, "I also like all of what you said. It's just hard for me to believe that all of what you said is true. How can you prove what you said is true? My name is Chad, by the way."

"Nice to meet you, Chad," Sophia said in a calm, understanding, and loving voice before continuing. "First of all, I have never been in the ER before, and the fact that I died and then came back to life shows you and everyone else that only God brought me back to life. He also told me a couple of things about Tess and Carl. I promise I have never heard of or seen the four of you before, especially Tess and Carl."

"Oh, all right," Tess began a bit sarcastically before going on. "Let's hear what this God told you about me and Carl. I don't remember ever hearing about or seeing you either, Sophia."

"Come on, Tess," Carl spoke up. "Let's just hear her out on what she knows about us. I'm kind of interested to hear what she knows."

"Okay," Sophia said before continuing. "To start with, God told me that Carl's older brother passed away from lung cancer and that he is investing a lot of time in his career as a medical team member."

"What? How did you know that?" Carl asked with equal amounts of frustration and amazement in his voice. "I haven't told anyone about my older brother passing away other than my family and close friends. None of them would share that information with anyone else."

"God told me," Sophia replied in a loving, compassionate, and sympathetic voice. She didn't mind telling Carl again that God told her about his older brother. "I'm deeply sorry for your loss of your older brother. I can't imagine how you must have felt when that happened and are feeling now."

"That's amazing," Carl said in awe and wonder before switching to a grateful tone. "Thank you for your condolences. My older brother passed away six months ago. His name was Frank."

"Oh, Carl," Tess responded in a sympathetic voice and then continued. "I didn't know about Frank passing away from lung cancer. I'm very sorry to hear that."

"That's so sad," Sabrina also said in a sympathetic voice. "I send my condolences to you and your family."

"Yeah, man," Chad responded in a similar voice as the others before continuing. "I'm really sorry to hear that. You and I can go to a bar and get some drinks sometime if you want."

"Thanks, everyone," Carl responded with gratitude. "Everything that you all have said means a lot to me. I think I might actually take you up on the drinks offer, Chad."

"For sure, man," Chad replied before continuing. "Just let me know what day and time that you want to go to the nearest bar and get drinks."

"I will definitely do that, Chad. Sabrina, Tess, and Sophia are welcome to come if they want. I now consider you all to be my friends. I had a difficult time letting you and other co-workers into my life. I only let my family and my closest friends, whom I've grown up with since childhood, know about my personal life. I guess I just wanted to bury myself in work. I'm sorry about not opening up to you all about my older brother sooner."

"There's no need to be sorry about not telling us about your older brother sooner," Tess responded in an all too empathetic tone before continuing. "I think I can speak for all of us that it would be a while before any one of us told anyone about a personal tragedy. As for getting drinks, I'm totally down for doing that."

"Thanks for your sympathy, Tess," Carl replied, not knowing that Tess said what she said with empathy in her voice.

"Yeah, I probably would've reacted in the same way as you did, Carl," Sabrina responded before continuing. "You can also count me in on getting drinks."

"Thanks, Sabrina," Carl said.

"I do have to say that I'm not twenty-one yet," Sophia chimed in between topic changes. "So, I cannot join you all in getting drinks."

"That's all right," Carl responded before continuing. "I was actually hoping that I could come to and try out your church sometime. I'm free next Sunday."

"You are always welcome to come to my church," Sophia replied kindly. "I think it will be great if you tried out my church next Sunday and you can see what you think. I'll tell you more about where I go to church and what time the service is on Sundays."

"Sounds great," Carl replied with some excitement in his voice. "I'm looking forward to coming to your church next Sunday."

"Nice," Sophia replied cheerfully.

"All right, Sophia," Tess began in somewhat of an impressed tone before continuing. "That was actually pretty impressive with this God telling you about the passing of Carl's older brother from lung cancer. I do have to admit that and that I am intrigued as to what this God told you about me as well when you were dead."

"Okay," Sophia started with a smooth voice before adding love, compassion, and sympathy to it. "I hope you don't mind that what God told me about you was from your personal life. He…told me that your husband cheated on you with another woman. That's why you are trying to bury yourself in work like Carl. I am truly sorry for what happened to you. It must have been devastating to you when you found out."

"Oh my God," Tess replied in total amazement and embarrassment at the same time. She clasped her hands, put them in front of her face, and began to tear up. "This God is really the one and only God. I never told anyone outside of my family that my husband cheated on me with another woman. He cheated on me eight months ago, and we are officially getting divorced in exactly a month from today. You couldn't have known something so personal to me unless God told you about it. I greatly appreciate your condolences."

Everyone else on the medical team and Sophia instantly moved over to where Tess was and embraced and comforted her. Sophia actually got off of the stretcher and came over to embrace and comfort Tess. Tess broke down and cried more, with her hands still clasped together and in front of her face. Her head was also bent down while she was crying. Everyone said their deepest condolences to Tess and kept embracing and comforting her for several minutes. Something lit up so brightly within the four hearts and minds of the medical team in those precious several minutes. God had indeed spoken to and started turning their hearts and minds to Him. It was just like the Scripture said in Romans 12:2: "Do not conform to the pattern of this world, but be transformed by the renewing of your mind. Then you will be able to test and approve what God's will is—his good, pleasing and perfect will."

Sabrina began to have a great interest in knowing more about God. She was planning on talking with her aunt and uncle tomorrow. Chad wanted to ask his Christian friends about God since he was an atheist. Tess was greatly thinking about coming to and trying out Sophia's church next Sunday with Carl. She could feel that there was more to be had with him and her.

The four medical team members went back to Debra Welsh and began having Sophia checked out of the hospital after the members had recomposed themselves. Sophia had to take some tests to make sure that she was fit to get out into the world again. She comfortably passed all of the tests that were carried out by Tess and the other three medical team members. Sophia gave Carl a piece of paper with the name of the church that she went to and the service time before she got out of the hospital. She called one of her dormmates/ friends to come and pick her up. Her dormmate/friend, Lucy Robinson, picked her up at 11:20 p.m. She was a slim White girl with curly blonde hair and brown eyes. Lucy was also a Christian but was starting to have some doubts about God's sovereignty because of all of the hurt that was going on in the world. Lucy asked if Sophia was okay and also asked her why she was driven to the hospital. Sophia said she just wanted to get to their dorm and just go to bed. She promised to tell Lucy everything after she came back from church the next day. Sophia's mission from Jesus had gone great so far. She planned and wanted to tell His messages to everyone that she met, which included her dormmates/friends and family as well. Sophia also wanted to ponder what Jesus said about Ben Lawson in terms of going out with and getting to know him more in terms of a serious relationship.

It was now 9:00 a.m. on Sunday, January 12th, 2003, at the Lawsons' house. Ben Lawson, the rest of his family, and Diego Sanchez chose to sleep in. Each person woke up and got up at various times, starting at nine with Ben. Diego was the last one to wake up and get up at nine thirty. It was as if everyone had the same nightmare from Saturday night. It actually started off as a nightmare on Saturday night just before 10:00 p.m., with Ben getting shot and dying. Then, several minutes later, it became a miraculous night with Jesus bringing Ben back from the dead. The Lawson family and Diego still had a lingering hangover from the events that happened and the revelatory information that Ben had told them from Jesus. Ben had written down everything that Jesus said about the messages that He gave to him to tell everyone that he met. The nineteen-year-old also had written down the life-saving information that Jesus told him, which was about how he and his wife would avoid the car crash on May 13th, 2005. Ben placed the piece of paper in a small and safe compartment in his backpack and made a mental note to himself to regularly look at the piece of paper. He thought that looking at the piece of paper once a month would keep his memory of it fresh.

The Lawson family and Diego made bacon, cheese, and hot sauce omelets for breakfast. It was a fast breakfast to eat, as the church service at the Lawson family's church, Light of the World, started at 10:30 a.m. In addition, Ben was also good with eating spicy things again. He actually enjoyed them. It was just those times in freshmen and sophomore year of college, the years that he struggled through personally, that he didn't want to eat spicy things. They reminded him of the fun things in life. His amputated legs were constant reminders that a lot of fun things were taken away from him. However, those times ended after Diego had helped him through his struggles. Anyway, Dave asked Diego if he would like to join him and the rest of the Lawson family at Light of the World, the church that they attended, and hang out at the house after that. Dave knew that Diego went to a different church called Holy Communion, but he wanted to invite him to Light of the World and hang out at the house afterward, given the events that had transpired the night before. The Southern Chilean native graciously accepted Dave's offer. The Lawson family and Diego separately showered, changed clothes, and got ready to go to church. They all left in the van at 10:20 a.m. and got to church a minute before the service started.

Light of the World church was a good-sized church that had 800 people of all ages in attendance each Sunday. A lot of people who were in the same age group sat together. Some columns and rows were filled with people of various age groups. The Lawson family and Diego chose to sit to the right of the middle of the congregation, where there were several teens, several young adults, and a lot of middle-aged people. Leslie took out one of the empty chairs in that row for Ben to park his wheelchair. Dave helped her in getting the chair out of the way of the people still coming into the church building. There was a kids' service in a different building on the church campus. The kids' service was specifically designed for them.

The service started with worship. Everyone stood on their feet and sang three songs of worship to God, which were played and carried out by an excellent and harmonious worship team. The church congregation expressed their worship to God in various and meaningful ways since Light of the World church was a more charismatic/Pentecostal/apostolic church.

The lead senior pastor, Pastor Derrell Watson, had recently preached a sermon two weeks ago about worship. The sermon was about how the church, which is really the people who gather together in a building, is the performer of worship to God. In addition, Pastor Watson said that God is the audience and the worship team is the director of worship. Pastor Watson also said in that sermon that God deserves and is worthy of all of our praise all of the time despite our wavering emotions, circumstances, and situations.

Ben had heard that sermon about worshiping God and didn't really take it to heart because of the hardships he had been through with losing his legs and having Sophia reject him and his offer for her to go out with him. However, the teen was now thinking back on that sermon as worship started. A sense of true gratitude towards God welled up inside him in that moment. Plus, he began to have a change of heart towards worshiping God, reading His Word, and being in His presence. Ben had been worshiping God and reading His Word in the past, but he didn't have the right posture of heart at that time. The teen always put God above everything, even when things around him were hard. However, the posture of heart issue still remained. Ben now realized what he was missing in his heart and desired to have more of that thing, which was the right posture of his heart towards worshiping God. The things that made the change all the more amazing were the flashing memories in his mind of being hugged by Jesus and seeing and experiencing the truly awesome, fulfilling nature of heaven. Ben closed his eyes and just fully embraced the true heart of worshiping God with his hands lifted as high as he could lift from his manual wheelchair. The teen's worshiping voice blended in with the rest of the congregation's voices and the loud sound of the worship team. Ben was totally enveloped in worshiping God and being in His presence. The rest of the Lawson family and Diego were doing similar things in worshiping God as Ben was doing.

The three songs of worship ended, and then there were some announcements on the two big screens that were flushed up behind the stage and hung high on the wall that was there. The announcements were about current church events and church events that were going to start in the coming weeks. Then, Pastor Watson came up on the stage, saying things about how good God has been with the plentiful harvest of people and their souls who were coming to know Jesus as their personal Lord and Savior. Pastor Watson also congratulated the church in volunteering at the current events that were helping their communities. He said that, above all, God had been and still is working greatly in those people who benefited from the church events. Lastly, Pastor Watson said to and told the church congregation to give praise to God for who He was, continued to be, and for all that He had been doing and continued to do. All of the church congregation, including the Lawson family and Diego, erupted in a united hand clap and shout of praise to God before the pastor encouraged them to greet people and sit down.

Pastor Derrell Watson began with the sermon of the day soon after all of the church congregation sat down. He sought God's help and guidance for each sermon and sermon series. Pastor Watson was a five-foot-eleven-inch tall African-American man with short dark brown hair and hazel-green eyes. He was mostly in shape. As for the sermon of the day, Pastor Watson preached on the first chapter of the book of James in the Bible, where it talked about considering it all joy when Christians go through trials of many kinds. Trials help Christians persevere and teach them to fully trust God. Ben was enraptured in the sermon, listening attentively to everything that Pastor Watson said. The teen was heavily pondering the part of the sermon about considering it all joy when Christians face trials. Ben certainly did not like that he got shot the night before in Diego's apartment. However, Ben was joyful that he was brought back to life by Jesus and that He entrusted him to share His messages with everyone whom he met.

Ben made sure to tell Jesus's messages to the people in church that he said hi to after introducing himself and talking with them a bit before the sermon had started. Ben didn't tell them what happened to him, though. Ben thought that showing them the scars from his shot wounds wouldn't help since they didn't see him die and be brought back to life. Jesus didn't say to tell everyone he met what happened to him. Jesus just said that he, Ben, was to tell His messages to everyone he met and interacted with. They thanked Ben and blessed him in the name of God. Dave and Leslie noticed all of those interactions and looked on their son with joy and a good sense of pride after Ben was done talking with the people.

Someone else was also semi-frequently looking at Ben and the Lawson family from the middle of the congregation. It was the old man that Dave saw in the main Evart hospital in 1984. The old man was about seventy-seven years old and now wearing a white shirt with light red and blue stripes and light blue jeans, but he still had the recognizable blue eyes and short gray hair that had mostly turned white. The sermon ended a few minutes after 12:00 p.m. Dave, the rest of the Lawson family, and Diego were just starting to get out of where they were sitting before Dave thought he might have seen someone that he had seen from the past. Dave did not fully recognize that it was the old man from the main Evart hospital. The old man stopped looking at Ben and the rest of his family when Dave went to look at him. Then, several seconds later, the old man got up and started walking toward the doors that led out of the church building.

"Is everything all right, honey?" Leslie curiously asked after she saw Dave look at the old man.

"I believe so," Dave replied confidently before continuing. "I just thought that I saw someone from a long time ago." Ben, Josh, and Diego were a few paces ahead of Dave and Leslie after leaving the place and seats that they were sitting in.

"What? Someone from a long time ago?" Leslie replied back with another question as she and her husband were just walking away from their seats.

"Do you remember an old man in a yellow shirt and light blue jeans who was at the main Evart hospital when we went there and you were ready to give birth to Ben?"

"I think I remember taking a glance or two at someone like that, but I was too busy dealing with the amount of pain that I was in at the moment. Do you think that he's trouble?"

"I knew and understood that you were in a lot of pain. I was just asking. Hmmm...my gut is telling me that he is not trouble nor intends to cause trouble. I think we are safe. I will be on the lookout for him next Sunday, and we can formally meet."

"That sounds like a good plan. Thank you for always doing your best to protect me, Ben, and Josh."

"You're very welcome. I do try to do my best at that." Then Dave and Leslie stopped walking and kissed each other a couple of times before going out of the church building doors.

Ben and Josh were already at the van when Dave and Leslie arrived there. Diego was beginning to start his car. The Lawson family and Diego picked up lunch from Wendy's, which was near the Lawsons' house, and then ate their lunch at the house and hung out there. Ben was still pondering the sermon that Pastor Watson preached. The teen didn't ponder the sermon as much as he had when the pastor had preached it. Ben was good and at peace with all of what had happened to him in the past couple of years. In addition, he was wondering where he would meet Hannah Rine and Anthony Markus at Evart University and how he would share Jesus's messages with them. As for the current moment, it was now 1:30 p.m., and the Lawson family and Diego were having a fun time watching TV and playing games after eating lunch.

Sophia O'Donnell and her dormmate, Lucy, were just finishing up their lunch that Sophia picked up at Eegee's after she got done with church. The other three dormmates had requested and got reassigned to a different dorm three months ago so that they could have more space for themselves in the new dorm. As for the current moment, Lucy was really starting to wonder why Sophia had gone to the hospital the night before.

"So, why the heck were you in the hospital last night before you called me to pick you up?" Lucy asked in a very curious and insistent tone that went quite well with her normal, moderately high-pitched voice, given the circumstances.

"Sorry, Lucy," Sophia replied calmly with some stress in her tone. "It was a very rough yet mind-boggling last night. The good part was the mind-boggling part."

"Sounds intense. Tell me more, if you want to share, of course," Lucy replied in a calm and compassionate voice.

"It's fine. I'll be totally honest with you. To start with, I was on my way back to the dorm from a late-night walk. As soon as I got to the art museum, I saw this guy in a white Beatles shirt, black jacket, and light blue jeans. I guessed that he stole one or two items from the museum because the left side of his jacket was sticking out, and his left hand and arm were holding it up. I was going to shout and wave to the police to arrest him, but he shot me twice in the chest, a little way to the right of my heart. I think it was actually two or three inches to the right of my heart. That was the start of my night's rough and quite freaky part. That was not fun at all. I think the police arrested the guy a couple of minutes after I got shot, but I didn't really see it happen because my feet and legs were facing the dorm when I fell down. I tried to look up and turn my head to see the police arrest that maniac. Then, I remember an ambulance picking me up two or three minutes later..."

"My God, Sophia," Lucy said in a totally shocked voice after Sophia took a pause to eat. "I am so deeply sorry that that happened to you. I should've been there to help protect you instead of taking a stupid shower in the dorm. How did you survive?"

"You shouldn't blame yourself for not being there to help protect me, Lucy. You couldn't have known what was going to happen. As for how I survived, I have to tell you that the story got worse before it got better. I remember this African-American woman and man putting me onto a stretcher and wheeling me into the ambulance. Then, the man put an oxygen mask on my mouth. He also put a bandage around the areas where I got shot. There were two other people in the driver's seat and passenger seat. I couldn't make out who they were because I was losing consciousness. I tried to hold on for as long as I could, which could have been a few or several minutes, but in the end, I died..."

"Okay, what the heck?" Lucy responded, completely stunned and baffled, after her dormmate took another pause to finish her lunch. "How are you here with me now? This story is really horrible at the moment. It must have taken a true miracle from God to bring you back to life if this is what really happened."

"Lucy, I assure you that all of what happened to me was true," Sophia replied confidently and assuringly before continuing. "Now, this is where the story gets better. I went to heaven after I died, and Jesus was standing several feet in front of me in a cloud-like atmosphere with a pearly gate behind Him. An angel was guarding the gate, and there was this magnificent and beautiful twelve-foundation wall made up of twelve gorgeous stones. I knew all of the names of the stones even though I had forgotten them before I died and went to heaven. I could also see some part of the tree of life and the river of the water of life. I knew who Jesus was and quickly walked up to Him, and we hugged each other..."

"What? You got to hug Jesus, and He hugged you back! I do have to say, this story is definitely getting way better, even though I'm still having a bit of a hard time believing that all of this happened to you."

"All right, then, I should show you something," Sophia said before revealing the scars from her shot wounds to Lucy. The scars were just above the top of her right breast, so they didn't reveal that breast.

"My God, are those shot wounds?" Lucy asked rhetorically, totally stunned. "So, everything that happened to you really was true. I'm so sorry, Sophia."

"Thanks," Sophia replied while pulling her shirt back up. "Getting shot was an awful experience. The moments after getting shot felt like something was gradually draining the life out of me."

"That must have felt awful, indeed. I can imagine that, but at the same time, I don't want to imagine it. Tell me the rest of the story after you and Jesus hugged each other."

"Yeah, getting shot is not something that I would have liked to imagine either. Getting shot in real life is way worse, and I don't ever want to repeat that experience again. Anyway, Jesus told me a few things after we hugged each other. First of all, He knew about my first and only boyfriend, Nate, and why we broke up. It was expected that Jesus would know about Nate because He's God. That was the part when I said that I would love to stay in heaven, although I didn't really accomplish all of what I wanted and desired to accomplish on Earth. Jesus knew that I wanted a Christian husband, and He even said that, but in different words. He wanted to give me a second chance at life on Earth to find and have a Christian husband and to also do something more important than that. Jesus told me to tell every Christian and nonbeliever I met, including you, that He will always love, provide for, and protect us and everyone else. He also told me to tell everyone that the kingdom of heaven and all of its goodness is in every born-again Christian who has a relationship with Him and does the will of His Father/God. I assure you, Lucy, that His messages are totally for you just as everyone else..."

"Wow! Thank you, God," Lucy replied in a reflective, pondering, and trembling voice. She was beginning to tear up. "I'm stoked that Jesus gave you a second chance of life! That's amazing! Also, that truly means the world to me that He said those messages to you to tell everyone you met, including me. You know that I was starting to have doubts about God and His sovereignty because of all of the hurt that I see that's going on in the world. I think I still have a pretty good relationship with Him, though. Plus, that started to affect my personal life in terms of not wanting to go out, be more social, and get into a serious relationship with a Christian guy. I thought that it was wrong of me to want to do those things all the while that other people were worse off than me. I got busy with volunteering at the church that I go to and at other charitable events. However, I now realize, thanks to God and you, that God will always love, provide for, and protect us, no matter what. We just have to put our faith in Him and have a true relationship with Him. We also have to completely trust Him for everything in our lives. Again, I'm truly grateful that Jesus entrusted you to tell His messages to everyone you meet. He probably was also thinking of me as well when He said that to you, and that gives me such great joy. Now, I will do all of the things that God wants me to do and have to the fullest. I will do God's will and tell people about His good news and the kingdom of heaven."

Lucy leaned over the smooth wooden table she and Sophia were eating their lunch on and met Sophia's right arm with her shoulder. Sophia placed her right arm on Lucy's left shoulder and comforted her while she was shedding some tears of joy and relief. Lucy finished up her own lunch a few minutes after recomposing herself and drawing away from Sophia. Then, the two girls went shopping at a nearby thrift store for a couple of hours.

Sophia and Lucy talked, watched TV, and made dinner for themselves after returning to the dorm from shopping at the thrift store. Sophia reminded Lucy about how she had previously met the guy, Ben Lawson, who had no legs and was in a wheelchair. The redhead also reminded her dormmate that she rejected his offer to go out with him to Starbucks because she didn't feel comfortable about his disability. Sophia went on to talk to Lucy about what Jesus had said about Ben when she went to heaven. Lucy thought for a couple of minutes about all of what Jesus had said to Sophia. Then Lucy said that Sophia should go out with Ben to Starbucks. The blonde girl thought that Ben and Sophia would be good together since Jesus had said that Ben was the best Christian guy in Evart. In addition, Lucy remembered going to see a Marvel movie with an older mutant guy in a wheelchair once. She thought that Ben would be a better, younger, and hotter version of the mutant wheelchair guy since Sophia had already described Ben's physical appearance.

Then, the two dormmates separately got ready and went to bed since it was almost 10:00 p.m. Sophia really began pondering in her head the possibility of going out with Ben. She wanted to think more about the situation during the upcoming school week, though. Sophia started feeling at peace and a little excited about going out with Ben right before falling asleep.

Monday, January 13th, came in a hurry for Ben Lawson. He was going to work eight hours that day at American Burgers and talk to the restaurant manager about him currently getting a server position. Ben was also going to talk to the manager about acquiring the cashier position after Alberto left. There was something more important that Ben was going to do at work today. He was going to tell Jesus's messages to a few of his co-workers. Those few co-workers would do the rest of the job of telling everyone else who worked at the restaurant, just like Jesus said.

Ben's morning routine of eating breakfast and getting ready before heading off to work came and went in a flash. He was showering and getting dressed one moment. Ben threw on his white American Burgers shirt that spelled out the name of the restaurant in blue and red letters. The "American" part of the restaurant name was in blue lettering, and the "Burgers" part of the name was in red lettering. Ben also put on dark blue shorts and blue and white sneakers. Then Ben was eating scrambled eggs and bacon with a side of toast another moment. Finally, he was being lifted up on the electronic van lift in the third moment. The teen was seemingly at his job in no time at all. It was now 9:00 a.m. Dave would be back to pick him up at 5:30 p.m. Ben had told his dad that he would stay at the fast-food restaurant for half an hour after his final shift was done.

Ben's first three hours of his dishwasher job came and went. It was like the nineteen-year-old got into the rhythm of thoroughly washing dishes and lost track of time. Ben knew that he did an excellent job washing each plate because he made sure that every one of them was spotless. The time now clicked to 12:00 p.m., and Ben began talking with Claire, the restaurant manager, about his desired future positions. American Burgers had an hour-long lunch break from 12:00 to 1:00 p.m.

Claire was an atheist but had heard some talk about God from a couple of her friends in the past. She was a five-foot-five-inch Hispanic woman who had recently turned thirty. Claire had curly, short brown hair, light brown skin, and hazel-green eyes. She was wearing her white American Burgers shirt that spelled out the name of the restaurant in red and blue letters. The Hispanic woman was also wearing dark blue jeans and black and white sneakers. Claire wanted Ben to stay as a dishwasher for the time being because he had always done a great job. However, the restaurant manager was agreeable to having him move up into the cashier position after Alberto left. Ben was a bit sad that he didn't get the server position, but he was thrilled that he would get the cashier position after Alberto transitioned to working at the Walmart that was near him.

The time now came for Ben to tell Jesus's messages to Claire. Ben remembered that Jesus told him that He would ignite the minds and hearts of the nonbelievers so that they would have a hunger for Him. The teen completely trusted Jesus and what He said and smoothly changed the topic of his and Claire's conversation to the topic of church. Claire was listening to Ben as he first talked to her about how extremely warm and welcoming the people at his church were. Then, the teen moved on to say that God is infinitely more warm and welcoming than all Christians. Finally, Ben told God's/Jesus's messages to Claire without showing her the scars that he had from his shot wounds. The teen compassionately talked to her about God wanting nonbelievers to repent of their sins and live for God. Ben also told Claire that God came to us on the earth two thousand years ago and is still with us so that we could have life and life to the full. Plus, the teen told the restaurant manager that everyone who comes into a personal relationship with God is supposed to love Him and people. Claire was definitely intrigued by the things that Ben said and would think more about them after she got home. She thanked him for wanting to talk to her about his desired restaurant positions and God's/Jesus's messages. Then, Claire went about eating her lunch. Ben followed suit and then got back to washing dishes at one.

Ben planned on interacting with and telling Jesus's messages to a co-worker who also washed dishes after their final shifts were over. He also wanted to do the same things with Alberto. Unfortunately, Alberto was too busy with his job as a cashier when Ben was done with his final shift at 5:00 p.m. Ben would see if he would encounter Alberto during the lunch break in his coming work days. As for now, he was going to talk to and tell Jesus's messages to another dishwasher who was just about to leave after his final shift was over. His name was Daniel. Daniel was also an atheist. He was a young White man in his mid-twenties with curly shoulder-length blonde hair and hazel-green eyes. Daniel was somewhat overweight for his age. He was also wearing his work shirt and dark blue jeans. The only difference in his work clothing was that he was wearing dark gray shoes.

Daniel was stationed approximately twenty feet to Ben's left. Ben and Daniel had some small talk in the past that was just about sports and what they were going to do on the weekends. The teen was going to use a similar but different conversation technique with Daniel as he used with Claire. The difference was Ben and Daniel's starting point in their conversation because of their past small talk. Ben told Daniel, at one time in the past, that he went to church every Sunday. Daniel didn't really think much about that church conversation when it occurred. However, that would be different today because Jesus would place a hunger for Him inside of Daniel as well as He did with Claire. Daniel would be slightly more interested in God after he heard Jesus's messages from Ben. That would be a spark that would catch fire in Daniel a little bit down the road. The same thing would happen for Claire. As for the current moment, Ben said hi to his co-worker, asked him how he was, and then proceeded to talk about sports with him for a few minutes. Then, Ben transitioned to the topic of church and Jesus's messages. He told the same things to his co-worker as he told Claire. As it happened, Daniel was indeed a little more interested in God after Ben talked to him. Daniel thanked Ben for talking to him and then walked out of the restaurant and drove home.

Ben only had to wait five minutes before his dad picked him up at five thirty. The nineteen-year-old felt good about telling Jesus's messages to Claire and Daniel as well as the dishwashing work that he did. Once Dave and Ben got home, Ben told Dave and the rest of his family about all of what he did that day, and they were very proud of him. Dave and Leslie cooked dinner, and then they and their children ate it and relaxed for the rest of the night. However, Ben had to do homework before going to his three classes the next day. The teen got ready and went to bed at 10:00 p.m. Ben thought about what lay ahead of him in terms of telling Jesus's messages to Hannah Rine and Anthony Markus after he prayed, talked to, and worshiped God in his bed. The nineteen-year-old fell asleep soon after doing those things.

It was now 8:30 a.m. on Tuesday, January 14th. Diego had left after dinner on Sunday night and was now on his way to his first college class of the week. Ben was moments away from getting into the van that would once again help him get to his college classes for the day. Dave was in the driver's seat, remotely hauling Ben up and into the van. Then, the ride to Evart University seemed to take on a different but good feeling for Ben. The teen thought and felt that he was finally doing the will of God by telling God's/Jesus's messages to everyone he met. He was wondering if he would get the chance to first tell the messages to Hannah Rine, Anthony Markus, or both of them at the same time.

It looked like Ben would not get to tell Jesus's messages to either of them for a while after he got dropped off at the university and went to his first junior-year advanced mechanical engineering class. There were no signs anywhere that pointed toward the two fellow students. Ben waited through his advanced engineering class, listening attentively to the professor or any number of students who might mention Hannah's and/or Anthony's names. The teen also did his best to take notes and memorize what the professor was teaching. Ben still wanted to do his best in learning how to make a pair of prosthetic legs for himself. He thought it would work out if God wanted him to have the resources to build the prosthetic legs. The teen had begun to make a list last semester that consisted of some of the resources that he would need. Ben thought he did a good job at multitasking. Then, the end of class came, and everyone started to flow out of the auditorium gradually. Ben wasted no time in packing up and putting away his notes. He still wanted to hear if anyone would mention the names "Hannah" and/or "Anthony." Ben did not have any luck hearing either name.

Ben's next class was one of his final two gen eds. It was a more in-depth Christian religion class. The teen didn't have any luck hearing Hannah's and/or Anthony's names for the first half of the class. However, Ben finally heard Hannah Rine's name being called on by the professor fifteen minutes before the end of class. He knew that she was Hannah Rine because the professor called her "Ms. Rine." Hannah was a five-foot-six-inch Chinese girl in her junior year of college. She just turned twenty years old. Hannah was mostly fit and had brown eyes and dark brown hair that reached down to the middle of her back. The twenty-year-old was wearing a solid pink shirt and light blue jeans. She was called on by the professor because the professor was asking her a question about the teaching topic. Hannah was sitting seven rows to Ben's right. Ben made a plan to see where she exited the auditorium; then, he would wheel up to her, introduce himself, and talk for a little bit. Then Ben would finally tell Jesus's messages to her. The Christian religion class came to a stop for the day, and then it was time for Ben to catch up with Hannah Rine. It was now 12:05 p.m.

"Hey," Ben started as he wheeled up next to Hannah. "How did you like today's class?"

"It was all right," Hannah replied plainly after she turned to look at Ben. "How are you doing today?"

"I'm doing good. You?"

"I'm fine. Are you sure you're doing good? I just noticed that you—"

"Don't have any legs. Yes, I'm doing good. It took me a long time to be at peace with my current situation. I used to have legs two years ago."

"My gosh, what happened, if you don't mind me asking? My name is Hannah, by the way."

"Nice to meet you, Hannah. I'm Ben. As for what happened to me, I don't mind sharing it. One day, my family took me to a NASCAR charity event on my birthday in 2001. I got to ride with Blake, a professional NASCAR racer, and then drive the same race car by myself with the driver in the passenger seat—"

"That's so cool that you got to ride and drive in a race car with a professional NASCAR racer," Hannah interrupted. "Sorry for interrupting you. Go on."

"You're fine," Ben replied calmly and compassionately before continuing. "That day was one of the best days of my life. I could feel the wind rushing by next to me. Plus, the adrenaline was pulsating through my veins. It truly was a rush of excitement. However, during the middle of my younger brother's ride, I felt twinges in both of my lower legs. I thought the twinges were nothing at first, but then they came back some number of minutes later. I told my mom what happened. Then the twinges got way more intense, and I collapsed and fell backwards. This all happened in the race car hangar that my mom, dad, and I were in at the time. My younger brother, Josh, and Blake got to me a minute later and helped carry me to my family's car. Josh had told my dad for someone to call a doctor before he and Blake carried me to the car. Blake said some encouraging words to me, and then my family and I headed over to the main Evart hospital. My doctor checked out my lower legs and then told me and my family that I had a rare disease, which was unknown. Then, my doctor told us that I would have to have my legs amputated just above my knees so that the disease would not spread any further. It took me about a year or so to get over what happened to me. God helped me in addition to another person, Diego, who is now my best friend."

"Oh my God, that's horrible. I'm glad that you're doing better now after God and Diego helped you."

"Yeah, I'm glad that they helped me. I was in a dark place during that time in my life."

"I'm sure that time in your life was very hard for you. Can I talk to you about something?"

"Yeah, you can tell me anything," Ben replied compassionately as he wheeled to one of the doors and opened it for Hannah to go through first before him. She thanked Ben for opening the door for her.

"Well, to start with," Hannah began before continuing, "I haven't told anyone this since this just happened three weeks ago. My parents got a divorce."

"I'm very sorry to hear that," Ben started to reply after he and Hannah headed over to an outside table nearby to sit. There were a couple of chairs to go with the table. Ben didn't need a chair, though. He just pushed aside one of the chairs and wheeled up to the table. Hannah sat in the other chair on the opposite end of the table. "I can't imagine what that must feel like. You can feel free to talk more to me if you want."

"Thank you, that means a lot," Hannah replied appreciatively. "You are such a kind guy even though you have been through a lot. As for my parents' divorce, it made me feel like I was by myself because my mom had moved out of the house. I had and still kind of have a great relationship with my mom. The fact that I have lived in an apartment near campus with my older sister for two years now helps a bit. I could not stand it if I were still living at my parents' house. I had a good relationship with my dad before the divorce, but now my relationship with him is broken. He was the one who wanted to get a divorce. That part of the story goes deeper, but I'm not comfortable sharing it now. Maybe sometime later down the road. In addition to all of the divorce mess, I have wanted to go out and have a serious relationship with a good and honest Christian guy for the past year. Then, you came up to me, and we started talking. I hope that I have not burdened you in any way. Maybe, if you want to, we can go out after we're done with all of our classes on Friday and see if there is anything more for us to have together. What do you say?"

"I would really like to go out with you. You look and seem like a really nice person. Let me pray about it tonight, and I will get back to you sometime after my classes tomorrow."

"Thanks. Sounds good. Here is my number," Hannah said before writing down her number on a torn piece of paper and giving it to Ben.

"Thanks as well," Ben said as he took the piece of paper and stuck it in the compartment of his backpack where he put the piece of paper that had Jesus's words on it. "Do you have time for me to tell you something before you go to your next class?"

"Definitely. I should be good on time. My next class is at twelve thirty. I probably should be heading over to it in five or seven minutes."

"Sounds good. What I have and want to say to you is not lengthy, so you will get to your class on time. What class is it, by the way?"

"It's an art history class. My major is art. Our Christian religion class is just one of the last gen eds that I have to take. What's your major?"

"Mechanical engineering. I'm also taking the Christian religion class as one of the last gen eds too. What about that? Well, what I wanted to say is to you are messages from Jesus/God. There's a wild and freaky story that goes with them, but I'll save it for another time. I'm telling these messages to everyone I meet. However, so far, although I haven't included the story. The first message is that Jesus/God will always love, provide for, and protect everyone. Secondly, He said that the kingdom of heaven and all of its goodness is in born-again Christians who have a relationship with Him and obey the will of the Father/God."

"Those are really good messages. I know that God will always love, provide for, and protect us Christians and every nonbeliever who turns to and comes into relationship with Him. It's just tough to really believe that when we experience hardships. I believe that the kingdom of heaven is in every person who does the will of God. I was doing my best before my parents' divorce in telling my nonbeliever friends and other people about the gospel, repentance from sins, loving God and people, and living for God. The whole mess with the divorce got me off track, and I stopped sharing God's good news with people. I'm sure that I'll get back to that sometime in the near future."

"I know. It was tough for me to really believe that when I was told by my doctor that I would have to have my legs amputated. That turn of events threw me down into a spiral of sadness, anger, and depression. I don't want to see you do the same thing as I did. You can know that I will always be there to help and talk to you if you want. I know that you will get back to sharing God's good news with people again when you are ready."

"Thank you for being so comforting to me. I really appreciate that and that you are willing to help and talk with me."

"You are very welcome."

"Well, I have to head off to my art history class now. It was good talking with you, and I look forward to hearing from you again. It's probably best to text me after I'm done with my classes any day of the week after 4:00 p.m. See and talk to you later, Ben," Hannah said as she was standing up.

"I had a good time talking with you as well. See and talk to you later, Hannah."

Hannah started walking off after she and Ben waved goodbye to each other. Then, Ben went off to have lunch in the student union. The rest of his day was only full of three more classes, which included two more of his higher-level mechanical engineering classes and a sports philosophy general education. There was no sign of Anthony Markus, so Ben would have to wait until Anthony showed up sometime during the rest of the week to tell Jesus's messages to him. Dave picked up Ben at 5:15 p.m., and then the two of them headed home.

Ben and Josh watched some TV and talked for a little bit after Ben got home. Dave and Leslie, as usual for the most part, made dinner at six, and then the whole family ate it at six thirty. Everyone shared the interesting things that happened during their days. Ben shared everything that happened with Hannah Rine, and everyone was proud and happy for him. Josh urged his brother to forget about Sophia and go out with Hannah. Dave and Leslie were slightly hesitant to say that Ben should go out with Hannah. However, in the end, the two parents said that their son should go out with Hannah and see where the two of them go. The first and main thing that Dave and Leslie advised Ben to do was to pray and talk to God about the situation beforehand.

Dinner came and went, and then it was time for Ben to do his homework for the night. It all went pretty well, except that he almost messed up on a few of the questions. That was because he was starting to feel a little bit uneasy. The teen didn't feel sick or anything like that. It was like two darts had been thrown at him. One of the darts shot into his mind, and the other shot into his heart. Both of the darts were definitely little darts of uneasiness, but Ben did not yet know what they were about.

Ben continued to feel the pings of uneasiness for the last hour of his night before getting ready for bed. It was now 8:45 p.m. The teen was playing the board game Stratego with his dad while Leslie and Josh were watching the rest of a *James Bond* movie on TV. Ben couldn't shake off the feelings of uneasiness, and Dave was beginning to notice them. That was because the teen hesitated in his board game moves a bit more so than the other times that he and his dad played the game. Dave asked his son if he was feeling uneasy. Ben said yes and then shrugged off the feelings of uneasiness as best as he could. However, he said he would pray and talk to God about the uneasiness and see what they were about. Dave agreed on that course of action, and then he and his son finished their game. Ben won by a thin margin.

The feelings of uneasiness came back a little bit stronger as Ben got ready for bed at 9:45 p.m. He began thinking again about his day, the fact that he shared Jesus's messages with Hannah, and the possibility of going out with Hannah on Friday. Ben was tempted to go out with her and leave Sophia behind. *Sophia did reject me and my offer for her to go out with me, right?* That was one of the thoughts that ran through Ben's mind as he got into his bed. *Surely, this turn of events with Hannah means that she is my wife. Hannah was so accepting of me. I think she likes me. She has been through a lot with her parents' divorce. I have also been through a lot with the amputation of my legs and the rejection from young women, namely Sophia. I don't think Sophia is going to give me another try.*

These thoughts swirled around in Ben's head for several minutes before he decided to put them aside and pray, talk to, and somewhat quietly and intimately worship God while he was lying on his bed. The teen had recently wanted to set aside a time to worship God for who He was and continued to be even though things in his life were not going as well as he thought that they would go. Ben wanted to worship God in the mornings for several minutes before getting out of bed. The teen also yearned to read the Bible every day instead of several times each week. As for the current moment, Ben continued to worship God. Then, he prayed and talked to God about the feelings of uneasiness and about going out with Hannah or not.

Ben still felt the strong pings of uneasiness after he worshiped, prayed to, and talked to God. The teen began to think that the uneasiness was connected to some nervousness about going out with Hannah. He thought it was no big deal and that the uneasiness, nervousness, or whatever the feelings were would be gone when he went out with Hannah. Plus, Ben thought that he would feel great after his and Hannah's time on Friday. Ben continued to think about Hannah, her attractive form, and how great he would feel when they went out together as he slowly drifted off to sleep. The teen finally fell asleep twenty minutes later.

Several hours had passed, and Ben had a dream, though it wasn't a dream entirely. He heard Jesus's voice in the dream, and He said these words: *"Wait until a bit after church on Sunday because Hannah is not the one."* Ben briefly woke up after the dream, and he knew that Jesus said the words that He just said. The teen was quite saddened by Jesus's words because Hannah had been so welcoming and accepting of him. However, Ben trusted Jesus and knew He only had the best for him. It was a bit hard for the teen to do this, but he knew that Jesus had a plan for him and knew who his wife would be. Ben felt that the uneasiness had suddenly begun to dissipate inside his mind and heart. He fell back asleep ten minutes later, wondering what and who lay ahead of him in his life journey.

Wednesday came, and it was another work day at American Burgers for Ben Lawson. His early morning flew by before he got to work. It was currently 9:00 a.m. The teen now found himself in a familiar position as he was washing dishes. Ben was wondering if he would run into Alberto sometime during the lunch break. The nineteen-year-old was expectantly waiting to see Alberto and tell Jesus's messages to him. Ben was also thinking about what would happen by or before the end of Sunday for him. *Maybe I will meet my wife at work or school during this week or at church on Sunday. Possibly sometime after church on Sunday, as Jesus said.* That thought swirled around in Ben's head for the last hour before the lunch break.

The lunch break came at 12:00 p.m., and Ben was fortunate enough to run into Alberto. Both Ben and Alberto finished their lunches at 12:30 p.m., and they went to throw away their trash at the same trash can. Alberto was a muscular twenty-six-year-old Hispanic man who was six-foot-three inches tall, with medium-length dark brown hair and brown eyes. He was wearing the usual work shirt for American Burgers, dark blue jeans, and dark blue and white shoes. Ben said hi to Alberto and asked him how he was doing. Alberto was actually doing pretty well. He and his girlfriend were happily celebrating their one-year anniversary on Saturday of the coming weekend. Ben congratulated him and then briefly talked to him about church and the church's intimate and loving marriage-type relationship with Jesus. The teen went on to tell Jesus's/God's messages to Alberto. Alberto was actually really interested in what Ben was talking about but didn't know and believe in God. However, the twenty-six-year-old felt a bit of hunger starting to well up in him to want to know more about God. That, in turn, would cause him to want a relationship with God down the road. As for the current moment, Alberto said thanks to Ben for talking to him, and then the two of them got back to work ten minutes before the lunch break ended.

The rest of Ben's day at work went by in a hurry. He continued to thoroughly wash dishes. It was like time sped up, and Dave was now at the fast-food restaurant to pick up his son at 5:15 p.m. Ben texted Hannah on the way home, saying that the two of them should talk in person tomorrow about them going out on Friday or not. The teen didn't want to simply text Hannah a message that said that he didn't think they should go out on Friday. Hannah texted back a reply five minutes later that asked if they could talk during their lunch break tomorrow at 12:30 p.m. Ben said that would work. Hannah replied with a final message that said that she looked forward to seeing and talking to him at that time. The message also said that she hoped Ben had a good night tonight and that they would talk later. Ben replied with a similar text before putting his phone back into his backpack.

Ben and his dad arrived at the house several minutes later. The teen decided to do some of his homework before dinner so that he would have more time to hang out with his family towards the end of the night. Ben told everyone about the dream that he had last night in addition to the usual family conversations. Dave and Leslie kind of knew that their son shouldn't go out with Hannah after they said that he should try out the experience and see where he and Hannah went. The two parents were still wondering if Ben still had the feeling that there was more to be had with him and Sophia. Ben said that he didn't exactly have that feeling anymore. It was more of a feeling that something or someone was coming by or before the end of Sunday of the current week. All three of Ben's family members believed him when he told them the words Jesus spoke to him in the dream. The rest of the Lawson family's night was filled with laughter, homework for Ben and Josh, relaxation and downtime for the four family members, and then getting ready and going to bed. Ben was already preparing himself for what he would say to Hannah after he prayed, talked to, and worshiped God in his bed. The teen was at peace with not going out with Hannah. Then Ben fell asleep.

Thursday came, and it seemed to go by in a flash. Aside from praying, talking to, and worshiping God, three other events felt like they went by at a slower rate for Ben. Ben was in his first class in no time after he got ready for the day, ate breakfast, and was driven to the university. The teen's two mechanical engineering classes were the first two events that seemed to slow down. These classes felt slower because Ben was soaking up information in his mind that would help him create his prosthetic legs. He wrote down some other materials that he would need in addition to efficient methods of building the prosthetic legs.

Ben's two mechanical engineering classes happened before and after the other slower event. This was because the other event was talking with Hannah about just being friends and not going out. Plus, Ben would talk with her at twelve thirty, which was after their Christian religion class. Ben and Hannah separately and quickly got something to eat before meeting and talking with each other. They started talking about how their days were going. Then, Ben smoothly transitioned to what he wanted to say to Hannah. He said that he didn't feel like the two of them were supposed to go out and have a relationship down the road. However, the teen said that he would like to be friends with Hannah. Hannah looked like she had somewhat expected what Ben said. She was totally good with being friends. Ben and Hannah talked about getting lunch sometime next week, and then they went their separate ways with the rest of their classes and days that day.

The remainder of Ben's day on Thursday blasted past him, and then it was Friday. Ben only had one higher-level math class on Friday at 9:00 a.m. that lasted for two hours since it was only on that day every week. Ben had arranged for his mom to pick him up at 12:30 p.m. when there was the lunch break at the private high school where she worked. The nineteen-year-old was fortunate enough to bump into Anthony Markus at 11:45 a.m. as the two of them were heading into the cafeteria for lunch. Anthony was a six-foot-two-inch African-American man who had thinly shaven black hair on his head and hazel-green eyes. He just turned twenty-one and was in his senior year of college. Anthony was wearing dark blue jeans, a blue and red Evart University football team jersey, and black shoes.

Ben only had forty-five minutes to talk to Anthony, tell Jesus's messages to him, and get some lunch. The one thing that Ben did not notice until that last second was that Anthony met up with one of his friends. Anthony and his friend did a fist bump and manly pats on each other's shoulders when they greeted each other. Ben stopped and stayed several feet behind the two friends, watching their interaction, all the while checking his messages on his flip phone. The teen somewhat heard what Anthony and his friend were talking about as other students were walking in between and around the three of them. The chatter amongst the students made it a bit hard to hear what Anthony and his friend were talking about. Ben picked up on topics that included football, girls/young women, and video games. Ten minutes went by, and then Anthony's friend left for his next class. Ben took the opportunity to wheel a few feet away from Anthony.

"Hey," Ben said casually after waving.

"Hey, man," Anthony replied as he was standing where he was, simultaneously thinking about where he wanted to eat in the cafeteria. "Dude, what happened to your legs?"

"It's a story within itself. I don't mind sharing it if you want to hear it. How are you doing today?"

"Pretty good. And, sure, I would be down for hearing your story."

"Sounds good. Do you want to get something to eat before I tell you my story? I only have about thirty-five minutes before I get picked up."

"For sure, man. We have plenty of time before you have to get picked up. I was actually just thinking about where I'm going to eat. I think I'm going to go with Burger King. Are you down with that?"

"Yes, that sounds great. By the way, I'm Ben," Ben said just before reaching out his hand to shake Anthony's hand.

"Cool. Nice to meet you, Ben. I'm Anthony," Anthony replied as he grabbed and shook Ben's right hand with his right hand.

"Nice to meet you, too, Anthony," Ben replied genuinely. The two of them put down their hands after a second. Then, Ben and Anthony headed thirty feet over to Burger King and got lunch there. They both ordered cheeseburgers, but they chose to have a couple of different things on the cheeseburgers. Ben got a small container of fries, and Anthony did the same. The only other difference in their lunches was that Ben got a medium-sized cup of Dr Pepper, and Anthony got a large cup of Coke. The two guys found and sat at an empty table on the outskirts of the cafeteria. Ben ate half of his lunch before telling Anthony his story of how he lost his legs.

"Man, that is one heck of a story!" Anthony exclaimed after Ben finished telling his story. "Ben, I'm truly sorry that that rare disease took your legs away."

"Thanks, Anthony," Ben responded before he started to eat the second half of his lunch. "It was hard to come to terms with what happened, but thankfully, God and Diego were right there to help me through that process."

"For sure, man. It's great that God and Diego helped you during that time. I want to let you know that we can go, if you want, to the gym or the recreation center to work out or play whatever rec center game you want whenever I'm free during the week. Would you want to do that?"

"That sounds good. I might have to take up your offer to play a game at the rec center sometime next week. I have a mean ping-pong swing."

"Really? Okay, man. It's on. I do know how to play ping pong pretty well myself. I should be free on Thursday of next week anytime from 12:00 to 1:15 p.m. Does 12:30 p.m. work for you?"

"That's perfect. I'm looking forward to it."

"Same here, Ben. By the way, how much time do you have before you get picked up?"

"Ten minutes," Ben replied after he pulled out his phone and checked the time. "Thanks for checking."

"No problem."

"Cool. Anyway, do you mind if I tell you a couple of messages I got from Jesus/God?"

"Sure. What does the big man want to say?"

"He said He will always love, protect, and provide for everyone. Jesus/God also said that the kingdom of heaven and all of its goodness is in every born-again Christian who has a relationship with Him and obediently does the will of His Father/God."

"Those are definitely good messages. They align with what Jesus/God says in His Word. Thanks for telling me that. I sort of needed it. I have a good relationship with God and have told some people about Jesus and His good news in the past. I guess life has just distracted me from doing more of that," Anthony said these things in somewhat of a somber and reflective tone. Ben knew the reasons behind Anthony's tone even though Anthony didn't tell him those reasons.

"Do you want to tell me what's going on?" Ben asked genuinely.

"Not really. Maybe some other time. Anyway, have you heard about the title of the next *Star Wars* movie in the prequel trilogy? It was just released on the internet on Wednesday."

"No, I haven't. I'm excited to know what will be included in it. We already know that Anakin Skywalker becomes Darth Vader because his son, Luke Skywalker, said that Darth Vader was formerly known as Anakin Skywalker."

"Yeah. It's kind of a buzz kill. It will be fun to see what George Lucas does with that part of the movie, though. Do you want to know the title of the movie?"

"Of course! Tell it to me."

"Okay, the title of the third and final movie of the *Star Wars* prequel trilogy is…" Anthony replied dramatically as he did a little drum roll with his hands on the table. Ben was waiting with great expectation and excitement for the title. "*Revenge of the Sith.*"

"No way, man!" Ben exclaimed. That is a cool title. I do like the titles of the other five movies a bit more, though."

"Same here, Ben. Plus, I do like the titles of *The Phantom Menace, Attack of the Clones*, and *The Empire Strikes Back* more than this new one."

"For sure. Well, I have to go now and be ready to be picked up. It's five minutes before my ride is supposed to be here, and I need to throw away my wrapper trash from lunch."

"Okay, man. I can throw away your trash for you if you want." Anthony was ready to get Ben's trash but waited for his reply.

"Sure, you can take it and throw it away. Thank you."

"You're welcome," Anthony said and then grabbed Ben's trash in addition to his own and threw it all away. Ben waited for Anthony to return to the table before starting to wheel out from underneath the table.

"Well," Anthony started before continuing, "my second class of the day is going to start at twelve forty-five, and it's a little ways away from here. The class is next to the art college. Anyway, it was really nice to get lunch with you and hear your story. Thanks for saying hi to me."

"You're welcome," Ben replied. "It was also really nice to get lunch with you. I look forward to playing ping-pong with you at the rec center on Thursday of next week. I hope you are ready for some heat."

"Keep on trash-talking, man. We'll see what you have then. I'm also looking forward to playing ping-pong with you. It'll be fun. I'll see you later," Anthony said and then fist-bumped Ben before heading off to his next class.

Ben began heading over to the place in front of the student union, where he usually got picked up. The teen arrived there one minute before twelve thirty. Leslie dropped the electronic ramp down with the remote as her son approached the van. She asked Ben how his day was after she got him into the van and tied his chair down. Ben said it was really good and told her about what happened with his conversation and lunch with Anthony Markus before she got into the driver's seat. Then, Leslie drove the two of them home.

It was still a bit weird for Ben to be home on Fridays by 1:00 p.m. The teen had two or three classes on Fridays for all of the previous semesters that ended by 3:00 or 5:00 p.m. This new schedule was also weird because he didn't have work on Fridays this semester. Claire was able to find two other current employees to work for all of the hours that Ben could not work for those days. The fast-food restaurant manager had said that this plan of action was better than having Ben work from 12:00 to 5:00 p.m. because the other two current employees were as good as Ben at washing dishes. In addition, Ben would not be able to get to work on time at twelve on Fridays because American Burgers was thirty-five minutes away from Evart University. That was because the two places were in completely opposite directions from the Lawsons' house. It would be futile to compromise Ben's parents' schedules. It was not possible. That is why Ben works all day from 9:00 a.m. to 7:00 p.m. on Saturdays this semester. He was allowed to get dinner at American Burgers before leaving at 7:00 p.m.

As for the current moment, Ben was home alone until 4:00 p.m., which was the time when Josh got home from high school. Leslie went back to the high school that she worked at to finish off her workday. Ben's parents would arrive at the house today around 5:30 p.m. after work. Dave and Leslie usually got home around 5:15 p.m., but they were getting the first season of *Smallville* together at the nearest Blockbuster store before that. Ben couldn't wait to watch three or four episodes of season one that night. He and his family would probably get through half of the season by the end of Sunday.

Ben texted an invite to Diego to come over and watch the first half of the season that night and on Sunday. Diego replied with a message that said he was able to and would absolutely love to do that. The two friends texted for a little while more. Ben told Diego about what happened with his interactions with Anthony, Hannah, Claire, Daniel, and Alberto and how he conveyed Jesus's messages to them. The teen also texted his friend about Hannah wanting to go out with him and being in a relationship. Ben told Diego that it didn't work out because of the words that Jesus spoke to him in the dream that he had.

The nineteen-year-old also texted his friend about the update on making his own prosthetic legs. Diego said that everything Ben said was amazing and that God was really working in Ben's life. The Southern Chilean texted his friend about what was going on at work and in his classes. Diego also texted Ben that he was going out on a first date with Vanessa after work on Saturday. Ben congratulated his friend on that great news and wished the best for him and Vanessa. Then, the teen ended the conversation by saying that he was going to work on most of his homework before Josh got home. Ben said he was looking forward to seeing Diego that night and watching *Smallville* with him and his family. Diego said that he was also looking forward to that and that he would talk to him later. Ben followed suit, texting his friend that he would talk to him later. Then, the teen put his phone away in his backpack, wheeled into his room, and started on his homework.

It was 6:30 p.m. on that Friday night, and Sophia O'Donnell was just starting to eat the spaghetti dinner that she and Lucy had made at their dorm. The two young women had decided to watch a romantic comedy movie that was on TV while eating dinner. They were eating at the kitchen table, which was ten to twelve feet away. Lucy and Sophia were enjoying watching their movie and eating dinner almost as much as Ben, Diego, and the rest of the Lawson family were enjoying watching *Smallville* and eating dinner. It was as if Ben and Sophia were connected even though they were miles apart. The storylines of both the romantic comedy movie and *Smallville* seemed to foreshadow similar endings, even though the beginnings of both *Smallville* and the romantic comedy movie were completely different from their endings. Both of the main characters in the movie and show ended up with different but more compatible people of the opposite gender. That looked to be the ending for Ben and Sophia after each of them had tried to be with who they thought they should be with. Surely, both of their encounters and conversations with Jesus would lead to that good ending.

Sophia was thinking more about not going out and being with Ben, even though she began to be a little excited on Sunday night before going to bed. The reality of the situation began to creep back into her head on Monday afternoon. She got distracted again by Ben's disability with his lack of legs. Sophia began to wonder once more if there was a different Christian guy out in the world for her.

Jesus, who was in heaven and knew her thoughts, started to bring her mind back to what He said about Ben as the romantic comedy movie neared its third and final act. Sophia thought back to what Jesus said about Ben being the best Christian guy in Evart and that life was more than a person's legs. Suddenly, Sophia began to feel a true and pure sense of peace and calm about going out and being with Ben. The senses of calm and peace were truly tangible in her heart and mind even before the main characters in the romantic comedy movie found and went on to be with the right partners of the opposite gender. Sophia felt the true and pure senses of calm and peace permanently solidify in her heart and mind as the main characters ended up with the people of the opposite gender that they were supposed to be with. She knew and felt that everything was going to work out and be even better than what she imagined. The young redheaded woman knew what she had to do, and she would do it with a true desire and passion. Sophia was going to look for, apologize to, and go out and be with Ben after she went back to her parents' house for the weekend. Her parents' house was twenty-five minutes away from the Lawsons' house, but she did not know that yet. Sophia only knew that she wanted to be with Ben, and nothing was going to stop her from doing that.

CHAPTER 6:

THE SEARCH

It was currently 9:30 a.m. on Saturday, January 18th, 2003, at Sophia O'Donnell's parents' house. Sophia had chosen to sleep in since it was the weekend. However, that did not impede her from her search for Ben Lawson a bit later in the day. She had texted her parents and her younger sister, Alicia, at 9:30 p.m. on Friday night that she was now heading over to the house and staying there for the weekend. All three of Sophia's family members were awake at 10:00 p.m. when she arrived at her parents' house, and they were very glad to see her. She talked to Alicia and her parents for ten to fifteen minutes before getting ready and going to bed along with the rest of her family. The young redhead did not tell them about Ben that night. Sophia wanted to save that for the time after she ate breakfast. As for now, she got up, put on some very casual Saturday morning clothes, and made her way across the purple-carpeted hallway and the living room to the family room.

"Good morning, Sis," Alicia O'Donnell said in a smooth teenage voice as she was at the counter in the family room, eating her sausage, toast, and fruit breakfast. Alicia was almost sixteen and was slightly thinner than Sophia. The fifteen-year-old was five feet four inches tall, had brown eyes, and wavy, mid-back length light brown hair currently styled in a ponytail with the help of a hairband. Alicia also was wearing very casual Saturday morning clothes.

"Good morning, Baby Sis," Sophia replied lovingly as she walked over to her sister to give her a hug. Alicia kindly obliged the gesture and hugged Sophia back.

"Good morning, sweetheart," Sophia's mom, Candace O'Donnell, said warmly in a smooth voice while handing her first-born daughter's breakfast. The plate had the same things on it as Alicia's plate. Candace was a forty-seven-year-old redheaded woman. She was five feet eight inches tall and had a normal body weight shape, just like her daughter Sophia. Candace had hazel-green eyes and was currently wearing her shoulder-length hair in a bun. She was wearing light blue jeans, a turquoise T-shirt, and light blue shoes with white bottoms.

"Good morning, Sophia. It's always a pleasure having you here," Sophia's dad, Sam O'Donnell, said in a smooth and somewhat deep voice as he was coming back into the house from the garage. Sam had eaten breakfast with his wife before Alicia and Sophia got out of bed. He went over to hug Sophia, kissed her on her forehead, and did the same thing with

Alicia. Then, Sam headed over to his wife, passionately hugged her, and kissed her on the lips before sitting down on a chair next to Sophia. Candace pulled up a chair next to her husband. Sam was a fifty-two-year-old man with brown eyes and short, light brown hair that was now mostly gray. He was wearing dark blue jeans, a blue and gold colored T-shirt, and black shoes.

"Good morning, Mom and Dad. It is very nice to see you two as well," Sophia responded warmly before hugging her mom and dad. Then, Sophia quietly prayed over her breakfast before starting to eat it. The young redheaded woman interspersedly talked with her parents and Alicia while eating her sausage, fruit, and toast breakfast. Sophia generally told them how her week was and how Lucy was doing. Sophia wanted to tell her family about the grave incident that happened to her after she ate her breakfast. That was also the time that she would tell Jesus's messages to them. In addition, she would tell her family about Ben. These stories and conversations were best said while not doing anything else.

The time had finally come for Sophia to tell her family about what happened before this current week. The story about when Sophia went to heaven and talked with Jesus after hugging Him would be the easiest part to tell her family. Nothing would be the same in the O'Donnell family after this. Sophia took the last bite of her toast, and then she was done with her breakfast. The young redhead swallowed a bit hard, and then she mentally prepared herself for all of the things that she was going to tell her family. Sophia's parents and sister noticed that she was a tad nervous at the moment and gently encouraged her to share what was going on. The nineteen-year-old said that she wanted to tell everyone some things that happened to her before this current week, and some things might be hard for them to understand and process. Sophia's family was really interested and anxious about what she had to say.

Sophia began to tell her parents and Alicia about how she was just heading back to her dorm on the night of January 11th before she noticed a suspicious guy who had come out of the art museum. Sophia told her family that she knew the guy had stolen one or two works of art from the museum. The police were heading in her direction from some other incident. Sophia told her family members that she was going to shout to the police to come and arrest the guy, but she didn't have time because he shot her twice in the right side of her upper chest. The looks from the teen's family said it all when they heard that part of the story. They were deeply sad and a bit grieved. Sophia showed her parents and sister her shot wounds to let them know that all of what happened to her was true. The three family members took turns hugging Sophia and comforting her as she told them what happened. Some tears streaked down Sophia's face. Sam, Candace, and Alicia were all wondering how Sophia survived.

Sophia recomposed herself and then told her family about the aftermath of her getting shot before going to heaven. All three faces of Sophia's family members lit up in great interest as she began to describe heaven and hugging and talking with Jesus. They all knew what heaven looked like, but they were amazed at how articulately and authentically Sophia spoke of the place. The young redhead talked to her family members about her wanting to stay in heaven. Sam, Candace, and Alicia all understood that feeling because of the perfection of heaven and being with the triune God and all believers. Sophia's three family members said that they would have been sad for quite some time if Jesus had not given her a second chance at life.

The teen's parents and sister wondered why Jesus gave her a second chance at life instead of just staying in heaven like she wanted to. Sophia explained by telling them that Jesus said that she would come back to heaven on May 14th, 2005, after she was married to her husband for about two years. Sam, Candace, and Alicia were more than a little anxious about Sophia going back to heaven in nearly two and a half years. They wanted to live the rest of their lives with her. However, they couldn't have known that she had gotten shot. The three family members were just happy that Sophia was with them now, and they were going to cherish every last minute with her. They were very happy to know that Sophia was going to have a husband for two years before going back to heaven. The teen's parents and sister were all wondering who her husband would be. Sophia went on to tell them that the most important reason why Jesus gave her a second chance at life was that He had messages that He wanted her to share with every Christian and nonbeliever she met. The young redhead went on to tell Jesus's messages to her parents and sister. They gladly received and rejoiced over Jesus's messages.

The nineteen-year-old started to end with the second but most important reason why Jesus brought her back to life. She began by saying that Jesus knew she wanted to have a godly Christian husband who would love her like He loved and still loves the church. Sophia told her family that was the second reason for Jesus bringing her back to life. Plus, she told them that she had said to Him near the beginning of His and her conversation that she had not done all of the things she wanted to do in her life on Earth. Sophia went on to tell her family members about the fact that Jesus knew about her one and only past relationship with Nate and why they broke up. Then, she told her parents and sister about the fact that Jesus had recommended that she try Ben Lawson again.

Sophia had to remind them that she had been in a Christian religion class with Ben during her second semester of sophomore year of college. She talked about how she had rejected his offer to go out with him after the two of them talked for a little bit. That led the teen to explain to her family members that Ben didn't have any legs and was in a wheelchair. Sophia told them she had no idea of how Ben had lost his legs.

The nineteen-year-old went back to talking to her parents and sister about her conversation with Jesus and the fact that He said that Ben was the best Christian guy in Evart. Sam, Candace, and Alicia were all intrigued by that. Finally, Sophia told her family members about how she was not that interested this past school week about going out and being with Ben even after Lucy talked to her about the situation. The teen finished the story by saying that she felt a true and pure sense of peace and calm about going out and being with Ben as she and Lucy neared the end of watching a romantic comedy movie last night at their dorm. The last thing that Sophia told her parents and sister was that she wanted to find Ben sometime this weekend, if not today, and start by going out with him to Starbucks on Friday of this upcoming week or next weekend.

"Wow, Sophia," Alicia said before continuing, "that was a lot to take in. I will need some time to fully process all of the things that you said. For now, I am just happy that Jesus gave you a second chance at life and that you are safe and with us now. Plus, I'm glad you are going to get married sometime in the future. It sounds like your husband might be this Ben guy. Above all, you get to do God's will and tell everyone you meet about Jesus's messages." Alicia came around to hug her sister a bit more tightly after saying these things.

"Absolutely, honey; we are ecstatic that you are safe and here with us now after Jesus brought you back to life," Sophia's mom said and then came around and hugged her oldest daughter like Alicia did. "Everything that you talked about was truly amazing, except the part of you getting shot. That scared me a lot and got my blood pressure through the roof for a minute."

"Yeah, sweetheart, you had us scared to death when you said you had gotten shot. Praise God that He brought you back to life and brought you back to us!" Sophia's dad responded before continuing. "God is good all the time, and all the time..."

"God is good. Amen," Candace, Alicia, and Sophia responded gladly in unison.

"You all are right. Always remember that," Sam replied. "As for this Ben guy, I want to meet him and give him a once over. It seems to me he should be a great guy, considering the fact that Jesus/God said that he is the best Christian guy in Evart. Sophia, you have my permission to go out with him on Friday or someday next weekend. Just make sure to bring him over here for dinner either of those nights."

"Okay, Dad. Sounds good," Sophia replied a bit nervously but with laughter in her voice.

"Sweet pea, there is nothing to be nervous about," Sam replied reassuringly. "I just want to make sure that this guy doesn't do anything to hurt you or make you upset. I doubt that he would do anything like that based on Jesus's recommendation of him. Plus, we will have to get to know him."

"I know. It's just that I have never really been in this situation with how I'm beginning to feel about Ben, going out with him and having him over here for dinner. It was somewhat different with Nate."

"That is to be expected. I have a feeling that it will go well with meeting and getting to know Ben."

"Yeah, I agree," Sophia's mom responded. "From what I heard from you when you were talking, Ben sounds like a pretty good guy."

"Me, too, Sis," Alicia said before continuing. "I wish you all the best for searching for Ben. Legs or no legs, anyone can be a great and godly Christian and a truly good person."

"Agreed," Sam and Candace responded almost simultaneously before Candace continued talking with Sophia. "Sophia, we all support you in finding and going out with Ben. As for today, your father, Alicia, and I are going to go see an action/comedy movie at one in the afternoon. Go and find Ben, and then you and the rest of our family can play volleyball before coming home for dinner. Your friends can feel free to come and play with us. I remember you telling your dad, Alicia, and me that you usually play volleyball with your friends on Saturdays. I think that we all can make it to the sand court at the Sports Hub at four. How does that sound?"

"That sounds great. I will tell my friends they are welcome to come and play volleyball with us. We all seemed to get along well the last time we played volleyball at the other facility," Sophia replied with happiness in her tone. "Do you all want to play a card game before I get ready to find Ben and before you three go to the movie?"

"I remember that. Sounds fun," Candace replied with excitement in her voice. "Let's do it."

"Yeah, that does sound fun," Alicia responded. "What card game?"

"Go fish," Sophia answered.

"Oh, go fish," Sam responded with interest in his tone. "I'm in."

"Okay, I will go get a deck of cards," Sophia replied before getting a deck of cards.

It was now 11:00 a.m., and the O'Donnell family played a few hands of go fish that lasted for almost an hour. Sophia won the first hand, and then her dad won the second hand. Alicia won the last hand. Candace came in second place in all three hands. The four family members greatly enjoyed playing the card game together and eagerly waited to play volleyball together later in the afternoon at the Sports Hub.

Sam, Candace, and Alicia wished Sophia all the best a second time for finding Ben. Alicia went first to shower in her and her sister's bathroom to get ready to go to the action/comedy movie with Sam and Candace. Then, Sophia took a shower to get ready for her search for

Ben. Her parents and sister were gone before she got dressed. They wanted to get to the movie ten or so minutes before it started in order to get some good seats and snacks. Sophia chose to wear light blue jeans, a light pink shirt, and white shoes with sky-blue bottoms.

It was now 12:40 p.m., and Sophia got a bit of a head start on her search for Ben. She remembered that Ben said that his major was mechanical engineering. The nineteen-year-old began by opening up her red-colored laptop in her room and searching for Ben on Evart University's website. Sophia scrolled and clicked on the mechanical engineering major page. Then, she went to the e-mail page for those students. It didn't help that there were not a lot of pictures of the students. Sophia saw that there were a dozen or so students with the name "Ben." There were only about half of the Ben-named students who had pictures to go with their names. Unfortunately, the teen did not see the right Ben she was looking for. That was a bit annoying to Sophia. The young redhead guessed that he did not want to be seen on the website. Fortunately, Sophia had another idea as to how to find her Ben. That idea would formulate into a longer search, though.

Sophia's second idea of finding Ben was to drive down to the mechanical engineering buildings, the student union, and the recreation center at Evart University and see if Ben or someone who knew him was there. Sophia grabbed her phone and car keys in her room and then made her way out of her family's house. She jumped into her red Lexus and began her drive to Evart University. Her plan was to start at the mechanical engineering buildings and then go on to search for Ben at the student union and recreation center if she needed to. Sophia thought that several zealous mechanical engineering students would be around those places to study or at least hang out at the recreation center. She thought that Ben might be one of those students.

Sophia parked her car in a small parking lot next to one of the mechanical engineering buildings. The building was called the Drake-Richards building, and it was four stories high and made of smooth, dark gray stone. Sophia got out of her car and started walking around the building. She was looking at the green plant life that was planted in a several-foot-long garden at the north side of the Drake-Richards building. The garden had yellow lily flowers in addition to white daisies and red roses. The green plant life was interweaved around the sections of flowers. Several trees surrounded the four-story building as well. There were four dark blue benches with matching back pieces to lay back on. They were positioned at the four sides of the building. All of the flowers and trees were great and relaxing sights to look at for Sophia, especially since she did not find Ben anywhere around the perimeter of the building. It took her ten minutes to walk around the Drake-Richards building. She only saw two students on two of the benches, surfing the internet on their laptops.

The next thing that Sophia did was go into the Drake-Richards building. She thought that Ben might have wanted to do a little homework before heading over to the recreation center to play ping-pong or some other game and hang out for a while. Maybe he was doing those things with a friend. It took Sophia a total of forty-five minutes to walk through all four floors of the four-story building. She did not have any luck finding Ben on either of the building floors. Sophia just found ten students spaced out on the second and third floors. The teen was pretty sure that Ben was a proactive person and wanted to spend some of the weekend doing a bit of his homework and studying. Then, Sophia thought that Ben would likely do most of his homework and study on Fridays. She was beginning to question herself on why she came to search for him at the university.

Sophia decided to change her plan of action. She was going to go search for Ben at the recreation center and the student union now instead of looking around and inside two other mechanical engineering buildings. The young redhead thought that Ben might still have wanted to hang out with a friend or classmate at the student union or play a game with that person at the recreation center. Sophia exited the Drake-Richards building, got into her red Lexus, and drove for four minutes until she parked in a parking lot next to the recreation center. It was now a few minutes after 2:00 p.m., and Sophia had almost an hour and a half before she walked back to her car and to the Sports Hub to play volleyball with her friends and family. That thought reminded her to text her friends to invite them to play at that facility with her family. Sophia got out of her car after texting her friends about the volleyball plan. Then, she spent forty minutes in the recreation center, trying to find Ben. The teen asked a dozen students if they knew or had seen Ben. Unfortunately, none of the students knew who she was looking for. Sophia returned and walked out of the recreation center, disappointed about not finding Ben at that place. However, she was bound and determined to find him, even if it took her until Sunday's end.

The last place that Sophia searched for Ben was at the student union. She now had a little less than forty-five minutes before she had to leave. The young redheaded woman quickly gazed around the outside of the student union while walking before she went inside the student union. She thought that she might have a better chance of finding Ben inside that place. Sophia was heading in the right direction with her guess, but Ben was still nowhere to be found. She checked the gaming room and the cafeteria area. The redhead talked to eight students in each place. Sophia had a stroke of luck when Anthony Markus overheard one of her conversations, even though she did not know that. They both were in the middle of the cafeteria area. Anthony was finishing up a late Panda Express lunch with a young, fit, and attractive African-American female student who had shoulder-length black hair and brown eyes. She was dressed in a dark purple shirt that had gold sparkles on it. She was also wearing dark blue jeans and purple shoes. Anthony said to her that he wanted to help out this young redheaded woman who knew who Ben was. Anthony excused himself for a few minutes and came up in front of Sophia.

"Excuse me," Anthony said as Sophia neared the end of talking to a student about knowing where to find Ben. The student said goodbye and started to walk away before Anthony continued. "Hi, my name is Anthony. I was wondering if I could help you. I couldn't help but overhear some of your conversation with that student."

"Hi, Anthony," Sophia replied with some excitement in her tone. "I would appreciate some help. I'm looking for a guy who goes to college at this university. His name is Ben; he has medium-length black hair and blue eyes. He is in a wheelchair and doesn't have legs. Do you know him? And where can I find him? I want to see Ben."

"It's nice to meet you, Sophia," Anthony replied warmly while giving her a little friendly handshake. "I do know Ben. He and I had lunch yesterday and had good and interesting conversations. You should ask him about what he has been through and what he has done recently. Unfortunately, I do not know where he is today. However, Ben and I are planning on playing ping-pong at the recreation center on Thursday at 12:30 p.m. this upcoming week. Would you like to join us that day? I'm sorry that I couldn't be of further help. I can tell by your eagerness that you really want to see and talk to him."

"I really appreciate your help, Anthony. I think I might take up your offer to join you and Ben on Thursday if I don't find him this weekend. However, I would prefer to talk to Ben alone after you two play ping-pong. I can give you my number, and I can text you if I do find Ben sometime this weekend. I hope that's okay with you."

"That's totally fine. You can give me your number just in case you find Ben sometime this weekend. I understand that you want to find and talk to him as soon as possible."

"Sounds good," Sophia replied as she typed out her phone number on her phone. She showed it to Anthony, and he took out his phone to type her number into it.

"All right," Anthony said as he put his phone away into his right jean pocket. "I'm glad that I was of some help to you in finding Ben. Text me if you find him this weekend. Otherwise, I will see you on Thursday of next week, and you can see and talk to Ben alone then. See you around. Bye."

"Sounds good. Bye," Sophia said as she and Anthony waved goodbye to each other. Anthony went back to finishing his late lunch with the young African-American female student. Sophia somewhat overheard Anthony saying to the young African-American woman that he just wanted to help Sophia find Ben. The redheaded teen walked away before Anthony and the other student began intimately talking to each other.

Sophia exited the cafeteria area and walked away from the student union to where she parked her car. She got into her Lexus and checked her phone. It was 3:15 p.m., fifteen or so minutes before Sophia drove to the Sports Hub. The young woman noticed that her friends replied to her message about coming to the Sports Hub to play volleyball with her and her family. Her friends said they would like to join her and her family at the sports facility to play volleyball. Sophia took five minutes to reply back to her friends, saying that she was looking forward to seeing and playing volleyball with them and her family at four.

Sophia used up another ten minutes in her car before she drove off to the Sports Hub. She was pondering where Ben was. The thoughts of him working at a job or hanging out with his family at home crossed her mind. The redheaded teen also thought that Ben might be hanging out with a friend at a place somewhere other than Evart University. Sophia did not know where he worked if he indeed had a job. In addition, she did not know where Ben lived. Lastly, she didn't know where Ben liked to hang out. Sophia only remembered that Ben liked to hang out with his best friend and other friends, go to movies, and play video games. She had a hard time remembering what else he had said that he liked to do. Sophia got a bit annoyed with herself as the ten minutes drew to a conclusion. The nineteen-year-old figured that she would go and play volleyball with her friends and family and do her best to get over the annoyance of not finding Ben yet. On a positive note, she did run into Anthony Markus, who knew who Ben was. Plus, Anthony would let her and Ben talk privately after he and him played ping-pong on Thursday of next week. That was if she did not find Ben during the weekend.

Sophia began to drive away from Evart University at 3:30 p.m. She was right in guessing that Ben was working at a job, but she did not know that. Sophia did not know that he had a job at American Burgers. The only thing that she knew was that she would search for anyone at her church, Holy Communion, who knew Ben. As for now, the young redhead was going to enjoy playing volleyball with her friends and family and having a good night with her family at home.

It was 9:20 a.m. on Sunday, and the Lawson family was finishing up breakfast before they got ready to go to church. Diego Sanchez called the family at nine thirty to invite them to Holy Communion, the church that he went to. Dave Lawson politely declined the offer because he and the rest of his family wanted to see the old man that Dave had seen last Sunday at their church, Light of the World. Dave had a feeling that he and the rest of his family should meet the old man. He thought that the meeting was for an important reason. The rest of the Lawson family had been told by Dave the night before about his feelings for the old man.

They all agreed they should see what this old man wanted with them. Diego understood their reason. Dave said he and the rest of the family would love to come to Holy Communion next Sunday, though. Diego said that was a great idea, and he was really looking forward to seeing them then. The Lawson family proceeded to get ready for church after they and Diego hung up.

The next two and a half or so hours went by in a flash. Ben and the rest of his family were getting ready to go to church at nine forty at one moment, and then they were at church at ten twenty-five the next moment. The worship and sermon parts of the service seemed to slow down, but it also went by in a hurry. However, the message of forgiveness in the sermon stuck with Ben. He was willing to forgive Sophia for rejecting him and his offer for her to go out with him, but he still found himself wrestling with that certain part of the situation.

Dave and the rest of the Lawson family did not see the old man during the entire service. They were ready to give up and head home right before he suddenly came walking towards them, fighting his way through an anxious crowd that was either going home or to lunch with their families. Dave recognized the old man and signaled for his family to stay where they were. The Lawson family was positioned to the right of the middle of the congregation. The old man was heading their way from the far right section of the congregation. It took a couple of minutes for him to get to where Dave and the rest of the family were, but he did make it there. He was wearing light blue jeans, a plain turquoise blue polo shirt, and white shoes. The old man looked just as healthy as he did in 1984, with his smoothly aged white skin and sharp blue eyes.

“Greetings,” the old man said in a chipper tone and a slightly deep voice before continuing. “I am Harold Trenton, and I am here to see about this young man. I know his name is Ben,” Harold said those last two sentences, all the while looking at Ben.

“Hello, Harold,” Dave said a bit hesitantly and with a questioning tone. “I recognize you from when my wife and I were at the main Evart hospital nineteen years ago. We were getting ready to have our firstborn son, Ben, come into the world. If you don’t mind me asking, how did you know Ben’s name?”

“I’m a prophet. God spoke to me in a dream two months ago,” Harold replied before continuing. “He told me that Ben was going to get shot. God also told me that He would give Ben a second chance at life with the task of telling His/Jesus’s two messages to every nonbeliever and Christian he met. Ben and his future wife, whom God also generally spoke to me about, will help lead many people to repent from their sins, turn to God, and have true relationships with Jesus. He also told me that Ben and his wife will return to heaven on May 14th, 2005, at 2:00 p.m. I can feel that the Holy Spirit is at work in Ben. Plus, I take it that he has already told Jesus’s messages to several people by now and that Ben has told you all of this.”

"Yes.....ummm...wow," Ben started in a little bit of an incredulous and amazed tone that was accompanied by a similar small smile and laugh. "Thank you, Mr. Trenton, for your very encouraging and insightful words. I have indeed told my family about what I went through and experienced. I'm amazed that God spoke to you in a dream about me and my future wife."

"Yes, I know," Harold said reassuringly. "It is a lot to take in. And, please, call me Harold." Harold extended his right arm and hand to shake Ben's right hand.

"Definitely is. Thanks, Harold," Ben replied as he extended his right arm and hand to shake Harold's right hand. "It is a pleasure to meet you."

"It is a pleasure to meet you as well, Ben," Harold said gratefully before he and Ben let go of each other's hands. "And excuse my manners, I believe I haven't met your mother, Ben. What is your name?" Harold asked this after he switched his attention to Leslie.

"I'm Leslie. It's wonderful to meet you, Harold," Leslie replied in more of an amazed and incredulous tone than Ben. The accompanying smile and slight laugh followed suit as she introduced herself and responded. She and Harold shook hands before she continued speaking. "Dave is my husband, and we also have our other son next to us. We are all amazed at what you said about Ben. It was a totally terrifying moment when I got a call from my husband at Ben's best friend's apartment last Saturday night, saying that Ben got shot. However, we are truly grateful that Jesus gave him a second chance at life with the task of telling His messages to everyone that he meets."

"I'm sure that must have been truly frightening to you. I'm so sorry that you had to experience that," Harold replied understandingly and sympathetically before turning his attention and focus to Josh. "What is your name, son?"

"My name is Josh," Josh responded as he went to shake hands with Harold. "It's cool that you are a prophet and had a dream in which God talked to you about what happened to my brother last Saturday night."

"It was cool indeed," Harold replied in an excited tone. "And quite amazing, actually."

"For sure," Dave responded in a voice that told Harold that he trusted him and believed all of what he said. "Sorry for the little tension, Harold. I just wanted to make sure that you had good intentions with my family."

"That is perfectly understandable," Harold said in an understanding tone. "I would have been like you if I were in your shoes. Consider it water under the bridge. As for Ben's mission, I want you and the rest of your family to continue to support him in this. Do the same when his wife comes about and stays with him. Finally, I want all of your family to take heart and know that Ben will have a great time in heaven once he gets there again with his wife. I know it will be tough for you, your wife, and Josh to process, but I'm sure that you three will find a way to go on. I pray that God brings you three peace and comfort after Ben and his wife return to heaven."

"Thanks, Harold," all four of the Lawson family members said gratefully and almost simultaneously.

"We are truly grateful that we got the chance to meet," Dave spoke again. Dave and Harold finally shook hands.

"You all are welcome," Harold replied before taking out his blue flip phone from his right jeans pocket. He typed out his number and gave his phone to Dave for a minute. "Here is my number if any one of you wants to reach out and talk to me."

"Thanks again, Harold," Dave said after he typed Harold's number into his phone. "When do you think we will see you again?"

"You're welcome. I think that we might run into each other soon," Harold said before continuing. "Plus, there could be some other times as well. As for now, I'm going to go out and have lunch with my wife. You all take care."

"Sounds good," all four Lawson family members responded in their own ways, a second or two apart from each other before they continued. "Have a great time having lunch with your wife, and have a great rest of your day with her."

"Thanks," Harold replied. "You guys all have a great rest of your day as well. Bye."

"Bye," Dave, Leslie, Ben, and Josh said as they waved to Harold, who was already starting to turn and walk away from them. However, Harold waved goodbye before meeting up with his wife in the church lobby. The Lawson family went out of the church lobby and out of the building, planning to get lunch and go home. They were also going to resume their *Smallville* marathon with Diego Sanchez once he got to their house after his church service was done. The one thing the four Lawson family members did not know was the one particular interaction with Sophia that Diego would have at his church beforehand. Things would get more interesting after that interaction occurred.

Sophia O'Donnell and her family were fully enjoying the church service at Holy Communion at 11:00 a.m. The four family members chose to sit in the middle of the left section of the congregation. All of the people in the church congregation were wearing various clothing, as usual. The clothing ranged from jeans or shorts with T-shirts and regular shoes to slacks, nice undershirts, coats, and dress shoes for the men. As for the women, they wore anything from jeans or shorts with T-shirts and regular shoes to one-piece dresses, heels, and jewelry. They loved being in fellowship with other believers in God's presence. Plus, the O'Donnell family often talked about God to nonbelievers that they came across on a couple of days of the week. One of the things they would say to people was that God loved them and only had good things for them, including personal relationships with Him. The four O'Donnell family members would also have discussions about their faith in God with their friends who were also believers. That was basically the case with Sophia as she told Jesus's/God's messages to the few people she met before the church sermon started the present day. Her other main objective was to find anyone else besides Anthony Markus who knew who Ben Lawson was and where she could find him. Sophia would get lucky after the church service ended.

It was 12:15 p.m., and the pastor of Holy Communion Church, Jack Hershel, had about five more minutes of his sermon before he blessed and dismissed the 600 or so people in the congregation. Jack was a six-foot-five-inch Hispanic man who had recently turned thirty-nine years old. He was mostly physically fit and had short, curly brown hair and hazel-green eyes. Jack was wearing a dark blue suit, a nice white undershirt, dark blue slacks, and dark blue dress shoes. The Hispanic man was nearly done with his sermon on the parable of the Good Samaritan. Sophia felt convicted by the sermon in a way because of the kindness that she should have shown Ben and gone out with him. The young redhead knew that the parable had a bit of a different meaning, but she couldn't help but think about what she should have done when she and Ben first met. That feeling inside her made her even more determined to find him.

The time came when Pastor Jack Hershel dismissed the church congregation. Most of the congregation steadily maneuvered their way out of the church service room, lobby, and building, which took several minutes. The O'Donnell family, Diego Sanchez, Carl Wendleson, and Tess Debor were among about thirty people who chose to stay and socialize with each other. Sophia was wondering in the back of her mind if Carl had come to today's service. Her mental question was answered two minutes after the congregation was dismissed. Carl walked toward her and her family from the back of the middle of the congregation with Tess on his right side. He was wearing a long-sleeved white button-down dress shirt with black slacks and black dress shoes; she was wearing a one-piece turquoise blue dress with blue heels with silver sparkles on them. The two of them were equally as well dressed as Sophia and her family.

"Oh, hey, Carl!" Sophia said excitedly and cheerfully as Carl and Tess stopped a few feet in front of her and her family. "I'm so glad that you came! I see that you brought Tess along as well."

"It sure is nice seeing you again, Sophia," Carl replied excitedly and kindly as he went in to give Sophia a friend-type hug.

"It definitely is great to see you again, Sophia," Tess said a bit more excitedly and kindly as Carl as she stepped forward to give her a hug that was the same as Carl's.

"Absolutely!" Sophia exclaimed excitedly a few seconds before she and Tess let go of each other. The young woman turned her attention to introducing Carl and Tess to her family. "Mom, Dad, and Sis, I want you to meet Tess and Carl. They were a part of the medical team that drove me to the hospital after my incident. Tess and Carl, meet my family."

"It is a pleasure to meet you two," Sam, Candace, and Alicia said with deep gratitude, appreciation, and warmness in their own ways. Sam continued to speak after he, his wife, and second daughter said those things and shook Tess and Carl's hands. "We are extremely grateful and appreciative for what you two did to help save Sophia's life after her incident. If either one or both of you need some help in any way, we can do that. It is the least that we can do."

"Definitely," Candace and Alicia responded almost simultaneously before Candace continued speaking. "We would truly be happy to help either one or both of you if you two need help with anything."

"Aww, that's so nice of you three," Tess said appreciatively. "We will let one of you know if we need help with anything. Thank you so much, Sam, Candace, and Alicia, for your guys offer."

"I can help as well." Sophia chimed in. "I would love to help in any way that I can."

"That is very kind of you, Sophia," Carl responded appreciatively before continuing. "You have already helped me and Tess more than we could have ever imagined. The choice is up to you. By the way, thank you for inviting me to your church today. Tess wanted to come too. We found the whole service to be quite fascinating."

"For sure," Tess responded gratefully. "Thanks so much for all of what you said back at the hospital, Sophia. I think that Carl and I will come here to church whenever we are free from work."

"You are so welcome!" Sophia replied gladly. "I'm happy that you and Carl are starting to like it here. Wait, are you and Carl seeing each other?"

"No," Tess said. "However, I think that sometime after my husband and I are officially divorced, Carl and I might start going out together."

"Definitely," Carl said to Sophia. "I'm willing to wait, as I had said to Tess a few days ago."

"I'm so happy for you two," Sophia responded. "I'm sure you guys will work things out."

"Thanks," Tess and Carl said almost simultaneously.

"Sounds like you and Carl have a bright future," Candace said happily to Tess after hearing all of what her daughter, Carl, and Tess talked about. "I'm sorry to hear about your and your soon-to-be ex-husband's divorce."

"Yeah, all the best for you and Carl," Sam chimed in. Alicia nodded in agreement.

"Thanks, you all," Tess responded.

"You're welcome," Candace said for all of her family. The rest of the church congregation had thinned down to fourteen people now. Ten minutes had passed, and Diego Sanchez was still among the group of fourteen people. Sophia waited a second before she switched the topic to Ben Lawson and how to find him.

"Well," Sophia spoke to Tess and Carl, "I think my family and I are going to head out in a few minutes. I was hoping I could ask you two a question. Do you mind if I ask you it?"

"For sure," Carl responded with a helpful tone. "What can Tess and I help you with?"

"Thanks," Sophia replied in a grateful voice. "Do you or Tess know a guy named Ben? He is in a wheelchair and doesn't have most of his legs. Ben has medium-length black hair and blue eyes. I want to find and talk to him, and I was wondering if you or Tess knew where he was."

"I don't know a Ben who meets your description," Carl replied. "I'm sorry. I will definitely let you know if I hear of him."

"Same," Tess said as she took half a piece of paper to write her number down and give it to Sophia. "We will let you know if we hear of him and find him."

"Thanks," Sophia replied to both Carl and Tess after Tess gave her the piece of paper. "I appreciate your willingness to help, guys."

"Always," Tess and Carl replied, almost a second apart from each other. Carl continued to speak a second later. "Well, Tess and I are off to get lunch now at Smashburger. Have a great rest of your day, O'Donnell family!"

"Thanks!" all four O'Donnell family members said nearly simultaneously. Candace continued to speak for the rest of her family. "Same to you two as well! Enjoy your lunch together!"

"Thanks!" Tess and Carl said nearly at once before they and the O'Donnell family waved goodbye to each other and walked away.

Sophia's family stuck around with her for five more minutes as she asked a couple of people about Ben and where she could find him. Sam, Candace, and Alicia asked a few other people about him as well. None of the O'Donnell family members had any luck and were starting to head out of the church room. The search at Holy Communion church seemed to be over, but the O'Donnell family were about to have the answer come to them. Diego Sanchez had heard Sophia and Sam ask a couple of people about Ben. He hesitated for a second, wondering if he should walk up to them and tell them about Ben. Plus, the Southern Chilean native didn't know if the young redheaded woman was Sophia. Diego took two more seconds to see if he wanted to tell Sophia and Sam about Ben because of what Sophia had done to him. Diego decided to figure all of that out once he caught up to the two people. He had to walk a little quickly to catch up to Sophia and Sam before they and the two other people that they were with reached the foyer. Diego finally got two feet next to Sophia on her right.

"Excuse me, my name is Diego Sanchez," Diego said in a slightly gasped voice after quickly walking up to Sophia, Sam, and the other two people. He looked directly at Sophia and continued to speak. "I couldn't help but hear you ask around about someone named Ben. Is Ben Lawson the person you're looking for? By the way, is this your family here?"

"Hello, Diego," Sophia started in a voice that had hope and excitement in it. She began to smile a bit. "Is Ben Lawson in a wheelchair and doesn't have most of his legs? Does he have medium-length black hair and blue eyes? And yes, this is my family. Diego, meet my family. Mom, Dad, Alicia, this is Diego. He may know who Ben is and where I can find him."

"It is very nice to meet you," Candace said warmly while shaking hands with Diego. Sam, Sophia, and Alicia followed suit as they introduced themselves as well. All four O'Donnell family members and Diego had stopped walking just seven feet outside of the church service room when Diego first spoke up.

Sam continued to speak after he, his wife, and his second daughter had introduced themselves to Diego. "I really appreciate you coming to us. Did I hear right when you said you know who this Ben guy is and where to find him? Sophia really wants to see and talk to him."

"Yes, I know Ben. He is my best friend," Diego replied to Sam before turning his attention to Sophia with a touch of dislike in his tone. "So, you are Sophia. You are the young woman who rejected Ben's offer for you to go out with him. I don't think it would be good if you met and talked with him. I don't want you to hurt him anymore." Diego offered his respects to Sophia's family after saying that. Then, he prepared to walk out of the church foyer. Sophia didn't even need a second before she responded to Diego.

"Diego, wait," Sophia pleaded with eagerness in her tone. Diego couldn't help but turn to her again. He was going to walk away, but he wanted to give Sophia one more chance since she pleaded with him. "I know that I hurt Ben when I rejected his offer for me to go out with him, and I am very sorry about that. I want to apologize to him in person and go out with him this upcoming Friday or Saturday if he is able to. A recent life-and-death incident that I experienced made me come to my senses."

"Okay, what was the life-and-death incident that you experienced?" Diego asked with great interest in his tone.

"This," Sophia replied as she pulled down her white and purple dress top just a little bit to show the scars from the shot wounds. "I got shot, died, went to heaven, and talked to Jesus."

"Oh my God," Diego said after he widened his eyes a bit. "I'm so sorry that happened to you. You need to see Ben now. You will understand why when you see and talk to him. I can take you to his and his family's house."

"Yes, please, take me to him," Sophia said with joy in her voice before turning to her family. "Can I go with Diego to Ben's family's house?"

"Absolutely," Sam, Candace, and Alicia answered almost simultaneously in each of their ways. Sam continued to talk to Sophia for a second after that. "Just make sure that Diego keeps you safe and that you ask Ben to come over to our house for dinner after you go out with him."

"For sure," Sophia replied assuringly.

"I will definitely keep your daughter safe, Mr. O'Donnell."

"Thanks, Diego," Sam said with ease and relief before speaking to Sophia again. "I wish you all the best for meeting and talking to Ben."

"Same here!" Candace and Alicia said in excited tones before Candace continued speaking. "Go get Ben! I know you will know the right things to say to him."

"Thanks, Mom!" Sophia said equally as excitedly before she went up to hug her, Alicia, and her dad. Sophia went on to speak one more time. "I will see you three back at our house after Ben and I are done talking! I'll tell Diego where we live, and he can drive me there."

"Sounds good!" all three O'Donnell family members said before they waved goodbye. Then, Diego and Sophia walked out of Holy Communion church. They got in Diego's car and began to drive towards the Lawsons' house. The Lawson family were going to be completely surprised when Diego and Sophia arrived at their house.

It was 1:10 p.m. on that Sunday, and the Lawson family was waiting for Diego Sanchez to arrive at their house with lunch from Eegee's. Diego had texted Ben at 1:00 p.m. that he would like to bring lunch for everyone before coming over to watch episodes of *Smallville*. The Southern Chilean native had also texted Ben that there was someone who he was bringing over for a little bit. However, Diego did not tell his best friend he was bringing over Sophia. Diego wanted to tell Ben in person that Sophia had a few important things to say to him. As for the time being, Ben and the rest of his family were waiting until Diego arrived, and they had no idea that Sophia would be with him. Diego texted Ben a final message that said that he would arrive at the house at 1:20 p.m. or so after getting lunch for both of them and the rest of Ben's family. The Southern Chilean native was also going to buy lunch for Sophia as well, but the Lawson family did not know that.

Time whizzed by, and then it was 1:23 p.m. Diego parked his car just outside Ben's family's garage. Sophia and Diego got out with the lunches from Eegee's and began to walk around to the front door. The young redhead wanted to wait to eat her lunch with Ben, the rest of his family, and Diego after she and Ben talked. Sophia walked behind Diego so that he could introduce her to Dave and Leslie. Then, Diego would let Ben know that she was here to talk to him. The Southern Chilean knocked on the front door two times and then waited for an answer.

"Hello, Diego," Leslie answered as she opened the door. Sophia had given Diego her lunch before Leslie answered the door because she wanted to be polite in waiting to be introduced and eat lunch. Leslie continued speaking as Diego handed her the Eegee's sandwiches and fries. "It was very kind of you to get lunch for all of us."

"I would say so," Dave said as he walked up behind his wife and offered to take the food and put it down. "Thank you very much for buying lunch. Eegee's is one of our favorites."

"You are very welcome, Mr. and Mrs. Lawson," Diego replied. Leslie took up her husband's offer, and he took the food and set it down on the kitchen table. Diego went on speaking after Dave returned to the door. "I would like to introduce you and Mr. Lawson to someone I brought over. She is going to be here for a while and really should talk to Ben. It is important that she and he do this. I would like to introduce you two to Sophia O'Donnell, who I know you two have probably heard about from Ben." Diego walked up the two steps and entered the house. He took a few steps to the left inside the house, and Sophia nervously waved hi to Dave and Leslie.

"Sophia?" Ben said in a very surprised tone as he emerged from the kitchen after overhearing Diego name-drop her. "Why is she here?" Ben was getting a bit annoyed, especially after all that he had gone through with Sophia.

"Sophia?" Josh responded, equally as surprised as he was entering the kitchen. "Ben, do you want me to get a squirt gun and squirt her with it? I'm totally down with that after what she did to you."

"No, Josh," Dave and Leslie interjected sternly before Leslie spoke again. "There is no need for that. I'm sure Sophia is here to talk with Ben about what happened, as Diego said and alluded to."

"Welcome to our house, Sophia," Dave said before he motioned with his right hand for her to come into the house. "I'm sorry for the awkward introduction. Have a seat on our couch, and I'm sure Ben will want to hear what you have and want to say."

"Thank you, Mr. Lawson," Sophia replied in a voice that still had some nervousness in it. She was a bit surprised at Josh's response, but she didn't mind because of what she wanted to talk about with Ben. Josh was slightly annoyed that he didn't get to squirt Sophia with a squirt gun, but he kept to himself as he walked around the inside of the kitchen. The young woman had not gotten two feet inside the house before Ben spoke again.

"Diego, I cannot believe you would even think of letting Sophia come over to my and my parents' house. Do you remember what she did to me and how it made me feel?" Ben said in a more annoyed tone.

"Ben, please hear Sophia out," Diego replied with emphasis on what he was saying. He also moved several feet towards Ben. "It is really important that she talks to you. I'm sorry that it had to be this way, but I thought this was the best way to do this. I overheard her and her dad asking about you at my church today after the service. It isn't a coincidence that Sophia also goes to my church. Just give her another chance. I promise you won't regret it."

Ben sighed but didn't say anything. Diego knew that Sophia was clear to continue on in and sit on the couch in the living room. Ben wheeled to meet her there. They were right next to each other. The rest of the Lawson family went to their rooms and would wait to eat lunch until Ben and Sophia were done talking. Diego asked Josh if he could hang out in his room for the time being. Josh said that was fine, and the two of them entered his room. Josh shut the door, and then Dave and Leslie followed suit by shutting their door.

"What do you have to talk to me about that is so important?" Ben finally asked Sophia in somewhat of a sarcastic but mostly frustrated voice. Sophia looked past his attitude, knowing that he had truly been hurt by her.

"Ben," Sophia began with a slight quiver in her voice, "I'm truly sorry for the way that I hurt you by not wanting to go out with you. I couldn't get past seeing you without most of your legs. It took me so long and so much to come to my senses and see that you are a really amazing guy. I want to get to know you more and go out with you."

"I don't know if I want to go out with you anymore, Sophia. You don't even know how I lost my legs and how that made me feel for a year after I lost them. I thought you were going to be the one for me because of the fact that God gave me a green thumbs up in a dream after I asked Him in a prayer about whether I should ask you out or not. As it turned out, I made a stupid decision."

"No, Ben, you didn't make a stupid decision. I love you," Sophia said that last sentence with an emphasis, and then she went in to kiss him on the lips. Ben did not need a second to think about the heartwarming thing that Sophia had just said. She went in most of the way to kiss him, and he went in the rest of the way. They both firmly and lovingly wrapped their arms around each other. Every hardship that Ben had gone through in his past, including losing his legs and Sophia's rejection to go out with him, melted away and didn't matter anymore. Ben felt in the current moment that he loved Sophia. He went back in his mind for a second and realized that he first started to love her when he saw her in their Christian religion class. That was why he was so attracted to her. The full and true love that he now felt for Sophia far surpassed the feeling of riding and driving in the NASCAR race car with Blake. Ben and Sophia continued to kiss each other for several more seconds. Every second they were kissing was just as passionate as the rest of the seconds. Ben drew back an inch from Sophia's face for a minute.

"I love you too," Ben responded with great love and passion in his voice. The annoyance and frustration that he had felt before Sophia said that she loved him instantly evaporated into thin air without the faintest trace. Ben wondered if Sophia wanted to say anything else. "Did you want to say anything else that was on your mind?"

"Other than the fact that I got shot, died, went to heaven, and talked to Jesus, no," Sophia said right before she showed her shot wounds to Ben.

"Oh my God, I'm so sorry that happened to you. That must have been terrifying when you got shot and died," Ben said with compassion and in total shock. Then, he remembered that Jesus had said in his most recent dream that he would have to wait until a bit after church to see who his wife would-be was because Hannah Rine wasn't her. Ben knew without a shadow of a doubt that Sophia would be his wife. "The same thing happened to me." Then, he showed Sophia his shot wounds as well.

"That is amazing," Sophia replied in total amazement. "How did we get so lucky to have Jesus give us a second chance at life together? Wait, did He task you with telling two messages to everyone you met? He did that to me."

"Yes, Jesus did do that to me as well."

"That is fantastic. We will bring a lot of people into His kingdom. I love you so much, Ben."

"We will definitely help a lot of people get saved. I love you so much, too, Sophia," Ben said as they passionately wrapped their arms around each other and kissed for a couple more minutes. The rest of the Lawson family and Diego heard that there was no more talking, so they gradually came out of their rooms. All of them were excited and happy, even Josh, to see the last few seconds of Ben and Sophia kissing each other. Dave got all of the sandwiches and fries and met the rest of the crew on the living room couch. Leslie asked if Sophia wanted to watch the first three episodes of *Smallville* and briefly described the show to her. Sophia absolutely wanted to watch the show in addition to eating lunch on the couch. She quickly texted her family about what happened after talking to Ben. Plus, Sophia said she was going to be home at six, which was later than she thought. Her family said that they were extremely happy for her and Ben and that her return time was totally fine. Ben, Sophia, Diego, and the rest of Ben's family spent the next three-ish hours eating lunch, watching the first three episodes of *Smallville*, and talking about all of what recently happened in Ben and Sophia's lives. Neither Ben, the rest of his family, nor Diego minded rewatching the three *Smallville* episodes with Sophia. The only thing that mattered to Ben in that moment was being with Sophia, with both of them hanging arms over each other. Ben couldn't help but wonder what exciting adventures were in store for him and his future wife, Sophia, before they went back to heaven.

CHAPTER 7:

PLANNING AND SHARING LIFE TOGETHER

All people, including quite a bit of Christians, think that they have the ability to create and plan out every part of their lives. They do their best to attain the American dream and want to be happy with every part of it. A large number of Christians believe that everything that they do by themselves according to what God's Word says is what He wants for them. However, God knows and speaks to us about what is best for us. Jesus says in the Bible, "'[...] I know the plans that I have for you,' declares the LORD, 'plans to prosper you and not to harm you, plans to give you hope and a future'" (Jeremiah 29:11).

God's ways and plans became clear in Ben Lawson and Sophia O'Donnell's lives. The two teens thought that life would be a certain way and that they would end up being in serious relationships with different people. Ben and Sophia's actual outcomes couldn't have been any more different than what they thought. However, as of the current moment, on Friday, January 24th, 2003, at the Starbucks near Ben's family's house, he and Sophia were very happy that God put them together.

Ben had a friendly lunch with Hannah Rine three days ago. He had told Hannah about his newfound, serious relationship with Sophia. Hannah was genuinely excited for Ben and Sophia. Ben said to Hannah that he knew and believed she would find the right Christian guy for her soon. She appreciated his words and would keep on living life, knowing that she would soon come across the right Christian guy for her. Ben was glad that he and Hannah had settled everything and were good friends now. She said the same.

Ben told Sophia about his and Hannah's friendship and everything else that happened between them later that day via text. Sophia understood why Ben had wanted to go out with Hannah. The young redhead had treated Ben badly when he first offered for her to go out with him. That was the reason why Sophia came to understand Ben and his previous desire to go out with Hannah. Sophia was very glad that Ben had listened to Jesus's voice in his dream about not going forward with going out with Hannah. The nineteen-year-old redhead told Ben about her previous up-and-down decision process of whether or not to go out with him. Sophia apologized again for being so blind and then excitedly said that she was overjoyed that she was with him now. Ben forgave her again and then texted her about what she was doing with her night and talked with her about that and the rest of his night before saying good night, thus ending the conversation.

Ben also made sure to tell his family and Diego about everything that had happened between him and Hannah. Plus, Ben told his family and Diego about the dream that he had of Jesus telling him that Hannah wasn't the one for him and that his wife would be revealed to him by the end of church on Sunday, January 19th. Everything was good between all of them.

Thursday the 23rd was a really fun day, in which Ben and Anthony Markus played ping-pong together and had good laughs. Sophia previously told Ben, who in turn told Anthony, that she had found him and that they were happy to be together now. Anthony was excited to hear the news about Ben and Sophia. Ben's week was filled with work and college classes other than those two events on Tuesday and Thursday. As for the current moment on that Friday at 1:00 p.m., Ben and Sophia were having a blast talking with each other, laughing, and drinking Starbucks coffee drinks. They had gotten lunch together at 11:30 a.m. at the Evart University Student Union before Ben's mom picked them up and dropped them off at the Starbucks coffee shop. Ben and Sophia chose to sit at an outside table that was about ten or so feet away from the nine other people who were also sitting outside of the coffee shop.

"I had no idea that you were this fun!" Sophia said while laughing and having a good time. Ben had told her about the professional baseball games that he, his family, and Diego had been to. Plus, he and Sophia talked about all of their individual and mutual interests. They found out that they had a lot in common. Those common interests included *Star Wars*, volleyball, superheroes, coffee, coffee drinks, various types of food and regular drinks, movies, TV shows, holiday celebrations, and swimming. Of course, both teens had great relationships with God and their families, and they went to church every Sunday. The black-haired nineteen-year-old had also made a joke about how Starbucks could have been everyone's favorite coffee shop to go to in *Star Wars*.

"You're too funny!" Sophia said while laughing. She knew everything that Ben talked about and referenced because she had seen all of the *Star Wars* movies.

"I'm glad that you think of me in that way," Ben replied honestly. "I can be funny a good majority of the time. I do know when to be serious, though."

"Yeah, learning how to be funny, fun, and serious in appropriate moments of life is a great skill to have." Then, Sophia changed the subject. She was genuinely interested in Ben's response to the question that she wanted to ask before she and Ben started making plans for their serious relationship and future marriage. "I believe you haven't told me about how you lost your legs and what your life was like before that incident. What was it all like? You don't have to fully answer if you don't want to. Then, we can go somewhere nearby, hang out, and begin making plans for our future together."

"It's all good. That sounds great. We can definitely go somewhere, hang out, and start making some plans for our future together after I answer your question. I'm good with telling you my story and what it was like before my incident. Sorry that I didn't tell you sooner. I have just been caught up in the moment and the other following moments after you first said that you loved me."

"No problem at all. I'm very happy that you have been caught up in our wonderful moment and subsequent moments since I said that I loved you. Tell me again, do you really love me, Ben Lawson?"

"I deeply love you, Sophia O'Donnell," Ben replied passionately before he scooted forward in his wheelchair and leaned forward to kiss Sophia. The two of them were sitting opposite each other. Sophia leaned forward and kissed him for a couple of seconds before leaning back. She was eagerly waiting for Ben's response to her other question about his incident with losing his legs and what his life was like before it.

"All right," Ben began as he was thinking about how to start his story. "Where should I start? Let's start with the bad part first. To start with, I got my legs cut off just above my knees in a procedure two years ago because of a rare disease. This disease, which neither my family nor my friends nor I have been told what it was, began as twinges in the backs of my lower legs on my 17th birthday. My parents surprised me with a trip to a NASCAR charity event for my birthday, in which I got to ride and drive in a professional race car with a professional racer named Blake. That was a total blast! It felt like I was living on the edge. I actually drove the race car at about 120 miles an hour at a few points on the five-mile race track that was almost shaped like two figure eights."

Then, Ben took a second to catch his breath before continuing his story. "Anyway, my younger brother, Josh, who came to the charity event, also got to ride in the race car with Blake. My dad was going to ride and drive with Blake in the race car after Josh's turn. However, I began to feel the twinges in the backs of my lower legs just as Josh was nearing the end of his ride with Blake. I thought that the twinges were nothing but some aftereffects of driving the race car. Then, the twinges got a little intense, and I told my mom about them. Unfortunately, it was too late by then. I think I remember that my mom was going to tell my dad about the twinges. The next thing that I know is that the twinges became super intense, my knees collapsed, and I fell back on my back. Luckily, I had enough sense to keep my head upright and not bang it on the hard hangar floor."

Ben took another second to catch his breath. Sophia was greatly interested in his story. She was excited in one moment when Ben said that he and his brother, Josh, got to ride in and drive a race car with the professional racer, Blake. Then, Sophia's facial expression changed to an expression that consisted of a mixture of concern, sadness, and nervousness. The black-haired teen continued to speak after the other one-second break.

"The following events went by in a blur. Blake and Josh came back into the race car hangar one or two minutes later. As soon as Blake and Josh got out of the race car, they rushed over to check on me and see what had happened. I remember how Josh came over to me, bent down, and asked me how I was doing. It was like he was an army soldier coming to check on one of his wounded fellow soldiers. I could see the deep concern that he had for me by the stress lines on his face and on his forehead. He said to my dad that someone should call a doctor, which my dad did. My dad was proud of Josh's recognition and suggestion that someone should call a doctor. Josh has had a bit of a hard time fitting into high school and finding out what he wants to do with his life, but I know and believe that he has improved in those areas of his life. Anyway, my dad called my personal doctor and explained everything that had happened to me. A crowd had already formed around me. It was full of people who were asking and wondering about what they could do to help me, which was very nice of them.

"In the end, my mom and dad thanked the crowd for their willingness to help but said that there wasn't a need for their help. My mom had Blake and Josh hoist me up in between them and carry me to my family's car. Blake took a complete hold of me after Josh opened the back right door, and Blake carefully and comfortably put me in the car. Blake made sure that my head was gently laid against the inside of the opposite door and that I was lying down on the car floor on my back. Those were the instructions that my mom gave to Blake and Josh. The thing I remember most is the comforting and encouraging thing that Blake said to me before my family got into the car and drove me to the main hospital. This is what Blake said to me: 'You're going to be all right, kid. Just stay calm and keep yourself in a positive state of mind.'

"The next thing I remember is the ride to the hospital. It was a bit bumpy, which greatly irritated my lower legs. That was super painful and honestly really sucked. Josh did his best to relieve the pain in my lower legs by keeping them in a comfortable position. The thing that totally sucked was when I heard my personal doctor say that I would have to immediately have a procedure done on myself, in which my legs had to be amputated just above my knees. My mom and dad were crying, and Josh and I were in total shock.

"The next year seemed to go on forever. I was completely stuck in a negative attitude and did not do as well in my college classes. It wasn't that much better in my personal life in terms of day-to-day stuff and making friends. Then, Diego was led by God to come to me and help me in the phase of life that I was currently in at the end of that year. God had told Diego to move to Evart from a part in Southern Chile, and he did exactly that. Diego and I had a mechanical engineering class together. He came up to me after one day in class and was friendly to me. Diego and I had lunch together one or two days after that. We talked for a few minutes about life in general and how we liked it. Then, Diego transitioned to the topic of my negative attitude and behavior that he had noticed. He also offered to help me navigate through what I was feeling. I got defensive and irritated and refused to accept Diego's help. Diego knew that I was hurting, and he said I could be like how I was and that he would be there for me when I was ready to accept his help. He gave me his number on a piece of paper, and that was it. We parted ways for the day.

"My mom and I ended up talking about what happened, my negative attitude, and my negative behavior in general that night. I prayed to God and realized something that I did not do. I did not put Blake's words into action in terms of keeping myself in a positive state of mind. The thing I made a mental note to do was to change my attitude and behavior and trust God to get me through what I had been feeling. I called Diego the following night, apologized for my rude and awful attitude and behavior, and accepted his help. He did an excellent job in helping me through all of what I felt about my current situation, with me having no legs. Plus, Diego taught me a lot of things about knowing God's will for my life. He was extremely helpful in that area as well. I'm greatly appreciative of all of what he did for me. We became best friends and started doing most things together, like hanging out at each other's houses, playing video games, and going to baseball events. Even so, I still wanted to walk again, and I started making a list in one of my mechanical engineering courses during my sophomore year of college last year. The listed included materials and building methods that I would need to build a pair of prosthetic legs for myself so that I could walk again." Ben finished this first part of his story after he said that last thing. He wanted to give Sophia a minute to think about and respond to the first half of his story if she wanted to respond to it. Ben did not have to wait twenty seconds before Sophia responded.

"Wow, I'm so sorry about how you lost your legs," Sophia began in an understanding and empathetic tone. "I'm disappointed in myself for not asking you that question when we first met. It must have felt like your heart and soul were crushed when you had to have your legs taken away from you because of the rare disease. Neither I nor the other hardships you faced after your incident helped. I never wanted you to feel that way. I'm willing, and I want, to spend the rest of my life with you, making up for what I did to you."

"Sophia, thank you for leveling with me and doing your best to know how I felt after everything that happened to me," Ben replied honestly and gratefully before continuing.

"That is one of the reasons why I love you. You have a lovely personality, and you want to be kind, compassionate, and empathetic to people who have been through tough times. Honestly, for me, every hardship and tough time that I had in my past is nothing compared to what we have now. I don't want to think about those rough times that I had. I learned my lesson, had God and Diego get me through how I had felt, and now I just want to be with you for the rest of my life."

"Thank you for being so honest and forgiving, Ben. Those are two of the reasons why I love you. I can't wait to spend the rest of my life with you. We have a bit more than two years, but we will absolutely make it the best time of our lives. Then, you and I will go back to heaven together. If I had to say one thing about how we came to be together, minus the tension between us at first and the experiences of getting shot, I would say that it was a heavenly romance."

"Hmmm...heavenly romance," Ben echoed Sophia's words in a greatly interested tone. "I like the sound of that." Sophia lovingly whispered the same thing, and then she and Ben leaned forward to kiss each other again for two more seconds. They were holding hands as well. Then, Sophia leaned back and waited for Ben to continue on with the other half of his story. Sophia began finishing drinking the pink passion fruit tea that she had bought earlier.

"All right, I have an idea of where to start with the other half of my story," Ben began again. "It was Christmas, and I was four years old or so at that time. I think it was the Christmas of 1998, but I don't specifically remember the year. The thing that I do remember is one of the presents that my mom and dad got me. They bought me a long, double-sided racetrack that came with two medium-sized hard plastic race cars. The race track was an orange-colored, five-foot high track that was level for about four or five inches on the top, then gradually started to curve downwards. The length of the track was approximately eighteen feet before reaching a hard plastic stopper that was nearly four inches high. My dad didn't mind doing the work of building the track for me because he knew that I would love it, and he was right. One of the race cars was royal blue and had black stripes from the edge of the hood to the edge of the trunk. The other race car was white and had red stripes that also ran from the beginning of the hood to the end of the trunk. I remember that my mom and dad would take turns racing the cars with me five to seven times per day for three or so months. I was so excited to walk up to the beginning of the track and do my best to send my race car down the track as fast as I could. Those times were among the best times for me when I had my legs."

Ben continued telling his story after a ten-or-so-second pause to drink the rest of his caffé moca and catch his breath. "The other things that were exceptionally memorable during the years of my life in which I had my legs were the sporting events that my mom and dad took me and Josh to. Josh and I each played in a junior little league baseball event when we were twelve years old. My mom and dad used to go to every one of our baseball games. I was the first person to try out and play in the junior little league since I was four and a half years older than Josh. Josh, who was seven and a half years old when I was twelve, came to all of my baseball games, as did my mom and dad. For me, playing baseball was one of the best things that I did. I played on a team called the Jaguars. Playing baseball felt like the best thing in the world when I used to run around the bases. Sliding onto home base felt like I was gliding on ice. I got really good at knowing when and how to slide onto home base because I didn't want to injure my feet and because I wanted to perfect the slide. My parents and Josh used to cheer very loudly along with the rest of the crowd when I hit home runs.

"The team was pretty good, and we ended up getting into third place at the end of the season when I was in seventh grade. I was excited when the rest of the team players and I got a bronze medal. It would've been great if we won the tournament and got gold medals, but I was still happy with my bronze medal. I stopped playing baseball when I got to high school. I wish I had played more baseball in junior high school, but I was overly focused on doing well in school in sixth grade and eighth grade. I ended up playing tennis and chess for the first two years of high school, which was really fun. Then, I focused on getting one year ahead in my schooling. That was because I wanted to get high school over with sooner, go to college, and move on with my life."

The black-haired teen took a second to catch his breath before progressing forward in his story. "Josh was so impressed with how well I did so much that he did his very best to copy my style of play. He even joined the Jaguars and took a practice swing each time right before he came up to bat. I was sixteen and a half years old when he was twelve, and I was busy at the beginning of my senior year in high school. I got moved up one schooling level after I learned all of the material for students in my junior year of high school during the summer of my sophomore year. Anyway, even with me being busy, I still made time to go to all of Josh's baseball games. I would cheer Josh on along with my family and the rest of the crowd as he hit home runs and balls past the basemen into the outfield. We all cheered for every solid hit that Josh made, which was the same case for me when I played baseball. Plus, I would encourage him when he had off days."

Ben went on to conclude his story after taking another second break to catch his breath. "In general, I loved to walk wherever and whenever I wanted to. No uneven or narrow pathways could ever stand in between me and where I wanted to go. I think that was one of the hardest things for me when I got my legs amputated. It hurt me to not be able to go to places that I had been previously able to go to. Anyway, the other exceptionally memorable experience I had in my childhood was hiking in and flying over the Grand Canyon for my thirteenth birthday. My dad bought two Southwest airline tickets and had him and me fly to Flagstaff, Arizona. He paid for us to hike in the Grand Canyon when we got to Flagstaff. Hiking in the Grand Canyon was simply fantastic. My dad and I hiked for a total of five miles over a period of about six hours. We started at 10:00 a.m. and went to approximately 4:00 p.m. My dad and I got to see a whole bunch of the various erosion-colored stones and walked around the inside of two caverns. The caverns were magnificent. They had rivers of blue turquoise water running in and out of them. My dad and I followed the rivers as much as we could before we had to start heading back to the hiking license shop. Then, he got him and me onto a helicopter ride, and we got to see way more of the Grand Canyon than we did on foot. All of these experiences in Flagstaff were spectacular. They were right up there with my baseball-playing year, riding and driving with Blake in the NASCAR charity event, and my other childhood experiences. So, that's the conclusion of my fun adventures, experiences, and memories before everything that happened to me."

"That sounds amazing!" Sophia responded. "I'm happy you got to have those experiences and go on those adventures. I'm so sorry that you were prevented from doing more of those things because of your legs getting amputated. I can only imagine how rough it must have been adjusting to your current situation."

"Thanks," Ben replied gratefully. "It's all good. I had great gifts that were given to me and even greater adventures that I went on before the rare disease took my legs away. However, having and being with you now is more precious than all of those other things combined."

"Awww....thanks, Ben," Sophia said in a completely flattered and warm tone. "That's the sweetest thing that you've said to me." She leaned forward again most of the way to kiss Ben, and he leaned forward the rest of the way. They held hands and kissed each other for about five seconds. Then, both teens leaned back and lovingly stared at each other for a second before Ben spoke again in a lovingly warm tone.

"You're very welcome, Sophia. So, what do you want to do now? My mom won't be back to pick us up until she is done teaching at the high school at three."

"Well, we could wander around the USA Fashion and Festivities Mall that is just two blocks away from here," Sophia suggested. "How does that sound?"

"That sounds fun," Ben said with excitement in his voice. "Let's do it."

"All right," Sophia said in excitement with a little giggle. The two of them threw away their empty drink containers in a nearby trashcan outside of the Starbucks that they were at before heading over to the USA Fashion and Festivities Mall together. Once they got there, Ben took a minute to text his mom to ask if she could pick him and Sophia up at the mall when she was done teaching. Leslie texted back a message within two minutes that said she could pick them up at the front entrance to the mall. Ben put his flip phone back in his backpack, and then he and Sophia started wandering around the USA Fashion and Festivities Mall.

The two of them bought one USA-themed sombrero and cap for each one of them. Ben and Sophia ended up participating in a few of the festivities and buying some shirts and jeans for themselves. The main thing they did together was make preliminary plans as to how they would go about their serious relationship and future marriage. Ben and Sophia had several laughs when talking about their plans. In addition, Sophia told him about her father wanting him to come over to the O'Donnell house for dinner that night. Ben was good with that and made the plan with Sophia.

On a more serious note, he told her about how he went to heaven on January 11th after getting shot. However, Ben fully described how amazing it was to be in heaven and to talk with Jesus. Then, Ben told Sophia about the potential car crash that he and she would have. Ben reassured Sophia that that wasn't going to happen because of the instruction that he received from Jesus in heaven. The black-haired teen also told her the other reasons why they were going back to heaven on May 14th, 2005, besides the fact that they wanted to go back. Sophia was scared at first because of the number of times that she and Ben could've died. However, she was grateful that they were going back to heaven before they would've died again.

It seemed like the next several hours flew by for Ben and Sophia. Leslie picked them up at 3:20 p.m. after she got done teaching at the high school at 3:00 p.m. and drove them back to the place at Evart University where Sophia had parked her car. Ben and Sophia kissed and parted ways for the time being. Both of them went back to each of their family houses. Dave helped Ben get out of his wheelchair, and Ben did his daily stretching routine on the living room couch for fifteen minutes. The teen just had to lay out and roll around a bit. He still wished that he had legs to stretch. Then, Dave helped Ben get back into his wheelchair before Ben did some of his homework for the weekend. Sophia took up about two-thirds of the time that she had at her parents's house to get ready for the family dinner date with Ben. Ben needed just one-third of the time that he had spent at his parents' house to get ready for the date. Then, Dave drove Ben to the O'Donnell's house, and they got there at 6:30 p.m., which was the agreed-upon time.

"I wish you the best of luck," Dad said to Ben as Ben got onto the powered ramp. "Have a great time tonight."

"Thanks, Dad," Ben replied gratefully while looking at his dad. Then, Dave dropped the powered ramp onto the sleek light gray sidewalk concrete that led to the O'Donnell house.

The two of them waved goodbye before Ben wheeled up to the front door of the house, which had two inclined wooden planks to help get up the two steps that led into the house. Ben guessed that one of the O'Donnell family members had put them there. He appreciated that gesture. The house was painted silver and had a dark gray door that had a gold-colored knob. There also was a gold-colored doorbell about one foot to the right of the knob. Ben pressed the doorbell, heard a quiet ding-dong sound that came from the inside of the house, and received an almost instant reply as the door was opened from the inside by Mr. O'Donnell. Ben had two medium-sized red rose bouquets that he wanted to give to Mrs. O'Donnell and Sophia.

"Hello! You must be Ben," Sam O'Donnell began after he opened the door all of the way. He was wearing a solid dark blue polo shirt, black slacks, and solid black dress shoes. "It's a pleasure to meet you. I've heard a lot of great and fun things about you from Sophia. Please, come inside. I appreciate the gesture of bringing both my wife and Sophia bouquets of red roses. You can call me Sam."

"You're welcome, Sam. It's also a pleasure to meet you," Ben replied graciously as he shook Sam's hand. Then, Ben wheeled up into the house. Sophia, Candace, and Alicia were standing together just about seven feet away, waiting to introduce themselves to him and say hi. Sophia was the first person to come up to him and give him a hug and a brief half-second kiss. She was wearing a beautiful, one-piece pink dress and white and pink shoes. Sophia had put on a sweet-smelling perfume and some makeup and had blow-dried her red hair so that it was styled in a straight but wavy fashion. Ben felt like he matched her fashion level with his stylish red and black striped polo shirt, black shorts, and black dress shoes. He had styled his hair back a bit in a young adult trendy way with smoothly efficient hair gel and put on a squirt of Versace cologne. Ben was also clean-shaven, as always.

"These are for you and your mom," Ben said to Sophia as he held out the bouquets of red roses.

"Awww...thank you, Ben!" Sophia replied in a thankful tone as Ben gave one of the bouquets to her. "That is very kind of you!"

"Definitely! Thank you, Ben!" Candace said gratefully as she approached Ben. She was wearing a one-piece white dress and white high heels. Ben gave her the other bouquet of red roses. "I'm Sophia's mother. It is very nice to finally meet you. You can call me Candace."

"You two are very welcome, Sophia and Candace," Ben responded gladly before shaking Candace's hand. "It is great to meet you."

"Hi! I'm Alicia, Sophia's younger sister," Alicia said as she took a couple of steps towards Ben. She was wearing a one-piece light blue dress and light blue sparkly shoes with white bottoms. "It's nice to finally meet you."

"It is nice to finally meet you, too, Alicia," Ben said as he shook Alicia's hand.

"Well," Candace began, "dinner is ready and on the dining room table. Sam grilled some steaks, and I made broccoli and white rice to go with the steaks. Please, wheel up to the table."

"Thank you so much, Sam and Candace," Ben responded gratefully while looking at them.

"You're very welcome, Ben," Sam and Candace replied almost simultaneously. Then, all five people walked over to the dining room table and sat down. They were only approximately twenty feet away from the table and accompanying chairs. The floor was made out of smooth mahogany wood, and the walls were painted with a smooth turquoise blue color. Ben wheeled up to an empty spot on the left side of the dining room table, made out of the same wood as the floor. The chairs at the table looked comfortable with their soft red cushions on top of solid dark brown wooden frames that had matching back pieces. Sophia sat in a chair directly opposite Ben on the right side of the table so that they could look at each other straight on. Alicia sat in a chair next to Sophia, and Sam and Candace sat on each of the other two ends for the same reason as Ben and Sophia. Sam was at the head of the dining room table, and he started out by saying a prayer of grace for dinner.

The O'Donnell family began intermittently telling Ben about Sophia's life and showing baby pictures of her while they and Ben ate dinner. All of them shared a lot of laughs, in addition to Sophia blushing over her baby pictures that were shown to Ben. Ben noticed several blue, red, and purple framed pictures on shelves that showed a combination of Sophia, her family, and friends during Easter, Christmas, playing volleyball, going to other events, and going to see movies. He listened to each story with great interest. The O'Donnell family even talked about their fun volleyball game at the Sports Hub six days ago. Then, the topic shifted to him and his and Sophia's plans for their future together.

"So, Ben," Sam started out, "Sophia told me and the rest of our family that you shared a similar experience as she in terms of a life-and-death accident and going to heaven. First of all, I'm deeply sorry that you were shot as well. That must have been really rough. However, tell me and the rest of us about what it was like talking with Jesus in heaven and what it was like there."

"Thanks, Sam," Ben replied after he finished eating half of his dinner. "I appreciate your condolences. I greatly appreciate that. As for telling you, Candace, and Alicia about my experience in heaven and talking with Jesus, it was truly amazing and breathtaking. I've already told Sophia all of this. First of all, I got to see the twelve foundational gates that had the twelve precious stones, as the book of Revelation talks about in the Bible. I also got to see three pearly gates that were in my line of sight. One gate was directly in front of me, and the other two were at the far ends of my left and right sides. I saw the three angels who were guarding the gates. In addition, I saw the river of the water of life and the tree that spanned the width of the middle of the river. All of these things were just spectacular to see. I had a unique glow all around me, like the angels and Jesus. I guess that is a part of the spiritual body that I had. Plus, I had my legs back, and I felt complete joy, fulfillment, and contentment. The truth is that I didn't want to come back to Earth, but Jesus had a different plan for me in terms of sharing His messages of love, protection, provision, and the kingdom of God to everyone I met. He also knew I wanted to get married to a Christian young woman. Jesus knew that I would end up with Sophia even after everything we had been through. I'm truly happy and glad that He set her and me up together."

"That is truly remarkable that you got to see and experience all of that in heaven, Ben," Sam responded after waiting a second to see if Ben was done talking. "I can only imagine what it must have been like to see Jesus and all of the other things. I guess that my wife, Alicia, and I will have to wait until the end of our lives to get to see and talk with Jesus and experience all of the things that you got to see and experience in addition to seeing and talking with Jesus."

"Definitely, Ben," Candace said in amazement. "It must have felt completely serene and peaceful to be in heaven, to see all of the things that you saw, and to talk with Jesus. All of that sounds a lot similar to what Sophia said to my husband, Alicia, and me about her experience in heaven. The things you said about your experience were truly amazing, and I know that I and the rest of my family will be completely fulfilled when we get to heaven. As for now, we are happy and content with where God has put us."

"For sure," Alicia responded. "I can only imagine how beautiful it must have been in heaven, Ben. It was very fascinating to hear about what you felt and experienced."

"Absolutely," Ben said after he ate some of the other half of his dinner. "All of it was really amazing when I was in heaven."

"Yep," Sam responded before changing the subject of the conversation. "Now, Ben, I want to ask you about your intentions for my daughter Sophia. I have a pretty good picture of what I think your intentions are with her based on both of your conversations with Jesus in heaven, but I want to hear them from you."

"For sure, I'm glad to speak about my intentions with your daughter, Sam," Ben replied confidently and gladly, even though he was a little nervous on the inside. He thought that the nervousness was because of the fact that he was hearing the question from Sam. Ben had expected the question, but the feeling of being in that moment caused him to be a little nervous. The teen did very well to keep the nervousness down. The love that Ben had for Sophia overwhelmed all of his emotions and feelings. "I want to marry Sophia sometime soon so that we can share a little more than two years of marriage together before the two of us go back to heaven. We are having a short, serious relationship at the moment, and I want to ask for your blessing to marry her." Sophia, Alicia, and Candace were all eagerly waiting in anticipation of Sam's response to Ben. The anxious, happy, and excited emotions were written all over the three women's faces.

"Well, I didn't expect you to be that confident and glad about your response to my question," Sam responded in a tone that sounded a little surprised. He used his knife and fork to cut up the last quarter or so of the steak that he had left before he continued speaking. Sam was trying to make Ben a little nervous, but it was to no avail. Ben kept calm and was still confident and glad about what he said. Even the nervousness inside the teen had disappeared after he had answered Sam's question. "Then, again, Ben, you heard from Jesus in heaven that you will have a wife, and Sophia heard from Jesus in heaven that she should try you out again. Combined with those experiences and all of what has recently transpired with you and Sophia, you can say that I am really impressed with you. I don't know you that much, Ben, aside from the things that Sophia told me and the rest of my family today before you came over. Plus, Sophia did mention you about a week ago and talked about how Jesus said that you were the best Christian guy in Evart. I cannot argue with what Jesus said about you, partially given your confident and glad response to my question. Also, I have a feeling that you will do whatever it takes to make sure that Sophia is happy, well provided for, well protected, and that she feels secure. I do want to get to know you more and get to know your family. In summation, I give you my blessing to marry my daughter."

"Yay!" Alicia and Candace said one time, each simultaneously clapping and smiling. They offered their congratulations to Ben and Sophia. Sam had started to clap a bit and nod his head in approval of all of what had happened in that one minute. Sophia was also smiling all the while that she got out of her chair and walked around to where Ben was sitting. Everyone still had a little bit of dinner left on each of their plates, but that didn't matter. They stopped eating for the momentous celebration. Sophia firmly and lovingly hugged Ben and kissed him for a couple of seconds or so after he wheeled away from the table to hug and kiss her. Alicia and Candace kept clapping and even cheering a bit when Ben and Sophia hugged and kissed each other for those two or so seconds.

"You did great," Sophia excitedly said to Ben. Ben acknowledged her compliment with a nod, and then the two of them hugged and kissed each other again for a brief second. Then, Sam stopped clapping and nodding his head. Alicia and Candace stopped clapping and cheering as well. Sophia returned to her seat on the opposite side of Ben, still smiling. Ben wheeled back the short distance to his place at the table, and he was still smiling as well. He and Sophia stopped smiling and went back to finishing up their dinner along with Sam and Alicia. Sam politely motioned for his wife, Candace, to ask one of the two questions that she had come up with earlier in the day with him in preparation for this moment.

"We are all very excited for you and Sophia, Ben," Candace said with a smile on her face and excitement in her tone. Then, the smile was mostly erased from her face before she asked one of her questions. "In saying that, Sam and I have some questions for you and Sophia in terms of you two moving forward into marriage. First of all, do you and Sophia have an idea of where you two want to live?"

"Well, Sophia and I came up with a couple of ideas of where we would like to live while we were hanging out at the USA Fashion and Festivities Mall earlier today," Ben responded gladly to Candace's question. "We definitely want to live twenty to forty minutes away from you and Sam. Anything from five to twenty minutes away is perfectly good as well. There are two apartments that Sophia and I looked at. She and I prefer to live in an apartment because we are only going to live there for two years before we go back to heaven. It would be too much to actually buy a house and maintain it only for those two years. Thus, Sophia and I would be more carefree with an apartment, except for the monthly rent and other little maintenances. I also told and talked with Sophia about getting an apartment that wasn't a part of my friend's complex, in which I got shot. In saying that, she and I will be totally safe in one of the two different apartments that we are looking at. Anyway, the first apartment is fifteen minutes away from your and Sam's house. The monthly rent is twenty-five hundred dollars, and the house has one bedroom, a kitchen, a living room, and one bathroom. We both like this apartment. Each of the two apartments is on the first story of their respective three-story high apartment complexes. Sophia and I will have to buy a king or queen-sized bed for us to sleep on. That's because the twin beds that the apartment rooms have are too small for us. Therefore, we will have to swap out the twin-sized bed with the king or queen-sized bed when we buy it. Sophia can tell you and Sam about the other apartment we discussed in addition to the color differences between the two apartments."

"For sure, thanks, Ben," Sophia responded warmly and gladly before switching her attention to her parents. "The other apartment is about thirty-five minutes away, and it's pretty good. I like it. This apartment is closer to Ben's family's house, and the monthly rent is only fifteen hundred dollars. It has the same rooms as the first house. The only differences between the two apartments are their colors. The first one has a white colored outside with a light blue colored roof and light green colored walls on the inside. Whereas the second apartment has a dark purple roof, a forest green colored outside, and a golden colored inside. Both apartments have really good light fixtures, TVs, dressers, and closets."

"Sounds like you and Ben did a pretty good job on your homework with the two apartments," Candace responded. "What resource did you and Ben use to look up the apartments?

Do they have good plumbing? Plus, which apartment are you two leaning towards getting? Sorry for the follow-up questions."

"You're fine, Mom. Ben and I looked up the apartments in an apartment catalog. Several catalogs were being sold at a stand near the USA Fashion and Festivities Mall. The apartments do have good plumbing, and I don't think that Ben and I will have to have either one of the plumbing systems majorly repaired because both of the systems are supposed to be good for at least three years. We might have to have some minor repairs during the two years that Ben and I will be married before we go back to heaven. As for which apartment we are going to get, we are still deciding on which one we like most and can afford."

"Sounds like a good plan so far," Candace responded reassuringly. "You and Ben are planning to move into one of those two apartments after getting married, right?"

"Yes," Ben and Sophia replied simultaneously with assurance in their tones.

"Great," Candace said in a glad voice. "My second original question is about college. Do you two plan on continuing your college careers?"

"Well," Ben began, "we were thinking of dropping out of college and getting entry-level jobs related to our current college majors. Sophia and I would have to get full-time entry-level jobs related to psychology and mechanical engineering, respectively."

"Okay. I guess that makes sense with you and Sophia getting an apartment," Candace responded confidently. "I have one last follow-up question. Do you two want to drop out of college because you two want to have more time to spend with each other and go on trips during vacation days from work?"

"Yes," Sophia responded confidently. "Plus, there is pretty much no point in continuing our college educations because we would just go back to heaven once we finished them."

"I want to say that your and Ben's plans are good so far, in my opinion," Sam responded before continuing. "It is sad that you two want to drop out of college, but I see the point. You and Ben will have enough money, depending on which apartment you two choose, to afford the monthly apartment rent and to go on two or three trips before going back to heaven. You two wouldn't be able to work enough hours to afford either one of the apartments you two are looking at and to go on the two or three trips if you two continue your college careers. I would do the same thing, and that is why I approve of your plans. One of my two questions for you and Ben is about where you two will get your entry-level jobs."

"That is a good question," Ben responded with a touch of uncertainty in his voice. He was still pretty confident that he could find an entry-level job that was related to mechanical engineering. "I think I remember seeing a company building called Aeromechanics Incorporated when I went to and from Evart University. I will look them up, in addition to other entry-level jobs at different companies, on my laptop when I get home from work at American Burgers tomorrow night. I was thinking of moving up to the cashier position at my current job when the current cashier leaves, but an Aeromechanics Incorporated entry-level job would probably have a higher pay than the cashier position at American Burgers."

"Definitely," Sam responded. "I'm sure you will get an entry-level job at Aeromechanics Incorporated or some other company within the next two or three weeks. I can see that you have what it takes to do an excellent job at whatever you do. I have heard and read good things about Aeromechanics Incorporated, including the fact that the hourly pay for entry-level job employees is thirty dollars."

"Thanks, Sam. I'll let you know how everything goes with my searches," Ben replied appreciatively and with sincerity, as always.

"You're welcome, Ben. I look forward to hearing about what you find," Sam replied warmly before switching his attention to Sophia. "Sophia, what ideas do you have about getting your entry-level job?"

"Yes, Dad, I have a couple of ideas of where I could get an entry-level job related to psychology," Sophia replied warmly with confidence. "First of all, there is a Christian counseling center called True Health that is only ten minutes away from here. I was thinking of getting an entry-level counselor aide job. My second idea was to get an entry-level desk job at the Psychology Department at Evart University. I can do some more digging if those two options don't work out. I think my entry-level counselor aide job at True Health would be my best option, though."

"Sounds like you and Ben have a good plan for providing for yourselves once you two get married," Sam responded with good pride in his voice. "My follow-up question is about when you two will get married. There will be quite a bit of money for you and Ben if you two get married in three or four months. That's if you and Ben get the entry-level jobs that you two want in two or three weeks."

"For sure, Dad," Sophia responded before continuing. "Ben and I are thinking of getting married on Saturday, April 26th, a couple of weeks after my birthday. Anyway, you and Mom know that I have about three thousand dollars in my savings account that was originally fifteen hundred dollars of birthday monies and allowances two years ago."

"Of course," Sam replied. "It was a smart move on your part to take my advice and put most of the birthday monies and allowances you've been collecting into a savings account."

"Nice," Ben responded to Sophia. "That will help us as we get closer to our wedding and marriage. I have about two thousand dollars in my savings account that I opened up a year and a half ago. My money is basically from the same things as your money was from."

"Sweet," Sam replied. "I'm glad you and Ben have thought about all of this, Sophia."

"Thanks, Dad," Sophia said happily and appreciatively.

"You're welcome. I will pay for the rehearsal dinner, wedding, and the reception," Sam said. "I just want you two to have enough money to go on trips and have fun with yourselves before going back to heaven. Anyway, my last original question is about how you and Ben will deal with Ben's disability."

"I was actually planning on building a pair of prosthetic legs for myself. Sophia knows this because I told her earlier today when we were at Starbucks. I made a list in one of my mechanical engineering courses during my sophomore year of college last year. The list contained materials and building methods that I would need to build a pair of prosthetic legs for myself. My best friend, Diego, is the only other person who knows about this besides you, Sophia, Candace, and Alicia," Ben responded confidently. "I'm now thinking about the financial implications of building my prosthetic legs as they relate to saving money for Sophia and I's future marriage. I'm confident that she and I can come up with alternative plans in our future marriage to accommodate my disability."

"That is all right for me, Ben," Sophia said reassuringly in a genuine, honest, and loving tone. "I remember you telling me this. We can definitely find ways to accommodate your disability. Just make sure that you are good with not building yourself a pair of prosthetic legs. I'm totally fine if you really want a pair of prosthetic legs or if you don't want prosthetic legs to avoid putting a financial dent in our future marriage. I think you should ask your parents about helping you make or get prosthetic legs. I will always love you, no matter what decision you end up making."

"Thanks, Sophia," Ben replied appreciatively in an equally genuine, honest, and loving tone. "That means a lot. I really appreciate it. I will let you know what I decide after I talk with my parents and Josh on Sunday. The conversation will be a little rough because I haven't told my parents about my potential plans to build a pair of prosthetic legs for myself. I should have told them when I first got the idea. I will deal with the consequences when I talk with my parents. The only person to whom I told my potential plans was my best friend, Diego, and that was about two months ago before I updated him a week or so ago. Anyway, do you want to come over to my parents' house on Sunday night, have dinner and dessert, watch more episodes of *Smallville*, and talk more about me possibly getting a pair of prosthetic legs in addition to the topics that you, your dad, your mom, and I have discussed tonight?"

"That does sound really nice," Sophia replied warmly. "It will be helpful to talk with your family about the things that my parents, you, and I have talked about tonight. Plus, I'm really looking forward to watching more of *Smallville* with you and your family." Both Ben and Sophia switched their attention to Sam before Sophia asked Sam's permission for her to go over to Ben's parents' house. "Is all of this okay with you, Dad?"

"Sure thing, Sophia," Sam replied. "Just make sure that you give me the full lowdown about the things that you and Ben discuss with his family." Then, Sam switched his attention to Ben. "Now, Ben, everything sounds good with you making your final decision on whether you want prosthetic legs or not with the help of your parents. I can tell that you and my daughter can make everything work out either way. Aside from that, can you ask your family about the day that works best for them and you to come over to my and my wife's house so that we all can get to know each other and talk more about your and Sophia's wedding and marriage?"

"Sure thing, Sam," Ben replied with excitement in his voice while looking at Sam. "I will ask my family about that tomorrow night at dinnertime. It will be fun to have our families get to know each other. Everything else is good. I will let Sophia and my family know my final decision on whether or not I want to get prosthetic legs with the help of my parents."

"Sounds like a plan," Sam said. "My second and last follow-up question is about your proposal to my daughter. You know you have to propose to Sophia someday soon in order to make all of this official, right?"

"Definitely," Ben replied with confidence, all the while concealing a growing spark of excitement inside himself. "I have an idea for a proposal. Sophia will have to wait and see what it is."

"Okay, sounds great," Sam replied, at ease with himself about everything that was going to happen with Ben and Sophia's engagement, wedding, and marriage.

"Ooohh! Sounds exciting," Sophia responded with great interest and excitement in her tone. "I can't wait to see how you will propose to me."

"For sure," Candace responded in an excited voice. "It will be fun to hear all of it from Sophia after she gets home from your proposal to her, Ben."

"I have been listening to all of the things that you and everyone else have been talking about," Alicia said to her sister in a very interested and excited voice. She was the first person to finish her dinner. "I'm so happy and excited for you and Ben! Congrats! Definitely tell me, Dad, and Mom everything about Ben's proposal to you."

"Thanks, Sis. Will do," Sophia responded gladly and with a big smile.

"Thanks, Alicia," Ben said appreciatively while looking at Alicia.

"You're welcome," Alicia said to both teens before continuing. "By the way, what is *Smallville?"*

"Yeah," Sam and Candace responded, almost in sync.

"I was thinking of what TV show that is ever since Ben mentioned it," Sam said.

"What is it about?" Candace asked Ben.

"*Smallville* is about the early adventures of Clark Kent, who is also known as superman," Ben answered.

"Sounds very intriguing," Candace replied in an interested tone. "How do you and your family like it?"

"It's really great," Ben said with excitement in his voice. "My family, Diego, and I just started watching the first three episodes of season one, which we bought. Plus, my family and I watched a couple of episodes in season two on TV. We are thinking of watching the rest of season one with Diego and Sophia before watching the rest of season two together. All four of us are waiting to watch the next few episodes of season one with Sophia when she comes over on Sunday night."

"Sounds fun," Alicia responded with some interest in her voice. "Could my mom, my dad, and I possibly borrow season one when you, Sophia, Diego, and your family are done watching it?"

"Yeah, that would be a ton of fun," Sam said with great interest in his tone. "Sophia, Alicia, my wife, and I all like the character of Clark Kent/superman. I'm glad Sophia is watching *Smallville* with you, your family, and Diego. I'm kind of jealous that Sophia is watching it first with you all."

"Absolutely," Ben replied with certainty. "We will let you all borrow season one when we're done watching it. Then, it's only a matter of getting caught up with season two before a potential third season starts. I still have to look up the possibility of there being a third season. I think *Smallville* has what it takes to last quite a while."

By this time, Ben and all of the O'Donnell family members had finished their dinner. They all expressed their eagerness to watch *Smallville*. Sam, Candace, and Alicia all said that they wouldn't keep any promises in not watching the current season two episodes on TV before Ben, Sophia, Diego, and Ben's family lent them season one. However, Alicia and her parents said they would rewatch the episodes in season two with them when all of them were caught up. Ben and the O'Donnell family ate apple pie and vanilla ice cream for dessert before playing one game of Scrabble. Then, Ben's dad picked him up and drove him home. The teen thought a lot about everything that happened that night besides thinking about work and the plans for Sunday. Ben knew that he and Sophia were in for a wild and fun ride from here on out before they went back to heaven.

Saturday went by in a hurry. At least, that's what it seemed to Ben Lawson. He worked at his job at American Burgers for most of the day, just like he scheduled it. Ben used the lunch break to talk with the manager, Claire, about leaving American Burgers in a week or two before he, hopefully, gets an entry-level job at Aeromechanics Incorporated. He also told her that he was getting married on April 26th. Claire congratulated Ben on the great news of him getting married and wished him all the best for it. The manager was also good with him leaving American Burgers and hopefully getting the entry-level job at Aeromechanics Incorporated. Claire told Ben that he would do great at the new job, and she wished him all the best for it as well as his future marriage. She even prayed for his new job opportunity and future marriage with him during the lunch break, which didn't come as a big surprise to Ben. Jesus had said to him that all of the workers at American Burgers would come to know and have relationships with Him. Jesus also said that would happen after Ben told a few of the workers about His messages about the kingdom of God, repentance, love, protection, and provision. The three-in-one Godhead knew that Ben would only be able to tell His messages to those few workers. God would do the rest in terms of having the few workers spread the word about the messages. Now, Ben was seeing the results of his obedience to Jesus. The teen knew that Daniel, Alberto, and all of the other workers had come to know and have relationships with Jesus as well as Claire based on her actions. Ben thanked Claire for her prayers, talked about how grateful he was for having his dishwasher job, said "God bless you" to Claire, and then returned to his job after the lunch break.

Sunday morning came, and Ben and his family went to Diego's church, Holy Communion Church. Sophia joined the group as well because she also attended that church. Plus, Sophia wanted to see Ben before she came over to his family's house that night. The group of people had a great time worshiping God and listening to the sermon. Time flew by, and it was now 6:00 p.m., which was the agreed-upon time for the redheaded teen to come over. Ben had texted Sophia around 4:00 p.m. to ask if it was okay to have Diego over at his family's house as well because Diego wanted to have a part of the conversations and watch *Smallville* with them and his family. Sophia had sent Ben a message saying that was fine and that she was looking forward to seeing Diego again.

"Hi, Mr. and Mrs. Lawson," Sophia said warmly after Dave opened the door of the turquoise-blue house. Leslie was on his right. The teen saw Ben, who was a few feet to Dave's left. Ben was wearing a plain royal blue polo and black shorts with black shoes. Sophia felt equally as dressed as she was wearing a solid one-piece red dress with red dress shoes. She noticed that Dave was wearing a plain white shirt with a collar, royal blue slacks, and royal blue dress shoes. Leslie had put on a one-piece light blue dress with matching dress shoes. Sophia also noticed that Josh, who was on Ben's left, was wearing a plain green collared shirt with black slacks and black dress shoes. The redheaded teen finally took in and intently looked at the royal blue walls and felt at ease being in the house under better pretensions. Diego was on Ben's left, wearing a red polo shirt with dark blue slacks and dark blue dress shoes.

"Hi, Sophia," Dave replied in a nice greeting tone. "Come in. Dinner is ready. You can call me Dave."

"Okay, thanks, Dave," Sophia replied kindly as she walked into the house.

"Hi, Sophia," Leslie said after Sophia got into the house. "Welcome again to our house. I know that the first time you were here wasn't as welcoming. You can call me Leslie, by the way."

"Thanks, Leslie. That means a lot," Sophia said warmly as she went in to hug her. Leslie hugged her back and then smoothly withdrew.

"Hi, Sophia," Ben said kindly and lovingly as he wheeled up to her. Sophia knelt down, and the two of them kissed and hugged each other for a second, then gently withdrew. Then, Ben continued on speaking. "It's really great to see you again today."

"For sure," Josh said as he fixed his attention on Sophia. "Sorry that I was a bit hostile to you in what I said when you first came here. I hope you can forgive me. I do really like and appreciate how things worked out for you and my brother."

"You are forgiven," Sophia replied. "I understand that you wanted to protect Ben. I'm glad you are good with the way that things are between him and me now."

"Thanks," Josh replied kindly.

"You're welcome," Sophia said warmly.

"Hi, Sophia," Diego said nicely. "It's very nice to see you again. I'm sorry for how it was between you and Ben when I brought you over here last Sunday."

"Hi, Diego," Sophia replied. "It's all good. I needed you to bring me over here last Sunday. Thanks for listening to me and doing that."

"You're welcome," Diego replied with sincerity in his tone. "I'm stoked that you and Ben are in a serious relationship now that's headed towards marriage. Ben told me last night that he got your father's blessing to marry you when Ben came over to your family's house for dinner on Friday night. Congrats, both of you!"

"Thanks, Diego," Ben and Sophia said a couple of seconds apart from each other with appreciativeness in their tones. Ben also patted Diego on his right shoulder a few times to show his appreciation.

"You two are welcome," Diego said kindly.

She, Ben, and Josh began to head over to the dining room table, with Dave, Leslie, and Diego a few steps behind them. A chicken Alfredo pasta dish was ready for the six of them to eat on six separate plates. They all sat down on their wooden chairs that had turquoise-green cushions on the bottoms and backs of the chairs. The seating arrangement was the same as at the O'Donnell house on Friday night. The six people prayed over their dinner and then started eating. Leslie got up for a minute, went to her and Dave's room, and brought back a book that had a lot of Ben's baby pictures. She showed them to Sophia, and Sophia had good laughs after seeing several of them. Ben actually laughed a bit when he saw some of his baby pictures. Then, Leslie closed the book, put it away, and asked Ben about what he, Sophia, and her family talked about and did on Friday night. Everybody took turns talking after eating a bit of their food. Ben and Sophia told everyone about what they and Sophia's family talked about and did on Friday night and did not spare any detail. However, Ben saved the conversation about the possibility of his parents helping him get a pair of prosthetic legs after the other conversations.

"Yeah, so the big day is on April 26th," Ben said with excitement in his tone. Sophia smiled again, obviously excited as well.

"Again, we are all excited for you and Sophia!" Dave responded to his son. "It seems like you two have good plans so far. My only follow-up questions are about which apartment you and Sophia are choosing to live in and your entry-level jobs."

"Well," Ben began, "Sophia and I texted for about five minutes last night about which one of the two apartments we would like to live in. We ended up choosing the second apartment that is closer to our house. That's because the rent is cheaper, and with our full-time entry-level jobs, we will have more money to go on two or three trips before going back to heaven. Sophia is totally good with our decision."

"Absolutely," Sophia responded. "We don't want to just get by from paycheck to paycheck with our entry-level jobs. We want to go on those trips. As for our entry-level jobs, Ben applied for the entry-level job at Aeromechanics Incorporated last night, and I applied for the entry-level counselor aide job at True Health Christian Counseling Center last night as well. We're waiting for the managers' responses."

"Sounds great," Dave said, confident in Ben and Sophia's decisions.

"For sure," Ben said confidently to his dad before switching the subject to the possibility of his parents getting him a pair of prosthetic legs. "On a different note, which I'm sorry that I didn't bring up with you and Mom earlier, during my sophomore year of college, I was planning on building myself a pair of prosthetic legs. I actually started making a list of the materials and building methods on a piece of paper that is in my backpack. That was as far as I got. Then, I got Sophia's father's blessing on Friday night for me to marry her. That got me thinking about the financial consequences to Sophia and I's future marriage if I built a pair of prosthetic legs for myself. Sophia heard this from me on Friday night at her parents' house during dinner, and she suggested that I ask you and Mom if you could buy me a pair of prosthetic legs. Now, I'm asking you two that question. I'm even willing to pay a quarter of the cost for my prosthetic legs after I get that amount of money from my new job, which I hope I get. I'm sorry that I'm not able to pay more, but that's the best that I can do with Sophia and I's future marriage approaching."

"Well, Ben," Leslie replied in somewhat of a disappointed voice, "you should have told me and your dad about your idea of building a pair of prosthetic legs sooner than this. I'm proud that you have really changed your attitude and behavior a year or so after learning that your legs needed to be amputated. I admire that you were able to do that, and I'm grateful for Diego helping you move forward when you accepted his help. Your dad and I are a bit disappointed that you waited this long to tell us your plan and ask for our help. However, I know that you would love to be able to walk again with the help of prosthetic legs. Your dad and I would be more than happy to buy you prosthetic legs so that you can walk again. The only thing we ask for is that you don't keep any more secrets from us, like the secret that you kept of the first incident with you and Sophia. Did you tell Diego or anyone else about your plans to build a pair of prosthetic legs for yourself?"

"I originally told Diego about my plans around two months ago, and then I updated him on my progress just a week or so ago. The only other people I told my previous plans to were Sophia and her family on Friday night during dinner at their house. God as my witness, I have no other secrets. I wouldn't use God as my witness if I were still keeping secrets. I have told everyone here about Hannah, Sophia, the dream that I had from Jesus, and my previous plans of building a pair of prosthetic legs for myself," Ben admitted reassuringly to his mom and dad.

"That's good," Dave responded with a little disappointment in his voice that turned to comfort. "I'm glad that you are coming to me and your mom now about your previous plans to build prosthetic legs for yourself and your request for us to buy you a pair of prosthetic legs." Then, Dave switched his attention to Diego for a moment. "Diego, did Ben tell you about his plans when he said he told you?"

"Yes," Diego replied confidently and reassuringly. "I remember that Ben first told me about his plans to build a pair of prosthetic legs for himself a couple of months or so ago. Honestly, I forgot the exact day that he told me about his plans. However, I do distinctly remember that Ben updated me about his progress a week or so ago."

"All right," Dave said in a self-assured voice. "It sounds like you and Ben are good now and will come to me and my wife if you two need help with anything." Dave turned his attention to Ben. "As your mom said, she and I would be happy to purchase a pair of prosthetic legs for you to be able to walk again. My wife and I are going to figure out a way how to get the prosthetic legs and decide when we will give them to you."

"Sounds like a plan, Dad," Ben responded in a relieved and grateful tone. "Thanks for having you and Mom do this for me. Sorry for keeping this secret from you and Mom for so long. I will never keep any more secrets from you two ever again."

"You're welcome," Dave and Leslie said to their son, a second apart from each other. They also told Ben how appreciative they were that he would not keep any more secrets from them ever again. Then, Leslie switched her attention to Sophia for a moment. "Sophia, I hope I didn't offend you when I generally brought up the first incident between you and Ben."

"It's totally fine," Sophia replied in a reassuring tone. "I know how badly I treated Ben when we first met. He forgave me after I told him how I felt about him last Sunday. Then, I told Ben again about how sorry I was on Friday while we were at Starbucks. He forgave me again. That's one of the reasons why I love him. Now, I just love being in a serious relationship with Ben."

"Oh, that's so sweet that my son forgave you both times. I helped raise him to be that way. Plus, I'm really happy you love being in a serious relationship with him. I know you and Ben will have a great marriage before you two go back to heaven."

"Thanks, Leslie," Sophia replied warmly and appreciatively. Then, the teen lovingly winked at Ben with her right eye. Ben returned the gesture.

"You're welcome, Sophia," Leslie said equally as warmly. "My only follow-up question is about where you and Ben will get married."

"Ben and I decided on getting married at a chapel next to Holy Communion Church," Sophia said excitedly. "It's called the Fellowship Chapel, and it has amazingly ornate, beautiful, and big glass windows. The windows have gorgeous shades of blue, purple, red, green, pink, and orange. The concrete walls on the inside and outside are nearly pure white color. Plus, the inside of the Fellowship Chapel has beautiful decorations."

"Sounds very beautiful, indeed," Leslie replied with amazement in her tone.

"For sure," Ben responded. "I saw the outside of the chapel when my family and I went to Holy Communion Church. It is really beautiful.

"You'll definitely love the inside of the chapel as well," Sophia replied to Ben before switching her attention to Josh. "Speaking of life plans, what ideas do you have of what you want to do after you graduate high school, Josh?"

"I appreciate you asking me about that, Sophia," Josh replied appreciatively. "Ummm...I think I want to be a healthcare provider, a soldier in the military, or a combat medic in the military. I don't think college is the right path for me after high school. I'll maybe go to college in my mid-twenties."

"Cool," Sophia replied in a supportive tone. "I'm sure you will do really well at whichever career you choose. College is not for everyone."

"Wow, Bro," Ben responded in a proud tone. "Those are really good career choices. Quite noble, if you ask me. I'm proud of you. You'll do great at whichever career you choose."

"Thanks, Bro. That means a lot," Josh replied genuinely.

"Absolutely," Dave responded to Josh about the career options he listed. "Leslie told me a few days ago that those were the career choices that Josh told her he was thinking of. Again, I would only suggest college because it opens a whole slew of career opportunities. However, it's your choice about what you want to do, and I will support you no matter what. I'm also proud of you. You are becoming a good young man."

"Thanks, Dad. I just don't think college is right for me now," Josh replied appreciatively. "I will let everyone know my choice as soon as I know for sure what career I want to pursue. The option of being a healthcare provider can be equally as long-term as being a soldier or combat medic in the military if I want to be a local healthcare manager sometime down the road. I could, on the other two hands, train soldiers or combat medics after I do two or three military tours."

"Sounds great. Those are good plans," Dave replied.

"I'm also so proud of you," Leslie said. "I'm glad that our conversations together have helped you grow."

"Thanks, Mom," Josh replied lovingly and appreciatively.

Ben, his family, Sophia, and Diego entered into a mostly quiet segment of their night as they finished dinner. Then, all six of them ate chocolate and coffee ice cream for dessert and talked with each other some more about their weeks. Finally, they gathered in the living room, sat down on the couch, and watched the fourth, fifth, and sixth episodes of season one of *Smallville*. It was just a few minutes after 10:00 p.m. when the six people finished the three episodes of *Smallville*. They eagerly wanted to watch another episode, but Sophia had to call it a night and drive home, especially since she lived twenty-five minutes away from the Lawson family house. Ben, his family, Sophia, and Diego agreed to eat dinner and dessert and to watch all of the other episodes of season one of *Smallville* every Friday and Sunday night at the Lawson family house. Then, Sophia left, and Diego followed suit and went back to his apartment. It was only then that Leslie gave her mother's engagement ring to Ben to give to Sophia when he proposed to her on Friday. Ben told his mom, dad, and Josh about his proposal plans, and they thought that the plans were really thoughtful and mindful. All four family members were excited about what was going to happen on Friday in terms of Ben's proposal to Sophia. The only trouble that Ben had that Sunday night was going to sleep because he was so excited.

That special Friday on January 31st came, and Ben Lawson was still really excited. His mom dropped him off at the Sports Hub at 12:45 p.m. Ben hid the little black square box with Leslie's mom's engagement ring in it in his right side shorts pockets. He was wearing a solid red polo, black shorts, and black dress shoes. The teen had texted Sophia to meet him at one of the more secluded indoor hardcourt volleyball courts next to a medium-sized window at 1:00 p.m. The window looked out onto the city of Evart. Plus, the Sports Hub was positioned on a concrete plateau seven feet above street level. Ben had also told her via text to wait to have a late lunch with him. He wouldn't tell her the name of the restaurant because he wanted to tell her that after the proposal. Sophia texted Ben a message that said she was really excited for whatever plans he had for the two of them. Those fifteen minutes gave Ben enough time to get onto the right side of the light blue volleyball court, pull out the little black box, and rehearse his proposal to Sophia by himself. The moment finally came for the real thing when Sophia walked over to him on the volleyball court. She was wearing a one-piece dark purple dress with fancy dark purple shoes to match the dress. Sophia had blow-dried her red hair so that it was straight and a bit curly.

"Hi, Ben!" Sophia said lovingly before kneeling, hugging, and kissing Ben for three or so seconds. Ben had put the little black box back inside his right side shorts pocket so that Sophia couldn't see it.

"Hi, Sophia!" Ben replied equally as lovingly after Sophia hugged and kissed him. "It's always wonderful to get to see and hang out with you. You look very beautiful, by the way."

"Thank you. It is very kind of you to say that!" Sophia said very appreciatively.

"You're welcome. You should see how beautiful the city of Evart looks on this cloudy day," Ben said as he waited for Sophia to look out onto the city of Evart through the window. That was when he took out the little black box from his right side shorts pocket, flipped it open, and turned it towards Sophia. Ben leaned forward and bent over in his chair a bit while holding the box. Sophia noticed the sound of the box flipping open, and she turned around to see what it was. Ben saw her priceless facial expression after she had turned around towards him and saw the silver three-karat diamond ring. Sophia's face was filled with excitement, joy, and happiness as she clasped her hands to her face.

"Sophia O'Donnell," Ben began, "will you marry me?"

"Oh my gosh, yes, yes!" Sophia exclaimed in pure excitement and joy before she knelt down, hugged, and kissed Ben very passionately for fifteen or so seconds.

"I thought you might want to play one game of volleyball before we headed to your favorite restaurant, Rebario's, for our late lunch," Ben said after he and Sophia were done hugging and kissing each other. Also, Ben had gently and lovingly put the engagement ring on Sophia's ring finger on her left hand right before he started talking.

"Both of those things sound absolutely fantastic!" Sophia said in a loving and thrilled voice as she was still kneeling down. Then, she and Ben proceeded to hug and kiss each other very passionately again for another twenty or so seconds. The two of them were in no rush and wanted to fully enjoy the heart-pounding, amazing, and thrilling moments that they were experiencing together.

Ben and Sophia proceeded to play one eleven-point game of volleyball before Leslie picked them up at 2:00 p.m. to go to Rebario's. The two teens played the volleyball game with great caution because they didn't want to mess up their outfits. Sophia won the game eleven points to seven. Then, they walked over to Ben and his family's van when Leslie came to pick them up. Ben, Sophia, and Leslie agreed to go back to the Sports Hub after Ben and Sophia's late lunch. That was because Sophia had to pick up her car. Anyway, the two teens were at Rebario's in no time. The drive over to Rebario's was mostly filled with excited and giddy conversations between Sophia and Leslie about Ben's proposal to Sophia, the volleyball game, and preliminary wedding dress plans. Ben talked to his mom and Sophia about how amazing it felt for him and Sophia when he proposed to her. Plus, he talked about how fun and nice his and Sophia's volleyball game was. Lastly, Ben was very supportive of where Sophia wanted to get her wedding dress and their wedding rings.

Leslie dropped Ben and Sophia off at Rebario's, which was a Mexican food restaurant, and said that she would pick them up at 4:30 p.m. That left Ben and Sophia two hours and fifteen minutes to eat their late lunch, hang out, and talk more about their interests and wedding plans. The two teens had a lot of fun doing those things. Finally, Leslie picked them up at four thirty and went back to the Sports Hub to drop Sophia off at her car.

"I had a wonderful time today, Ben! Thank you!" Sophia said after Leslie had let Ben out of the van. Ben had wheeled the few feet over to where Sophia was, next to her car. His mom had given him and Sophia ten minutes to talk and say their goodbyes for that moment. The two of them were going to see each other again that night at Ben's parents' house for dinner and dessert, and they would be watching Smallville starting at 6:00 p.m.

"You're very welcome, Sophia!" Ben replied lovingly and genuinely.

"Yeah. It was a ton of fun trying out your very spicy shredded beef tacos at Rebario's," Sophia said while laughing a bit.

"For sure," Ben said while laughing. "Your facial expression was unforgettable when you tried my tacos. They had quite a bit of hot sauce on them. You literally drank your whole glass of water just to get the heat and spice out of your mouth and throat."

"Oh yeah, that's right," Sophia said funnily while laughing. "I remember that I also took your glass of water and drank half of it before my mouth and throat calmed down from having that much spice in them. You were good with me drinking half of your glass of water, which I appreciated. I must admit, Ben Lawson, you eat more spicier food than me. I usually have half the amount of hot sauce on my food from Rebario's and the other Mexican food I eat, which is a moderate amount."

"You're welcome," Ben began. "I'm glad that you were able to purge the spice from your mouth and throat with your glass of water and my half glass of water. It can get pretty annoying when some hot sauce stays in your mouth and the back of your throat for longer than usual. I don't know why; I just like hot sauce and spicy food in general with a good amount of fervor. Plus, I love the spices of life, if I can use that phrase."

"You're always kind, Ben. That is one of your characteristics that I appreciate the most. I have a question about your spices of life analogy/phrase. Am I the best spice that you have in your life? I know that you are a great spice in my life," Sophia said those last three sentences in a humorous and loving way.

"Absolutely," Ben replied definitively, with humor and love in his tone. "You are the best spice that I could've asked for. You shouldn't be compared to spice, though. Sophia O'Donnell, you are way better than any spice in the world."

"I'm so happy that you said that," Sophia said with a smile on her face before she and Ben hugged and kissed each other for seven or so seconds. Nine minutes had passed since Leslie had let Ben and Sophia talk and say their goodbyes for now.

"See you tonight," Ben said lovingly.

"See you tonight," Sophia replied equally as lovingly. "I'm really looking forward to seeing you again, having dinner and dessert with you, your family, and Diego, and watching more episodes of *Smallville.*"

"Definitely," Ben said. "I love you."

"I love you too," Sophia replied. "See you and everyone else in about an hour and a half."

Ben and Sophia waved to each other after Sophia got into her car and started the engine. Then, she drove off and went home to her family. The house was only ten minutes away from the Sports Hub, which was on the way to Ben's parents's house. Leslie drove her son back to the Lawson family house, and the hour and a half passed by in a flash. That amount of time let Sophia drive to her family's house and excitedly tell her family about Ben's proposal to her and everything else that followed. Also, that hour and a half gave Sophia time to freshen up before heading over to Ben's family's house. The Lawson family, Sophia, and Diego had a ton of fun eating dinner and dessert, talking, and watching *Smallville*. Then, it was time for Sophia to head back to her family's house at 10:30 p.m. Ben and Sophia had noticed that time flew by so fast that night while they were having fun with Ben's family and Diego. However, the two teens had made the most of the time that they had together with everyone else. It seemed that, for a while, that time had slowed down while Ben and Sophia were holding, hugging, and kissing each other on the living room couch. They wanted to make sure that the two of them thoroughly soaked up every minute that they had with each other before going back to heaven.

Time had indeed begun to speed past Ben and Sophia like a train that was moving at high speed. On the flip side, the two teens were making sure that they tightly held onto and fully enjoyed every precious minute that they had together. That was easier to do after they had officially dropped out of college on February 1st and waited to be interviewed for the entry-level jobs that they had applied for.

In addition, Ben left his dishwasher position at American Burgers on that same day of February 1st. He had said his final goodbye to Claire and had prayed that she would continue to do really well as the manager of the fast-food restaurant. Claire had thanked him for that and told Ben that she would keep him in her prayers. Plus she also said that she would do her best to cultivate strong, Christ-centered relationships with all of the new believers working at the restaurant in addition to strengthening her relationship with Jesus. Ben couldn't help but smile at the fact that Daniel, Alberto, and the other employees at American Burgers came to know and be in relationships with Jesus, just as Jesus had said to Ben. Ben had said his final words of gratitude and appreciation for being able to work at the fast-food restaurant before he permanently left it.

Ben and Sophia took full advantage of the sixteen days of fun that they had on their hands. The two of them went out on more dates together, which included going to a movie, hanging out and checking out books at Barnes & Noble, hanging out at the USA Fashion and Festivities Mall, and cuddling together on each of their family's living room couches while watching TV shows.

Ben and Sophia still stayed in contact and hung out with Anthony Markus and Hannah Rine as well, even after dropping out of college. The teen couple started to become good friends with Anthony and Hannah. Ben and Sophia told them everything about what happened to them in terms of getting shot, going to heaven, talking with Jesus, and entering into their serious relationship. Anthony and Hannah were totally baffled and truly amazed about everything that the two teens had told them, except for the parts in which Ben and Sophia got shot. Hannah and Anthony ended up telling them everything that had happened in their lives as well. All in all, the sixteen days of complete fun and relaxation for Ben and Sophia was a blast.

The day of February 17th finally came for Ben and Sophia to start their entry-level jobs at Aeromechanics Incorporated and the True Health Christian Counseling Center, respectively. That was, of course, after very successful interviews with the respective company managers and directors on February 10th and 12th. So, Ben started an entry-level desk job at Aeromechanics Incorporated.

Sophia also got started with her entry-level counselor aide job at the True Health Christian Counseling Center on February 17th. The counselor aide job began smoothly as Sophia was assigned to a great psychologist, Dr. Beatrice Altred. However, Sophia knew that the aide job would become hard.

Days passed by, and days turned into weeks. Ben and Sophia were working full-time, Monday through Friday, at their respective entry-level jobs. The two teens worked for eight hours each day from 9:00 a.m. to 5:00 p.m., and they got really good at their jobs. There were low moments that came with more stress in Ben and Sophia's entry-level jobs, just like any other job. However, they knew that they were building a better life for themselves. The two teens were saving money to provide for themselves once they got married. As for job decompression, Ben and Sophia would hang out with their families and friends on many days after they got home from their jobs. In addition, the two teens made sure to still go out on dates together and spend quality time with each other.

Ben and Sophia were also planning on where they would have their wedding invitations made in addition to the wedding dress, wedding rings, and wedding suit tryouts. In addition, Sophia chose her sister, Alicia, to be her maid of honor, and Ben chose his brother, Josh, to be his best man. The two siblings were completely stoked about Ben and Sophia's decision to pick them. Ben and Sophia made their guest list, groomsmen list, bridesmaid list, wedding gifts list, and the Fellowship Chapel's floral surroundings list for the wedding. Plus, the two teens made order preparations for the wedding cake at a wedding cake bakery. They also planned the bachelor and bachelorette parties. Finally, they chose April 19th to be the day of their rehearsal dinner. The two teens were proud of themselves for the plans they made, and they knew God was going before them.

Saturday, March 29th, came, and it was going to be a great day. That was because Ben and Sophia had their bachelor and bachelorette parties on that day. Ben, his dad, brother, Diego, Anthony Markus, and Sam O'Donnell were going to play a best-of-five paintball tournament at an outside concrete paintball course called Franklin's Paintball Course. Then, the six men were going to see a comedy movie together. These two events took over most of that Saturday. Meanwhile, Sophia, her mom, sister, Sophia's previous dormmate Lucy Robinson,

Hannah Rine, and Leslie Lawson were going to drive in seven high-quality bumper kart races at a nearby place called Randall's Arcade & Bumper Kart Alley. Then, the six women were going to get manicures and pedicures together. These events also took over most of the day.

Ben, Dave, Josh, Diego, Anthony, and Sam had a total blast playing paintball at Franklin's Paintball Course. The course had many block-sized obstacles in addition to towers where players could snipe other players. All six men were wearing black or gray full-body protective gear. Dave, Anthony, and Sam were on one team, and the only things that distinguished them from Ben, Josh, and Diego's team were their black gear. Ben, Josh, and Diego's team took full advantage of the block obstacles, no matter how big, small, wide, short, or long the obstacles were. They needed to do this because Dave, Anthony, and Sam's team took full advantage of the towers in addition to sometimes using the block obstacles for cover. Josh and Diego did their best to protect Ben as they fought off Anthony, Dave, and Sam. In the end, Ben, Josh, and Diego beat Dave, Anthony, and Sam three games to two. Then, the six men had a fun time watching the comedy movie they went to see after going to their respective homes, showering, and getting redressed.

Sophia, Candace, Alicia, Lucy Robinson, Hannah Rine, and Leslie Lawson had a thrilling time racing bumper karts at Randall's Arcade & Racing Alley. Lucy Robinson, Sophia's dormmate at Evart University, was really excited to be a part of Sophia's bachelorette party. The race course at Randall's Arcade & Bumper Kart Alley was half a mile long and swerved in and out like musical notes and ocean waves. There were a few straightaways as well. Sophia, Candace, and Alicia were in red, pink, and blue bumper karts, respectively. Leslie, Hannah, and Lucy were in orange, yellow, and purple bumper karts, respectively. It felt like the video game *Mario Kart*, as the six women revved up their small engines before they started the first race. That feeling continued on each race.

Sophia, Candace, and Hannah were the people who took turns bouncing back and forth from first place, second place, and third place during four of the seven races. Lucy, Alicia, and Leslie vied for fourth, fifth, and sixth place during those four races out of the seven races total. The other three races were more competitive. In the end, Sophia got in first place one time. Hannah ended up in first place two times. Finally, Candace got in first place one time. Leslie ended up in second place for two races. Alicia got in third place for two races. Lucy ended up in second place one time. The rest of the rankings were a wild combination for the six women. Then, they returned back to their own homes, showered, and redressed before getting their manicures and pedicures together.

A couple of things happened before Ben and Sophia's rehearsal dinner on April 19th. First of all, Sophia's birthday was on Saturday, April 12th. Ben came over to Sophia's family's house for her birthday celebration at 3:00 p.m. Lucy Robinson was also invited to Sophia's birthday celebration. The O'Donnell family, Lucy, and Ben played Scrabble and a couple of card games before having red chili enchiladas for dinner and chocolate cake and vanilla ice cream for dessert. Then, they watched the newest episode of season two of *Smallville*, which was on TV again. Sophia had told Lucy about *Smallville*, and Lucy had binge-watched season one over five days. Lucy was going to buy season two when it came to Blockbuster since she was jumping into season two midstream. She didn't mind doing that. As for the rest of the Lawson family and Diego that night, they were watching the same episode at the Lawson family house. Ben and Sophia took turns watching the new episodes at each of their family's houses with their family members and Diego.

The second thing that happened before Ben and Sophia's rehearsal dinner was that Sophia, the rest of her family, and Diego were introduced to the prophet, Harold Trenton, at Light of the World Church by the Lawson family on Sunday, April 13th. All of them had agreed to come there, meet Harold, and talk with him. God had finally revealed the identity of Ben's future wife to Harold on April 5th in a dream. In addition, God said that Harold was also going to meet Sophia's family and Diego someday soon. However, God did not reveal the day that he would meet them. So, on April 13th, Harold was introduced to Sophia's family and Diego after the church sermon, and he told them about the many people whom Ben and Sophia were going to help bring to God. Harold also told Sophia, her family, Diego, and the Lawson family words of wisdom. All of them were amazed and greatly interested in everything Harold had to say. Harold would continue to meet with Diego and the Lawson and O'Donnell families after meeting one or two times per month after the church sermon at Light of the World Church when they came there. The prophet would speak numerous words of wisdom to them in addition to getting lunch with them.

Ben and Sophia's rehearsal dinner finally came on April 19th, and everyone who was invited to it was extremely excited to be there. Diego, Anthony Markus, Hannah Rine, Lucy Robinson, Tess Debor, and Carl Wendleson were among the guests who were invited to the rehearsal dinner, in addition to Ben and his family and Sophia and her family. Sophia wanted to invite Tess and Carl to the rehearsal dinner, wedding, and reception because they were good people, and they helped her on the way to the main Evart hospital after she got shot. Ben was good with inviting them. Some of Ben and Sophia's extended families were also at the rehearsal dinner. The men were wearing an assortment of solid-colored suits and ties in addition to dark blue, black, or silver gray slacks and black or silver gray dress shoes. As for the women, they were wearing various one-piece dresses and matching dress shoes. Sophia was wearing a plain white one-piece dress and white dress shoes because she was saving her wedding dress, which she and Ben got with both of their families for her and Ben's wedding next Saturday. Ben wore a black suit, tie, and a fancy white undershirt that was accompanied by black shorts that were made to cover his amputated legs.

As Dave and Leslie looked at Ben, they thought about the plan they had to give Ben a pair of prosthetic legs a few days before his and Sophia's wedding. The two parents would deliver the prosthetic legs to their son on time. They had used a significant amount of money from their joint retirement savings account in addition to a little bit from their joint checking account to buy the $180,000 pair of prosthetic legs. Both parents' and Ben's insurances didn't expense prosthetic legs that would last several years. Their insurance company only paid for prosthetic legs that usually broke and wore out after six months because the insurance company didn't want to pay for sturdier prosthetic legs that would last longer. The reason why Dave and Leslie were waiting to give them to Ben was that they wanted it to be a transformation from Ben and Sophia's rehearsal dinner to their wedding.

The location of the rehearsal dinner was held inside a wooden building at Crystal Park, which was two blocks away from the Fellowship Hall and Holy Communion Church. Crystal Park had finely cut green grass, and it overlooked a small river on its right side. Everyone, including Ben and Sophia, had a fantastic time eating the grilled chicken, rice, and asparagus dinner. That was after Sophia and her soon-to-be husband had acted out their entry into the wooden building, preparing for their first time as husband and wife. Ben and Sophia had chosen the *Smallville* introductory song as their entry song because they liked it a lot. Ben and his soon-to-be wife had the song start at the one-minute mark and played it for thirty-four or so seconds on an overhead speaker. They entered the wooden building in a more dramatic way at a slower pace to accommodate the time. There was only one thing that Ben and Sophia didn't know, which was Dave and Leslie's plan to give Ben the pair of prosthetic legs that they had bought. This turn of events would really excite Ben and Sophia. Even with the rehearsal dinner, wedding, and prosthetic leg plans, the young, soon-to-be-married couple was still determined to tell everyone they met about Jesus's messages of love, protection, provision, and the kingdom of God. As for Diego, Ben, Sophia, and the rest of the Lawson and O'Donnell families, things were about to get even better.

CHAPTER 8:

THE BIG DAY

Ben Lawson felt like a changed young man as he was getting dressed in one of the dressing rooms inside the Fellowship Chapel an hour before his and Sophia's wedding ceremony began. It was 4:00 p.m. on Saturday, April 26th, 2003, and the weather was very nice, with a high of eighty-five degrees and a sky that only had a small number of clouds. There would not be any rain again until June 8th. The weather conditions were simply perfect, according to Ben and Sophia, as they were getting dressed in different dressing rooms. That thought about the weather conditions was just a small thought in Ben's mind at the moment. The most lingering thought in his head was that he was getting married. It excited him the most out of the three thoughts that were swirling around in his head. Aside from that and the perfect weather conditions, he was ecstatic about the fact that he now had a pair of prosthetic legs that enabled him to walk again.

It was a little tough to get used to walking again when his doctor, Dr. Shiela Blisk, had attached the pair of black prosthetic legs to Ben's leg stubs at her office at the main Evart hospital three days ago.

"I'm so happy for you!" Sophia had exclaimed to Ben when he was shown the prosthetic legs by his parents and Dr. Blisk.

"Thanks, Sophia! I'm extremely excited about this! I can't contain my excitement!" Ben had replied very enthusiastically to Sophia before Dr. Blisk had attached the pair of prosthetic legs to him and talked to him about what he could and could not do with them. Diego, Ben's family, and Sophia's family were there, and everyone was super excited. Even Dr. Blisk showed her overwhelming happiness for Ben, Sophia, and the rest of the crew.

There were some things that Shiela revealed to everyone as well. The rare disease that ended up taking away Ben's legs was called Ewing sarcoma,[1] and it would have killed Ben after a couple of days as it would have crept up into his heart. It was a relatively fast-spreading disease, and it was triggered by Ben driving the race car at the NASCAR charity event

1 Ewing sarcoma is a type of cancer that begins as a growth of cells in the bones and the soft tissue around the bones. Ewing sarcoma mostly happens in children and young adults, although it can happen at any age. Ewing sarcoma most often begins in the leg bones and in the pelvis, but it can happen in any bone.

on his seventeenth birthday. There were strands of his DNA that had the disease embedded in them, which had been passed down from his great-grandfather on his dad's side of the family. Dave had never heard much about his dad's father, and the hospitals didn't have that many files on him. That was the main reason why Dr. Blisk and the other doctors had so much trouble figuring out what the disease was. They gave up on the search after a year of digging through electronic and hard-copy files. However, Shiela and the other doctors were bound and determined to figure out what the disease was that ended up taking away Ben's legs. They figured out that it was Ewing sarcoma after a six-month break. Then, Shiela and the other doctors had to run some tests and learn more about the disease. Shiela was sorry that it took them so long to identify the disease and its deadly effects. Diego, Ben, Sophia, and the rest of the Lawson and O'Donnell families understood the research difficulty and agreed that there was nothing that they could have done to prevent it from infecting Ben. They were just overjoyed that Ben and Sophia were getting married in three days and that Ben would be able to walk again with the help of the prosthetic legs.

Ben was now thinking back on that revelation in the dressing room inside the Fellowship Chapel with a big mirror in front of him. He thought about how sudden the disease had appeared in the NASCAR race car hangar. He was a little sad that there was nothing that anyone could have done to prevent the disease from taking away his legs. However, the teen knew that Jesus would work everything out for his good, and Jesus was right. Ben was getting married to Sophia, and he now had a great pair of prosthetic legs to help him walk. Life brings people many troubles, but God always has plans to prosper people who love, follow, and are in relationships with Him.

Ben came out of the dressing room and reentered the waiting room that faced the back right side of the Fellowship Chapel hall. He was dressed in a fancy white undershirt, a black suit, a black bow tie, black dress pants, and black dress shoes, just like his best man and groomsmen. The groomsmen who were waiting there included Diego, Anthony Markus, and one of Ben's good high school friends, Brandon Heraldez. Brandon was an eighteen-year-old Hispanic/Asian Christian man who was six feet two inches tall, was pretty fit, and had short dark brown hair with no facial hair. Ben's best man and brother, Josh, was also waiting in the waiting room. The door that led to the hall of the Fellowship Chapel was closed. That was because, as of tradition, the bridegroom was not allowed to see the bride on the wedding day. Ben and Sophia had made sure to not cross paths with each other that day.

"Looking sharp, man!" Diego said enthusiastically to Ben. "Congrats on your and Sophia's big day today, which is officially going to start in forty minutes! Plus, your prosthetic legs fill those dress pants pretty nicely."

"Thanks, Diego!" Ben replied equally as enthusiastically. "I'm super excited for our big day today! Today is really Sophia's big day with me. It feels great to be able to walk again with the help of these prosthetic legs!"

"I know. I'm sure it does feel great to be able to walk again, man!" Diego replied before he reached out a bit to excitedly and proudly pat Ben's left shoulder. Ben returned the gesture by patting Diego's right shoulder. Then, Ben, Josh, and the three groomsmen sat down on a long blue leather couch in the waiting room.

"Hey, Bro," Josh began. He was sitting next to his older brother on his right side. "I want to say that I'm very happy that you and Sophia are getting married in forty minutes! Also, I want to say that I'm proud of how well you navigated your previous situation with not having legs. You took Diego's help and trusted that God only had the best for you. I really look up to you as my older brother. Finally, I want to say that you and Sophia will have a fun and great marriage before you two go back to heaven."

"Thanks, Bro," Ben replied gratefully before giving Josh a good side hug that lasted for a second. "That means a lot. You have grown a lot in your character these past couple of years. I know that high school hasn't been easy, but I know that God will bless and help you in everything you do."

"You're welcome. Thanks too," Josh said gratefully as well before giving Ben a one-second-long side hug.

"Dude, I'm stoked that you and Sophia are getting married very soon today!" Brandon said to Ben. He was sitting on the left side of the couch, two spaces away, with Diego right next to Ben. "Congrats! Sorry that I wasn't able to attend your bachelor party and your and Sophia's rehearsal dinner because I was helping take care of my dad, who broke his arm six months ago. Also, thanks for filling me in on all of what happened to you and Sophia recently. It was really scary to hear about you two getting shot when you told me two days ago at my house. However, it was very exciting to hear about the experiences that you and Sophia had in heaven, especially the parts where you two talked to Jesus. That was awesome! You and Sophia are richly blessed with the time that you two have together now to live life together and tell Jesus's messages to everyone you two meet. It's nice to think that you and she will not die in the numerous life-ending events starting on May 14th, 2005. That was kind of Jesus to save you and Sophia from those events and welcome you two back to heaven."

"You're welcome, Brandon. Thanks as well. I do really appreciate that Sophia and I will not experience the life-ending events. That's a huge relief. Everything else about you helping your dad is good." Ben replied in a thankful and understanding tone. "Family is more important, and I'm glad you helped take care of your dad. It's good to hear that he is doing a bit better now. I'm sure that God will heal his arm soon."

"Thanks, Ben," Brandon said appreciatively. "That means a lot. I know that God will heal his arm soon. It's only a matter of time."

"For sure," Ben replied confidently. "Your dad will be back to his construction work in no time."

"I sure hope so," Brandon said in a hopeful tone before there was a second of silence.

"Ben, I want to say that I'm truly amazed at how much you have overcome and how much God has blessed you and Sophia." Anthony Markus was the next person to speak. "I know and believe that you and Sophia will have a greatly blessed marriage before you two go back to heaven. It has been a privilege to be one of your good friends, and I will miss you and Sophia when you two are gone."

"Thank you for saying those things, Anthony," Ben responded gratefully and meaningfully. "It has been great to be good friends with you as well. We will have some time to hang out more before Sophia and I go back to heaven. Speaking of which, you, me, Sophia, and everyone else in this room should definitely go to see *Star Wars: Revenge of the Sith* when there is a private showing before it officially comes out in theaters."

"That is a sure thing, man!" Anthony replied excitedly. "On a short side note, do you, Josh, Diego, and Brandon want to stand up again in this waiting room? I just don't want our suits, shirts, and pants to get wrinkles in them."

"Absolutely," Ben said before getting off of the blue leather couch and standing up. The rest of the crew understood and followed suit. Then, Ben continued on speaking. "Thanks for reminding me, Josh, Diego, and Brandon about that. We were just taking a break from standing. We definitely don't want wrinkles in our outfits. That wouldn't have been good."

"Yeah, wrinkles are not good," Diego responded before switching the subject back to the upcoming *Star Wars* movie. "Anyway, I think it is a great idea for all of us and Sophia to go see *Revenge of the Sith* at a private showing before it officially comes out in theaters. That is if there is a private showing. We may have to do some digging on the internet for that."

"We can do that. I'm sure we will find a private showing of *Revenge of the Sith*," Brandon said. "I'm looking forward to seeing the movie!"

"Sounds like a plan!" Josh said excitedly. "That will be fun! We still have to see *Bruce Almighty* and *Secondhand Lions* as well when they come out this year."

"Definitely!" Ben responded assuredly and enthusiastically. Then, he, Josh, and Ben's groomsmen progressed on talking about *Bruce Almighty* and *Secondhand Lions* in addition to getting hyped up for Ben and Sophia's wedding and reception dinner. Ben's dad had joined them in the waiting room and had talked with all of them about those topics, as well as how proud and happy he was for Ben and Sophia.

It is said in the Bible that the Christian church is the bride and wife of Christ, namely in the book of Revelation. John, who wrote Revelation, said, "I [He] saw the Holy City, the new Jerusalem, coming down out of heaven from God, prepared as a bride beautifully dressed for her husband" (Revelation 21:2).[2] The covenant relationship of marriage between husband and wife is a direct representation of that. Sophia O'Donnell was about to enter into the covenant relationship of marriage with Ben Lawson. She would no longer be known as Sophia O'Donnell but as Sophia Lawson. Sophia and Ben will become as one body, as also said in the Bible in the book of Genesis when God had made Adam and Eve. Sophia and Ben's transformation would begin in thirty minutes. The redheaded twenty-year-old, her sister/maid of honor, and her mom were helping with the last parts of the wedding dress as the minutes ticked down. Sophia had told her sister, mom, and dad, too, about the life-ending reasons why she and Ben were going back to heaven. The three family members were very grateful that Jesus would spare Ben and Sophia from experiencing death again. However, like the rest of the Lawson family and Diego, they would miss Ben and Sophia. Anyway, Sophia, Alicia, and Candace were in the dressing room opposite Ben, Josh, Diego, Anthony, and Brandon. This dressing room was on the left side of the Fellowship Chapel, which connected to another waiting room. That waiting room faced out towards the back left side of the Fellowship Chapel hall.

Lucy Robinson, Hannah Rine, and one of Sophia's other college friends, Selina Cogle, served as Sophia's bridesmaids. Selina was a nineteen-year-old, five-foot-three-inch Hispanic Christian young woman. She had green eyes and long black hair that reached down to the middle of her back. Selina was also extremely fit. She and the other bridesmaids, along with Sophia's sister/maid of honor, Alicia, were dressed in elegant pink wedding dresses and matching heels. They were talking and hanging out in the adjacent waiting room.

"You know, Mom and Sis, I'm extremely happy that I get to share this moment with you two!" Sophia began as her mom and sister were finishing up the final touch-ups on her white wedding dress. The twenty-year-old was also looking into a big mirror as her mom and sister were helping her. "Even more so, I'm excited that I will spend the next two and some years with Ben! Is it good if I am still a bit nervous now, though?"

"I am so happy that I can be a part of this moment with you, too, my little sweet pea!" Candace responded happily and emotionally as she stopped doing the touch-ups on her daughter's wedding dress for a moment. She was wearing a fancy one-piece light purple dress with matching heels. Sophia's mom sniffled a little bit right before a happy tear started to

2 Hereinafter, brackets added for clarity.

drop down from her left eyelid. "I'm very appreciative that Jesus allowed your sister and me to help you on your big day with Ben. It would have broken our hearts if you had permanently died on the night of January 11th, along with Ben. Anyway, it is perfectly normal that you are feeling a bit nervous right before you and Ben get married. That is to be expected. The nervousness will evaporate and become an overflowing well of joy and happiness once you and him say your 'I do's.'"

"What she said?" Alicia responded funnily before getting sincere. She also stopped touching up Sophia's dress for a minute. "Truly, Sis, it means a lot that I get to help you. I'm so happy and excited that I have shared these moments with you. You chose me to be your maid of honor, and it made me really happy. I know that I, Mom, Dad, Ben, and everyone else will cherish these next two and some years with you. I want you and Ben to take up most of the time with you two doing life and having fun by yourselves, of course. Our families will share a lot of time with you and Ben during this season of life, though."

"What she said as well?" Candace said funnily, all the while showing emotion. Alicia emotionally laughed for a second at her mom's quip.

"Aww...thanks, Mom and Sis," Sophia said sincerely and emotionally. "Don't make me cry. I'm super grateful that you two have gotten to share these special moments with me. I was so blessed by Jesus when He gave me a second chance at life to get married to Ben, share Jesus's messages with everyone whom Ben and I meet, and share these moments with you two and Dad."

"You're welcome, my beautiful daughter," Candace responded with a few happy and joyful tears beginning to streak down her eyes.

"You're welcome, Sis," Alicia said before a happy tear began to form underneath her left eyelid. "I'm always glad to help you and be by your side. I'm going to be with you all the way until you and Ben go back to heaven."

"Awww....you two..." Sophia responded emotionally as two joyful and happy tears slid out of both of her eyes. "I didn't want both of you to make me cry. But, whatever. I love you, Mom and Sis."

"I love you, too, Sis," Alicia said lovingly and emotionally.

"I love you, too, my baby," Candace said equally as lovingly and emotionally as Alicia before the two women gave Sophia a group hug. Sophia fully embraced and hugged her mom and sister. This moment lasted for half a minute or so before Candace and Alicia finished the touch-ups on Sophia's wedding dress. Then, the three women walked out into the next-door waiting room. Sam was in there with Lucy, Hannah, and Selina. He was wearing the same outfit as Ben, Dave, Diego, Josh, Anthony, and Brandon. Of course, Ben and his crew were waiting in the other waiting room.

"Oh my gosh, you look so amazing!" Lucy exclaimed happily, right before going up to and giving Sophia a hug. Sophia completely obliged and hugged her back. Sam was looking at Sophia with happiness, joy, pride, and a touch of nervousness in his eyes and facial expression. She quickly walked up to him after she and Lucy let go of each other.

"Dad!" Sophia exclaimed happily and lovingly before they hugged each other for several seconds. "Thank you for coming in here!"

"You're welcome, sweet pea!" Sam responded lovingly and enthusiastically before they finally separated from each other. "Look at you! You look absolutely beautiful! I know that Ben will think the exact same thing as you and I walk down the aisle together!"

"Thanks, Dad!" Sophia said appreciatively. "I was telling Mom and Alicia that it has been a blessing to have shared all of these recent moments with you three!"

"Definitely!" Sam replied gratefully. "God has really blessed you and Ben and the rest of our family in addition to the rest of the Lawson family."

"That is as true as it comes," Candace responded gratefully and lovingly as she quickly walked up to, hugged, and kissed her husband. "I'm very happy and excited that you chose to come in here with us!"

"Absolutely! I'm also happy and excited that I came in here!" Sam said lovingly and excitedly before he hugged and kissed her as well. Then, he turned his attention to Alicia, Lucy, Hannah, and Selina. The five of them talked for a few minutes and then checked if Sophia needed any touch-ups on her wedding dress. They addressed the few small touch-ups that popped up after Sophia hugged Lucy and her dad. Then, it was fifteen minutes before the wedding ceremony started. Leslie Lawson came into the waiting room where Ben, her husband, Josh, and the others were waiting. She greeted everyone, hugged and kissed Dave, and hugged Ben. Leslie also told Ben about how proud she was of him for the many things that he had overcome. In addition, she told her oldest son about how happy and joyful she was about him and Sophia getting married soon.

Five minutes passed by, and then Leslie, Dave, Ben, and Josh came out of their waiting room and proceeded to get into their positions. Diego, Brandon, and Anthony stayed in the waiting room until the wedding ceremony started. Dave and Leslie sat in the two family-only seats on the far right side in the front row with their parents next to them. Josh made his way down the red-carpeted aisle with Ben, and they went up to the top of the altar together. The Holy Communion Church pastor, Jack Hershel, was right behind and just to Ben's right. Jack was given the honor of marrying Ben and Sophia. The pastor was wearing a white suit, a good-looking gray undershirt, a black tie, white slacks, and white dress shoes. Jack's short, curly brown hair was neatly styled for the wedding ceremony. The ceremony was about to begin in ten minutes. Forty-seven out of the fifty guests had arrived.

The ten minutes passed by in a hurry, and Ben and Sophia's wedding ceremony began. All fifty guests were sitting in their white, hard plastic chairs. The inside of The Fellowship Chapel looked incredible. There were two long brick containers that spread the entire length of the two sides of the inside of the chapel. They were positioned against the inside edges of the building, spreading from the front walls of the waiting rooms to the altar. Each of the two long containers was filled with red, white, and pink roses that were neatly arranged in single-file rows. The inside walls of the Fellowship Chapel were lined with a few long green wreaths. All of the bridesmaids and groomsmen fully took in the surroundings after they exited their waiting rooms and elegantly walked down the aisle and up onto the altar. Each bridesmaid was paired with a groomsman, as in all weddings. Lucy was paired with Brandon. Hannah was paired with Diego. Finally, Selina was paired with Anthony. The ten-year-old flower girl walked to and down the aisle, spreading white rose petals all along the aisle from a round basket. Her name was Olivia, and she was the youngest daughter of Sam's brother and sister-in-law. Olivia was a Hispanic girl with brown eyes and light brown hair that reached the middle of her back.

Sophia O'Donnell and her dad watched all of this unfold right before they walked out of the waiting room. Dave, Leslie, their parents, and the rest of the guests stood up and watched as the bride, Sophia, and her father made their way to and down the aisle. Sam was holding his daughter's left hand as they were walking together. A lot of the guests quietly oohed and awed at Sophia and her wedding dress. The white dress fit her perfectly and gently flowed down from her body and made a trail behind her that was two or three feet long.

Sophia knew that Ben was attentively looking at her with pure love, amazement, and wonder in his eyes and facial expression. She could see all of that in him as plain as day. The redheaded twenty-year-old knew that Ben was thinking that she looked absolutely beautiful. In addition, Sophia could not see any hint of an expression on his face that told her that he still had any lingering memory of their first conflict when they first met at Evart University. That certainly was true from Ben's point of view. He did not care about what had transpired when he and Sophia first met and talked. Sophia's rejection of Ben's offer for her to go out with him didn't really exist in Ben's mind anymore. Each step that Sophia took with her dad down the aisle and up onto the altar was a step closer to a happy and joyful future with Ben. Also, each step was a step further away from that controversial first meeting between Ben and Sophia. They were only thinking about the wonderful moments that they had shared with each other ever since they entered into a serious relationship that led to this moment. One thing was for certain: Ben and Sophia were going to have a great marriage before they joyously spent all of eternity with Jesus, the angels, and the other Christians who were in heaven.

"Dearly beloved, we are gathered here today to witness the covenant relationship of marriage between Ben Lawson and Sophia O'Donnell," Pastor Jack Hershel addressed the crowd after Sophia made it up to the altar.

Sophia's dad lifted up the veil on her face and put it over her head before he went back to where his wife and Alicia were sitting. Now, she was standing face-to-face with Ben.

Pastor Hershel went through all of the marriage discourse. Ben and Sophia patiently waited through all of it. The wait was nothing compared to them waiting for this day. Nobody in the crowd objected to the two young people getting married. Then, the pastor got to the "I do" part of the marriage discourse.

"Ben," Jack said before continuing, "do you promise to love and cherish Sophia as your lawfully wedded wife for better or for worse, for richer or poorer, in sickness or health until death do you part?"

"I do," Ben said confidently and lovingly to Sophia while glancing at Jack. "I, Ben, promise to love and cherish Sophia as my lawfully wedded wife for better or for worse, for richer or for poorer, in sickness and in health until death do I part." The black-haired teen was thinking about the irony of him and Sophia getting shot and dying on the night of January 11th. Those events and all of the amazing and wonderful events and moments that followed them were shaping up to be a beautiful symphony orchestrated by Jesus. Ben and Sophia were always meant to get married, even with all of the tragedies and conflicts in their life journeys.

"All right," Jack said before switching his attention to Sophia. "Sophia, do you promise to love and cherish Ben as your lawfully wedded husband for better or for worse, for richer or for poorer, in sickness or in health until death do you part?"

"I do," Sophia said equally as confidently and lovingly to Ben as he said to her while glancing at Jack. "I, Sophia, promise to love and cherish Ben as my lawfully wedded husband for better or for worse, for richer or for poorer, in sickness and in health until death do I part." She was also thinking about the irony of her and Ben getting shot. Jesus indeed orchestrated a heavenly romance between them.

"All right," Jack began, "now you and Ben can put on your wedding rings. Josh, you can give them the rings."

"Coming right up," Josh said quietly. He came up from behind and to the left of Ben and handed him and Sophia their wedding rings. Ben put one of the rings on Sophia's ring finger on her right hand, and Sophia put the other one on Ben's ring finger on his right hand. Then, they signed the marriage papers.

"Nice exchange. We're all good now," Jack said quietly to Ben and Sophia before addressing them and the crowd. "Now, by the power of God first and foremost and then the power invested in me by God, I pronounce you two husband and wife. You may kiss the bride."

That special moment finally came. Ben leaned forward to kiss Sophia. The kiss felt unique for the newlyweds because of the moment. All of the previous kisses were on the lips, just like the kiss that they were now sharing for a second. However, this kiss felt more passionate than the other kisses that Ben and Sophia shared together. In addition, this unique kiss was more meaningful on a higher level. All fifty guests stood up, cheered, and clapped their hands. Then, Pastor Hershel closed out the wedding ceremony. It was official: Ben and Sophia were married. The other fun part of the day was going to be the reception, which was going to be in a half hour. However, Ben and Sophia were going to have several pictures taken of them, their families, friends, and a few of the guests just outside the Fellowship Chapel on a neatly lawned area of grass. They were also going to have some more pictures taken of all of them by the river at Crystal Park.

It was approximately 5:45 p.m. when the reception began. Ben and Sophia Lawson made their dramatic entrance into the wooden building at Crystal Park. They had the introductory song to *Smallville*, "Save Me," play from one minute into the song for thirty-four or so seconds. Sophia and her husband timed their entrance perfectly as the song was being played on an overhead speaker inside the wooden building. The announcer declared Ben and Sophia as Mr. and Mrs. Lawson as they entered the building. Then, the dinner of grilled chicken, rice, and asparagus was passed around to Ben, Sophia, and the fifty guests. Dave Lawson said grace on a microphone before everyone started eating. He was sitting with Leslie, Josh, Ben, Sophia, Sam, Candace, and Alicia at one of the white cloth-covered round tables. Diego, Brandon, Anthony, Hannah, Lucy, and Selina were sitting at a table next to them. Dave, Leslie, Josh, Diego, Brandon, Sam, Candice, and Alicia stood up at various times a little while into dinner time to deliver speeches to the bride and bridegroom. Ben's parents were the first ones to do their speech.

"Ladies and gentlemen..." Dave began after clinking his nonalcoholic sparkling cider glass with his fork. Leslie stood up at the same time as her husband. Then, Dave continued to speak for a minute. "My wife and I just want to raise a toast and say some things about Ben and Sophia. To start with, we are so proud that you two, Ben and Sophia, chose to embark on this marriage journey. We know that God has His favor on you two. Ben and Sophia are two great and godly people. Our son has grown into an amazing young man of God. My wife and

I were honored to raise and teach him. We know and believe that Ben will be a great husband to Sophia."

"Absolutely," Leslie continued after Dave had stopped speaking for half of a second. Then, she continued on speaking about Ben and Sophia in front of the crowd. "We are so happy for our oldest son and his wife! These two have grown into amazing young adults who love God! It was an incredible privilege to raise my son with my husband to become the great young man he is now! Ben and Sophia have been through long and tiring life journeys that have also been really interesting. You all can ask them about that part. It will blow your minds. Anyway, my husband and I know and believe that Ben and Sophia will have an amazing marriage. A toast to the bride and bridegroom!"

All of the guests raised their sparkling cider glasses and made a toast to Ben and Sophia. Then, all fifty of the guests drank a sip of the drink from their glasses. Ben and Sophia expressed their thanks for Ben's parents' very nice, meaningful, and kind words after Dave and Leslie sat back down. Josh was the next person to stand up and deliver his speech to his brother and Sophia ten or so minutes later.

"Ladies and gentlemen..." Josh started before continuing. He had also clinked his sparkling cider glass with his fork. "I want to raise another toast to my brother and his wife, Sophia, and say a few more things about them. First of all, I want to say that I am extremely proud of them for choosing to get married. Ben and Sophia are two of the people who I really look up to. I'm also very proud of how they have overcome all of the hardships in their lives, with God helping them each step of the way. As my mother said, you all should really ask my brother and Sophia about the interesting things they have experienced. They have wildly amazing stories to tell you all. A toast to the bride and bridegroom!"

The rest of the guests raised their sparkling cider glasses and made another toast to Ben and Sophia. Then, they drank another sip of the sparkling cider from their glasses before Josh sat back down. Ben and his wife thanked Josh for the very meaningful things that he said about them. Brandon stood up about fifteen minutes later to deliver his speech to Ben and Sophia and to raise a toast to them.

"Ladies and gentlemen," Brandon started before continuing, "I want to raise another toast to Ben and Sophia and say some more things about them. First of all, I want to say that I'm proud that they made this choice to get married. God definitely guided them to this point. I want to say this next thing to Sophia. Sophia, you are in for a ton of fun, as you have probably already learned a bit. This guy you just married knows how to go on trips and vacations. Just ask him about the time that our high school church youth group and I went on the trip to Dolaris Beach and the amusement park next to it in northern Michigan during sophomore year. Ben is the master at knowing how to visit places and do all of the things that you want to do and relax at the same time. Finally, I just want to say to you two, in front of these guests, that I know you two will have a richly blessed marriage by God. A toast to the bride and bridegroom!"

All of the guests repeated the same thing by raising their sparkling cider glasses in a toast to Ben and Sophia and drank a sip from each of their glasses. Brandon sat back down, and Ben and Sophia expressed their thanks for his nice, fun, and meaningful speech about them. Diego was the next person to make a speech to Ben and Sophia and say some more things about them in front of the other guests five minutes later.

"Ladies and gentlemen," Diego began, "I want to make a toast to Ben and Sophia and say a few more things about them. They have been through some rough hardships in their lives, but God has seen them through all those hardships. God meant to bring Ben and Sophia together, and this moment tonight is the culmination of all that led them here. However, the journey doesn't stop here. I also know and believe that these two people will have a great and beautiful marriage that was orchestrated by God. A toast to the bride and bridegroom!"

Diego and the rest of the guests repeated the same action as in the other toasts. Ben and Sophia thanked Diego for his very meaningful and kind words after he sat back down. Sam and Candace O'Donnell were the next people to deliver their speeches to their daughter and Ben. Sam sniffled one time once he stood up. Candace wiped a happy tear from her left eye before she stood up with her husband.

"Ladies and gentlemen," Sam said as he recomposed himself, "my wife and I want to raise another toast to my daughter and her husband and say several things about them. To start with, we want to say to my daughter that it was an absolute pleasure and honor to help raise you to be the amazing and godly young woman you are now. Your mother and I absolutely know and believe, without a shadow of a doubt, that you and Ben will have an abundantly blessed marriage by God. Ben, I'm happy and proud to call you my son-in-law. Our daughter is very lucky to have you as her husband."

"You are definitely extremely lucky to be Sophia's husband, Ben," Candace said as she was fighting back tears in her eyes. Sam had given her a slight pause to let her know that she could finish their speech. Candace would get more emotional as she continued on speaking. "Sophia, it was an absolute joy to raise you with your father. You are the most kind and compassionate person I know. Time has definitely flown by incredibly fast. I fully enjoyed all the times I have spent with you, your dad, your sister, and your friends. You pack a mean punch when you hit the ball during our volleyball games. I know that you and Ben will have a fun, beautiful, and amazing marriage. A toast to the bride and bridegroom!"

Candace, her husband, and the rest of the guests repeated the same actions as in the other toasts. Then, Sam and Candace sat down. Ben and Sophia expressed their thanks for the heartfelt and kind words that Sophia's parents said about them. Nearly all of the guests were done with dinner by now. Alicia was the last person to give her speech to her sister and Ben before the wedding cake slices were handed out.

"Ladies and gentlemen," Alicia began, "I want to give one last toast to my sister and her husband and say some things about them. They are truly remarkable people, especially considering all of what they have been through. If it hasn't been said enough tonight, you all really should ask Ben and Sophia about the things that they have experienced. There are several parts of their stories that are amazing. Those parts are not about the hardships that Ben and Sophia have experienced. The hardships that they have experienced have only made them stronger. God certainly knew how to work all of it out for their good. I mean, look! My sister and her husband are extremely happy that they are together! They are two of the people I really look up to. I know and believe that Ben and Sophia will have a greatly blessed and happy marriage, which God orchestrated from the start of their life journeys. A toast to the bride and bridegroom!"

Alicia and the rest of the guests raised a toast to Ben and Sophia. Then, Sophia and her husband thanked Alicia for the very nice and meaningful things she said about them. Ben and Sophia took turns feeding a few bites of cake to each other from their plates. Then, the fifty guests were each served one slice of the rest of the wedding cake.

The father and daughter dance started about ten minutes after everyone fully enjoyed eating their slices of the wedding cake. Sam and Sophia danced to a slow, meaningful, fun, and heartfelt song that was picked by the DJ. They completely soaked in all of the emotions that came with it. Then, it was time for the mother and son dance. Leslie and Ben walked onto the dance floor and danced to a different song that was a bit similar to the song for the father and daughter dance. Leslie was more emotional dancing with her son than Sam was when he danced with his daughter. Ben's mom had a couple of happy and sad tears that had found their way down her face. All in all, the mother and son dance was very nice for the two of them. Leslie and her son fully took in all of the emotions that came with the dance. Then, Ben, Sophia, the bridesmaids, and the groomsmen got onto the dance floor and danced to a fun and upbeat song.

The DJ took a few minute break after the fun and upbeat song to allow Ben and Sophia to gather all of the single young men, single young women, the bridesmaids, and the groomsmen on the dance floor. Ben and Sophia proceeded to throw two bouquets of flowers behind their backs and then see which young man and young woman caught the bouquets. The activities, of course, tried to hint at which young man and young woman would get married next. Hannah Rine ended up catching the bouquet that Sophia threw behind her back into the group of young women. Then, Brandon Heraldez caught the bouquet that Ben threw behind his back into the group of young men. Hannah and Brandon locked eyes with each other for a second after these activities, and there could only be one thing that could be said. They were going to test out that next marriage theory by talking to each other and starting out as friends. The rest of it would take care of itself. Hannah and Brandon were indeed going to talk with each other and start out as friends. Brandon came up to Hannah, introduced himself, and asked if they could hang out as friends sometime. Hannah said yes and gave her phone number to Brandon. They would figure out all of the other details at a later time. This night belonged to Ben and Sophia.

This next part of the night was a free-for-all dance party. All of the guests were invited onto the dance floor by the DJ. A lot of fun, upbeat, and jazzy songs were played. Diego Sanchez ended up dancing with Vanessa Lopez, the young woman he was talking to and hanging out with. He had requested from Ben and Sophia that Vanessa be his plus one. Vanessa was also at the wedding ceremony, and she was okay with Diego being paired with Hannah for the introductory part of the ceremony. Vanessa was a five-foot-six-inch Mexican/Hispanic young woman with brown eyes and shoulder-length black hair. She was twenty years old, and she was mostly physically fit. Selina Cogle had found a different young man to dance with during the reception.

Ben and Sophia had a blast dancing with each other. Sam O'Donnell took Sophia for a song or two to dance with her, which Ben was totally good with. Candace did the same thing with her daughter for one song. Then, Ben and Sophia danced away to the rest of the songs with each other, lovingly gazing into each other's eyes. The young married couple only stopped dancing when some guests pulled them aside and asked them about their stories. Ben and Sophia told the guests a shortened version of the amazing things in their stories after the parts about them getting shot. The guests were completely baffled and amazed at Ben and Sophia's stories. Sophia and her husband made sure to tell Jesus's messages to the guests, and the guests were grateful for Jesus's messages. Then, those people let Ben and Sophia get back to dancing with each other.

Josh Lawson mingled around on the dance floor, dancing with a couple of young women for three songs. However, he didn't feel at home with the two young women. Josh left them and wandered around the dance floor for a couple of minutes until he found Alicia O'Donnell. He felt more attracted to her than the other two young women. Alicia was just watching everyone dance while she watched on the right sideline. Josh came up to her, introduced himself as Ben's brother, and asked if she wanted to dance. Alicia said yes, even though she was slightly nervous. Then, she loosened up and had fun dancing with Josh. Alicia didn't know what it was, but she felt safe and happy dancing with Ben's brother. Josh's experience dancing with Sophia's sister was one of the most exciting things he had done in his life. Then, it got more exciting and fun at the end of the dance party, where there were slower songs. Everybody, including Josh and Alicia, fully but appropriately enjoyed the three songs they slowly danced to. Josh could feel that there was more to be had with him and Alicia at a later time. Tonight was a celebration of Ben and Sophia's marriage.

It was almost 10:00 p.m. when the dance party was done. The reception was drawing to a close. The final event of the night was that all of the guests would make two lines that formed a tunnel on the grass outside of the wooden building. The guest tunnel ran alongside the river. Each guest was given a sparkler stick, and then Sam O'Donnell lit every one of them, including his own sparkler stick. Then, Ben and Sophia dramatically and happily walked through the guest tunnel that had a sparkling line of light on the two sides of the tunnel. Ben and his wife made their way through the grass and onto the parking lot. Sophia's red Lexus was waiting for her and Ben on the near side of the parking lot. The redhead insisted on driving the two of them to the cheaper of the two apartments that they signed a two-and-a-half-year lease for two days ago. Ben said yes, but he also said that he would work on his driving skills to be able to drive her and himself to work and events.

The fifty guests gathered near Sophia's Lexus and waved goodbye to her and Ben as she started up the car. Ben and Sophia waved back to the guests, especially their parents and siblings, as they drove away from the parking space and out of the parking lot. Dave, Leslie, Josh, Sam, Candace, and Alicia were doing their absolute best to hold back their inner emotions, but a little bit of their emotions slipped out in the form of one or two happy and sad tears from each person. They were still really happy for Ben and Sophia, just like the rest of the guests. The newlyweds' parents, Diego Sanchez, Brandon Heraldez, Anthony Markus, and Hannah Rine kept waving to the young married couple, even as Sophia's red Lexus shrank to a red dot on the concrete streets. The reception ended after Ben and Sophia totally disappeared from everyone's sight. Then, the announcer, the DJ, and the fifty guests went back to their homes.

It was 10:30 p.m., and Ben and Sophia arrived at the apartment that they were living in for a little over two years. They got their luggage and walked towards their apartment room. The forest green colored outside of the apartments was a nice touch, along with the dark purple colored roofs. Ben and Sophia's apartment room was located inside an apartment building that was closer to the middle of the complex. Sophia and her husband headed inside their first-floor apartment room and began to unpack. They put their room key in a little compartment on top of the dresser along with the piece of paper that had the information Jesus told Ben to write down. The piece of paper also had Jesus's messages on it. The first part of the information was going to save Ben and Sophia's lives on the night of May 13th, 2005.

Once the young married couple left their luggage suitcases inside their bedroom, they got ready for bed. Ben and Sophia were going to enjoy each other's company in their king-sized bed after praying to and worshiping God. They already had the king-sized bed moved into the bedroom two days ago. The young married couple got rid of the twin-sized bed. Ben and Sophia had figured out how they were going to intimately interact with each other, even with Sophia's shot wound scars and Ben's prosthetic legs. They had talked about it during their time at the USA Fashion and Festivities Mall. The black-haired teen didn't mind his shot wound scars that much, but he took Sophia's thoughts and feelings about her scars into serious consideration and was sensitive to her when interacting with her. Ben would take off his prosthetic legs every night after going onto the bed with Sophia. Then, Ben would put his prosthetic legs back on in the mornings. As for this night, Ben and Sophia completely enjoyed each other's company before falling asleep. They couldn't wait for the adventures that they knew lay ahead of them before they went back to heaven.

CHAPTER 9:

A Time of Pure Joy, Love, and Happiness (Part 1)

Ben and Sophia Lawson felt like they died and went to heaven again, in a good way. However, it was nothing compared to their amazing experiences in heaven after they got shot. The marriage connection that they now shared with each other in every way came as close as anything on Earth to their experiences in heaven. That certainly was true as Ben and Sophia woke up at 9:30 a.m. on Sunday, April 27th, 2003, and lovingly gazed into each other's eyes. This part at the beginning of their first year together as a married couple was definitely a time of pure joy, love, and happiness in addition to the rest of their first year. Both Ben and Sophia had asked God during their times as single people that they would find a person of the opposite sex to have a serious relationship and marriage with. It is written in Philippians 4:6: "Do not be anxious about anything, but in every situation, by prayer and petition, with thanksgiving, present your requests to God." Ben and Sophia had not been too anxious about the desires of their hearts, but they had prayed to God that they would find their spouses sometime soon. Now, they were truly joyful and happy that they ended up as a married couple.

"Good morning, Ben," Sophia said in a loving tone.

"Good morning, Sophia," Ben responded in a loving tone as well.

"Yesterday and last night were amazing with the wedding, reception, and our time here at our apartment," Sophia said in an amazed, relaxed, and loving tone.

"I completely agree with all of that," Ben responded in a similar tone before he and Sophia hugged and kissed each other for several seconds. Then, Ben continued speaking. "Are you ready to get ready to go to church together at Holy Communion Church and prepare for our weeklong honeymoon in San Diego?"

"Absolutely! I can't wait!" Sophia said excitedly and lovingly. Sophia and her husband had planned to have their weeklong honeymoon in San Diego, California. Ben and Sophia had already arranged their American Airlines flight to leave that night at 6:45 p.m. for the city in California when they talked about it three weeks ago. Plus, the young married couple had already made an over-the-phone reservation at a reasonably priced hotel, the Marion Hotel, after looking it up online. Their honeymoon was also going to serve as one of their two trips before going back to heaven on May 14th, 2005. The young married couple had already requested and gotten the next work week off from their entry-level job managers. The two of them promised their managers that they would work hard when they got back.

Sophia only got seven days of marital leave/personal time off that year from her counselor aide entry-level job at the True Health Christian Counseling Center, which she and her husband would take full advantage of. She would get another seven days off for personal time the following year. Ben only got seven days off of personal time per year at his entry-level job at Aeromechanics Incorporated. He and his wife would have to make do with the two additional days of personal time that each of them had off after their honeymoon trip this year. They were yet to decide on where they wanted to go for their second trip next year in 2004. For now, the young married couple got out of bed and got dressed for church. They planned on getting two omelets at a Denny's nearby Holy Communion Church before going to the church. Ben and Sophia had decided that Holy Communion Church, which was the church that Sophia attended, would be their home church.

The minutes flew by in a wonderful hurry. One minute, Ben and Sophia got dressed for church. Then, before they knew it, they drove off in Sophia's red Lexus to the Denny's near Holy Communion Church. Ben and Sophia thoroughly enjoyed the bacon, cheddar cheese, and hot sauce-induced omelets that they had for breakfast, along with a cup of coffee for each of them. Ben and Sophia got a few lovely comments from the waitress and several of the other customers about them being married. Finally, the time came for Ben and his wife to drive to the 11:00 a.m. service at Holy Communion Church. They left Denny's at ten forty and had five minutes to spare when they got to the church.

Ben and Sophia found Diego when they came into the church and ended up sitting next to him on the far left side of the church congregation. The worship team came up onto the stage and began the first of four worship songs after an associate pastor welcomed the church congregation and prayed over the service. It was a pure joy for Ben, Sophia, and Diego to worship God together with their arms and hands lifted high. Ben was wearing light blue jeans, a nice solid white polo, and white shoes that had two blue lines on each shoe. Sophia was wearing light blue jeans as well but with a nice solid pink shirt and white and pink shoes. Diego had chosen to wear black jeans, a solid green polo, and black shoes.

Pastor Jack Hershel came up onto the stage, praised God for all that He was doing through the church, and told the congregation to greet people next to them. Then, Jack began the sermon. The sermon was about God wanting to bless His people and take care of them in the covenant relationship that He had with them. In addition, the pastor talked about the fact that God's kindness leads unbelievers to the repentance of their sins. Thus, Jack said that God would invite the newfound believers into the same covenant relationship that He had with the other believers. There were other things that the pastor dove into. Finally, near the end of Jack's sermon, he said that God had a plan to prosper His people and to not harm them, just as it is written in Jeremiah chapter 29, verse 11, even though this Earth was a fallen world because of sin. Pastor Jack Hershel blessed the church congregation before dismissing them around 12:30 p.m.

"Did you and Ben enjoy the service today?" Diego asked Sophia after they and Ben started walking out of the church room together.

"Definitely," Ben and Sophia responded almost simultaneously.

"It just comes to show that Jesus/God always has the best intentions for our lives despite this fallen world and the sinful acts that people commit," Sophia continued speaking. "Look at me and Ben! God blessed us with the covenant relationship of marriage even after all of the craziness Ben and I have been through! Then, we will get to spend eternity with God, the angels, and the other Christians who are in heaven when we go back there in 2005."

"Amen to that!" Ben said gratefully to Sophia before continuing. "I'm truly grateful that Jesus gave you and me a second chance at life to not only share His messages with everyone we meet but to be married as well!"

"Certainly!" Diego said in an amazed tone. "It has been great to watch this awesome story unfold for you two! On a bit of a different note, I have a surprise for you, Ben, if you and Sophia want to swing by my apartment for a minute."

"Absolutely, man!" Ben responded excitedly. "I can't wait to see what my surprise is! Thanks in advance!"

"You're welcome, my good friend!" Diego said before he patted Ben on his right shoulder. "I think both you and Sophia will enjoy it. I will meet you two at my apartment."

"Sounds good, Diego!" Ben responded. "See you again soon."

"For sure!" Sophia said excitedly. "I can't wait to see what Ben's surprise is as well! See you again soon, Diego."

"See you soon again, Sophia. Same to you, Ben," Diego responded kindly before exiting Holy Communion Church and going to his car. Ben and Sophia followed suit as they walked out of the church and towards Sophia's red Lexus. It took the young married couple and Diego about fifteen minutes to drive to Diego's apartment. The thing that Ben and Sophia saw in the parking lot took their breaths away.

"No way! Is this what I think it is?" Ben excitedly asked after he and Sophia got out of Sophia's car. Diego was already on the left side of the electric blue Ford truck that was parked next to his sleek dark blue Honda. Sophia was also excited.

"Yes, it is what you think!" Diego exclaimed excitedly before continuing. "This is my other wedding gift to you and Sophia! This truck is mainly for you to get to and from work, Ben, but you and Sophia can share it. Congrats again on getting married, you two!"

"Wow! Thanks, Diego!" Ben said in a super excited voice. "You didn't have to do this. I....I don't know what else to say! This is great! Thanks again!"

"Oh my gosh, Diego!" Sophia began. "It's wonderful! Thanks for buying this for us!"

"You and Ben are absolutely welcome!" Diego responded.

"How did you get it?" Ben excitedly asked.

"Well, I talked with your parents nearly three weeks ago and asked about your experiences with them before you lost your legs," Diego replied before continuing to speak. "Your parents said they were heartbroken, as you well know, when they, you, and Josh heard the news from your doctor that your legs would have to be amputated. Dave and Leslie had saved enough money to buy you an electric blue Ford truck, but they had to spend that money to get the van that you currently have. Plus, they were already busy paying for Josh's high school tuition. So, an idea hatched in my head after I saw that your parents had gotten you a pair of prosthetic legs three days before your and Sophia's wedding. I wanted to get you the electric blue Ford truck that you always wanted, and I did exactly that. I went to a nearby car dealership and earnestly searched for that specific truck, and, certainly enough, I found one. The car dealer came to me and asked if I wanted to buy it. I said I wanted to buy it and that I just had to get the cash for it. I don't like to pay for cars and other big things with my checking account and credit cards. Anyway, I drove to the bank to get enough money from my savings and checking accounts to buy the truck. My savings account was completely drained, and I had to withdraw a good amount of money from my checking account, but it was totally worth it. So, I've had the electric blue Ford truck for almost three days now, excitedly waiting to give it to you and Sophia. I hope you both enjoy it! It was the least I could do with everything that has happened with you and Sophia."

"Man, you are the best!" Ben excitedly exclaimed before he came in for a friend hug with Diego. Diego accepted the gesture, hugged Ben back, and patted him on his left shoulder. Then, Ben continued speaking after he and his friend let go of each other after a second. "I can't believe you did this! Thank you again! Sophia and I will take great care of it."

"Absolutely!" Sophia said with excitement in her voice. "It was so generous of you to buy the truck for Ben and me! Thank you again, Diego!"

"You're very welcome again, you two!" Diego responded to both of them before focusing all of his attention on Sophia. "I'm glad that you and Ben really like it!"

"Yeah!" Ben said before changing the subject. "Well, we can have lunch together at a nearby Eegee's if you two want. How does that sound, Sophia?"

"Sounds fun," Sophia responded gladly.

"What about you, Diego?" Ben asked.

"I'm down for that," Diego said assuredly. "By the way, are you and Sophia ready to go for your flight to San Diego tonight? I remember that you two told me and both of your families about that honeymoon plan two days ago."

"Yep," Ben responded confidently, "we are all packed up and ready to go. Sophia and I didn't need to unpack our things when we got to our apartment last night."

"Yeah, we are just using up our time before we have to head to Evart International Airport," Sophia said confidently as well before letting excitement creep into her tone. "The trip is going to be a blast!"

"Definitely!" Ben said excitedly and lovingly to Sophia before the two of them gave each other a side hug.

"I'm happy for you two!" Diego responded with gladness and excitement in his tone. "I know that the trip will be a trip to remember. It's bound to be fun!"

"For sure!" Ben said with excitement still in his voice. Then, he asked Diego a question. "Diego, do you mind if Sophia and I spend quality time together at our apartment after the three of us get lunch?"

"Absolutely. Don't feel like you and Sophia have to have lunch with me at Eegee's," Diego replied reassuringly.

"Okay, thanks," Ben said before requesting a few seconds from Diego to speak with his wife quietly. Then, Ben continued on speaking. "Sophia and I want to get lunch with you at Eegee's. Plus, as a token of our appreciation for you getting us the truck, we would like to pay for your lunch there."

"Definitely," Sophia agreed after Ben spoke to Diego. "Ben and I want to do this for you because of your generous gift. Plus, thanks for understanding that Ben and I want to spend quality time together after the three of us get lunch."

"Thanks, you two! Also, I understand that you and Ben want quality time together before you two go to the airport, Sophia," Diego responded appreciatively and with an understanding tone before focusing his entire attention on Ben. "You and Sophia don't have to do this."

"We insist," Ben said.

"All right, thanks for doing this!" Diego responded.

"Absolutely," Sophia said. "It's our treat to you."

"Okay, it's settled," Ben said assuredly. "If it's all right with you, Sophia, we can drive both of our cars to our apartment, and then we can hop into my new truck and meet Diego at the Eegee's on Piedmont Drive and River Road."

"Sounds like a good plan, my love," Sophia replied happily and lovingly before she gave her husband a front hug and a brief kiss on the lips. Ben hugged and kissed her back for a couple of seconds. Then, Ben and Sophia separated from each other.

"My gosh, you two! Get a room!" Diego responded, poking fun at Ben and Sophia. The three of them laughed for about half a minute before getting into each of their cars. Sophia got into her red Lexus, and Diego got into his dark blue Honda. It was a completely different feeling for Ben as he stepped into his electric blue Ford truck. The teen was taken back to the time when he got into the orange and yellow NASCAR race car with Blake on his seventeenth birthday. It was an incredible feeling for Ben to be able to get into the truck, even with the nuances of his prosthetic legs. However, it took a minute for him to get used to putting his hard plastic feet and shoes onto the brake and gas pedals. As for wearing shoes, Ben wanted to feel a sense of normality even though he had the hard plastic feet. His shoes were smaller and well-fitting to accommodate the difference. He and Sophia proceeded to go off to their apartment to drop off Sophia's Lexus. Diego drove to Eegee's and patiently waited for the young married couple in Ben's electric blue Ford truck to arrive there. Truthfully, just as his truck was both his and Sophia's truck, so Sophia's Lexus was also both her and Ben's Lexus. The young married couple agreed on those things as they drove to Eegee's.

Ben and Sophia bought their and Diego's turkey grinder sandwiches with wheat bread, turkey, mustard, lettuce, house dressing, and pepperoncini. The black-haired teen also got three small fries and three lemon Eegee's drinks for all of them. Then, Ben, Sophia, and Diego sat down at a red square table in the inside corner of the fast-food restaurant. They waited seven or so minutes for their food, talking about Ben and Sophia's honeymoon trip to San Diego and what Diego had planned for the rest of his day and night. The young married couple told the Southern Chilean native that their families, Hannah Rine, and Anthony Markus were meeting them at the airport to say their goodbyes and best wishes. Ben and Sophia said that Diego was more than welcome to come to the airport to also say goodbye and best wishes to them. Diego said he would do that before hanging out with Vanessa at his apartment and watching a show with her, which the two of them had recently planned on doing. Ben and Sophia said that they were happy that Diego was spending more time with Vanessa and asked him about how they were doing. However, before the Southern Chilean had time to think of his answer, the sandwiches, fries, and lemon Eegee's drinks were ready for him, Ben, and Sophia. Ben walked over to the counter, picked up their food, and walked back to the table. The teen prayed over their food and time together before the three of them dove into the sandwiches, fries, and Eegee's drinks.

The young married couple and Diego proceeded to talk about how Diego and Vanessa were doing. The Southern Chilean said that he and Vanessa were doing really well. Diego said that the two of them had met at Holy Communion Church about four months ago. They wanted to start out as friends before entering into a serious relationship that would hopefully lead to marriage. Diego also said he and Vanessa had been going on dates and hanging out at each other's apartments for the past four weeks. Diego told Ben and Sophia that his and Vanessa's dates and hangout times had been going great. However, the six-foot-four-inch Southern Chilean said that Vanessa wanted to take the dating and hanging out process as slow as she and Diego wanted and needed in order to know if God really wanted them to be together. Diego had told Vanessa he was willing to do that. Ben and Sophia were really happy that things were going really well for him and Vanessa. The young married couple also said they would pray that it would be God's will for the two of them to get married someday. Then, Ben, Sophia, and Diego ate the rest of their lunches in silence.

It was about 3:30 p.m. by the time the young married couple and Diego were done eating their lunches and talking inside the Eegee's fast-food restaurant. Ben and Sophia said goodbye to Diego and said that they would see him again at the Evart International Airport at 5:30 p.m. The young married couple wanted to have enough time before their 6:45 p.m. flight to get checked in at the airport, say goodbye to their families, Diego, Hannah, and Anthony, and get on the plane. As for now, Ben and Sophia went back to their apartment on Oakland and 1st Street. Meanwhile, Diego returned to his apartment by Evart University and hung out by himself. Ben and Sophia had fun watching a show together and enjoying each other's company. The time flew by, and the clock struck five o'clock in the late afternoon. Ben and Sophia made sure that they had everything that they needed in the suitcases and plane carry-ons that they were taking. Then, the young married couple carried their suitcases and carry-ons to and inside their electric blue Ford truck. The one other thing that they did was notify the apartment complex manager that they were going to be gone on their honeymoon for a week and that they would be back after that. Then, Ben and Sophia were ready to make their twenty-minute drive to the Evart International Airport.

"Have a blast on your honeymoon trip in San Diego!" Dave Lawson excitedly said to Ben and Sophia in the Evart International Airport waiting room area next to the flight terminal. The young married couple had already gotten checked in. Dave hugged his son and Sophia before continuing to speak. "We will miss you!"

"We all are definitely going to miss you and Ben," Candace O'Donnell said to her daughter and Ben. A couple of happy and sad tears were starting to streak down her face before she hugged the young married couple. "Stay safe, have fun, and take a lot of pictures!"

Ben and Sophia expressed their thanks to Dave and Candace and told them that they would be safe, have fun, and take a lot of pictures with both of their Polaroid cameras. Then, the rest of the Lawson and O'Donnell families, Diego Sanchez, Hannah Rine, and Anthony Markus said their goodbyes and best wishes to the young couple. Ben and Sophia thanked them all for their best wishes and said their goodbyes to them. The digital clock above the flight terminal drew to 6:30 p.m., and everyone could hear the plane engines revving up for the four-and-a-half-hour flight to San Diego. Ben and Sophia waved their final goodbyes to their families, Diego, Hannah, and Anthony before they and the other passengers walked through the terminal and onto the plane.

The American Airlines flight was filled with entertainment, snacks, drinks, and a wonderful view of the countryside and other areas of the states that the passengers were flown over. Ben and Sophia Lawson were having fun listening to music with headphones on their heads and ears, watching a couple of movies, and eating snacks. The only drinks that they drank were water, orange soda, and pink lemonade. The pilots only had to stop in Kansas City to refuel. Ben, Sophia, and the other passengers were allowed to get off the plane for the amount of time that it took for the plane to get refueled. The young married couple had a nice time wandering around the Kansas City International Airport for ten minutes, looking at several of the items that were there. They even saw posters for the football team, the Kansas City Chiefs. Then, Ben, Sophia, and the other passengers that got off the plane got back into it and sat down. The rest of the flight was straightaway to the San Diego International Airport.

It was 8:15 p.m. when Ben, Sophia, and the other passengers got off the plane because San Diego was three hours behind in time compared to Evart. The young married couple got a shuttle that arrived two blocks east from the Marion Hotel. However, Ben and Sophia didn't get checked into the hotel and their hotel room until 9:45 p.m. because the shuttle had arrived fifteen minutes late for their 9:00 p.m. ride. Then, the shuttle took twenty minutes to get to the spot where the driver dropped off Ben, Sophia, and the other riders. Finally, the married couple walked for about ten minutes in the dark, using two flashlights to guide their way to the Marion Hotel. They found the hotel, walked into the front entrance, and checked in at the front desk. Ben and Sophia went to their hotel room on the second floor and ordered two burgers and small fries for dinner via room service. The young married couple ate their dinner, got ready for bed, and worshipped and prayed to God for a few minutes before taking showers in the bathroom. The shower was a walk-in shower. Therefore, Ben had to walk in it with his prosthetic legs, sit on the shower bench, and then take off his prosthetic legs before getting ready for the shower. This process was only a small routine that the teen and his wife had to go through as they got ready for bed each night. The most predominant thoughts the young couple had when they finished their showers and got into bed were about the amazing adventures they were going to embark on during their honeymoon trip.

"Good morning, my love," Ben said lovingly and genuinely as he and Sophia woke up in their comfortable king-sized bed at 9:00 a.m. on Monday, April 28th. The silky white bed-sheets were refreshing to wake up under.

"Good morning, my love," Sophia responded equally as lovingly and genuinely after rolling towards Ben. Then, they hugged and kissed each other for five or so seconds. Sophia continued to speak after she and Ben let go of each other. "I was thinking that we could go to the San Diego Zoo today and spend most of the day there before wrapping the day up with going out to dinner at a nearby Olive Garden. How does that sound?"

"That sounds great!" Ben replied in an excited and relaxed tone. "Then, we can go to Mission Beach tomorrow and just stay there for most of the day as well. The beach is only a ten-minute walk west of our hotel. We can figure out what we will do for dinner that night when the time gets closer. How does that sound?"

"That sounds absolutely fantastic!" Sophia replied in an equally excited and relaxed tone. "The thing is that we will have to rent a beach wheelchair for you because your prosthetic legs can't get sand on them."

"That is true." Ben sighed in slight frustration. He was good with the beach wheelchair action, though. "I feel like Anakin in *Attack of the Clones* when he was telling Padmè about his dislike of sand while they were on Naboo."

"You're too funny!" Sophia laughed. Ben laughed with her at his comment. Then, Sophia got more even-toned and hopeful. "Hey, you know that you are able to do a lot of things with your prosthetic legs, but not everything. I know that it will be a fun adventure with you being in a beach wheelchair on Mission Beach. Just take it as it is and make the best of it."

"I know that," Ben responded in a positive and hopeful tone. "It is a bit disappointing that I don't have my regular legs to walk on Mission Beach and play in the sand and ocean with you. However, I know that we will come up with fun ways to interact with each other on the beach while I'm in the beach wheelchair. I can wheel myself along the shoreline as the waves come up to us. You can do a fast walk or slow run beside me while I wheel myself in the beach wheelchair. As for my speed, it depends on how fast I can go while moving those big beach wheelchair wheels. It's totally fine if we don't go at a relatively fast speed. The thing that matters is that we do it together. It will be exciting, considering all of what we have been through. I think that a movie should have a scene in which someone is excitedly running along the shoreline of a beach. Who knows, maybe there is a movie that has that type of scene in it."

"Now, there is the Ben I married," Sophia responded gladly and lovingly. "You always find a way to enjoy life even when some things are not in it. That's one of the many reasons why I love you. Plus, I'm sure that there is a movie that has a scene with a person or two excitedly running along the beach. We just haven't seen it yet."

"Thanks, Sophia," Ben replied gratefully. "I credit God and my parents for teaching me that lesson. That certainly wasn't the case when I just lost my legs to the stupid Ewing sarcoma. However, God, Diego, and my parents really brought me through that season of my life. I will never not adhere to that lesson God and my parents taught me ever again. I have an amazing and beautiful wife, an amazing relationship with Jesus/God, a great family, and great friends."

"Awww...that's great to hear!" Sophia happily and lovingly responded. "I'm also happy you think I'm amazing and beautiful!"

"I meant every word," Ben said lovingly and genuinely. Then, he and Sophia hugged and kissed each other for almost ten seconds before they worshiped and prayed to God for a few minutes and got ready for their fun day.

It was about 10:00 a.m. when Ben and Sophia got breakfast from a restaurant called Nelly's Breakfast Diner, which was only a five-minute walk west of the hotel where they were staying. Ben was wearing his *Star Wars: A New Hope* T-shirt, well-fitting dark blue jeans, and dark blue shoes. Sophia had chosen to put on a white T-shirt, well-fitting light blue jeans, and white shoes. The young married couple searched the Internet on Sophia's laptop for a shuttle to get them to the San Diego Zoo. That was what they did. The zoo was a twenty-five-minute drive from the diner that they were at. Ben and Sophia rode to the zoo with the other riders on the shuttle at 11:00 a.m. after it arrived at a block near Nelly's Breakfast Diner. The young couple had made sure to have both of their Polaroid cameras to take pictures of themselves and the animals at the San Diego Zoo in addition to their wallets, laptops, backpacks, sunscreen bottles, phones, and plenty of water bottles. Ben and his wife enjoyed looking at the scenery as they rode on the shuttle. Then, they and the other riders arrived at the zoo.

Ben and Sophia walked out of the shuttle and went towards the ticket booth to buy their ticket passes and one of the maps of the zoo. Sophia grabbed the map after her husband paid for their ticket passes and the map. Then, the two of them entered the large zoo. The young married couple began their sightseeing tour by visiting the tiger exhibit cage. It was twenty-nine feet in front and to the right of the ticket booth. Ben and Sophia planned on taking at least one picture in front of the tiger exhibit cage and every other animal exhibit cage. As for now, the young married couple was staring at the beautiful orange and black stripes on the two tigers that were in the exhibit cage. They did this for several minutes before taking a picture in front of the tigers with Sophia's Polaroid camera.

Sophia and her husband walked seven or so feet more in front of them and to the right of the tigers. They came upon the monkey exhibit cage with four orangutans. The young married couple took less time looking at and taking a picture with the monkeys with Ben's Polaroid camera. Ben and Sophia were off to the lion exhibit cage that was in front and to the right of the monkey exhibit cage. The two of them gazed upon the amazing features of the two lions and two lionesses that were there. Ben and his wife were reminded of the Bible Scripture that describes Jesus/God as the Lion of Judah. They spent about twelve minutes at the lion exhibit cage before taking a picture with Ben's Polaroid camera and heading off to see the next set of animals.

Ben and Sophia walked towards the panda bear exhibit cage and stayed there for fifteen to twenty minutes. There was one long blue bench that ran along the right side of the inside of the exhibit cage. A larger and longer rock overhang covered the young married couple and the other people who were there. Ben and Sophia oohed and awed at the two panda bears that were walking in the exhibit cage, stepping over and between grass, dirt, bushes, and bamboo tree branches. They saw the two animals climb up a few short trees to eat some leaves on a couple of branches. The young married couple was surprised at how green the grass, bushes, and leaves were inside the panda bear exhibit cage. Then, Ben and his wife took a picture in front of the two panda bears with Sophia's Polaroid camera.

Sophia and her husband wandered around the San Diego Zoo and saw a variety of other animals. The animals ranged from giraffes, elephants, and rhinoceroses to otters, flamingoes, and other types of birds. Ben and Sophia made sure to drink plenty of water and take breaks, which included bathroom breaks. During some of the breaks in which the young married couple stopped walking and sat down on nearby benches, the two of them reflected on the fun times they were having. The two of them made sure to revisit the lions, lionesses, tigers, and panda bears near the end of their time at the San Diego Zoo. Then, Ben and his wife, along with the other people at the zoo, had to leave at 4:30 p.m. This was because 4:30 p.m. was when the zookeepers started feeding dinner to the animals.

The young couple walked out of the zoo and sat down on a nearby bench. Sophia pulled out her laptop and started looking for a shuttle that would take her and Ben to an Olive Garden restaurant that was relatively close to their hotel. Ben pulled out his laptop and searched for that specific Olive Garden while Sophia was searching for the shuttle. They couldn't rent a car because they had to be twenty-five years old to do that. Anyway, Ben and Sophia found the respective items they were looking for, and each person paid for the item that they found. The shuttle was going to arrive one block west from the San Diego Zoo at 5:15 p.m. On the other hand, Ben had found an Olive Garden that was a five-minute walk away from the hotel, and he had Sophia message the shuttle driver to take them close, if not directly, to the Olive Garden that he found. The black-haired teen had also paid online for a 7:00 p.m. reservation. Ben made that later reservation just in case the shuttle driver was late and if the driver had to drop off some other riders at different locations.

Everything mostly worked out the way that Ben and Sophia had planned. The shuttle driver only had to drop off two other riders at different locations. Ben and Sophia met and talked to the driver, in addition to a few of the other riders, and they told them about Jesus's messages. The driver and the riders were intrigued about what the young married couple told them. These people would ponder what Ben and Sophia said to them when they arrived at their destinations. The young married couple was sure that those people would eventually repent of their sins and come into personal relationships with Jesus. Anyway, Ben and Sophia enjoyed the ride that brought them to a block next to the Olive Garden they planned to go to. They got to the restaurant at 6:35 p.m. with plenty of time left before their 7:00 p.m. reservation that Ben made.

The young married couple thoroughly enjoyed their dinner at Olive Garden after they were seated at a mid-restaurant table at 6:55 p.m. and served dinner at 7:20 p.m. Ben had ordered a chicken parmigiana pasta dish for himself and a chicken Alfredo pasta dish for Sophia, which she wanted. Sophia insisted that she would pay for dessert for the two of them. Ben accepted his wife's offer, and she got herself and Ben a big slice of lemon meringue pie, which was absolutely delicious. Then, at 8:15 p.m., the young married couple paid the dinner and dessert bill and added a twenty-five dollar tip before heading out of the restaurant. Ben and Sophia made their short five-minute walk back to their hotel and hotel room.

It was nearly 8:25 p.m. when the two love birds got inside their hotel room and cuddled up together on the bed after Ben grabbed the TV remote and paper guide for the remote and TV. Once Ben and Sophia figured out how the TV and TV remote worked, they began searching the channel guide for a movie to watch before getting ready for bed later in the night. There were three movies that caught their eyes: *Ocean's Eleven*, *Miss Congeniality*, and *The Count of Monte Cristo*. The young married couple hadn't seen any of them. *Ocean's Eleven* was on channel 36, and it was going to start at 8:45 p.m. *Miss Congeniality* was on channel 38, but it was already a half hour into the movie. *The Count of Monte Cristo* was on channel 42, and it was going to start at the same time as *Ocean's Eleven*. Ben and Sophia were not in the mood to watch *Ocean's Eleven* after reading the synopsis on the TV channel, and they didn't want to jump in the middle of *Miss Congeniality*. That only left *The Count of Monte Cristo*, which starred Jim Caviezel, Guy Pearce, and Dagmara Dominczyk, in addition to the other actors and actresses. Ben and Sophia really liked the synopsis of that movie and decided to watch it when it came on. They didn't care that the movie ended at 11:35 p.m. The young married couple was on a relaxed schedule.

Ben and Sophia made sure to get on channel 42 two minutes before the start time of *The Count of Monte Cristo*. They were not going to miss a second of the movie even though it had commercial breaks throughout it. The start-time came, and the young married couple was already greatly interested in the history storyline that was in text form on the TV screen. Ben and Sophia also made sure to turn on closed captions to see everything that the characters said. As the movie progressed, Sophia and her husband were engrossed in the story of Edmond Dantès and Mercedes.

A while into the movie, the beach scene Ben and Sophia were talking about that morning came on. Edmond had swum to an island that was a couple of miles away from the Château d'If. He woke up on the shoreline of the beach and felt the wet sand beneath his hands. Edmond stood up and gave thanks to the previously deceased priest for his help in escaping the prison. Then, Edmond excitedly ran along the shoreline of the beach, flailing his arms and hands in the air and shouting in pure joy and excitement. Ben and Sophia couldn't believe they finally saw the scene that they were talking about. The young married couple could feel Edmond's excitement and a deep connection to his story. Sophia and her husband held each other a bit more tightly and lovingly as the beach running scene was playing. The two of them kissed each other for a second, not wanting to miss any part of the movie that they had grown extremely attached to on an emotional level. Then, Ben and his wife saw the pirates in the front part of the TV screen. Edmond began to slow down his excited running and came to a complete stop when he saw the pirates. The young couple laughed at that scene, in addition to past scenes in the Château d'If with Edmond and the priest. Ben and Sophia agreed that the movie incorporated good, comical scenes in it. The two of them laughed during other particular future scenes in the movie.

Ben and his wife thoroughly enjoyed all of what happened during the rest of the movie. The young married couple thought it was fitting to show the message on the one wall of Edmond's former prison cell before the movie credits began rolling. Ben and his wife got emotional and talked about how great the movie was, especially in relation to their lives. Then, they turned off the TV, got ready for bed, prayed to and worshiped God, and enjoyed each other's company on the bed before falling asleep. Tomorrow would be a blast for the young married couple as they hung out on Mission Beach.

Tuesday morning came, and another fun adventure lay ahead for Ben and Sophia Lawson. The young married couple woke up at 10:00 a.m., said good morning to each other, worshiped God for a few minutes, and then got ready for the day. Ben was kind of getting used to putting on his prosthetic legs every morning, but it still felt a little weird. Nonetheless, he was super happy and grateful that his parents bought and gave the prosthetic legs to him. Ben always kept the legs next to his side of the bed, lying down flat on the ground.

Ben and Sophia walked out of their hotel room and the hotel itself after getting ready for the day. The teen was wearing a white T-shirt that had several blue and red horizontal stripes, a different pair of dark blue jeans, and a pair of dark blue shoes that had white bottoms on them. Sophia had chosen to wear a light purple T-shirt, a different pair of light blue jeans, and light purple shoes that had white bottoms on them. They went to Nelly's Breakfast Diner for breakfast. The young married couple thought it would be less expensive and somewhat convenient to just get breakfast every day at that restaurant. Ben and his wife had stockpiled a large amount of snacks for their lunches on their honeymoon trip from a store close to their apartment in Evart. The two of them had put a lot of the snacks in the pantry in their hotel room and strategically planned how many snacks they would eat for their lunches every day. Ben and Sophia put the snacks they would eat each day in their backpacks. Money was not an issue because Dave Lawson had completely financed Ben and Sophia's honeymoon trip. Dave had sent enough money into the young married couple's joint checking account before the two of them embarked on their trip. Sophia and her husband were able to receive the money from him because they had set up their joint checking account four days before they got married. Ben and his wife were going to use all of the money in their joint savings account for their second vacation/trip.

Ben bought breakfast for himself and his wife at Nelly's Breakfast Diner. Sophia told her husband she wanted to get blueberry pancakes, scrambled eggs, and a glass of orange juice. He ordered that in addition to chocolate chip pancakes, chicken sausages, and a glass of orange juice for himself. The two of them sat down at a small blue circular table in the middle and to the right of the inside of the restaurant. They had their backpacks, which held their laptops, sunscreen lotion bottles, water bottles, glasses, phones, cameras, four smaller rolls of paper towels in total, Sophia's beach towel, sunglasses, and beach clothes. All of these items were going to be used for Ben and Sophia's time at Mission Beach.

Sophia and her husband fully enjoyed eating their breakfast meals after they were served to them. Then, Ben did some Mission Beach beach wheelchair research on his laptop for himself and called the workers at one of the beach stations before he and Sophia got changed into their beach clothes in the restaurant bathrooms. They had decided to not be in their beach clothes when they were at the restaurant. Plus, Ben and Sophia were going to put their day clothes back on after they were done at the beach for that day.

Ben and Sophia got changed and put on sunscreen lotion in the men's and women's bathrooms, respectively, and then they walked out of Nelly's Breakfast Diner. Sophia was wearing a pink one-piece bathing suit with matching pink sandals, and Ben was wearing a light blue T-shirt and white swimming shorts that had waves on them. The dark-haired teen's black prosthetic legs were showing, but he didn't mind that since he was going to take them off before he got onto the sand and into his beach wheelchair. One of the beach station workers at Mission Beach, Miguel, was going to meet him and his wife just before the sand line began.

It was almost 12:30 p.m. when Ben and Sophia arrived at Mission Beach after changing out to their beach clothes inside the men's and women's bathrooms at Nelly's Breakfast Diner. Miguel, the beach station worker, a six-foot-five-inch thirty-five-year-old Hispanic/Mexican man, got to the young couple. All three people introduced themselves to each other. Miguel had shortly shaved brown hair, a little mustache and goatee, and hazel-green eyes. Plus, he was physically fit. In addition, he was wearing plain red swim shorts and a white shirt. Miguel winced when he saw Ben's prosthetic legs and said that he was deeply sorry for whatever happened to him. Ben appreciated that and told him a one-sentence explanation about the disease that took his legs. Miguel told him how awful that must have been for him. Plus, the Hispanic/Mexican man said he was very proud that Ben was still living life to the fullest.

Ben and Sophia started talking to Miguel about how God wants everyone to have a full and blessed life. The young couple proceeded to tell him about Jesus's/God's messages of love, protection, provision, and the kingdom of God. The thirty-five-year-old was really intrigued by what Ben and Sophia said to him. Then, he said that he would look more into God after he got off of work. Finally, Ben got into the big beach wheelchair, took off his prosthetic legs, and gave them to Miguel to keep safe inside the beach station. Miguel said he would do his absolute best to keep Ben's prosthetic legs safe, and then he went back to the station. Ben strapped himself into the beach wheelchair, and he and Sophia began their fun adventure at Mission Beach.

Ben and his wife began their fun at the beach by just staring out at the Pacific Ocean after Ben wheeled onto the sand in the beach wheelchair. Sophia stood beside him on his right side, sharing in their ocean-gazing experience for the moment. The sight of the Pacific Ocean took their breaths away. Then, after several minutes, the young married couple made their way down the beach. It took Ben longer to wheel himself over the sand with Sophia because of the big beach wheelchair wheels and the sand. Sophia laid down her beach towel on an unoccupied sand area sixteen feet above the shoreline. Then, Sophia and her husband headed down to the shoreline and paused there for a few minutes. They felt like Edmond Dantès as they stared at the ocean, with the waves coming up to them and hitting their legs and feet. The saltwater of the ocean felt slightly cool against their skin. The water would warm up a bit in a month or so since summer was approaching. Ben and Sophia could feel the remnants of the past tension between them at Evart University, them getting shot, and the tense part of their first meeting at the Lawson family house get washed away from their minds and hearts. It was just like the ocean waves taking away the top part of the sand on the shoreline. The two of them began to love each other more as they were holding hands.

The young married couple acted out their version of Edmond Dantès excitedly, running along the beach shoreline. Ben and Sophia were going along the beach shoreline at a relatively fast pace, excitedly shouting into the sky. The black-haired teen found that it was easier to wheel himself because of the wet and smooth sand. Sophia and her husband excitedly ran and shouted for a minute before stopping. They went ten feet above the shoreline so as to not have Ben be swept away by the waves. Then, the young couple hugged each other tightly and lovingly and kissed each other for five or so seconds before they casually headed back to their spot on the beach. They didn't mind that people were looking at their display of love and affection for each other.

Ben and Sophia returned to their spot after going along the beach for several minutes, taking in everything they saw. The black-haired teen wheeled right next to his wife, who was already sitting on her beach towel that had an accurate drawing of a dolphin on it. She also had her sunglasses over her eyes. Ben followed suit and put on his sunglasses. Both of their backpacks were on Sophia's beach towel. They had the two smaller rolls of paper towels in each of their backpacks so as to help clean themselves off after they were done with their time at the beach that day. The young couple would also make sure to drink ample amounts of water and to frequently use the bathrooms on the top of the beach. In addition, Ben and Sophia had some snacks left over from the previous day at the San Diego Zoo that they were going to eat on the beach today. Finally, the two of them would make sure to reapply more sunscreen lotion on themselves every forty-five minutes.

"This is so amazing, Ben!" Sophia exclaimed in excitement after turning her head to the left to look at her husband. Ben was already looking at her. Then, Sophia continued to speak. "I'm so glad that we chose to go here for our honeymoon and first trip together as a married couple!"

"Absolutely, Sophia!" Ben responded with a ton of excitement in his tone before he reached out his right arm to hold the top of his wife's right shoulder. "This was a great choice!"

The young married couple spent the next five hours at Mission Beach. The first hour was filled with Ben and Sophia watching the ocean, completely mesmerized by the beautiful waves that came up and then crashed down on the shoreline. Some of the waves moved up to three feet below where Ben and his wife were. The two of them stayed on their area, which was still sixteen feet above the shoreline. Sophia and her husband tried to catch some of the saltwater that came closer to them, but they were not able to do a lot of that. However, the young married couple took out their Polaroid cameras and took a few pictures of the ocean. A young woman walked by, noticed that they were taking pictures, and offered to take some pictures of the two of them. Ben and Sophia took up the young woman's offer and had her take two pictures of them. The young woman took one picture with each camera. The young married couple thanked her for taking the pictures before she left.

Ben and Sophia moved themselves four feet down the beach when the second hour of the rest of the first day at Mission Beach started. They wanted to feel more of the ocean saltwater against their skin. However, the young married couple didn't want Ben to be carried away by the waves. Sophia and her husband were going to go to the farthest part of the shoreline at the beginning of the third hour so that they could fully immerse themselves in the water as the waves came crashing down on them. The young woman was going to have to keep a firm grip on the back handle of the beach wheelchair that Ben was using when they did that. Ben and Sophia talked about it, and they thought that it would be a fun adventure. As for now, they were completely enjoying being twelve feet above the shoreline, feeling the cool water that the waves brought to them. The water was only reaching just below Sophia's thighs. Sophia made sure to horizontally arrange her dolphin towel so as to not have the waves wet it and try to sweep it away. She was sitting on her towel with her legs in the sand, waiting for the water to wash against them. Ben was a little jealous that his wife was able to do that, but he enjoyed it as the water from several of the waves splashed up in front of him.

The third hour came, and the young couple was ready for their daring and fun adventure of going down to the farthest point of the beach shoreline. Ben wheeled himself down to that point, with Sophia right behind him, ready to grab the back handle at any given moment. They were going to have fun with this, even with Ben not being able to have his prosthetic legs on the beach and in the water. Ben and Sophia excitedly prepared themselves for the barrage of waves from the ocean that would somewhat soak them.

One middle-aged, fit, six-foot-three-inch White man watched the young couple twenty-five feet away on the left side of them as they embarked on their fun and daring adventure. The man's name was Michael Alans, and he had short blonde hair and hazel-green eyes. He was with his wife and three children. Ben and Sophia were ecstatically enjoying a few waves as they fell on them at this point. Sophia was tightly holding onto the back handle of the beach wheelchair that her husband was using. Once Michael saw that Ben did not have any legs, he had compassion on him. Plus, the middle-aged man was proud that the teen was enjoying life to the fullest, even with his situation, which was what Miguel had thought as well. Michael wanted to help the young woman, who he thought was Ben's friend or girlfriend at that time. He asked his wife, Abigail, if it was all right if he came over to the two people and helped them out for a little while. Abigail was a mostly fit, five-foot-six-inch, middle-aged White woman who had shoulder-length black hair and green eyes. She said that her husband could help out the young couple for a while. Abigail understood the reasons why Michael wanted to help the young married couple when she saw the situation.

Sophia was having a little trouble firmly holding the back handle of the beach wheelchair that Ben was using as the waves forcefully crashed down on the two of them on the edge of the shoreline. However, the young married couple was still having a blast, feeling the ocean waves on a good portion of their bodies. They were shouting in excitement as the water hit and splashed on them. Sophia's arms were getting tired of holding the back handle of her husband's beach wheelchair after five minutes. She and Ben talked about the situation and were about to go back to their spot farther up the beach. Then, Michael Alans approached them and introduced himself. He said that he noticed their situation. Ben and his wife appreciated that and introduced themselves to Michael before he continued on speaking. He said that he wanted to help hold Ben's beach wheelchair for Sophia and have her take a break so that she could go farther into the ocean if she wanted to do that. Ben and Sophia greatly appreciated and took Michael's offer to help.

Michael held the back of Ben's beach wheelchair as Sophia headed farther into the ocean. The teen told Michael how grateful he was for him doing this. The middle-aged man said it was no problem at all and that he was glad to help him and his wife. Michael also said that Ben was really lucky to have Sophia as his wife, and Ben totally agreed with that and said she was amazing. The nineteen-year-old told Michael about what had happened to him in relation to losing his legs. Michael was truly amazed at Ben's story and said that he was truly blessed. In addition, the middle-aged man said he was glad to hear that Ben now had a pair of prosthetic legs to help him walk. Ben completely agreed with him on everything he said. Then, Michael said that he was here at Mission Beach with his wife, Abigail, and their three children. He also said that Abigail had noticed the situation with Ben and Sophia. Ben said that Michael's wife was a great and compassionate woman since she had noticed the situation and allowed her husband to come and help.

Michael thanked Ben for the comment before asking if he would like to go farther into the ocean with Sophia. The teen said yes and thanked him for doing that. Ben and Michael went so far down beyond the shoreline that the waves splashed up and onto most of Ben's body. The teen even had several trickles of saltwater splash into his mouth as he was laughing and talking with his wife, who was just four feet in front of him and Michael. The three of them had a ton of fun playing there for several minutes. Michael had to pull Ben ten feet back every one or two minutes so as to get stabilized again. The middle-aged man would proceed to push Ben to where the two of them were before, behind Sophia. This process stopped and started for fifteen more minutes. Then, Ben and Sophia talked to Michael about the abundant life that God wanted for everyone. The young couple proceeded to tell him about Jesus's messages. In the end, Michael was interested in wanting to know more about God with his wife and children when the five of them got home. He said they were an agnostic family, but they always had friends who talked about God. Michael told Ben and Sophia that their story pushed him over the edge and that he and his family would definitely look more into God.

The middle-aged man thanked the young couple for all of what they said to him. Ben and his wife said that Michael was welcome before thanking him again for helping them out and having fun with them. Michael also told the young couple that they were welcome before heading back to his wife and children. Abigail had a big smile on her face, and she patted her husband's left shoulder before they went back to playing with the kids. Ben and Sophia were confident that Michael and his family would come to know God and have personal relationships with Jesus sometime down the road. Jesus's words to the young couple while each of them was in heaven confirmed that.

The young couple spent the rest of their time on their area of sand, which was twelve feet above the shoreline. Sophia vertically arranged her beach towel so she could lie down and relax as the smooth sound of the ocean waves and air comforted her ears and calmed her mind even more. Ben sat in his big beach wheelchair on the left side of his wife. He completely allowed the sound of the waves crashing on the shoreline to relax his mind. The teen thought about how wide, deep, and great Jesus's/God's love for him and everyone was, just like the unknown depth and width of the Pacific Ocean. Ben and Sophia lovingly held hands as the tide came in a few inches around 4:00 p.m. They enjoyed the water that splashed onto them.

Sophia sat up and dug a medium-sized hole in the sand on the right side of her towel, searching for ocean water. Sophia found the water after digging several inches into the beach sand. She and Ben only had a few minutes before more waves came and deposited sand into the hole. Sophia turned her towel around under her into a horizontal position again so as to not have it get wet by the waves. She didn't cover the hole because she wanted to splash her husband with the water in it. Ben got the idea and knew what was coming. He and Sophia thought it was a nice idea because he couldn't get into the ocean without help. Sophia had fun splashing her husband with the saltwater. The two of them wanted to have more time to do this on a different day during their honeymoon trip. Ben enjoyed playing along with his wife before they had to move up seven feet from where they were on the beach. The tide was coming up farther onto the beach. The young couple spent the rest of their day on Mission Beach, staring out onto the ocean. There were a few barges out in the distance on the ocean. Then, Ben and Sophia packed up their things at 5:00 p.m. and headed back to the beach station to get Ben's prosthetic legs back from Miguel. The teen had dried himself off and got rid of the sand on him with a lot of paper towels from inside his backpack.

"Hey, guys," Miguel said to Ben and Sophia after he saw and came out to them from the garage-like area of the beach station. "Did you two have fun today?"

"Hey, Miguel," Sophia replied. Ben wheeled up next to his wife before she continued speaking. "We had a blast today! We are planning on coming back here two or three more times before the end of Saturday. Ben and I are on our honeymoon trip after we got married this past Saturday."

"Definitely!" Ben began to add. "Sophia and I thoroughly enjoyed every minute of our time here! We are looking forward to coming back here as many times as we can before the end of our honeymoon trip."

"Sweet! I'm glad you and Sophia had a great time today," Miguel responded. "It's even more great that you two chose to come here during your honeymoon trip! Congrats on getting married!"

"Thanks!" Ben and Sophia said almost simultaneously in appreciative tones.

"You two are very welcome!" Miguel replied before switching the subject and turning his full attention to Sophia. "You and your husband are here to pick up his prosthetic legs, if I'm not mistaken. I took great care of Ben's prosthetic legs in our storage area, in which we keep our equipment and things that beachgoers drop off here. Let me get your husband's prosthetic legs. I'll be back in a minute."

"Thank you!" Ben and Sophia responded just before Miguel went to get Ben's prosthetic legs.

"Don't mention it," Miguel said graciously. "It's my pleasure to do this for you two."

Miguel brought Ben's prosthetic legs back to him, and then Ben put them on. The Hispanic/Mexican man thought that it was neat how the teen put his prosthetic legs back on himself. Then, Miguel took the beach wheelchair back and said goodbye to the young married couple. In addition, he said that he wouldn't forget to look up more information about God. Miguel was excited about what he would find. Ben and Sophia were very glad about that, and then they walked over to a little clothes-changing room twenty feet to the right of the beach station to change out of their clothes. They further cleaned themselves off so as to make sure that there was no sand on them. Ben had to be more careful in cleaning and wiping himself off because of his prosthetic legs. He had done a quick check to see if there was any sand in his shorts right before he put on his prosthetic legs. There was a little bit of sand in his shorts that was probably from the ocean waves. The teen was making sure that he had no more sand on him as he cleaned and wiped himself off in one of the small bathrooms with more paper towels that he dampened with the shower hose that was there.

Ben and Sophia proceeded to walk to a nearby Mexican restaurant for dinner. Sophia insisted that she would pay for dinner, and her husband gladly accepted her offer. However, Ben insisted that he would pay for dessert, and his wife happily accepted his offer. The young married couple spent the next two hours eating dinner and dessert and talking with each other about the fun day they had had. Then, they made the journey back east towards The Marion Hotel and walked inside it and towards their hotel room. The two of them had made sure to keep their room key in a small compartment in Sophia's backpack while they were at Mission Beach. Ben and Sophia entered their hotel room, enjoyed each other's company on the king-sized bed, and watched three episodes of a show there. Sophia and her husband now made plans to visit an aquarium the following day, which was called the Sea Trench Aquarium. Ben and his wife proceeded to worship and pray to God for five to seven minutes before getting ready for bed and falling asleep together on their bed. There were still four more days of exciting adventures for the young couple before they flew back to Evart.

"Good morning, my love," Ben Lawson said genuinely and lovingly to his wife after the two of them woke up on their hotel bed at 9:30 a.m. on Wednesday, April 30th. He had turned to the right to face Sophia.

"Good morning, my love," Sophia said equally as genuinely and lovingly to her husband after she turned to the left towards him. She had let out a little giggle as she said good morning to him. "Are you ready for our next adventure at the Sea Trench Aquarium today?"

"Absolutely!" Ben replied enthusiastically. "Let's get up, get breakfast, and head over to the aquarium!"

The young couple proceeded to do their usual things with God before they got ready for the day. Ben and Sophia made sure to bring their laptops in their backpacks in addition to their room key, phones, wallets, cameras, and plenty of water bottles. Then, the two of them walked over to Nelly's Breakfast Diner for breakfast. Sophia was wearing a plain red T-shirt, well-fitting dark blue jean shorts, and dark blue shoes that had white bottoms on them. Ben was wearing a green T-shirt, black jeans, and black shoes. The two of them were both in the mood for bacon, cheese, and hot sauce omelets, which Ben ordered for them. Sophia also had her husband order hash browns, a piece of cinnamon toast, and a glass of apple juice for her. The teen did that in addition to ordering a bagel and a glass of milk for himself after ordering his omelet. Ben and Sophia waited about twenty minutes at a table in the middle of the diner before the waiter brought out their breakfast meals. The young couple prayed over their food and then began to eat it. It was nearly 11:15 a.m. when the two of them finished their meals.

Ben took out his laptop from his backpack, placed it on the table, and then searched for a shuttle to drop them off near the Sea Trench Aquarium. The aquarium was a twenty-five-minute drive east from a block next to Nelly's Breakfast Diner. Once the teen found and paid for a shuttle that would pick him and Sophia up one block east of the diner, he checked to see if the Sea Trench Aquarium allowed visitors to buy passes/tickets online or strictly in person by looking on their website. Ben found that the aquarium only offered passes/tickets to visitors in person, but they accepted debit cards in addition to cash. Sophia had been looking at her husband's laptop all the while he was searching for information about the shuttle and the aquarium, which was totally good with him. He and his wife were one. They made decisions together and always put God in the center of their marriage. Anyway, the young couple started to walk out of Nelly's Breakfast Diner and kept on walking east for one block. Then, they stopped and stood, patiently waiting for the shuttle. It was almost 12:20 p.m. when the shuttle arrived at the block.

Sophia and her husband took in all of the sites as the driver of the shuttle drove them and the other riders to a block near the Sea Trench Aquarium and other places. The young couple didn't talk to any of the other riders for the entirety of the ride. They wanted to sit right next to each other, enjoying every minute of their honeymoon trip. The two of them would meet other shuttle riders and tell them about Jesus's messages within the next three days. As for now, it took them fifty minutes to get to the aquarium. This was because the shuttle driver had to drop off several other riders at various locations before dropping Ben and Sophia off at a block near the Sea Trench Aquarium.

It was almost 1:10 p.m. when the young couple thanked the shuttle driver and walked out and towards the Sea Trench Aquarium. All of the outside walls of the aquarium were an ocean blue color. Two dolphins were painted onto the front of the roof overhang, with each dolphin facing the other. There was a trench in between and below the dolphins. Several different fish were painted on each side of and above the trench. Ben and Sophia approached the ticket/pass handler and paid for their tickets/passes. The aquarium closed at 5:30 p.m. Therefore, the young couple and the rest of the visitors had four hours and twenty minutes to wander around the aquarium.

Ben and his wife entered the Sea Trench Aquarium and gasped at the wide expanse and sites of the place. They felt like they had been swept into a world within their world. There were several huge tubes and rectangular tanks that ran up, on top, and along the inside of the aquarium. The young couple couldn't see an end to the vast number of huge tubes and tanks they saw as they slowly walked through the Sea Trench Aquarium. The building even had a trench forty or so feet inside it, which had a long and wide rectangular tank that had a span of seventy feet. Ben and Sophia first saw a big tank on their right side. The lighting in the aquarium made it feel like they and the other visitors were underwater. As for the big tank, the young couple saw fifteen to twenty catfish, pufferfish, and starfish. There were other various types of fish in the large tubes and tanks as the two of them leisurely made their way through the aquarium. These types of fish included sturgeons, clown fish, parrotfish, and many other colorful fish. Ben and Sophia even saw turtles and a few types of sharks in very large tanks and tubes as well.

The first two hours and fifteen minutes seemed to pass by without Ben and Sophia noticing it. They were having a blast looking at all of the numerous types of sea life in the huge tubes and tanks. The thing was that the young couple walked so slowly and took a lot of water, snacks, and bathroom breaks that they only had walked through three-quarters of the Sea Trench Aquarium. The area of the aquarium was approximately 130,000 square feet. Ben and Sophia were bound and determined to enjoyably see every inch of the aquarium before they and the other visitors had to leave at 5:30 p.m. In addition, the two of them wanted to take several pictures of themselves and the sea life. Finally, they wanted to revisit several of the large tubes and tanks before the closing time. Sophia and her husband really liked the sturgeons, clown fish, catfish, turtles, and puffer fish. They spent the rest of the time doing these things, thoroughly enjoying every minute of them. Then, at 5:20 p.m., it was time for Ben and his wife to walk towards the exit of the Sea Trench Aquarium. A lot of the other visitors followed suit.

Ben and Sophia found a bench several feet outside of the aquarium and sat there for a moment. Sophia took her laptop out of her backpack and searched for a shuttle that would take her and her husband to a block near their hotel. The young married couple had decided that they were just going to order room service for dinner once they got back to their hotel room. That was exactly what they did after Sophia paid for a shuttle that brought them to a block east of their hotel. The shuttle dropped Ben and his wife off at that block around 6:30 p.m.

Ben ordered two chicken pasta dishes for himself and his wife, which they both wanted, on the phone after they got into their hotel room. The two of them ate their dinners when they arrived. Then, they cuddled up together on their bed and watched three episodes of a cop show before they got ready for bed. This process included taking showers and brushing their teeth. The young married couple proceeded to pray to and worship God for several minutes once they got back onto their bed. Ben had done his usual thing of taking off his prosthetic legs after he got onto the bed with his wife. He left his prosthetic legs on the ground next to his side of the bed. It was nearly 11:30 p.m. when Ben and Sophia fell asleep.

Thursday morning came, and the young couple were ready to dive into their adventure for the day. Ben and Sophia said good morning to each other at 9:15 a.m. and then came up with an idea to go to SeaWorld that day. The two of them proceeded to do their things with God before getting ready for the day and heading over to Nelly's Breakfast Diner for breakfast. Sophia was wearing an ocean blue T-shirt that had a mini beach, ocean, and palm trees on it, in addition to light blue jeans and light blue shoes that had white bottoms on them. Her husband had chosen to wear a white T-shirt that had similar things on it as his wife's shirt, in addition to light blue jeans and white shoes. Ben bought two breakfast burritos and two glasses of orange juice for himself and his wife once they got inside the restaurant. They were in the mood to have breakfast burritos. Anyway, the young married couple ate their breakfast meals before starting the process of looking up a shuttle that would take them near SeaWorld.

Sophia took the honors of searching and paying for a shuttle on her laptop. Then, Ben and Sophia exited Nelly's Breakfast Diner and walked west towards the block where the shuttle would pick them up. The shuttle arrived at 11:45 a.m., and it took thirty minutes for the shuttle to head south towards a block near SeaWorld. Ben and his wife met the driver of the shuttle, in addition to a couple of the other riders, and told them about Jesus's messages of love, protection, provision, and the kingdom of God. The driver and riders had similar reactions and responses to everyone else to whom the young married couple told Jesus's messages.

Ben and his wife arrived at SeaWorld at 12:20 p.m. after walking one block from where the shuttle dropped them off. The black-haired teen paid for his and Sophia's passes before officially entering SeaWorld. Sophia and her husband had made sure to put on enough sunscreen lotion since SeaWorld was held in an outside location. They were ready for the cool weather with their backpacks on their backs. The young couple was truly amazed at all of the sights and ocean life that they saw. Ben and Sophia saw the Shamu orca whale and two of her offspring after walking toward the huge open tank that held them. The two of them were completely amazed at the sight of the whales. The black and white colors on their blubber made for a spectacular contrast. Ben and his wife were awestruck at how God wonderfully made the orca whales, just like they thought about the lions in the San Diego Zoo. They made sure to take several pictures of the three sea creatures with both of their Polaroid cameras. The young couple stayed on the left side of the open orca whale tank for fifteen minutes before viewing the sea creatures from a big underground cavern. Sophia and her husband were even more amazed at seeing Shamu and her two offspring swimming in the water. The young couple took two more pictures of the orca whales and remained in the underground cavern for almost twenty minutes, along with a lot of other visitors.

Sophia and her husband continued to walk around SeaWorld's grounds for the next hour. Then, the two of them took a break and sat down on a black bench that was fifteen feet away from the huge, open, ground-level dolphin tank. They were awestruck at the sight of the dolphins as they swam in the tank. Ben and Sophia had this thought in common: *God is an incredible creator!* One dolphin trainer, Rebecca Dillons, noticed that the young couple was staring at the dolphins while she was watching over them. More specifically, Rebecca noticed that Ben had prosthetic legs, and she had compassion for him. Rebecca was a fit, five-foot-seven-inch, middle-aged woman who had blue eyes and shoulder-length dirty blonde hair. She was half White and half Hispanic. The middle-aged woman left her watch post and walked towards Ben and Sophia. Rebecca and the young couple introduced themselves to each other before Rebecca said that she noticed by the very bottom of Ben's jeans that he had prosthetic legs. She also said that she had compassion for him and offered him and his wife to swim with the dolphins for half an hour. Ben and Sophia were extremely grateful to Rebecca and took her offer.

The young married couple gave their backpacks to Rebecca to put inside the lifeguard station. Ben and Sophia proceeded to change their clothes in a nearby bathroom and put on dark blue and black swimsuits that Rebecca gave them to borrow. Rebecca notified the other dolphin trainer, Gerard Wilkins, that she gave Ben and Sophia the opportunity to swim with the dolphins for half an hour. The two dolphin trainers were also wearing similar swimsuits to the swimsuits that Rebecca gave to Ben and Sophia to wear. Gerard was good with that and waited for the young married couple to come out of the bathroom. He was a fit, six foot-three-inch, middle-aged African-American man who had thinly shaved dark brown hair and brown eyes. Sophia and her husband walked out of the bathroom and stopped four feet before the edge of the pool. Rebecca and Gerard were there, waiting for them. The young married couple and Gerard introduced themselves to each other. The middle-aged man saw that Ben was wearing his swim shorts when he and his wife were at Mission Beach two days ago. Rebecca and Gerard said they were okay with him wearing the swim shorts. Then, Gerard offered to take his prosthetic legs and put them in a safe place in the lifeguard station in addition to getting him two floating devices for his forearms. The teen obliged and proceeded to sit on the ground with his back towards the tank. He took off his prosthetic legs and gave them to Gerard. Rebecca, Ben, and Sophia patiently waited for Gerard to come back to them after dropping off Ben's prosthetic legs inside the lifeguard station. Then, Ben shuffled around to face the tank and put on the floating devices on both of his forearms. Rebecca and Gerard guided Ben into the large ground-level tank. Sophia proceeded to smoothly slide down into the water by herself.

The young married couple had a complete blast swimming with the dolphins along with Rebecca and Gerard for the next half an hour. Rebecca and Gerard made sure to swim on both sides of Ben to make sure that nothing went wrong. Sophia and her husband swam in between and next to the three dolphins that were in the large tank. The names of the dolphins were Misty, Missy, and Betsy. Ben and his wife both strongly agreed that swimming with the three dolphins was a highlight of their honeymoon trip. The young married couple was amazed at how sleek and smooth the blubber on the dolphins was as they gently ran their hands along them. Ben and Sophia wished that they could swim with Misty, Missy, and Betsy for just a bit longer. Fortunately, their wish was granted after they asked Rebecca and Gerard the question. The two dolphin trainers said the young couple could swim with the dolphins for an extra fifteen minutes. Sophia and her husband were extremely grateful for the additional time, and they said that they wouldn't ask for any more time.

Ben and Sophia made the best of the fifteen extra minutes. They tried their hardest to make the time slow down. The two of them were thoroughly enjoying their time as they swam with the three dolphins. Misty, Missy, and Betsy had gotten equally as fond of the young couple as the young couple had gotten fond of them. Finally, Ben and Sophia's forty-five-minute swim with the dolphins drew to its end. The young couple asked if Rebecca and Gerard would quickly take a picture of them with the three dolphins with each of their Polaroid cameras. Rebecca and Gerard kindly obliged Ben and Sophia's request. Sophia and her husband thanked the two dolphin trainers before they told them that the cameras were in their backpacks. Gerard and Rebecca swam the four feet of distance that was between them and the edge of the tank. Then, they got out of the tank and headed towards the lifeguard post to get the cameras. The two dolphin trainers got the cameras, headed back to the edge of the tank, and took a picture of Ben and Sophia with Misty, Missy, and Betsy. Rebecca and Gerard took one picture with each of the cameras. Ben and Sophia thanked Rebecca and Gerard for taking the pictures. Then, the two middle-aged people set the cameras down ten feet behind the edge of the tank.

Rebecca and Gerard proceeded to help Ben get out of the large tank after Sophia got out of it first. The young couple remained by the edge of the tank as the two dolphin trainers headed back to the lifeguard post to grab four towels for all of them to get dried off with.

Once the four of them were dried off, Gerard went back to the lifeguard post to get Ben's prosthetic legs and backpack, along with Sophia's backpack. The young couple thanked the middle-aged man for doing those things, and then they started talking to him and Rebecca about Jesus's messages. Ben and Sophia made sure to connect their conversation starting points with Jesus's messages, as they usually did with everyone else they met. Gerard and Rebecca knew all the things the young couple was talking about because they were also Christians. The two dolphin trainers waited to reveal that after Ben and his wife were done talking, though.

Once Sophia and her husband were done telling Jesus's messages to Rebecca and Gerard, the two dolphin trainers told them that they greatly appreciated the reaffirming messages and that they were Christians as well. Gerard and Rebecca also said that they attended a nearby church every Sunday. The young married couple was a little surprised, but they had seen different facial complexions on each of Rebecca's and Gerard's faces that told them what they needed to know. Ben and his wife kept talking because they just wanted to fully deliver Jesus's messages to the two dolphin trainers. As if to make everything more interesting, the three dolphins were swimming closer to where Ben, Sophia, Rebecca, and Gerard were several feet behind the tank. Misty, Missy, and Betsy looked at the young married couple as if to say goodbye and that they really enjoyed swimming with them. Ben put his prosthetic legs back on himself. He stood up, and he and Sophia headed over to the nearby bathroom to change back into their day clothes and give the two swimsuits back to Rebecca and Gerard. Then, Sophia and her husband shook Rebecca's and Gerard's hands and said goodbye to them. In addition, Ben and Sophia expressed their huge thanks to the two dolphin trainers for letting the two of them swim with the dolphins. The young couple waved goodbye to Misty, Missy, and Betsy before they put their cameras back into their backpacks, strapped up, and continued to walk around SeaWorld.

Ben and Sophia wandered around SeaWorld for the next three hours, looking at everything they came across. They felt that everything they did and looked at didn't come close to their forty-five-minute swim with the three dolphins. The two of them continued to see and experience new things after that, though. The young married couple wanted to see as many ocean creatures as possible, try out various snacks, visit the on-site museum, and participate in a few of the activities at SeaWorld. They made sure to hydrate and reapply more sunscreen lotion as needed. The two of them really enjoyed walking through the on-site museum. Ben and his wife actually had a man take a couple of funny pictures of them while they were in a large shark mouth model.

The time on a nearby clock on a wall inside the museum struck 5:00 p.m., and it was time for Ben and Sophia to head out of SeaWorld. This was because Rebecca, Gerard, and the other ocean creature trainers and caretakers had to feed the creatures. Other visitors, in addition to Sophia and her husband, were already walking towards the exit. The young couple walked out of SeaWorld, sat down on a nearby bench, and began the process of searching the Internet on their laptops to get a shuttle to drive them to a block next to the hotel where they were staying. In addition, they were searching for a restaurant near their hotel to have dinner at.

Once Ben and Sophia were dropped off at a block, which was on the east side of the Marion Hotel, the two of them headed towards an American cuisine restaurant for dinner. This restaurant was a seven-minute walk southeast of their hotel. Sophia and her husband entered the restaurant, got seated at a table within fifteen minutes, and ordered two cheeseburgers, two small fries, and two Dr Pepper sodas ten minutes after getting seated at the table. Then, Ben and Sophia had fun eating their dinner together and talking with each other for the next two or so hours. The young couple proceeded to exit the restaurant after having two slices of key lime pie for dessert. They strolled towards their hotel, went inside it, and headed to their second-floor hotel room. It was almost 10:00 p.m. by the time that Ben and his wife got inside their hotel room. The two of them cuddled up on their king-sized bed and enjoyed each other's company before getting ready for bed at 10:45 p.m. Sophia and her husband did their usual thing of praying to and worshiping God in bed before falling asleep.

It is said that time flies by when you are having fun. That was certainly the case for Ben and Sophia Lawson, as they thoroughly enjoyed every minute of the last two full days of their honeymoon trip. The past four days seemed to go by in a hurry for them, but those days were extremely fun. As for the last two days of Ben and Sophia's honeymoon trip, the young married couple began each of the two mornings waking up together around 9:30 a.m., lovingly saying good morning to each other and gazing into each other's eyes. Each of them had regularly thought about how lucky they were that God had put them together in a covenant marriage relationship. Those thoughts never diminished, not even in the slightest. Ben and Sophia were especially thinking about how lucky they were to have each other as they had begun to wake up on Friday, May 2nd. It was just like Dave Lawson had thought about himself being the luckiest man to have his wife, Leslie, as Dave drove her to the hospital to have Ben.

As for the beginning of the last two days of Ben and Sophia's honeymoon trip, they did the usual things they did in the mornings. Then, the two of them headed over to Nelly's Breakfast Diner to get breakfast. Finally, the young couple spent the majority of the last two days of their honeymoon trip at Mission Beach. They would eat the rest of their snacks over those two days while staring out at the beach. In addition, the two of them made sure to put on and reapply ample amounts of sunscreen lotion as needed. Sophia and her husband sat twelve feet above the shoreline, with Ben in the big beach wheelchair and Sophia on her dolphin-imprinted beach towel. They gave Miguel Ben's prosthetic legs each day before going to their spot on the beach.

The young couple adventured out farther down the shoreline at various times during their final two stays at Mission Beach. Ben and his wife wanted to feel as much of the saltwater of the Pacific Ocean as they could feel. Sophia dug medium-sized holes in the sand when she and her husband were a little farther down the shoreline so as to funnily splash him with the water that she found. Ben really enjoyed and appreciated that. The young married couple also took two pictures of the ocean with both of their Polaroid cameras. In addition, the two of them made sure to tell Jesus's messages to the people they met on the beach. They would continue to do that everywhere they went. Anyway, once Sophia and her husband were done with each of their two other visits to Mission Beach, they returned the beach wheelchair to Miguel at the lifeguard station and thanked Miguel for helping them with the beach wheelchair. Then, the two of them got Ben's prosthetic legs back from Miguel, cleaned themselves off, and changed themselves back to their regular day clothes.

The young couple walked to the nearby Mexican restaurant to have dinner and dessert. Finally, Ben and Sophia returned to their hotel and hotel room each of the two nights after eating at the Mexican restaurant. Ben and his wife were profoundly thankful and grateful to God for the amazing honeymoon trip that they had as they worshiped and prayed to God in their bed on that Saturday night. The young couple would return to Evart, Michigan, the next day when their Southwest flight left San Diego at 12:45 p.m.

Ben and Sophia drove into the parking lot of the apartment complex that they were staying at in Evart, Michigan, on a clear night on Sunday, May 4th. Dave Lawson had driven their electric blue Ford truck back to their apartment right after the two of them left for San Diego a week ago. In addition, Dave had driven the truck to the airport in Evart on the Sunday that Ben and Sophia came back to Evart and left it there in a protected parking spot at 7:45 p.m. Then, the father had Leslie come to the airport in her car and drive him back to their house. Anyway, Ben and Sophia had already had dinner that Sunday night on May 4th, at the drive-through of a Chipotle that was near their apartment.

As for Ben and Sophia's prior activities, the young couple had checked out of the Marion Hotel at 9:00 a.m. that day. Then, Sophia and her husband had gotten their last breakfast at Nelly's Breakfast Diner at 9:30 a.m. Finally, they found and took a shuttle to the San Diego

National Airport at 10:30 a.m. The two of them had arrived at the airport around 11:15 a.m., which had been enough time for them to get checked for their Southwest flight to Evart at 12:45 p.m. Ben and his wife enjoyed their flight back to their hometown, even with the stop along the way in Kansas City.

Now, the young couple were back at their apartment in Evart. It was almost 9:00 p.m., and the two of them had let their families know that was the time they would return to their apartment. The thing that Ben and Sophia didn't know was that both of their families would be waiting just outside of their apartment room on the first floor. There were numerous new things that the young couple's families would reveal to them. The two of them were about to discover one of those new things as they approached their apartment building. Sophia and her husband heard a dog bark as they opened the door.

"Stop, Buster!" a familiar voice said as Ben and Sophia entered into their apartment building. It was Leslie. She was telling the dog, Buster, to stop barking. Buster stopped barking for a few seconds but then started barking again once Ben and his wife were well and clear into the apartment building. The young couple saw that Buster was a male black Labrador retriever and was well-fed. They also saw the rest of their families, who were standing against and next to the nearest corner that led to their apartment room. Leslie continued to reprimand the dog and introduce him to her son and daughter-in-law. "Buster, sit! Be quiet. We got special clearance to bring you in here for half an hour. This is Ben and Sophia. All of us are very happy to see them after their honeymoon trip to San Diego."

"Hello, my son!" Leslie excitedly exclaimed as she turned her full attention to Ben and his wife. Buster was still barking a bit, but Leslie didn't care as she came up to her son and embraced him in her arms.

"Hey, Mom!" Ben responded, equally as excited. He had fully embraced his mom in his arms as well. "It's so great to see you again!"

"It sure is!" Leslie said before she and her son let go of each other. She turned toward Sophia and began to stretch out her arms again to hug her. "How is my one and only favorite daughter-in-law!? Welcome home, Sophia!"

"I'm doing great, Leslie!" Sophia excitedly responded and laughed a little bit as she and Leslie hugged each other. The twenty-year-old continued to speak. "Thanks for the homecoming gathering. I see that you have a new furry member of the family."

"You're welcome!" Leslie happily responded as she and Sophia let go of each other. "And yes, this is Buster."

"Yeah, Buster is a bit of a rowdy dog," Sam O'Donnell said as he approached his daughter. Sophia forgot about Buster and quickly walked towards her dad. Sam continued to speak as he embraced Sophia in his arms. Sophia embraced him in her arms as well. "Hi, my wonderful daughter! Welcome home, kiddo! It's great to see you again!"

"Hi, Dad!" Sophia excitedly and lovingly exclaimed while she and her dad hugged each other. "It's so nice to see you again as well! Thanks for coming here along with everyone else!"

"You're welcome, my sweet pea!" Sam responded lovingly.

Ben and Sophia spent the next half an hour greeting and catching up with their families. Everybody was very happy to see the young couple again. Even Buster had calmed down and begun to like Sophia and her husband after they became acquainted with him. Ben also thanked his dad for financing his and Sophia's honeymoon trip. Dave said that it was nothing big and that Ben was welcome. Dave, Leslie, and Josh told the two of them that they had gotten Buster from the nearest animal shelter four days ago. The dog was four years old, and they got really attached to him. So, Dave, Leslie, and Josh bought Buster, took him to their house, and started caring for him. It was fortunate that the Lawsons' house had a backyard with a medium-sized area of grass in it. Buster had been happy to have a backyard full of grass to play and go to the bathroom on. The dog had rolled around on the grass on the first day that Dave, Leslie, and Josh brought him to their home. The three of them had invited the O'Donnell family over to their house after work and school on Thursday of that week to see and play with Buster. The three Lawson family members had made sure to buy several top-grade teeth-protective tennis balls in addition to beaver and sheep squeak toys for the dog at a PetSmart next to the animal shelter. Anyway, all three of the O'Donnell family members had begun to grow quite fond of Buster when they first met him at the Lawsons' house.

There were several other new things that the Lawson and O'Donnell families told Ben and Sophia that night in the apartment building. Sam, Candace, and Alicia had lunch with Tess Debor and Carl Wendleson after they saw each other at Holy Communion Church that Sunday morning. Tess and Carl told the three family members that they had become Christians, were baptized, and were now dating each other. Ben and Sophia were extremely happy to hear all of the good news about Tess and Carl.

The Lawson and O'Donnell family members were eager to see the pictures from Ben and Sophia's honeymoon trip after talking about Buster, Tess, and Carl for the past ten minutes. Thus, Ben and his wife took out their Polaroid cameras from their backpacks and showed the pictures to everyone, all the while providing the incredible stories that came with the pictures. All of the six Lawson and O'Donnell family members were completely captivated by the amazing pictures that Sophia and her husband showed to them. Even more so, they thoroughly enjoyed listening to the stories behind the pictures. The six family members loved every picture and story the young couple told them about. Josh thought that the funny pictures of Ben and Sophia inside the giant shark mouth model was hilarious. The other five Lawson and O'Donnell family members did indeed think that those pictures were very funny. Once all was said and done, the six people agreed that the pictures with Ben, Sophia, and the three dolphins at SeaWorld were the best pictures. The pictures from the San Diego Zoo and Mission Beach were right behind those from SeaWorld, in their opinion.

Finally, the six Lawson and O'Donnell family members told Ben and Sophia that each one of them had increased the number of people they shared Jesus's good news with each week. The young couple were proud of their families. They told them that every one of those people would eventually come to know Jesus and have relationships with Him. Ben and Sophia's families agreed, and then the young couple told them about the people they had shared Jesus's messages with in San Diego. Dave, Leslie, and the rest of the six family members were extremely proud of the young couple for doing that. It was a few minutes after the half an hour that they all expected to be catching up with each other. So, the six Lawson and O'Donnell family members said goodbye to Ben and Sophia so as to let them unpack and go to bed. The young couple also said goodbye to their families in addition to petting Buster and saying goodbye to him. Then, after Sophia's and her husband's families left along with Buster, they unpacked and checked back into their apartment room after talking with the apartment complex manager on the phone. Ben and Sophia proceeded to get ready for bed, do their usual things with God, and then fall asleep. Tomorrow was the first day back to their assistant jobs.

Time started to fly by really fast for Ben and Sophia Lawson. They went back to their entry-level jobs at 9:00 a.m. on Monday, May 5th. It only took the young couple a few hours at their jobs that day to get back in the groove of the work that they had to do. Ben continued to excel at his entry-level desk job at Aeromechanics Incorporated. Sophia also continued to do extremely well as an aide for Dr. Beatrice Altred at the True Health Christian Counseling Center. Anyway, almost a month passed by, and Ben and Sophia were still completely enjoying every minute they had together after work. The weekends were the best since they didn't have to work then. As for Saturday, May 31st, the young couple drove to a theater in Evart to see *Bruce Almighty* with their families, Diego Sanchez, Vanessa Lopez, Anthony Markus, Lucy Robinson, Hannah Rine, and Brandon Heraldez. The group really liked the movie. They thought that it was super funny, especially in the soup scene at the diner and the scene around the middle of the movie in which Bruce indirectly makes fun of Evan Baxter. After the movie, Ben, Sophia, and the rest of the group learned that Hannah and Brandon were planning on going on a date with each other next Saturday. Everyone in the large group was extremely happy for Hannah and Brandon.

Church was always one of the highlights of the weekends for Ben and Sophia. They were really invested in Pastor Jack Hershel's sermons after the worship time each Sunday. The two of them found out that Jack and the rest of the pastoral team had incorporated weekly baptism sessions during the worship times each Sunday. In addition, they incorporated an altar call for people in the church congregation who wanted to be saved and follow Jesus/God. These two things began happening on Sunday, June 1st. Sophia and her husband thought that those additions were excellent ideas. The two of them rejoiced and clapped their hands with the rest of the church congregation when people got baptized and accepted altar calls.

Now, days turned into weeks, and weeks turned into months for Ben and his wife. They had heard on Saturday, June 7th, that Hannah Rine's date with Brandon Heraldez went extremely well and that the two of them would continue dating each other. Sophia and her husband were really excited to hear the great news about their two friends. Then, time continued to rush forward, and Ben and Sophia did their best to thoroughly enjoy every minute of it that they had together. It was the 4th of July before they knew it. That night's celebration was fun as the young couple ate burgers for dinner with their families at the O'Donnell house and watched fireworks go off from a somewhat far away site. Then, the days began culminating until it was Saturday, September 27th. Once again, Ben, Sophia, their families, Diego, Vanessa, Hannah, Brandon, Lucy, and Anthony headed over to a theater to see *Secondhand Lions*. They all agreed that the movie was hilarious but a bit weird. The group thought that *Bruce Almighty* was better.

Time flew by so fast because of Ben and Sophia's amazing marriage and entry-level jobs that it was Thanksgiving weekend. The young couple, in addition to everyone else, had that special day off from their jobs because it was Thanksgiving Day. Sophia and her husband only had two more days off of work for the rest of the year. Anyway, they hung out with their families and friends in the early afternoon on Thanksgiving Day at the Lawson family house. The group also ended up playing with the Lawson family dog, Buster, in addition to playing various board, card, and video games with each other.

Thanksgiving dinner was being prepared all the while these things were happening. Dave, Leslie, and Josh had bought a bigger dining room table so as to have everyone sit at the table. Each person in the large group helped out with Thanksgiving dinner that day, whether it was a small or large contribution. Dave prayed over Thanksgiving dinner when it was ready and on the table at 6:30 p.m. Then, everyone completely enjoyed eating the food. Even Buster got several pieces of turkey mixed into his dog food. He was really well fed and cared for by Dave, Leslie, and Josh. Anyway, the large group of people also ate pumpkin pie for dessert. Buster got three small cubes of pumpkin pie as well. Everyone talked with each other about numerous things after dessert. Then, at 10:30 p.m., the O'Donnell family, Ben, Sophia, Diego, Vanessa, Anthony, Hannah, Brandon, and Lucy headed back to their respective houses and apartments.

Christmas came, and the end of the year was speedily drawing to a close. The gathering was just like that of Thanksgiving Day's gathering, except that it was at the O'Donnell house. Dave, Leslie, and Josh brought Buster as well. Everyone came over to the house that morning on December 25th for a late brunch at 11:00 a.m. They saw that there were a lot of presents under the tall and large O'Donnell Christmas tree. Each person had gotten a gift for someone, wrapped it up, and headed over to the O'Donnell house to place that gift under the tree. There were also stockings over and on each side of the fireplace in the family room for each person. The O'Donnell family had provided the stockings that were full of small gifts. As for that Christmas morning, everyone sat at the table in the dining room. Sam O'Donnell prayed over the food before he and the rest of the group dived into it. Blueberry pancakes, bacon, and sausages were what they had for brunch.

The large group walked into the family room and sat down on the burgundy carpeted floor and dark brown couch. Everyone first recognized and gave thanks for Jesus because he was the ultimate gift and reason for Christmas. Then, they waited to receive their stockings from Alicia O'Donnell. All of them had a blast taking out all of the fun small gifts that were in the stockings. Even Buster got a stocking full of dog treats and a few toys too. Once the large group was done, they headed into the living room, which was covered in green carpet instead of the wood in the dining room and kitchen area. All of them sat down on the floor on a different dark brown couch and began tearing the gift wrapping off of their presents. Their presents included various Star Wars items in addition to gag gifts and sports items. Buster got a gift-wrapped box that had tennis balls in it. Everyone hung out, talked, and played with their gifts in and outside of the O'Donnell house after opening their gifts. The fantastic day was capped off by a ham, broccoli, and rice dinner that night. Then, everyone, except the O'Donnell family, headed back to their houses and apartments around 9:30 p.m.

Ben, Sophia, their families, and the rest of the crew gathered at the Lawson family house for New Year's Eve. Everyone had taken that day off from work. They had a great time on December 31st. The group ate an Eegee's lunch, talked, and hung out with each other. Two thousand and four was only hours away, and everyone was going to stay up for the very start of the new year.

Two thousand and three had been a fantastic year for Ben, Sophia, and their families and friends. Ben and Sophia got married and traveled to San Diego for their honeymoon trip. Hannah Rine and Brandon Heraldez entered into a serious relationship with each other after being in the dating phase. Tess and Carl also ended up going the way of Hannah and Brandon. Diego and Vanessa had just entered into a serious relationship as well two months ago. Josh became an A-student in several of his high school classes. Plus, he and Alicia were starting off as friends after not seeing each other for good chunks of time between Ben and Sophia's wedding, the 4th of July, Thanksgiving, and Christmas. Dave and Leslie were still very happy in their marriage, and they were doing great at their jobs. The same things could be said of Sam and Candace. Everyone went to each other's birthdays as well. Anthony was doing well in college even though things had not worked out well for him and the African-American young woman he had been dating. Finally, Lucy began finding out what other things she wanted to do with her life in addition to going to college. Only time would tell if Lucy and Anthony became a couple.

All in all, everyone was truly grateful for the many blessings that God had poured out on them. As for Ben and Sophia, they were happy about all of the people they told Jesus's messages to. The young married couple wanted to more thoroughly enjoy the time that they had together and at work before, during, and after their trips, though. They also wanted to spend as much time with their friends and families as they could. The two of them completely enjoyed their vacation in San Diego, but they didn't completely savor every minute of their time at work and their time together after work each day of every work week. Everything flew by so fast. Speaking of vacations/trips, Sophia and her husband decided on where to go for their second trip before going back to heaven. They missed seeing the ocean. Therefore, Ben and Sophia agreed to go to Atlantic City in New Jersey to see the Atlantic Ocean.

CHAPTER 10:

A Time of Pure Joy, Love, and Happiness (Part 2)

Jesus said in John 16:24, "Until now you have not asked for anything in my name. Ask and you will receive, and your joy will be complete." The context of this verse refers to the time that Jesus's disciples asked Him about what He meant by His disciples not being able to see Him for a certain period of time. This time that Jesus was referring to was when He would go back to heaven. However, Jesus also said that His disciples would be able to see Him again after a certain period of time. He was talking about the time after His resurrection and the other times that they would go to heaven and see Him again after laying down their lives for the kingdom of God and Jesus's good news of the forgiveness of sins. As for this particular Bible verse, Jesus was likely telling His disciples that they could ask for any spiritual gift from His Father/God while they were still on Earth. Jesus was also probably telling them they could ask for any other good gift from God as well. This is supported by John 14:13-14, which says, "And I [Jesus] will do whatever you ask in my name, so that the Father may be glorified in the Son. You may ask me for anything in my name, and I will do it." In conclusion, God wants to give many good gifts to His people to make them prosper on Earth.

Those verses definitely rang true for Ben and Sophia Lawson as they reflected on everything that happened in 2003. It was 9:00 p.m. on New Year's Eve of that year, but 2004 was fast approaching them. The young married couple wanted to soak in the final three hours they had together in 2003 as they cuddled next to each other on the right side of the sectional couch in the living room of the Lawson house. In addition, Sophia and her husband wanted to completely enjoy the first full year that they had together before going back to heaven on May 14th, 2005. It didn't matter if it was a usual work day, weekend, or their Atlantic City vacation. The two of them wanted to get as much as they could get out of their lives on Earth. This time period of seventeen and a half months was definitely going to be another time of pure joy, love, and happiness for Ben and Sophia. As for the current moment, on December 31st, 2003, Diego Sanchez, Vanessa Lopez, Hannah Rine, Brandon Heraldez, Sam O'Donnell, and Candace O'Donnell were sitting next to Ben and Sophia on the couch. They were coupled together based on their relationship and marriage statuses. All of the couples on the couch were enjoying their time together. Dave, Leslie, Josh, and the rest of the group members were standing and talking with each other in the family room.

As for Ben, Sophia, and the rest of the people on the couch in the living room, they were watching *Star Wars: Return of the Jedi* on TV. The movie started at 9:00 p.m. and went until 11:45 p.m. That end-time gave the eight people, in addition to the rest of the group, enough time to switch the channel to a channel where announcers were counting down the minutes until 2004 arrived. As for the current moment, the couples on the living room couch were having fun talking with each other and watching the Star Wars movie. Dave, Leslie, Josh, and the rest of the group in the family room came into the living room and watched the second half of the movie. Some of them stood, while others swapped spots with two of the several couples.

The time came to switch the channel to a news channel to see the local ball drop from a high tower. The event was being held at the Evart Fair Grounds, which was forty minutes west of the Lawson house. It was 11:45 p.m., and everyone geared up for the countdown. Ben and Sophia were still cuddled up next to each other on the right side of the living room couch, in addition to Diego and Vanessa on the far left side of the couch. However, Josh, Alicia, Anthony, and Lucy were sitting in between the two couples. They had swapped places with Hannah, Brandon, Sam, and Candace. Josh and Anthony had talked with Alicia and Lucy about friends and relationships in the family room beforehand, respectively. Now, Josh was sitting on the couch a few inches away from Alicia. Anthony and Lucy had followed suit. The four of them, in addition to the rest of the group, started to count down the seconds until 2004 at the five-minute mark.

Each person in the group in the living room, whether standing or sitting, knew what was coming as part of the New Year celebration. Everyone was going to kiss a person of the opposite sex once it turned midnight. That was easy enough since there were seven men and seven women. Even more so, there were three married couples, two couples in the relationship phase. It could not have been any better, except that Josh, Alicia, Anthony, and Lucy were not in relationships with someone among them who was of the opposite sex. The four of them were a bit nervous, knowing that the moment was almost upon them. It could be said that Josh and Alicia were less nervous than Anthony and Lucy, though.

Anthony scratched his thinly shaved dark brown hair on top of his head and silently tapped his feet on the carpet for about ten seconds. Lucy fiddled with her fingers and ran her fingers along her now long blonde hair for nearly half a minute. Josh only stared down at his feet for approximately five seconds, pretending to notice something that was on his shoes.

Alicia just pushed back farther onto the couch. However, Josh and Alicia looked at each other familiarly several times during the final five minutes of 2003. It was just like the way the two of them looked at each other when they were dancing together at Ben and Sophia's wedding. They thought of that night as they looked at each other again at the two-minute mark. Anthony and Lucy were ready to dive into the kiss tradition after getting over their nervousness. The young African-American man and young blonde woman were doing the other things that they wanted to do in life besides going to college. This time belonged to them in addition to the rest of the group.

The ten-second countdown began, and all of the fourteen people in the living room counted down the seconds in chorus. Then, the last two seconds came and went. Two thousand and four finally arrived. Everyone shouted in celebration for two or three seconds. Ben and Sophia proceeded to kiss each other, and all of the other couples followed suit. Josh and Alicia felt a connection start to grow between them after they kissed each other. The same could be said for Anthony and Lucy. The nervousness inside the four of them evaporated into thin air while they took part in the New Year's Eve tradition. All the while this was happening, Buster was eating several dog treats that Dave had given him five minutes before midnight. The treats were part of Buster's celebration of the New Year after he had dinner at 6:30 p.m. that night.

Ben and Sophia couldn't help but notice the newfound connections between Josh and Alicia and Anthony and Lucy after the kissing tradition. The young married couple was happy for their siblings and friends. Then, they and everyone else, except Dave, Leslie, Josh, and Buster, headed back to their homes and apartments. Relationships would start to blossom between Josh and Alicia and Anthony and Lucy down the road. However, this new year would mark the year and five months that Ben and Sophia had left together before they went back to heaven. The young married couple would savor every minute they had at their jobs, with each other, and with their families and friends during that time period.

New Year's Day arrived, and the group of fourteen people gathered at the O'Donnell house. They ate a strawberry waffle, bacon, and sausage brunch at 11:30 a.m. at the dining room table in the living room. Then, the whole bunch of them watched movies and played all sorts of games with each other. Sophia got a net volleyball and volleyball from her husband for Christmas. So, everyone in the group helped set up the net in the grassy backyard and played volleyball for an hour in the afternoon after playing chess, checkers, and the *Star Wars* plug-and-play video game that Ben brought over from his and Sophia's apartment. The Lawsons' dog, Buster, had fun running in the backyard and chasing after tennis balls that Leslie had brought over from their house. Buster wasn't really interested in the volleyball game, so that was good for everyone. There wouldn't be anyone who tripped and fell because of the dog.

Dave had gotten a dark green Prince tennis racquet from Leslie for Christmas, and he used that to hit the tennis balls to Buster during a few breaks in the volleyball game. The fourteen people wrapped up the day by sitting and watching more TV on the couch and love seats in the O'Donnells family room around 5:00 p.m. before having a steak, broccoli, and noodle dinner at 6:30 p.m. Ben and Sophia thoroughly enjoyed spending time with their families and friends that day. Now, Sunday the 4th was coming in three days, and everyone was going to attend Light of the World Church, which was agreed upon by each person in the group. As for that night, everyone hung out and talked with each other after dinner. Then, around 10:30 p.m., everyone except the O'Donnell family drove back to their homes and apartments.

Sunday morning came, and all of the fourteen people in the group got ready at their respective places to go to Light of the World Church. In addition, the prophet Harold Trenton got ready to go to the same church as usual with his wife, Esther. Esther was a slender, five-foot-three-inch tall seventy-six-year-old Hispanic woman with hazel-green eyes and wavy white hair that reached down to the middle of her back. She and her husband would be sitting seven rows behind Ben, Sophia, and their families and friends.

At 10:30 a.m., Ben, Sophia, and their friends and families were sitting in the middle of the far left column of the church congregation. The men in the group were wearing light blue, dark blue, or black jeans or slacks with various polo shirts, T-shirts, and shoes. The women in the group had chosen to wear different colors of one-piece dresses with matching shoes or heels. However, some of the women, like Sophia and Hannah, were simply wearing light or dark blue jeans with various colors of T-shirts and regular shoes. Harold and Esther Trenton could see most of the backs of the fourteen people as the service was starting because the two of them were sitting on the far right of the left column. In addition, there were several empty seats in front of Harold and Esther.

The worship part of the service was amazing for everyone at Light of the World Church. Ben, Sophia, and their family and friends were completely absorbed into worshiping God. The same thing could be said for Harold and Esther as well. The rest of the church congregation was also really in tune with worshiping God. Then, Pastor Derrell Watson preached a sermon about Jesus's sermon on the mount, which lasted for a little over an hour. Everyone in the church congregation thought that the church sermon was helpful and insightful. Ben, Sophia, their families and friends, Harold, and Esther met and talked with each other after the service ended with the altar call for nonbelievers to become believers. Esther and her husband were wearing fancy clothes. The two of them told Ben, Sophia, and their families that they had expected that the group was going tell more people about Jesus's good news and messages. Harold and his wife were proud of them. Other than that, the whole bunch of them talked about what was happening in their lives. Then, the group of sixteen people split up and headed back to the houses and apartments that they lived in.

The next day came, and it was Ben's twentieth birthday. He and Sophia woke up on a slightly overcast day in their king-sized bed in their apartment. It was 9:30 a.m., and the two of them enjoyed each other's company for a little while before getting ready for the day. They had taken that day off of both of their entry-level jobs. Sophia and her husband wouldn't take more time off from work until Sophia's birthday on April 12th, in addition to their one-year anniversary on April 26th and their trip to Atlantic City in May.

As for today, Sophia would treat Ben with making his favorite breakfast for him, which included chocolate chip pancakes, bacon, and sausages. She was also going to have the same breakfast. Sophia insisted that her husband just sit on their purple love seat in their living room area, watch TV, and relax until breakfast was ready for the two of them. The medium-sized TV was situated on a gold-colored wall ten feet in front of the love seat. Ben noticed that there were three gift-wrapped presents and a card in an envelope for him on a coffee table that was in front of the small couch. The now twenty-year-old knew that Sophia must have gone to a store or two on Saturday to purchase his card and presents. Ben would wait until he and his wife were done eating breakfast before opening his presents and card.

An hour and a half passed, and the young married couple was done eating breakfast. Sophia watched her husband as he first took the card-filled envelope off of the coffee table, opened the envelope, and took the card out of it. Ben was really touched by the message in his birthday card after reading the message. The message was about how amazing it was for Sophia to marry Ben and spend the time they had together before going back to heaven in 2005. He and his wife shared a ten-second kiss with each other before Ben started opening his presents. The black-haired twenty-year-old found out that Sophia had bought him a metal baseball bat, mitt, and four baseballs that were concealed in a box. Ben loved his presents and thanked his wife for them.

Sophia and her husband cuddled up and watched TV on their purple love seat at their apartment until 2:00 p.m. Then, the two of them spent the rest of the day at Crystal Park, playing baseball with their families and friends. The young married couple drove to a nearby Olive Garden for dinner at 6:30 p.m. Finally, they returned to their apartment and apartment room at 9:30 p.m. Ben and Sophia enjoyed each other's company again in their bed after getting ready for bed and worshiping and praying to God. They proceeded to fall asleep after all of these things.

Ben and Sophia made sure to soak up and fully enjoy every minute that they had together and at their entry-level jobs, even though time was flying by. The rest of January 2004 was filled with a lot of work during the weeks. The young married couple took pride in what they did at their jobs. However, after work each day of the week, Sophia and her husband would have fun making and eating dinner together. In addition, the two of them thoroughly enjoyed cuddling up next to each other on their purple love seat in an intimate and loving way in the blue-carpeted living room area of their apartment room during the nights after they ate dinner. They would watch *Smallville* and other TV shows. Ben and his wife were all caught up with watching *Smallville* as well as their friends and families. They looked forward to watching the new episodes on TV every Thursday night.

January was a fun blur, and before Ben and Sophia knew it, it was February. The young couple was having a blast living life together and experiencing everything. The first fourteen days of February hurried by, and then it was the day after Valentine's Day. Sophia and her husband planned on doing something fun for their Valentine's Day since the actual romantic holiday was the previous day, and they didn't want to spend a lot of money. As for this Sunday morning, the two of them woke up around 8:45 a.m. in their apartment bed and turned towards each other. They lovingly gazed into each other's eyes and hung out in bed for a little while before getting ready to go to Holy Communion Church since it was Sunday. Ben and Sophia made and ate scrambled eggs with bacon, toast, and fruit for breakfast before going to church.

The church service was always great for the young married couple, no matter what the sermon was about. Ben and his wife completely enjoyed every worship, sermon, baptism, and altar call time. Today was not any different as the two of them got really in tune with worshiping God and fully listening to the sermon. In addition, Sophia and her husband clapped their hands and rejoiced with the rest of the church congregation when nonbelievers got baptized during worship time and when other nonbelievers accepted the altar call at the end of the service. As for the sermon, Pastor Jack Hershel preached on the parable of the good Samaritan. Ben and Sophia thought that the sermon was helpful and encouraging to them when the service was over.

Sophia and her husband drove over to the USA Fashion and Festivities Mall and had lunch at a sandwich deli that was in the middle of the mall. The young married couple spent a few hours of the afternoon eating lunch, trying out different Valentine's Day outfits, and participating in several fun activities at the mall. Then, Ben and Sophia headed back to their apartment and apartment room at 5:00 p.m. Sophia thought that it was kind of weird that her husband seemingly hadn't gotten her anything for that day. She was willing to wait a couple of hours for any last-minute surprises.

"I know what you are thinking," Ben said in a knowing tone after he and his wife sat together on their living room area love seat. "Why hasn't he gotten me anything for today? You might also be thinking that I could've gotten you something or some things while we were at the mall today. I didn't do that, but I did something better."

"Okay, I'm listening," Sophia responded in a loving tone as she leaned against the right side of Ben's chest and looked up at him. "What was the better thing that you did?"

"You will see. I'm going to get up and get those things from a special hiding place of mine," Ben responded in an anonymous voice before Sophia sat back up straight to let him get off of the love seat. He walked into the other small living/family room area and got some things that Sophia couldn't see because of the long corner wall that fed into that room. The second living/family room area was twenty-four feet in front and to the far left of where Sophia was sitting on the purple love seat. Then, Ben continued to speak. "Close your eyes."

"Okay, I closed my eyes," Sophia said after closing her eyes. She was getting excited.

"All right, open your eyes," Ben responded after he got back from the other room and sat down next to his wife on the love seat.

"Oh my gosh," Sophia gasped in excitement as she saw the medium-sized bouquet of red and pink roses in a glass vase on the coffee table in front of her. She also saw a white rectangular box of See's Candies and an envelope with a card in it. These items were also on the coffee table. "Thank you so much, babe."

"You're welcome, babe. Happy Valentine's Day," Ben lovingly said.

"Happy Valentine's Day," Sophia responded in a loving tone as well before she and Ben hugged and kissed each other for approximately ten seconds. Then, she continued to speak, "This See's Candies box should be full of those yummy coffee truffles and milk chocolate patties."

"It is," Ben said reassuringly. "You had told me about two months ago that those were your favorite candies from See's. So, I bought a box of them when I went out yesterday before making dinner with you. Plus, I got the flowers and card at Walgreens that time yesterday as well. I put the flowers in a vase and stuck them in a discrete corner next to the window in the other room. As for the candy and card, I placed them in a big empty box in the pantry in that room. You haven't bothered to look in that corner or in the pantry since Friday night."

"Ooohhh, that's what you have been up to," Sophia responded in a funny but impressed tone as she lovingly leaned against Ben's chest again. "Very nice. That is true. I haven't looked in that window corner or in the pantry since Friday night. That is nice enough for each of us to have one truffle and one patty before we make our chicken parmigiana dinner."

"Sweet," Ben said. "Let's do it!"

Ben and Sophia proceeded to eat their share of the truffles and patties after Sophia opened her card and thanked her husband for it. Then, the two of them began to make their chicken parmigiana dinner together. Time passed, and the young couple completely enjoyed eating their dinner at the kitchen counter in the second living/family room area. Sophia and her husband savored eating the rest of the See's truffles and patties as they watched TV on the love seat after dinner. The young married couple watched a romantic comedy movie before getting ready for bed and doing their usual things with God. Ben and Sophia hung out in bed for a little while before falling asleep at 10:15 p.m.

The rest of the events in February included the young married couple having fun with each other after work each day of the week. In addition, the two of them went to and participated in volleyball and baseball events on the weekends. Even though the days were passing by in a fun flurry of events and amazing moments, they always made time to tell Jesus's messages to everyone they met. That was a thing that Ben and Sophia would continue to do until the day and hour that they went back to heaven.

March came, and it was filled with work for the young married couple in addition to spectacular times between the two of them. Sophia and her husband continued to thoroughly enjoy each other's company after work each day of the week and on the weekends. The two of them absolutely loved every minute of everything they did together, even though they sometimes had to work a few extra hours at their entry-level jobs on a couple of Saturdays. Ben and his wife visited a small, local aquarium on one of their completely free weekends. Their visit to that aquarium reminded them of their time at the Sea Trench Aquarium in San Diego. The young married couple sure hoped they would visit another aquarium in Atlantic City during their second vacation.

The end of March seemed to blur and flow into the first eleven days of April. It is said several times that when days blur and flow into another month, it's because nothing that exciting happens during those days. People get stuck in their work routines and doing chores at home. That was the complete opposite for Ben and Sophia. The young married couple kind of enjoyed their work and chore routines. In addition, they absolutely enjoyed spending time with each other when they were not working or doing chores.

It was about to get even more enjoyable for Ben and Sophia Lawson because the next day was Sophia's twenty-first birthday. The young married couple woke up around 9:00 a.m. on

Monday, April 12th. Ben lovingly said happy birthday to his wife before the two of them got ready for the day. He hugged Sophia after he put on his prosthetic legs and stood. Then, Ben insisted that she just relax on their purple love seat in the living room area while he made her favorite breakfast. Sophia's favorite breakfast was strawberry waffles and chicken sausages. So, the twenty-year-old made that breakfast for his wife and himself while Sophia laid down on her side on the love seat and watched TV. She looked very comfortable because she put a blanket on herself and rested her head on the right armpiece of the love seat.

At 10:00 a.m., Ben and Sophia completely enjoyed and indulged themselves as they ate their strawberry waffles and chicken sausages while watching a comedy TV show on their purple love seat in their pajamas. The two of them watched TV, talked, and cuddled up next to each other until 2:00 p.m. Then, the young married couple got casually dressed before driving over to Sophia's family's house. They stayed there from 3:00 to 9:00 p.m. All three of Sophia's family members got off of work and school by 2:30 p.m. and were home by 2:45 p.m. that day. The five people played some volleyball in the backyard for almost an hour before going back inside the house. Ben, Sophia, and Sophia's family hung out, talked, and watched TV during that other part of the afternoon. Their conversations ranged from work and school to friends, family, and *Smallville*. Finally, at 6:30 p.m., the five of them had dinner at their house with Ben's family, who were invited to join them. The Lawsons' dog, Buster, was also invited.

Chocolate cake had been made by Candace O'Donnell while she and the rest of the family hung out and talked with Ben and Sophia. Now, after dinner, everyone at the dining room table thoroughly enjoyed eating the chocolate cake for dessert after they sang "Happy Birthday" to Sophia. Then, Ben, Dave, Leslie, Josh, and the O'Donnell family each gave one present to Sophia. The eight people and Buster proceeded to spend time and talk with each other in addition to watching some more TV. It was 9:00 p.m. before everyone knew it, and it was time for Ben and Sophia to head back to their apartment. Dave, Leslie, Josh, and Buster also decided to go back to their house when Ben and Sophia left.

Time flew by once again, but the young married couple held on tightly to every minute that they had with each other. One moment, Ben was spending time with Sophia once the two of them had gotten back to their apartment on the night of Sophia's birthday. The next moment, Ben and Sophia were working at their entry-level jobs on Tuesday, April 13th. That second moment blended into a blur, and it was Monday, April 26th, before the young couple knew it. This day was very special because it was Ben and Sophia's one-year marriage anniversary. The young couple began their day by lovingly saying good morning to each other and hanging out after waking up together around 9:00 a.m. Then, the two of them got ready for their fun day. Ben already had a great and memorable plan for his and Sophia's one-year anniversary. As for now, the two of them had a good time making a wonderful strawberry waffle, bacon, and sausage breakfast for themselves in the kitchen of their apartment.

Ben and Sophia had a blast as they ate their one-year anniversary breakfast and watched a romantic comedy movie on their purple love seat. Both of them couldn't believe that one year had passed since they got married. The young married couple mentally and emotionally reflected back on their first year of marriage together as they ate breakfast and watched the movie on TV. Little memories stuck out for them as much as the big memories. They remembered the little memories of waking up to each other every morning and lovingly saying good morning to each other before getting ready for work or a day on the weekend. In addition, Sophia and her husband remembered every interaction they had with each other in that first year of marriage. Then came the big memories, such as their honeymoon trip to San Diego, which included wandering around the San Diego Zoo and seeing all of the various animals. Ben and his wife also remembered and thought about their visits to SeaWorld, the Sea Trench Aquarium, and Mission Beach during that vacation in San Diego. The other big memories the young couple remembered and thought about were the times that they spent with their friends and families during holidays and birthdays. Ben and Sophia were even more intent on making more long-lasting and wonderful memories with each other during their second year of marriage, in addition to the extra two and a half weeks before they went back to heaven.

The young couple finished eating their strawberry waffles, bacon, and sausages forty minutes before the romantic comedy movie ended. They quickly washed their plates and utensils and put them in the dishwasher before cuddling up next to each other on their love seat to watch the last half hour of the movie. Then, after the movie was over at 1:00 p.m., Ben and Sophia gave anniversary presents to each other. Sophia first opened the card that her husband gave her. She read the very touching message inside the card and thanked him for it. The twenty-one-year-old proceeded to open her four presents.

Sophia gasped in excitement after she unwrapped four very meaningful gifts from her husband. Two of the gifts were medium-sized pictures from her and Ben's honeymoon trip that had rectangular, gold-colored frames around them. The other two gifts were additional medium-sized pictures from their honeymoon that had rectangular silver-colored frames around them. Each of the four framed pictures was from an activity that Ben and Sophia had done in San Diego. One picture was of themselves at the zoo. Another picture was of themselves at Mission Beach. The other two pictures were of the two of them swimming with the three dolphins at SeaWorld and walking around the Sea Trench Aquarium. Sophia absolutely loved the framed pictures and passionately hugged and kissed Ben for nearly five seconds after thanking him for her presents.

The young redhead gave her husband his card and three presents. Ben read the extremely touching message inside the card that Sophia gave him, and he thanked her for it. Then, the black-haired twenty-year-old opened his presents. Ben let out a gasp of excitement as he opened each of his presents. One of his gifts was a picture of him and his wife as they funnily posed inside the huge shark mouth model inside the SeaWorld museum. The picture had a rectangular dark blue frame around it. The other two gifts were a medium-sized *Star Wars* poster and a black *Star Wars* T-shirt from *Attack of the Clones*. Ben thanked Sophia for the meaningful card and presents that she gave them.

The young married couple relaxed and hung out with each other from 1:30 to 3:45 p.m. at their apartment. During that time, Sophia wondered if her husband had any more surprises for her for their one-year anniversary. Ben kept the plans that he had for an unforgettable anniversary dinner in his mind. He had arranged for Sophia to hang out with her mom and sister from 4:30 to 6:00 p.m. at the O'Donnell house while he and Sam O'Donnell set up the special dinner at a special place. The two guys had already talked on the phone yesterday and had bought everything that they would need except for the anniversary dinner. Sophia didn't even know that her husband had called her dad that day. The black-haired twenty-year-old had called Sam yesterday while Sophia was taking a shower in the late afternoon. She would be completely caught by surprise and would totally be enraptured in what Ben and Sam had done. Ben secretly ordered the dinner at 3:30 p.m. while Sophia and he relaxed and hung out with each other on the day of their anniversary. Then, at 3:45 p.m., Ben drove over to the O'Donnell house with his wife to drop her off there for the time being. As for now, he and Sam headed to the restaurant where he had ordered the special dinner. Finally, the two guys drove over to the special location and set up everything.

"Oh my goodness, Ben!" Sophia excitedly exclaimed after she was led blindfolded into the wooden building at Crystal Park. It was 6:40 p.m. on a cool and cloudy night on that Monday, which was perfect for Ben and Sophia's dinner event for their one-year anniversary. She saw several light cords on top of the inside of the building that were arranged in wonderful and beautiful patterns. The light cords had a vast assortment of colored lights on them. Then, Sophia saw a medium-sized silver-gray circular table in the center of the interior of the wooden building. The table had dinner entrees on it, which were from Rebario's, her favorite restaurant. In addition, there was a medium-sized vase of red, white, and pink roses in the center of the table. Two silver-colored chairs at each end of the table had thin red cushions on them. Sophia continued to speak in amazement after seeing all of this. "This is absolutely amazing and beautiful! Thank you very much!"

"You are very welcome, Sophia," Ben lovingly responded before he and her passionately hugged and kissed each other. Then, he proceeded to speak again, "Your dad and I did all of this today while you were hanging out with your mom and sister. I bought everything, and Sam helped me set up the lights. I set up the table, chairs, and flower vase. Plus, I insisted that I help set up a good portion of the lights with your dad. I'm very happy that you love what we did. I even brought one of our Polaroid cameras to take pictures of ourselves throughout the night."

"Yes, I absolutely love all of it!" Sophia said with excitement in her voice. "This is even more romantic because you got us dinner from Rebario's, which is my favorite restaurant, and the restaurant that we ate a late lunch at after you proposed to me and played volleyball with me. Plus, you bought the same flowers that were used at our wedding and put those flowers in a beautiful vase! You are such a romantic! I love it! It'll be great to take pictures of ourselves tonight as well! I love you so much!"

"I love you so much too!" Ben lovingly exclaimed before he and Sophia passionately hugged and kissed each other again for several seconds. Then, he continued speaking in an excited tone, "Well, let's dive into our food and enjoy our special night together!"

"Definitely!" Sophia excitedly agreed before she and Ben sat down at the table.

The young married couple ate a very special dinner from Rebario's at the table inside the colorfully lit wooden building at Crystal Park. They ate fancy tacos that had all sorts of Sophia's favorite items. The two of them also split a very nice burrito that was covered in smashed bean paste, several touches of sour cream, and hot sauce. In addition, the burrito had shredded beef, pepper jack cheese, more bean paste, sour cream, and hot sauce on the inside. Ben and Sophia also poured themselves glasses of orange cream soda from a big plastic container. There was no need for dessert because of the orange cream soda, which was one of Sophia's favorite soda flavors. They would refill their glasses a few times.

As for the young couple's attire, Ben was wearing a snazzy dark blue polo shirt, black slacks, and black dress shoes. The slacks and shoes almost perfectly fit over his waist and prosthetic legs. Ben had also made sure to put on a good-smelling cologne and to style his medium-length black hair with gel. He was clean-shaven, as usual. Sophia was nicely dressed in a one-piece turquoise blue dress with matching dress shoes. She had her red hair tied back in a long ponytail. Sophia had also made sure to put on a sweet-smelling perfume.

Once Ben and Sophia had finished their dinner together at the table, they stayed there and talked and laughed with each other about their life together, especially the great and fantastic memories that they shared together during their first year of marriage. They drank more orange cream soda in between their conversations as well. Sophia and her husband also talked about the fun times with their friends and families before and during their marriage. Lastly, the two of them conversed about their plan to go on vacation in Atlantic City, New Jersey, in the middle of May. The young married couple finished off the last part of their night by dancing with each other. All in all, Ben and his wife had a lovely time talking and laughing with each other after dinner.

Time flew by, and it was 8:45 p.m. before the young couple knew it. The two of them had so much fun together in all that they did in the wonderfully lit wooden building at Crystal Park. They even took several pictures of themselves at various points of the night with the Polaroid camera that Ben had brought into the wooden building. It helped that there was a timer on the camera because Sophia and her husband took pictures of themselves from farther away. Now, Ben and Sophia gathered up and threw their trash away before heading back to their apartment. They drove in the red Lexus that they had. The young couple were back inside their apartment room by 9:10 p.m. The two of them got ready for bed and worshiped and prayed to God. Then, Ben and Sophia lovingly and intently looked into each other's eyes as they turned off their apartment room lights and closed their bedroom door.

The morning of Tuesday, April 27th, came, and it was time for Ben and Sophia Lawson to get back to work. Ben continued to excel in his entry-level desk job at Aeromechanics Incorporated, and Sophia did the same thing as Dr. Beatrice Altred's aide at True Health Christian Counseling Center. The young married couple ate a Chipotle takeout dinner, talked, and spent time together in their apartment room after each of them got off of work. Then, that fun and interesting mixture of work and quality time blended together in a spectacular way.

It was Tuesday, May 18th, and it was time for Ben and Sophia's trip to Atlantic City, New Jersey. The young married couple could only take four days off from each of their entry-level jobs. That was because of the other three days that they took off for Ben's birthday, Sophia's birthday, and their one-year anniversary. The two of them would not have any more days off after their Atlantic City vacation. That was okay for them since they automatically would have Thanksgiving and Christmas Day off from work. Those two days were the days that they were going to hang out with all of their friends and families, in addition to a lot of weekends throughout the year.

As for the present moment, on May 18th, Ben and Sophia were in the waiting area behind the terminal of their Southwest flight to Atlantic City at the Evart International Airport. It was 3:30 p.m. on a mostly sunny day in Evart. All of Ben and Sophia's friends and families, even Diego, Vanessa, Lucy, Anthony, Hannah, and Brandon, were in the waiting area with the young married couple to say goodbye to them. Sophia and her husband's flight was at 3:45 p.m., which left about ten minutes for the two of them to say goodbye to their friends and families and vice versa.

Once everyone said goodbye to each other, Ben and his wife walked into and down the terminal tunnel into the airplane at 3:40 p.m. along with the other passengers. The young married couple had bought seats seven rows behind the front of the airplane. As for the pilots, they took an additional ten minutes to do a flight check, as usual, after the scheduled departure at 3:45 p.m. Then, at 3:55 p.m., the pilots revved up the airplane engines and began to move away from the terminal tunnel. It took just below thirty seconds for the pilots to fly into the air after driving down the runway at a gradually increasing speed. For Ben and Sophia, the takeoff parts of the two flights they had been on were the most exhilarating moments of the flights. Now, they and the other passengers were on their way to Atlantic City.

"Good morning, Ben," Sophia lovingly and genuinely said to Ben after they both woke up in their king-size bed around 9:15 a.m. on a sunny Wednesday morning in their first-floor hotel room at the Eastern Seaboard Hotel in Atlantic City, New Jersey. The two of them had gotten a shuttle at 6:45 p.m. after their two-hour-and-fifteen-minute flight to the East Coast city. Then, they ordered dinner inside their hotel room via room service. Finally, Sophia and her husband watched TV before going to bed and doing their usual things with God.

"Good morning, Sophia," Ben responded in an equally loving and genuine tone before getting excited. "Are you ready to see and go into the Atlantic Ocean today?"

"You bet I am!" Sophia excitedly replied with a big smile on her face. "Are you ready?"

"Sure am!" Ben said with a smile on his face as well.

"All right, let's get ready for our fun day at one of those beaches!"

Sure enough, that is what the young married couple did. Ben and his wife walked out of their room and the hotel and continued walking east for five minutes with their backpacks strapped onto their backs until they found a breakfast diner that they thought sounded good. The diner was called the Flip-House Breakfast Diner. Ben ordered two bacon, cheese, and hot sauce omelets for himself and his wife in addition to four pieces of cinnamon raisin toast and two glasses of milk. Then, after waiting twenty minutes for their order, Ben and Sophia prayed over their food and thoroughly enjoyed eating it.

Sophia and her husband grabbed their backpacks, which they had laid on the smooth tile floor next to their chairs, and began searching on their laptops for a good beach to go to and a beach wheelchair for Ben. Once Sophia found a nearby beach on her laptop called Pebble

Beach, Ben searched the Internet on his laptop for a beach wheelchair at Pebble Beach. The beach was a ten-minute walk east of the Flip-House Breakfast Diner. So, when the young married couple had squared everything away, they went into the men's and women's bathrooms inside the diner to change into their beach clothes.

Once Ben and Sophia changed their clothes, they headed out of the diner and towards Pebble Beach. Ben was wearing a short-sleeved light blue T-shirt with plain white swim shorts and white shoes. Sophia had chosen to wear a red one-piece swimsuit and matching sandals. The two of them both had sunglasses on and had made sure to put enough sunscreen lotion on themselves. They also had plenty of snacks and other necessities to get them through the day. As for the beach wheelchair, the young married couple would go down to the pier near Pebble Beach, drop off Ben's prosthetic legs, and grab the wheelchair.

Sophia and her husband got to the Pebble Beach pier around 12:30 p.m. The walk to the pier had been an extra ten minutes. The two of them called out for a lifeguard once they walked inside the lifeguard station. A six-foot-five-inch White man walked out of the inner door to the station and approached Ben and his wife. He was a muscly thirty-five-year-old man with medium-length brown hair and a neatly trimmed beard of the same color. The lifeguard was an atheist but had heard things about God from his friends and strangers who passed by. He was wearing a bright orange lifeguard shirt and green board shorts.

The lifeguard introduced himself as James, and then Ben and Sophia introduced themselves to him. James noticed the black prosthetic legs that Ben was wearing and had compassion for him. The thirty-five-year-old was impressed by Ben's desire to do everything that he could in life, even though he was limited in what he could do with his prosthetic legs. James even said that before going to get the beach wheelchair. Then, after James brought the wheelchair, Ben proceeded to sit in the wheelchair and take off his prosthetic legs. The lifeguard was a little surprised by how well the twenty-year-old took off his prosthetic legs. James took the prosthetic legs and said he would take great care of them while the young married couple was having fun on the beach. Finally, before the thirty-five-year-old man walked off and placed Ben's prosthetic legs in a safe spot fairly deep within the lifeguard station, Ben and Sophia told him about Jesus's messages. That was after the two of them talked about how God loves everyone and wants them to have abundant lives. James was really involved and interested in everything the young couple had to say. He said he wanted to look into God after he was done with working at the lifeguard station for that day. Ben and his wife were glad to hear that. Then, the two of them said goodbye to James and began their fun adventure at Pebble Beach.

Ben and Sophia's day at Pebble Beach was amazing. The two of them realized how much they missed the ocean as they gazed upon the Atlantic Ocean from a spot on the beach twelve feet above the shoreline. Sophia, once again, dug a hole in the sand and found some of the saltwater from the ocean. She funnily splashed her husband with the water. Ben had fun with that but wanted to be with his wife on her beach towel for a little while. The twenty-one-year-old redhead noticed that longing in her husband's eyes and felt bad she couldn't lift him out of the beach wheelchair and put him onto her beach towel. Sophia had chosen to bring a different beach towel than the one she brought to Mission Beach in San Diego. This beach towel was a plain pink beach towel.

The young married couple got lucky after a Hispanic married couple walked towards them and noticed Ben's condition. They had compassion on him, just like James did. The couple was in their late twenties and were pretty fit. They introduced themselves as Fernando and Leticia Guartez. Fernando was six feet three inches tall and had short dark brown hair and brown eyes. He was only wearing a dark blue Speedo. Leticia was five feet six inches tall; she had hazel-green eyes and black hair that came down to the middle of her back. She was wearing a lime green two-piece bikini. Ben and Sophia also introduced themselves to Fernando and Leticia.

The Hispanic couple proceeded to talk about how much they were inspired by Ben's willingness to do all that he could without legs. Ben said he had prosthetic legs but couldn't bring them onto the beach because of the sand and ocean. Fernando and Leticia understood his reasons for not having his prosthetic legs at the moment. The couple was also gladly surprised that Ben and Sophia were married. The two couples exchanged brief stories about when they got married and had their honeymoon vacations. Fernando and Leticia were genuinely happy that Ben and Sophia had an amazing honeymoon vacation. In addition, the Hispanic couple loved the short story of how the young married couple married.

Ben and Sophia told Fernando and Leticia about their desire to sit next to each other on Sophia's beach towel. The young married couple wondered if it was possible for Fernando to take Ben out of the beach wheelchair and sit him next to Sophia. Fernando absolutely agreed to their wish, and Sophia and her husband were extremely grateful for his help. The Hispanic man was glad to help. So, he picked up Ben from the beach wheelchair and hoisted him over his right shoulder before walking to Sophia's right side and putting him down next to her. Ben and Sophia's backpacks were directly behind them. Leticia offered to take some pictures of the young married couple with any cameras that they had. Ben and his wife accepted the generous offer and took out their Polaroid cameras from their backpacks. Then, Leticia took two pictures of Ben and Sophia with each camera.

Fernando and Leticia proceeded to talk more to Sophia and her husband about married life, in addition to offering to do anything else for them. Ben and Sophia came up with another idea after talking with the Hispanic couple for fifteen minutes. The young married couple asked Fernando if he could put Ben back in the beach wheelchair and wheel him down the shoreline so as to have the ocean water splash onto him. Fernando was glad to offer his help to the young couple again. So, he picked Ben up and put him back into the beach wheelchair before wheeling him down the shoreline. Leticia and Sophia followed the two men and walked a few feet farther in front of them. Then, the four people played in the ocean for nearly twenty minutes before heading back up to where Sophia's beach towel was.

Ben and Sophia thanked Fernando and Leticia again for helping and playing in the ocean with them. The Hispanic couple was very happy they could help and provide a fun time for the young married couple. Then, Sophia and her husband eased into a conversation in which they told Jesus's messages of love, provision, protection, and the kingdom of God to Fernando and Leticia. Leticia and her husband were intrigued by all of what the young married couple told them. In addition, Fernando and his wife said that they grew up learning about Catholicism and didn't know some of what Ben and Sophia were talking about. Fernando and Leticia also said they wanted to learn more about God and become Christians. Ben and Sophia declared they were very glad to hear that. Then, the two couples said goodbye to each other and went about their own things.

The rest of Ben and Sophia's day at Pebble Beach was filled with them just staring out at the Atlantic Ocean and holding hands. They had made sure to reapply enough sunscreen lotion on their skin and drink plenty of water. It was 5:00 p.m. before the young married couple knew it, and they packed up their stuff and headed back to the lifeguard station near the pier. The two of them gave the beach wheelchair back to James after James gave Ben's prosthetic legs back. Sophia and her husband thanked James for allowing them to borrow the wheelchair. Then, Ben and his wife walked over to a nearby bathroom to clean themselves off and change back into the clothes that they had on before going to the beach. Once all was said and done, the young married couple headed over to an Italian restaurant to have dinner. It was 8:20 p.m. when Ben and Sophia were done having dinner and dessert at the restaurant and talking with each other. Finally, the two of them walked seven minutes west back to the Eastern Seaboard Hotel, entered it, and went into their hotel room. The young married couple enjoyed each other's company before calling it a night.

The morning of Thursday, May 20th, arrived, and Ben and Sophia were ready to completely savor their next adventure. The two of them woke up and lovingly gazed into each other's eyes around 9:20 a.m. Then, Sophia and her husband hatched a plan to go to an aquarium that day. The young married couple got ready for the day and searched the Internet on Sophia's laptop for aquariums in Atlantic City. As it turned out, there was the Sea

Anemone Aquarium, which was a twenty-minute walk southeast of the Eastern Seaboard Hotel. Ben and his wife finalized their fun plan before heading to the Flip-House Breakfast Diner for breakfast after making the five-minute walk there.

Once Ben and Sophia were done eating a blueberry pancake and chicken sausage breakfast, they made the fifteen-minute trek to the Sea Anemone Aquarium. Ben was wearing the black short-sleeved *Star Wars: Attack of the Clones* T-shirt his wife bought him as one of his one-year anniversary presents. He also had chosen to wear black jeans and black shoes. Sophia had chosen to wear her light pink short-sleeved T-shirt along with light blue jeans and white shoes that had light pink stripes on them. The young married couple had their backpacks, which were full of everything that they needed for the day.

Sophia and her husband quickly found out why the aquarium was called the Sea Anemone Aquarium after they entered the ocean-blue-colored building and bought their passes. There were a ton of sea anemones along with various types of fish in the huge sidewall and floor-level tanks. Ben and his wife also saw overhead tanks and other sidewall tanks that held sea horses, catfish, zebra fish, clown fish, and sharks. There also were manta rays and sturgeons. The Sea Anemone Aquarium was bigger compared to the Sea Trench Aquarium in San Diego. The young married couple had a blast looking at all of the extremely colorful and beautiful fish, sea anemones, and other sea creatures for the next few hours from 11:45 a.m. to 2:45 p.m.

The young married couple took a break in the middle of the Sea Anemone Aquarium at 2:45 p.m. and sat on a red bench. They fully took in and gazed in wonder upon all of the sights of the fish, anemones, and sharks in the huge tanks. The Sea Anemone Aquarium closed at 5:00 p.m. for feeding time for all of the sea creatures. Ben and Sophia planned on taking a nice chunk of the rest of the time they had to just sit on the bench and thoroughly enjoy looking at all of the sea creatures. So, that is what they did from 2:45 to approximately 3:25 p.m. Then, Sophia and her husband took several pictures of themselves and a lot of the fish, sea anemones, and sharks, in addition to walking throughout the rest of the aquarium.

Minutes piled on minutes, and it was 4:45 p.m. before Ben and Sophia knew it. A few minutes passed, and they began to walk towards the exit of the Sea Anemone Aquarium. Once the two of them exited the building, they walked to a Mexican restaurant to have dinner. The restaurant was only a five-minute walk north of where they were. Ben and his wife savored a chimichanga and taco dinner at the Mexican restaurant before heading back to the Eastern Seaboard Hotel. It was nearly 7:15 p.m. by the time the young married couple got inside their hotel room on the first floor. Sophia and her husband cuddled up next to each other on their king bed and watched three episodes of a cop show on TV before getting ready for bed and marking the end of their night.

Thursday night turned into Friday morning. Ben and Sophia woke up together at 9:00 a.m. and got ready for the day. Ben chose to wear his red and blue *Star Wars: A New Hope* T-shirt with dark blue jeans and dark blue sneakers with white bottoms on them. Sophia chose her white shirt with light purple patterns on it to wear along with light blue jeans and white shoes with light purple stripes. Now, the young married couple gathered up all of the items they would need for the day and put those items in their backpacks. Sophia and her husband wanted to go to an amusement park or a national park. They would further discuss their final plan after they ate breakfast at the Flip-House Breakfast Diner.

It was approximately 11:30 a.m. when Ben and his wife were done eating breakfast and talking at the diner. The two of them had chosen to go to an amusement park. They wanted to participate in fun activities and ride the Ferris wheel at the park. The catch that Ben and Sophia found out while searching the Internet was that there were only two amusement parks in Atlantic City. The first park was a forty-five-minute drive southeast of where they were at the Flip-House Breakfast Diner. However, the second amusement park was only a half-hour drive northeast from the diner. The young married couple would need to find and get a shuttle to drive them to either one of the parks. Ben and his wife decided to go to the amusement park that was a half hour away before searching the Internet for a shuttle to drive them there.

Sophia and her husband arrived at the amusement park, which was called Mountain-High Amusement Park, a few minutes after 12:45 p.m. The shuttle that they had taken dropped them off one block south of the park. The young married couple had shared Jesus's messages with the shuttle driver and two of the riders on the way to Mountain-High Amusement Park. All three people were greatly interested in all that Ben and Sophia talked to them about. Ben and his wife were sure that those three people would eventually come to know Jesus/God and have relationships with Him. As for now, Ben and his wife were going to have a ton of fun at the amusement park.

The young married couple began their time at Mountain-High Amusement Park by participating in a table-grounded squirt gun contest, in which contestants tried to shoot at circular targets that ran up and down along the back wall of the contest table. Sophia ended up shooting the most targets after the end of the contest was signaled by the ring of a bell. Ben was just one target shy of outperforming his wife. The other two contestants came in third place and fourth place. Sophia had the choice of choosing which prize she would get. There was a pink watch, a medium-sized stuffed sea turtle, a medium-sized stuffed dolphin, and a purple purse. It was a tough choice for the twenty-one-year-old, but she finally and decisively chose to get the purple purse.

Sophia wanted Ben to play in the squirt gun contest again and win her the stuffed dolphin. Ben was fully intent on getting the dolphin for his wife as she stepped aside to let another contestant participate in the contest. There were three different contestants other than Ben. He focused in once the contest started again. He dialed in on every target and shot them. Then, the twenty-year-old was announced as the winner at the end of the contest. Sophia was super happy as the announcement was made and as Ben told the contest director to give him the stuffed dolphin that he would give to his wife.

Ben and Sophia participated and contested in other games and contests at Mountain-High Amusement Park for most of the rest of the afternoon. Then, at 4:30 p.m., the young married couple headed towards the red Ferris wheel. Once the two of them paid to go on the Ferris wheel, they had a great time gradually going up and around the contraption at a slower pace as other people hopped onto it. Sophia and her husband began to talk more with each other as the two of them were one-quarter of the distance to the top of the Ferris wheel. The adjustable side-by-side blue seats made it easy for Ben and his wife to talk intimately with each other and hold hands.

"You know what, Sophia," Ben said in a reflective tone, "I've been thinking about a few things as we approach the top of this Ferris wheel. You remember when we were flying high in the airplanes as we traveled to and from San Diego and to Atlantic City?"

"Yes," Sophia replied with a hint of curiosity in her voice. "What have you been thinking about?"

"I have just been thinking about how amazing and breathtaking it was to fly high in the sky on those airplanes with you and the other passengers," Ben replied with wonder in his tone. "Those times got me thinking about what it will be like to see a lot of Atlantic City once we reach the top of this Ferris wheel. And..."

"What it will be like once we go back to heaven..." Sophia finished her husband's sentence after he paused for a second. "I was catching on to what you were talking about. It will be amazing and awesome to look down on the Earth from whatever height we choose and from whatever time we want. That will be truly spectacular. I'm sure Jesus will allow us to do that. For now, you and I will just have to settle for the sights from high-up-in-the-sky airplanes and this Ferris wheel."

"Absolutely," Ben agreed. "It will be amazing to see all of the Earth from whatever height and time we choose once we go back to heaven. As for now, let's just completely absorb and soak in every second of this ride that we have. Plus, let's continue to totally enjoy every minute that we have together."

"Definitely," Sophia said assuredly. "You know just what to say at the right time. I have absolutely loved every minute that we have had together since I said that I loved you at your parents' house. And I will absolutely love every minute that we will have together from now on and into eternity with you, Jesus, the angels, and all of the other Christians who are in heaven."

"Man, you also have the knack of knowing just what to say at the right time too," Ben genuinely and lovingly responded. "I love you."

"I love you too," Sophia said equally as genuinely and lovingly as her husband.

Ben and Sophia lovingly held each other's hand in silence as they slowly rose further up and around the Ferris wheel. They were just five seats away from reaching the top. It was approximately 4:55 p.m. on a mostly cloudy day at Mountain-High Amusement Park. Sophia and her husband found out just why the amusement park was called what it was called once they reached the top of the Ferris wheel. The young married couple saw that the amusement park was nearly thirty feet away from a fifty-foot ledge. Even more so, the two of them could see a portion of the Atlantic Ocean in front of them in the distance. Ben and his wife also twisted their torsos a bit to the left, and they could see a majority of the city behind them. They turned back and faced forward again to thoroughly enjoy looking upon the portion of the ocean that they could see in addition to some of the city. Ben and Sophia soaked in all of the sights that they could while they were at the highest point on the Ferris wheel. Then, slowly but surely, the young married couple circled down to the bottom of the amusement park contraption.

It was nearly 5:25 p.m. by the time Sophia and her husband got down from the Ferris wheel. They proceeded to head back towards the exit of Mountain-High Amusement Park. The two of them sat down on an orange bench near the exit of the amusement park. Then, the young married couple took out their laptops from their backpacks and searched for a shuttle to drive them to a restaurant that was close to the hotel they were staying at.

Approximately two and a half hours passed by, and Ben and Sophia were back in their hotel room at the Eastern Seaboard Hotel, cuddled up next to each other on their king bed. They had eaten a chicken and pasta dinner at an Italian restaurant around 6:30 p.m. after the shuttle that they had taken dropped them off at the restaurant. Now, the young married couple was watching a romance/action movie in their bed inside their hotel room. The movie ended at 10:30 p.m., and then the two of them got ready for bed and did their usual things with God before calling it a night.

The morning of Saturday, May 22nd, came, and Ben and Sophia Lawson planned on staying at Pebble Beach for most of the day since it was the last day of their Atlantic City vacation. The young married couple began their wonderful morning around 9:30 a.m. and got ready for the day before heading over to the Flip-House Breakfast Diner for breakfast. They ordered two hot sauce-induced bacon and cheese omelets along with two bagels and a couple of glasses of orange juice. Sophia and her husband completely enjoyed their breakfast before changing into their beach clothes in the men's and women's bathrooms inside the restaurant. Then, the two of them walked out of the Flip-House Breakfast Diner and made the ten-minute trek east to Pebble Beach.

It was approximately 11:45 a.m. when Ben and Sophia arrived at the lifeguard station next to the pier at the beach. The two of them exchanged Ben's prosthetic legs for the big beach wheelchair that James let them borrow again. Once those things happened, the young married couple settled down on a spot on the beach that was twenty-two feet above the shoreline, where there was dry sand. Ben and his wife just stared at the Atlantic Ocean for nearly an hour and a half in addition to talking with each other. Then, at 1:30 p.m., Sophia grabbed the handlebar on the back of the beach wheelchair that Ben was in and wheeled him fifteen feet down the shoreline. Wave after wave came and splashed a bit onto Ben's dark blue swim shorts. The waves also splashed onto and against Sophia's feet and the bottom parts of her thighs. Ben's plain dark blue short-sleeved shirt and his wife's green one-piece bikini stayed clear of the ocean water.

Sophia wheeled her husband back to where they were twenty-two feet up on the shoreline every five minutes for twenty minutes. The young married couple thoroughly enjoyed this fun activity for the time that they did it. Ben and his wife especially liked it as the waves came up the shoreline, splashed up, and smoothly and gently caressed Sophia's feet and Ben's upper leg areas. Once the thrilling twenty minutes were done, Ben and Sophia came back up to their spot on the beach again. They spent the next three and a half hours gazing upon the Atlantic Ocean, eating snacks, and relaxing on their spot on the beach. The two of them finished their exciting day at Pebble Beach around 5:45 p.m. before exchanging the beach wheelchair for Ben's prosthetic legs with James at the lifeguard station. Finally, the young married couple cleaned themselves off and walked towards a Mexican restaurant for dinner.

The next twenty-six hours and fifteen minutes flew by in a spectacular way for Ben and Sophia Lawson. They were having a delectable chicken enchilada dinner at the Mexican restaurant in Atlantic City one moment. Then, the next moment, Sophia and her husband watched a cop show in their hotel room. The young married couple went to bed at about 11:00 p.m. that Saturday night. They woke up on the morning of Sunday, May 23rd, and ate breakfast at the Flip-House Breakfast Diner before returning to their hotel room and enjoying each other's company. Ben and his wife checked out of their hotel room and hotel at 1:30 p.m. Then, they got a shuttle to drive them to the airport in Atlantic City for their 3:15 p.m. American Airlines flight. The young married couple was back in their apartment room in Evart, Michigan, by 8:00 p.m. after their flight came into the city and after the two of them bought groceries at a nearby Whole Foods. Now, at 8:00 p.m., Ben and Sophia cooked and ate dinner inside their apartment room before winding down their night.

Time blurred together in a wonderful and beautiful way for Ben and Sophia. They went back to work on Monday, May 24th, and worked hard at their jobs. Work turned into quality time between the young married couple around 5:30 p.m. on each day of the work week. Then, on the weekends, Sophia and her husband participated in a variety of baseball, volleyball, and video game activities by themselves and with their friends and family. In addition, Ben and his wife spent a lot of quality time together on the weekends and did everything together. June came and then turned into July. The young married couple and their friends and family had a ton of fun interacting with each other and watching a fireworks show at the Evart Fair Grounds for the 4th of July. July continued to speed by after that event. Ben and Sophia always made sure to savor and soak in every precious minute they had together, in addition to their time at work and with their friends and families.

August 7th arrived, and it was a very special day for Ben's brother, Josh. It was Josh's birthday, and the rest of the Lawson family, the O'Donnell family, and all of Ben's and Josh's friends gathered at the NASCAR charity event that was being held in Southern Michigan. Josh wanted to drive a race car ever since he saw Ben drive one with Blake in 2001. The sixteen-year-old was now going to learn to drive a NASCAR race car. It helped that he had practiced driving Leslie's Honda several times during July. Now, the group was gathered in a gun metal gray colored race car hangar along with other people who wanted to ride and drive in a professional race car with a NASCAR racer. Everyone had completed the hour-and-a-half-long safety and procedure class in a lecture-style room in a different building. Josh was first up on riding and driving in a red and purple colored race car. He didn't know which racer would accompany him because it was a surprise that only Dave and Leslie knew. There was a completely new set of racers except for one.

"Is that you, Ben?" Blake said surprisingly but excitedly as he walked towards Ben, Josh, and Sophia.

"Hey, Blake," Ben said with surprise in his tone. "I'm a little surprised to see you here after these past few years. It's good to see you."

"You, too, man," Blake responded after walking up to Ben and giving him a hug. Ben hugged him back. Then, after the two men let go of each other, Blake continued to speak, "I was waiting these three years to see if you and Josh would come back to this event and give it another go. Then, I heard from the event director that you and Josh would indeed be coming back for Josh's sixteenth birthday courtesy of your parents, and here you two are. I also noticed that you now have prosthetic legs, Ben. It's great to see you up and walking around again."

"Thanks, Blake," Ben said genuinely. "Truthfully, I did not do that well for the first year or so after my incident, but thanks to God and my friends and family, I am back to a good spot in my life. Speaking of family, I would like to introduce you to my wife, Sophia."

"That is awesome stuff to hear, Ben, especially the fact that you have a wife!" Blake enthusiastically responded before switching his attention to Sophia, who waved to him a little bit since they were not that far apart. "It is a pleasure to meet you, Sophia."

"It is also a pleasure to meet you, too, Blake," Sophia responded kindly and genuinely as she and Blake shook hands. "Ben told me good things about you, especially about the time that you and Josh helped carry him to his family's car right as his incident started. It was also very kind of you to share those encouraging words with Ben."

"I was glad to be of help to him," Blake said genuinely before turning his attention to Josh. "Now, here is the birthday boy! Happy sixteenth birthday, Josh!"

"Thanks, Blake!" Josh responded gratefully and enthusiastically before shaking Blake's hand. The sixteen-year-old hadn't minded that Blake first talked to Ben. He was good with that. "It's good to see you again!"

"Same here, man!" Blake excitedly said. "Now, let's get ready for our ride and drive together."

"Definitely, let's go!" Josh responded excitedly.

Blake and Josh got suited up for their ride and drive. Then, Blake drove the sixteen-year-old in the red and purple race car across the circular four-mile-long racetrack for almost ten minutes at an exhilarating rate of one hundred miles an hour for the most part. Finally, after

Josh and Blake regrouped and switched positions in the race car hangar, Josh drove the race car out onto the racetrack and stepped on the gas. The next fifteen minutes were the most thrilling and exhilarating minutes of Josh's life as he sped around the long racetrack from eighty to one hundred miles per hour with Blake in the passenger seat. These fifteen minutes took Ben down a trip to memory lane when he drove the orange and yellow race car with Blake in the seat next to him. The events that followed Ben's outing with Blake didn't bother him anymore. The twenty-year-old was at peace with all of what happened to him in relation to his incident. Now, Ben was having fun watching his brother zoom around the racetrack. This part was even more fun as Sophia lovingly rested her head against Ben's right shoulder.

Time seemed to slip by yet again. One minute saw Ben, Sophia, the rest of the Lawson and O'Donnell family members, and Ben's and Josh's friends head home from the NASCAR charity event. That moment on that day was instantly followed by a birthday celebration for Josh at the Lawson house. The Lawson family dog, Buster, had been watched over by a good and trustworthy neighborhood friend while the family and friend group were gone in southern Michigan. The next moment after Josh's birthday celebration, Ben and Sophia were back at their entry-level jobs again. Then, the beautiful and spectacular mixture of work and quality time together after work turned into October of 2004. This month was filled to the brim with work, quality time, baseball and volleyball activities by themselves and with friends and family, and Halloween. Ben and Sophia dressed up as Casey and April from the *Teenage Mutant Ninja Turtles* animated series and handed out candy at a neighborhood next to Crystal Park.

November arrived, and the days in that month seemed to blur together. It was Thanksgiving again before anyone knew it. Ben, Sophia, and all of their friends and families gathered at the O'Donnell house for Thanksgiving at 1:30 p.m. Even Carl Wendleson and Tess Debor were there. The dog, Buster, was also brought to the gathering. He eventually warmed up to everyone after barking at them. Anyway, the large group of families and friends played volleyball in the backyard in addition to playing with Buster. They also rewatched a couple of episodes of *Smallville* from season one. Each couple took turns sitting on the living room couch and standing as they watched the show and talked.

Four o'clock came, and everyone helped prepare Thanksgiving dinner. Once everything was said and done by 6:30 p.m., the group ate dinner together at the elongated dining room tables that the O'Donnell family had bought. Even Buster had some little pieces of turkey and pumpkin pie mixed into his dog food. Each person at the two tables intermittently talked about a few things they were grateful for. Once everyone was done talking about that, Ben asked his brother if he had chosen a career to go into after graduating high school. Josh said he still didn't know which career he wanted to go into. However, the sixteen-year-old said that he had been thinking for a few days about becoming a healthcare provider for one or two people.

The night continued to seemingly fly by while everyone in the huge group ate dinner and dessert and talked with each other. Then, all of the people flocked to the living room to rewatch more episodes of *Smallville*. Anthony Markus and Lucy Robinson officially announced that they had just entered into a serious relationship with each other five months ago after dating each other for nearly five months. Alicia O'Donnell and Josh also announced they have been in a serious relationship for three months after dating each other for approximately seven months. Everybody was very happy about the news concerning the four people. Finally, around 10:15 p.m., everyone except the O'Donnell family headed back to their houses and apartments.

The next four months seemed to pile onto each other. To start with, the rest of November and the majority of December came and went. Then, it was Christmas Day. Ben, Sophia, and their friends and families, including Carl and Tess, gathered at the Lawson house for that day. It was nearly 11:00 a.m. when everyone arrived to eat a strawberry waffle, bacon, eggs, and sausage brunch. Even Buster received several little pieces of all the food items that were mixed into his dog food. Then, after brunch, everyone walked the short distance towards the sectional couch and fireplace in the family room to open their stockings, which were provided by the Lawson family. Each person had a blast picking out every little thing that was in his or her stocking. The little gifts ranged from little pieces of candy to fun everyday items. Finally, everyone flocked to the living room to open their presents. Each person, including Tess and Carl, got each other one to three presents. The presents ranged from Smallville, Superman, and Justice League bobblehead figures, coffee mugs, and posters to Star Wars collectible items and sports stuff. Buster even got a Krypto the Superdog cape and a few more dog toys and treats.

The rest of Christmas Day was filled with everyone hanging out and talking with each other, in addition to walking around the Lawsons' neighborhood at night after dinner to check out the lights that the neighbors had. There were dazzling lights of most colors and shapes. Everyone thoroughly enjoyed looking at the lights and intermittently talking with each other. Then, at 8:30 p.m., Ben, Sophia, and their friends and families returned to the Lawsons to talk with each other a bit more and watch TV. Finally, everyone except Dave, Leslie, Josh, and Buster headed back to their own houses and apartments by 10:15 p.m.

January soon arrived after everyone in the large group spent New Year's Eve together at the O'Donnell family house. Ben's twenty-first birthday came on January 5th, and it was the second special event that kicked off the year of 2005. The New Year's Day party at the Lawson house was the first special event. As for Ben's birthday, he and Sophia took off the day from work since it was on a Wednesday. The young married couple woke up in their king bed in their apartment around 9:15 a.m. and spent some time together before getting ready for the fun day. Sophia drove herself and her husband to a nearby Denny's restaurant to have Ben's birthday breakfast. Once the two of them finished eating a delicious chocolate chip, hash browns, and sausage breakfast, they headed to the movie theater to see a comedy/action movie.

The latter part of the day was filled with a fun game of baseball with the two of them and Ben's family at Crystal Park. Finally, Ben and his wife returned to their apartment around 7:00 p.m. to eat an Olive Garden take-out dinner that Sophia bought after playing baseball. The young married couple watched a few rerun episodes of Smallville from season three while eating dinner before wrapping up their night. Ben and Sophia lovingly and intently looked into each other's eyes before turning off their apartment room lights and closing their bedroom door.

February came rushing to Ben and Sophia Lawson like a roaring ocean wave after the rest of January flew by in a fantastic flurry of work and quality time together. The days leading up to the day before Valentine's Day were filled to the brim with work, family time, and the usual fun times between the young married couple. Then, Sophia and her husband's celebration of Valentine's Day came on that Sunday, February 13th. The day began like usual before Ben and Sophia drove to Holy Communion Church for the church service. The O'Donnell family, Diego Sanchez, and his girlfriend, Vanessa Lopez, were next to the young married couple. All of them had a great time worshiping God and listening to the sermon from Pastor Jack Hershel about God's plans for healthy Christian relationships and marriages.

Sophia and her husband drove in their red Lexus to a nearby Eegee's to have lunch there after the church service was over. Then, they returned to their apartment, cuddled up on their purple love seat, and watched a romantic comedy movie on TV. Lastly, Ben and his wife drove to a somewhat nearby Cheesecake Factory for dinner at approximately 6:30 p.m. After having a delectable chicken and pasta dinner and cheesecake dessert, they headed back to their apartment. The young married couple spent more amazing quality time together before hitting the hay.

The rest of February and the entirety of March were filled with work and quality time together for Ben and Sophia Lawson, as well as hanging out with friends and family. April arrived before the two of them knew it, and it was more of the same fun mixture of work and activities for the young married couple until Sophia's birthday arrived. Today was going to be a special occasion, and it started out with Ben making and giving his wife a strawberry waffle and sausage breakfast in bed around 9:30 a.m. The two of them took the day off from work since Sophia's birthday was on a Tuesday. She had plenty of time to eat breakfast in bed.

Sophia and her husband headed to Rebario's to have a nacho lunch after spending time with each other at their apartment until eleven fifty. The Lawson and O'Donnell families had decided to only let Ben and Sophia celebrate Sophia's birthday that day. However, the O'Donnell family dropped off her presents from them at her and Ben's apartment before they went to work. Sophia opened her presents from her family right after eating breakfast in bed. As for now, Ben gave Sophia her first of three presents from him.

"I thought that this would be a good time to give you your first birthday present from me," Ben said with some enthusiasm and excitement in his tone. "Close your eyes."

"Ooohhh, I like the sound of this," Sophia responded excitedly before closing her eyes.

"Okay, you can open your eyes now," Ben said after pulling out a red $250 Serenity Spa gift card from the right pocket of his light blue jeans.

"Oh my gosh!" Sophia excitedly exclaimed. "Thank you so much, Ben!"

"You're welcome, Sophia!" Ben responded excitedly out of a happy heart.

"This is so great!" Sophia said with excitement in her tone. "Is it possible for me to go to Serenity Spa now, or should I go some other time?"

"I can drop you off there now," Ben responded genuinely. "It's only two forty-five, and Serenity Spa is only twelve minutes west from here. Plus, the spa is open until six."

"Fantastic!" Sophia said excitedly. "You can drive and drop me off there. I will definitely be at Serenity Spa until they close. Thank you again for my present, babe! I love you very much!"

"I love you very much, too, babe!" Ben responded lovingly and genuinely right before he and his wife passionately hugged and kissed each other for several seconds.

The young married couple arrived at Serenity Spa at 3:00 p.m. Ben asked Sophia if he could stay with her for a little while, and she kindly obliged. So, Ben stayed at the spa for an hour while his wife received a relaxing massage. Then, he walked out of the spa and headed into a nearby movie theater/mall that had an arcade in it. He played some video games before heading back to Serenity Spa to pick up Sophia at 6:00 p.m. She had gotten into a spa and received a pedicure and manicure after the massage. Now, Sophia and her husband drove to an Olive Garden fifteen minutes southwest of their apartment. The young married couple had a wonderful dinner at the restaurant before going back to their apartment. They spent the next hour cuddling up next to each other on their bed while watching an episode of a cop show. That was when Ben surprised his wife with her other two birthday presents from him. One of her presents was a silver necklace, and the other was a silver bracelet. Then, with that same loving and passionate look that Ben and Sophia gave each other, they called it a night and closed their bedroom door after turning off their apartment room lights.

Two weeks flew by, and it was Tuesday, April 26th. Today was Ben and Sophia's second-year anniversary, and it was going to be a spectacular day. The young married couple planned on staying in a hotel room at the Tree Lodge Hotel in Evart City, which Ben had reserved a week ago. As for the morning of their second-year anniversary, the two of them woke up together around 8:45 a.m. and lovingly gazed into each other's eyes. Then, Sophia and her husband got ready for the day at 9:10 a.m. and prepared breakfast for themselves fifteen minutes later since they took that day off from work.

The two of them drove to Rebario's for lunch at eleven forty-five after spending quality time with each other. They ate and talked with each other before heading to the Tree Lodge Hotel at 2:00 p.m. Their hotel room check-in time was at two thirty, and they were twenty-five minutes away from the hotel. So, Ben and his wife drove to the Tree Lodge Hotel and got there at 2:25 p.m. The young married couple noticed why the hotel was called what it was called. There were a lot of redwood trees around the entire hotel, and there were smaller trees in a huge courtyard-like area. The two of them also noticed that there was a large pool in the middle of the courtyard area after they checked into their hotel room. Ben and Sophia were staying in a first-floor hotel room that was northeast of the courtyard and pool. The inside of their hotel room was completely laid with sleek and smooth white tile and had a kitchen, living room area, bathroom, laundry room, and master bedroom. The living room area was laid with comfortable white carpet and had a gray couch, a few potted plants on coffee tables, and a fifty-inch TV.

"This is absolutely amazing, babe!" Sophia said excitedly to Ben as the two of them walked towards the pool area. The walkways to that area were strewn with pretty-looking trees, bushes, and flowers on both sides of them. The young married couple had their backpacks strapped to their backs. They had everything in their backpacks that they would need for their time at the pool.

"For sure!" Ben responded, equally excited as his wife. "This is definitely incredible!"

"Definitely!" Sophia enthusiastically agreed. "Happy second-year anniversary, my love!"

"Happy second-year anniversary as well, my love!" Ben said with love and enthusiasm in his voice just as he and his wife stopped in the middle of the walkway with the trees, flowers, and bushes on either side of them. The two of them passionately hugged and kissed each other for nearly twenty seconds.

The rest of Ben and Sophia's lovely day at the Tree Lodge Hotel flowed over with tons of fun. They changed their clothes to swimming clothes when they entered their hotel room. So, now the young married couple walked the rest of the way down the walkway towards the pool area. It was almost 3:15 p.m. on a somewhat cloudy but sunny day in Evart City. Sophia and her husband spent the next three hours swimming in the pool with the other people who were there as well. In addition, Ben and his wife sat in pool chairs next to the pool and ordered a couple of snacks and two glasses of pink lemonade. Ben had made sure to take off and put on his prosthetic legs at the appropriate times.

Ben and Sophia changed back into their day clothes around 6:15 p.m. in a family bathroom after they thoroughly enjoyed their wonderful time at the pool area. Then, they walked into a very nice Italian restaurant inside the hotel and had dinner there. The young married couple ate dinner and dessert and reminisced about their amazing two years together. Finally, Sophia and her husband exited the restaurant at approximately 8:45 p.m. and slowly strolled back to their hotel room on the scenic outside route, taking in everything that they saw. Once the two of them got back inside their hotel room, they got ready for bed and worshiped and praised God earlier than usual. Ben and his wife proceeded to go inside their bedroom and spend some more intimate quality time with each other before falling asleep on their king bed.

As it has been said repeatedly, time seems to fly by when you are having fun. That saying definitely had been the case for Ben and Sophia Lawson time and time again throughout their marriage. The two of them gave one present to each other once they got into their hotel room bedroom on the night of their second anniversary. Then, as it happened, Sophia and her husband spent more intimate time with each other before falling asleep on their bed. Those moments, in turn, turned into their check-out time of 8:00 a.m. of Wednesday, April 27th. Ben only had reserved their hotel room at the Tree Lodge Hotel for one night because of the expensive price and because of work on that Wednesday. Now, after checking out, Ben dropped off his wife at True Health Christian Counseling Center for her entry-level aide job. Then, he drove over to Aeromechanics Incorporated for his entry-level desk job. Once

Ben got off of work on that Wednesday and picked up Sophia from her job, everything began to blend together again in one beautiful mixture.

The last three days of April passed by in a beautiful blur, and then it was May. Ben and Sophia had reminded themselves during those last few days of April about what Jesus said to Ben so that he and her could avoid the car crash on the night of May 13th on the way to Rebario's. The young married couple was not afraid to go out to the restaurant that night. They were not going to hide themselves and live in fear. The two of them were going to do what they wanted to do to the fullest before going back to heaven.

One other event occurred for Ben, his wife, and their friends and families before May 13th, in addition to the usual fantastic mixture of work and quality time with each other. The large group drove in several of their cars to a film festival in western Michigan on the afternoon of May 7th to go see one of the very first screenings of *Star Wars: Revenge of the Sith*. Tess Debor and Carl Wendleson were among the friends in the moviegoing group. In saying that, a trusted and good neighbor of the Lawson family watched and took care of Buster while they were gone.

Ben, Sophia, and the rest of the group arrived at the film festival an hour before the 6:00 p.m. screening of the movie. All of them were hyped to finally watch the third and final installment of the Star Wars prequel trilogy as they were eating an early dinner. Then, the time came to sit down in their chairs along with the rest of the huge crowd. The movie began, and every single person at the film festival was already enraptured by what they saw. Time passed by, and then the movie was over at 8:20 p.m. Ben, Sophia, and their friends and families, in addition to a large portion of the rest of the crowd, really liked the movie even though it had a darker tone. The group especially liked the lightsaber battle between Obi-Wan and Anakin Skywalker on the planet of Mustafar towards the end of the movie, even though it saddened them to see the two characters fight each other. Now, they knew everything about how Anakin became Darth Vader. As for the current moment, everyone walked to their own vehicles to drive back to their houses and apartments.

Six more days hurried past, and they blended into Friday, May 13th. Ben and Sophia Lawson stayed inside their apartment room and enjoyed each other's company throughout the morning and afternoon. This was because the two of them had amicably quit and left their entry-level jobs effectively and immediately the day before. The young married couple had been really thankful and grateful to their bosses for their entry-level jobs when they announced that they were leaving them. Ben and Sophia's bosses understood that they were ready to go to another job and level up. Even though the young married couple didn't say where they were going, the two of them knew they were going to help rule nations in heaven with Jesus and everyone else there. As for the current moment, Sophia and her husband cuddled up next to each other on their purple love seat in the living room area of their apartment and rewatched Smallville episodes. They couldn't wait to celebrate their final night on Earth at Rebario's. The great thing was that the two of them knew how to avoid the car crash on the way to the restaurant.

Ben and Sophia drove to Rebario's for dinner in their electric blue Ford truck at 6:00 p.m. The young married couple made sure to take the longer route on North Waterfront Avenue instead of the fastest route. Sure enough, a drunk driver in a big semitruck flew in front of them in the distance to the right, approximately five minutes before Sophia and her husband would have been hit by the semitruck. Once Ben and his wife safely arrived at Rebario's, the two of them walked into the restaurant. Then, the young married couple ordered and ate dinner and dessert that outdid what Ben provided for his and Sophia's first-year anniversary. The two of them didn't drink any alcoholic beverages, nor did they ever drink any because they were not fans of alcohol. Anyway, Sophia and her husband were dressed in just as nice clothes as they had on for their first-year and second-year anniversaries.

Finally, when Sophia and her husband were done eating their delicious dinner and dessert and talking with each other, they returned to their apartment. It was approximately 9:15 p.m. when the young married couple got into their apartment room and got ready for bed. They were going to spend some more special quality time with each other in their bedroom before falling asleep on their king bed. Ben and Sophia wanted to wake up at 7:00 a.m. on Saturday and completely savor and cherish every last minute they had with each other on Earth, just like they always did.

CHAPTER 11:

The Final Destination

The Bible is clear that Christians who believe in God and have relationships with Jesus go to heaven when they die. Heaven is a far better place than Earth because it is perfect in heaven. As Jesus had said to Ben when He talked with him in heaven, God wipes away every tear from a believer's eyes and that there will be no more pain, death, suffering, and heartache. Jesus had been grieved that Ben and Sophia had been shot by Yennik and Erik Dragano. He had known that those unfortunate events had been bound to happen. So, Jesus had given Ben and Sophia a second chance at life to find and marry each other in addition to the most important thing of all. That thing was to tell His messages of love, provision, protection, and the kingdom of God to everyone they met.

Now, it was 7:00 a.m. on a bright and sunny day in Evart on Saturday, May 14th, 2005. Ben and Sophia Lawson had thoroughly savored every minute they had together in their marriage. The young married couple did an excellent job in telling Jesus's messages to everyone they met. Even more so, the two of them had worked at great entry-level jobs and spent a lot of time with their friends and family. Ben and his wife had also gladly and joyfully attended church every Sunday and had tithed on every paycheck they got. Finally, Sophia and her husband had a date to meet Jesus/God/the Holy Spirit, the angels, and the other Christians in heaven. Ben and his wife were very grateful that Jesus would spare the two of them from all of what He told Ben.

"Good morning, my love," Sophia genuinely and lovingly said to Ben after the two of them woke up at 7:00 a.m. in their king bed in their apartment room. They had also turned towards each other.

"Good morning, my love," Ben responded in a voice that was equally as genuine and loving as that of his beautiful wife. The young married couple passionately hugged and kissed each other for nearly ten seconds before Ben spoke again. "Today is the day that we go back to heaven. Can you believe it?"

"Honestly, I cannot believe it," Sophia said. "Time has just gone by so fast. Where did it all go?"

"Me too," Ben said in agreement. "I cannot believe that this day is already here. Time went by too fast."

"Agreed," Sophia responded. "However, it was one heck of a lovely ride."

"Definitely. It indeed was a heavenly romance."

"Absolutely. I just have one thing to ask. You will remember this question from when I first asked it. Ben Lawson, do you really love me?"

"I remember that time," Ben responded happily and lovingly. "I will say the same thing I said then because it has never been more true. I deeply love you, Sophia Lawson."

"Awww....thank you, babe," Sophia lovingly said. "It means just as much, if not more, as when you first said it."

"You're welcome, babe," Ben said in that similar loving voice before he and Sophia passionately hugged and kissed each other for nearly half a minute.

Ben and Sophia got ready for the rest of their morning and short afternoon at 8:15 a.m. after spending intimate quality time with each other. The young married couple just sat on their king bed after getting ready for their shorter day. Sophia was wearing her light purple, short-sleeved shirt with light blue patterns on it in addition to light blue jeans and white shoes that had light blue bottoms on them. Ben had chosen to wear his black short-sleeved *Star Wars: Attack of the Clones* T-shirt along with black jeans and black shoes that had dark blue bottoms on them. He smiled to himself after he had seen what his wife was wearing. It was like Ben was just seeing Sophia for the first time during the second semester of his sophomore year of college at Evart University, minus the negative interactions that the two of them had at the university sixteen days later. The black-haired twenty-one-year-old was very grateful for the amazing two years of marriage he and Sophia had. Now, they were just sitting right next to each other on the front edge of their bed. The young married couple was reminiscing about the adventures they had in San Diego and Atlantic City. That was certainly true as Sophia and her husband looked at the colorfully framed pictures they gave each other for their marriage anniversaries. Those framed pictures were on a shelf in front of them.

"Great times," Ben said in a happy and reflective voice to his wife.

"They sure were," Sophia agreed in a similar voice. "I wonder what those places will look like from heaven."

"That is something to wonder about," Ben responded. "All that I can say is that it all should be heavenly."

"Definitely," Sophia said. "Hawaii and the entirety of Europe must be absolutely beautiful from up there."

"Yes, it will be amazing to see Hawaii, the entirety of Europe, and all of the other countries from heaven," Ben responded. "The best thing of all is that we will get to do that and many other good things with Jesus and all of the angels and Christians who are there."

"Those things will truly be awesome. I have missed seeing Jesus. He is the greatest."

"Amen. I have missed seeing Him too."

"Yep. It will be really great to see Him again. For the time being, let's just savor and cherish every last minute that we have together, like we have always done."

"For sure," Ben responded before standing up on his prosthetic legs. Sophia followed suit before Ben spoke again. "Speaking of which, how would you like to make our final and favorite breakfast of strawberry waffles, bacon, and sausages together?"

"I'd absolutely love that!" Sophia happily and excitedly said before she and Ben headed out of their bedroom and walked into the kitchen area. The young married couple took forty-five minutes to prepare their favorite breakfast in addition to texting their friends and family to meet them at the wooden building at Crystal Park at noon or a few minutes after that. Then, at approximately 9:20 a.m., Ben and Sophia took their beautiful red plates that had their breakfast, walked over to the living room area, and set their plates down on the coffee table that was in front on the purple love seat. Sophia and her husband proceeded to sit on the love seat, pray over their breakfast and day, and then grab their plates and eat their breakfast in silence for a few minutes.

"You know what has got me thinking, Ben?" Sophia asked her husband after eating some strawberry waffles and sausages.

"What, Sophia?" Ben asked in a genuinely curious tone after taking bites of a strawberry waffle, bacon, and sausages.

"I was wondering how this type of breakfast will taste in heaven," Sophia responded in wonder. "I mean, there is going to be the banquet with Jesus and all of us Christians in heaven who are collectively His bride and wife. Plus, since that's the case, we will eat all kinds of things in heaven."

"Valid point," Ben said after eating more of his breakfast. "I bet this type of breakfast will be absolutely and perfectly delicious in heaven, along with all of the other food that all of us will eat. That's one of the things that I'm looking forward to doing once we go back to heaven. Also, we will not gain any pounds from the things that we all will eat, if I understand heaven correctly. It will simply be awesome."

"I think the whole idea of not gaining any pounds in heaven is very true," Sophia agreed. "It will be great."

"For sure," Ben responded before changing the subject. He had that look that he and Sophia both had at the end of the nights of their marriage anniversaries. "Do you want to rewatch one last episode of *Smallville* before we do other things and drive to Crystal Park to meet our friends and families?"

"Oh, yes," Sophia passionately said with that similar look in her eyes and on her face. "First of all, I would like to rewatch the season one finale. That episode is one of my favorites."

"Same here," Ben agreed. "The season one finale is also one of my favorite episodes. Before we start, I want to say that we could watch the rest of the *Smallville* series in heaven if there are any more seasons after season four. Plus, I thought that seasons three and four were all right."

"I would have to say the same about seasons three and four," Sophia said in agreement. "Lois Lane made season four better. Also, it would be amazing if we could watch the rest of the series in heaven if there are any more seasons."

"Absolutely," Ben responded in agreement. "Lois Lane definitely made season four better. Well, are you ready to rewatch the finale of season one?"

"Yes, my handsome Clark Kent," Sophia said in a comical voice right as she put her left arm around her husband's waist.

"All right, my beautiful Lois Lane," Ben responded in a similar voice right before he and his wife kissed each other.

Ben and Sophia proceeded to rewatch the season one finale of Smallville. It was nearly 10:30 a.m. by the time the episode was over, and then the young married couple had some more special time with each other. Time passed by, and then the two of them were ready to drive to Crystal Park in their electric blue Ford truck to meet up and hang out with their friends and families. The Lawson and O'Donnell families, in addition to Ben and Sophia's friends, had only worked a couple of hours at their jobs in order to have one last time to spend with the young married couple. Then, Sophia and her husband would go back to heaven at 2:00 p.m. There was a change of mind by both Ben and his wife as they stopped at a stoplight seven minutes west from Crystal Park. Little did they know that going back to heaven was the best possible solution because of some events that were going to happen during the second life-threatening occurrence that day.

"Ben, I first want to say that it was an amazing morning today," Sophia said happily and lovingly as she sat in the passenger's seat, waiting for the stoplight to turn green. "There is one thing I want to talk with you for a minute and then talk with everyone at the park. It is amazing to think that we can spend eternity with Jesus, the angels, and all of the other Christians in heaven starting in just over two hours. However, I want more time to spend with you and our friends and families on Earth. You and I can figure out ways to navigate the future hardships in our marriage with God's help. What do you think?"

"I feel the same," Ben responded as there were ten more seconds left for the stoplight. He made sure to look at Sophia for those ten seconds. "I know the two of us can handle anything that life throws at us and our marriage. We should definitely talk with our friends and families when we get to the park in addition to praying to God."

"Sounds like a plan," Sophia said just as the stoplight turned green. Ben turned his head forward and focused on driving again. The seven minutes to Crystal Park seemed like a long time. Maybe it was just because the young married couple was caught in suspension due to their anxiety about talking with their friends and families and praying to God for more time on Earth. Sophia and her husband were good with either outcome of going back to heaven at 2:00 p.m. or later in life. They were truly grateful for the precious two years of marriage that the two of them had. As for the current moment, the young married couple was just on their way to Crystal Park. The seven minutes finally passed by, and Ben and Sophia parked next to Leslie Lawson's silver Honda.

"This is a great place to potentially spend the last two hours of our lives on Earth," Ben said in a reflective and grateful tone after he and Sophia got out of their truck and started walking towards the wooden building in which they had had their reception two years ago. It was approximately a fifty-foot walk towards the building, and all of Ben and Sophia's friends and families were gathered at the entrance.

"Absolutely," Sophia responded in a similar tone as she walked on Ben's left side. The two of them were holding hands. "This is where it all began for us as a newly married couple after our wedding."

"Yep," Ben said as he and his wife continued to hold hands and walk towards the wooden building. "That was an amazing day. You looked so beautiful in your wedding dress for our wedding and reception."

"Awww...thank you, babe," Sophia responded in a genuine and appreciative tone.

"You're welcome, babe," Ben said.

"Plus, you looked very handsome and stylish in your tux and slacks," Sophia said.

"Thanks,"

"You're welcome,"

"All right," Ben began before bringing up a new conversation topic. "On a different note, I was wondering how it would feel as we transition from being on Earth to being in heaven if we do indeed go back to heaven in a couple of hours."

"That is an interesting topic," Sophia responded before continuing to speak. "I would think that it would just be a smooth transition without any feeling at all. I would best describe the occurrence as a water vapor that instantly gets evaporated and disappears."

"Nice description," Ben said as he and Sophia closed in on the wooden building and their friends and families. The two of them were only fifteen feet away from the group. Leslie was the first person to excitedly run up to the young married couple. Ben shifted his attention to his mom as she came up to him with happy tears in her eyes. The mother and son hugged each other and remained in their embrace for almost twelve seconds.

"My son, it is so wonderful to see you again," Leslie said with great happiness and emotion in her voice.

"It is so great to see you, too, Mom," Ben responded in a happy and emotional voice as well. "Thank you so much for coming here along with the rest of our families and friends."

"You are so welcome, Ben," Leslie said with that same emotion in her voice. "We wanted to see and spend time with you and Sophia one last time before you two go back to heaven."

"Yeah," Ben began. "Sophia and I wanted to talk to you and the rest of the group about us going back to heaven."

"Oh, all right," Leslie responded in a curious voice. Then, she walked to Sophia and greeted her in a similar fashion as she did with her son. Once that happened, all of the rest of Ben and Sophia's friends and families quickly ran up to and greeted the young married couple, with Dave Lawson, Sam O'Donnell, and Candace O'Donnell leading the pack. Josh was holding a leash that had Buster at the end of it. Dave, Leslie, and Josh had thought they were going to surprise Ben and Sophia with one last visit from their dog. Josh was one of the last people to greet the young married couple.

"Hey, Ben," Josh excitedly said as he walked up to his brother and gave him a hug with both of his arms. Ben gladly accepted his gesture and hugged him back. Dave had stuck close by and grabbed Buster's leash from Josh. Then, the sixteen-year-old high school graduate continued to speak. "It's so great to see you again, Bro."

"I have to say the same," Ben responded genuinely and excitedly after he and Josh let go of each other. "It is so great to see you again, too, Bro. I also want to say again that I'm so proud of you for finishing your high school career strong. I know the first two years were tough, in addition to seventh grade. You have grown into a great young man."

"Thanks," Josh said appreciatively.

"You're welcome," Ben responded gladly. Then, Josh turned his attention to Sophia while Ben happily greeted Buster.

"I'm so glad that I get to see you one last time, Sophia," Josh said in a grateful tone as he and Sophia hugged each other as friends.

"Me, too, Josh," Sophia responded gratefully as well. "I know that I've said this before, but I'm so proud that you have grown so much mentally and emotionally since we first met each other."

"Thanks, Sophia," Josh said in an appreciative tone. "That means a lot. You have been like an older sister ever since we resolved the tension between us."

"Awww...Josh," Sophia began as she got emotional. "That's very sweet. You were also like a younger brother to me. Come here."

"That's really kind of you to say," Josh responded as he and Sophia shared another brief hug. "Thank you."

"You're welcome," Sophia said before she turned her attention to Buster and her husband. "Now, who do we have here? It's a pleasure to see you again, Buster."

"Buster has definitely been wanting to see you two one last time," Dave said as Ben and Sophia continued to rub Buster. Then, Dave continued to speak after pulling a tennis ball out of his light blue jeans. "I think he would like it if you two played with him one more time."

"Absolutely," Sophia happily said before she politely grabbed the tennis ball out of Dave's right hand. She shifted her attention to Buster once again after Dave unhooked the leash from Buster's harness. He knew that the dog would be good with playing fetch with Ben and Sophia one last time because he, Leslie, and Josh had trained him to do just that.

"All right, Buster," Sophia said in a playful tone before throwing the tennis ball fifteen feet to the left of the wooden building. "Go fetch."

The black Labrador retriever sped off to retrieve the tennis ball. Ben, Sophia, Dave, and the rest of the people who were watching could tell that Buster was loving this. Then, once Buster came back to Sophia with the tennis ball in his mouth, Sophia told him to drop the ball. She proceeded to give the ball to Ben. Buster noticed this and waited for Ben to throw the ball.

"All right, Buster," Ben said in a playful tone as well as he winded up his arm to throw the tennis ball twenty or so feet in the same direction as Sophia threw the ball. "Go fetch."

Ben and Sophia took turns throwing the tennis ball for Buster for almost twenty minutes, with a few of their friends and families joining in on the activity. The young married couple stared out into the distance at the baseball field as they threw the ball for the dog. Sophia and her husband remembered and reminisced about all of the fun times that they played baseball with their friends and families. That, in turn, made Ben and his wife remember all of the other thrilling times in which they and everyone else played volleyball, went out to see movies, and hung out at the O'Donnell and Lawson houses for the holidays. The other fond memories of the 4th of July celebrations with the two of them and their friends and families also came up to the surface of their minds.

Time passed by, and it was nearly 12:25 p.m. Several other people besides the young married couple and their friends and families were also at Crystal Park. Ben and Sophia stopped playing with Buster, and the rest of their friends and families who were doing so also stopped playing with the dog. Dave called Buster over to him and hooked the leash on the dog. Sophia and her husband were about to announce their change of mind about not going to heaven yet to all of their friends and families.

"If Sophia and I may say something to all of you," Ben began as he and Sophia stood next to each other a few feet in front of the building. All of the young married couple's friends and families were gathered several feet in front of them, eagerly awaiting to hear their announcement. "We would like to announce that we have had a change of mind about going back to heaven in an hour and a half."

"Yes," Sophia continued, "Ben and I want to have more time on Earth with each other and with all of you. We all have grown into a big family, both literally and figuratively. Our friends feel like additional family members to us. Again, Ben and I would love to have more time with all of you as well as with each other."

"Definitely," Ben said in continuation. "You all mean so much to us in addition to Sophia and I's marriage connection. We all have bonded so much in these past two years and even before that with each of our families. So, as my wife said, we would absolutely love to have more time with all of you and go back to heaven some other time in the future."

"I think I can speak for all of us here," Leslie Lawson said to Ben with emotion creeping into her voice. Then, she continued to speak. "We deeply appreciate what you and Sophia have said. I think we all would agree that we want to have more time with you two. Surely God knows what we all have been thinking."

"For sure," Diego Sanchez responded to Ben, Sophia, and Leslie while walking up to the front of the group of friends and families. "I only have one question. What would you two do about the inevitable life-ending events that Jesus specifically said would happen several times per month from tomorrow until June 4th, 2006?"

"Sophia and I could move to another city," Ben said to his best friend while addressing the crowd.

"We would go wherever you and Sophia go," Dave Lawson said, jumping into the conversation. He was saying that he, Leslie, Josh, and Buster would go wherever the young married couple moved to. Leslie and Josh agreed, and Buster wagged his tail. Then, Dave continued to speak. "However, I don't know if everyone else is able to move to a different city."

"Carl and I could move to a different city," Tess Debor said to Ben as she moved to the front of the crowd with her boyfriend, Carl Wendleson. "It would take some doing, but we would be happy to move to anywhere you two go. You and Sophia and your other friends and family have been very kind to us, especially with inviting us over for Thanksgiving and Christmas last year in addition to your rehearsal dinner, wedding, and reception, guys."

"Definitely," Carl contributed to the conversation before continuing. "Tess and I deeply appreciate the hospitality that you two and everyone else have shown us. We would be more than willing to move to a different city."

"Ben and I really appreciate your willingness to move to a different city to be closer to us and our families and friends who would be there," Sophia responded appreciatively to Carl and Tess. "We did enjoy having you two over at each of our family's houses for Thanksgiving and Christmas last year and my and Ben's rehearsal dinner, wedding, and reception."

"Absolutely," Ben jumped in on the conversation. "Our rehearsal dinner, wedding, and reception, in addition to last year's Thanksgiving and Christmas and the other holidays and events that you two were a part of, were tons of fun. Sophia and I would love to be close to you two again should we choose to move to a different city. However, my wife and I are good if we go back to heaven in about an hour and twenty minutes or some other time in the future because of some unforeseen reason. Otherwise, we want to stay with you all for a longer time."

"For sure," Sophia agreed before continuing to speak. "I think it is best if we all pray and ask God what should happen."

"Sounds like a great idea, sweet pea," Sam O'Donnell said to Sophia while standing with his wife in the front left side of the crowd.

"Absolutely," Candace O'Donnell agreed with her daughter. "Let's do it."

Ben also agreed, and the rest of the group of friends and family members jumped on board with the idea after saying whether or not they would be willing to move to a different city with the young married couple. Then, Dave started the group prayer. Leslie, Sam, and Candace, in addition to Ben and Sophia, also contributed to the group prayer, as did other group members. The people prayed with different words, and some of them used fewer words than others, but the main thing was that they wanted God's will to be done even though they wanted Ben and Sophia to stay with them for many more years to come. It was 12:55 p.m. when the young married couple and their friends and families were done with their group prayer. Then, as if in answer to prayer, the prophet, Harold Trenton, and his wife, Esther, decisively drove into the parking lot at Crystal Park at 1:00 p.m. in a red Honda. It only took five minutes for the two of them to walk over to the crowd of friends and families. Everyone in the group was surprised to see Harold and Esther as they all had puzzled faces.

"Harold, what are you doing here?" Ben asked as the elderly man walked up to him and Sophia with his wife. Harold was wearing a plain white short-sleeved shirt along with light blue jeans and white shoes. Esther had chosen to wear a red short-sleeved shirt, black jeans, and black shoes that had red bottoms on them.

"Hello again, Ben," Harold said in an even tone as he and Esther shook hands with Ben and Sophia and waved to everyone else in the large group. Then, Harold continued to speak. "I see you have your family and friends here, along with your wife's family and friends. My wife and I are here to tell you about a vision I had from God two and a half hours ago."

"Oh, that's timely," Ben responded in a curious and even tone. "What was your vision from God about, and what did God tell you?"

"Yes, please do share," Sophia said in a similar tone. Her and Ben's friends and families were also curious about and eagerly waited for what Harold had to say.

"All right," Harold began as he addressed Ben and Sophia. "My wife and I were at the end of finishing a delicious brunch at 10:30 a.m. at our house when, suddenly, God spoke to me and gave me a vision about you two and your friends and families. I stopped eating the rest of my meal and just sat still in my chair, listened to God, and paid attention to what He showed me. My wife was good with what I was doing and stopped eating the rest of her meal as well. As for the vision, God showed me that you two and your friends and families would gather at Crystal Park at 12:00 a.m. Then, I heard God say that you two had changed your minds about going back to heaven that day, which He said He knew would happen. God just wanted to respect your and Sophia's choices of going back to heaven when you two first met and talked with Him in heaven.

"Then," Harold continued, "the Lord told me again about the potentially life-ending events that would happen to Ben and you last night and today, in addition to the definite life-ending events that would happen to you two from tomorrow until June 4th, 2006. I see that you and Sophia heeded God's instruction in avoiding the first potentially life-ending event that happened last night with the drunk driver in the semitruck, which is great. However, you two will not be able to prevent the other life-ending event that happens today, as the Lord said to Ben when he was in heaven. Someone in your group of friends and family will prevent the event for you and Ben. God told me the name of that person, and I will not tell any of you who that person is. The thing that I will tell you is that person will confront a Middle Eastern/American man named Rajim Nemas, who would've otherwise shot you and Sophia in this park at 1:50 p.m. because of a personal reason. God didn't tell me the reason why Rajim would shoot you two, but I guess that I will find out soon. Nobody else would deter Rajim from accomplishing his goal. As for the definite life-ending events for you and Sophia, there is no escape from them, even if you two move to a different city. God told me that Rajim would have his uncle and some other men, who are experts at hiding and tracking people, track you two no matter where you two are.

"So," Harold started to conclude, "I told my wife everything I heard and saw before we ate the rest of our brunch and got ready to drive over here to tell you all of this."

"Yes," Esther said to Ben, Sophia, and their friends and families before continuing. "My husband and I are very sorry to break this terrible news to you all. It is the best solution for Ben and Sophia to go back to heaven in about forty-five minutes."

"Definitely," Harold agreed when addressing the group of friends and families in addition to Sophia and her husband. "We are extremely sorry, and we want to keep this wonderful and amazing young married couple from experiencing death again."

"That was a lot to unload on us, Harold," Dave Lawson said as he was standing ten feet away from the prophet. "So, it is better for Ben and Sophia to go back to heaven."

"I guess it is," Leslie responded in a somewhat disappointed but grateful tone. She was sad that it was finally time for her oldest son and his wife to go back to heaven. However, Leslie was grateful for the great twenty-one years she had with Ben and the two wonderful years she spent with him and Sophia. As for the current moment, Dave, Leslie, and Josh walked up to Ben and Sophia to hug them. In addition, Leslie, Dave, and Josh switched their attention from Harold and Esther to Ben and Sophia as she stood next to Dave in front of the crowd. Leslie's voice was now full of emotion. Dave was still holding Buster by his leash. "We will dearly miss you two, but we are very grateful to have cherished the time that we had with you two. Ben, my oldest son, it was an absolute privilege to be your mother and friend. We sure had a ton of fun with you all throughout the years, even with the challenges we all faced. I'm so proud of the godly young man you have become. You have been a great husband to Sophia in addition to a fantastic son and role model. Sophia, you are an amazing and godly young woman, and I absolutely loved getting to know you all throughout your and Ben's marriage. Dave and I look forward to seeing you and Ben once again when we go to heaven."

"What she said?" Dave joked, doing his best to manage his emotions that were rising up to the surface. "Really, Ben, I am tremendously proud of the godly young man you have become despite the very tough challenges you faced. You sought God in the midst of those challenges, and He blessed you in many ways. I am also really grateful to have had you as my oldest son and to have been your earthly father. You and I had great and fun father and son times and great family and friend activities with all of us. Plus, you have been an exemplary husband to Sophia. Sophia, I think I can say for all of us here that you have brought such a joy into our lives. I'm extraordinarily happy that you and Ben have had a great and happy marriage that has had God at the center of it. I look forward to seeing you and my son again one day in heaven."

"Absolutely," Josh started before sniffling a few times. Then, he continued to speak. "Ben, my big brother, you have always been there for me in my highs and lows, even when I made fun of you. You are the best older brother any sibling could ask for, and I am so proud to have been your younger brother. You have been such a role model to me throughout the years. God has truly blessed you with an amazing life and with your wife, Sophia. Sophia, as I said earlier to you in private, you have been like an older sister to me. I thank God that He sent me you. You have been such a blessing to me and as my brother's wife. All of us here had a spectacular two and some years with you while you were married to Ben. I will miss you a lot, and I really look forward to seeing you and my brother again in heaven."

"Man..." Ben responded as emotion swelled up inside him. The rest of his and Sophia's friends and families were beginning to form a big circle around them. Ben continued to speak to his family. "You all are such blessings. I'm so fortunate to have had you three as my mom, dad, and brother. You three have put up with me in our good times and bad times. I had so much fun doing everything with you guys, Sophia, her family, and the rest of our friends. I can't wait until all of us are united again in heaven. I love you all so much."

"Awww...you guys," Sophia began as happy tears started to roll down her face. "You all are going to make me cry. I am so happy and grateful that I was a special part of your lives, in addition to the lives of all of our families and friends who are here. These past two and some years have been the best years of my life, especially with our marriage. Also, the two of us have had a blast doing various fun activities with you guys in addition to the rest of our friends and my family. Ben and I will await the time when we all will be together in heaven with Jesus."

"We all are very appreciative of the time that God has graced us with you and Ben and everyone else in this great group of friends and families," Sam O'Donnell said to Sophia as he, Candace, and Alicia walked up towards her, Ben, Buster, and the Lawson family. Sam sniffled four times before he called in a big group hug with everyone in the huge group of friends and families. Even the dog nestled his head against Sophia's right lower leg. Harold and Esther also joined in on the group hug and delivered very meaningful speeches to Ben and Sophia. The elderly couple also gave individual hugs to Ben and his wife.

Sam, Candace, and Alicia proceeded to give heartfelt speeches to Ben and Sophia after the big group hug. The three of them also gave individual hugs to the young married couple. Then, all of Sophia and her husband's friends walked up to the two of them and delivered more heartfelt and deeply meaningful speeches in addition to individual hugs. The first friend to deliver his heartfelt and expressively meaningful speech and individual hugs to Ben and Sophia was Diego Sanchez. Lucy Robinson followed suit after Diego. Then, Brandon Heraldez came up to Ben and his wife to give his very meaningful and expressive speeches to them, in addition to hugging the two of them.

The order of all of the following friends who did these things goes like this: Hannah Rine, Anthony Markus, Tess Debor, and Carl Wendleson. Even Vanessa Lopez, Diego's girlfriend, walked up and expressed her meaningful appreciation of the friendships between herself, Ben, and Sophia. Vanessa had decided to come to Crystal Park with Diego and the rest of the large group. In addition, she had been friends with Sophia and her husband during the entirety of their marriage. Then, after everyone spoke and gave hugs to Ben and Sophia, the young married couple talked to their families about which of their possessions would go to each family member. It was 1:40 p.m. by the time all of these things were said and done.

"You know what, everyone," Diego said to the group, "let's give Ben and Sophia one last time to dance with each other inside this wooden building."

"That sounds like a fitting way to end their time here on Earth before all of the craziness starts in about ten minutes," Josh responded in agreement.

"Absolutely," Alicia agreed before starting a chant. "Dance, dance, dance."

"Dance, dance, dance." Josh continued the chant as he moved toward his girlfriend, Alicia.

The rest of Ben and Sophia's friends and families joined in on the chant, egging the young married couple on to dance in the wooden building. Sophia and her husband quietly and humorously laughed with their heads tilted down a little bit for a second before walking into the wooden building and indulging the crowd with the dance. The young married couple did think that this was a fitting way to end their time on Earth with each other and their friends and families. So, the two of them entered the wooden building while holding hands, left the door open, and stopped ten feet into the building. They began to do a slow dance, and their families and friends erupted in joyful cheer and resounding claps of hands as they watched the two of them dance. Ben and Sophia quietly laughed again in the same manner as they had before while dancing close to each other. Sophia's head gently and lovingly rested on the right side of Ben's neck as they swayed away.

It was as if time stood still from 1:41 to 1:49 p.m. for Ben and Sophia Lawson. Each precious minute seemed to go on forever. As the young married couple danced, the two of them began to have flashbacks of their marriage. The first flashback took Sophia and her husband back to the dances that they shared together during their wedding reception in the exact same building that they were dancing in now. Every detail of those fun and wonderful wedding reception dances slowly ran through Ben and Sophia's minds. There was even a similar slow dance that came into the young married couple's minds with Sophia's head nestled against the right side of Ben's neck.

The second flashback of Ben and Sophia's marriage came just after 1:42 p.m. This flashback was of the two of them signing the lease of their apartment in Evart for two and a half years. The memory also came with everything that the two of them did during the first day of their marriage. It took Sophia and her husband back to them going to Holy Communion Church that day and having Diego there with them. The lunch with Diego also flashed through Ben and his wife's minds. Finally, the time when the Southern Chilean native gave Ben and Sophia the electric blue Ford truck passed by on memory lane.

The other amazing flashbacks of Sophia and her husband's two-year marriage included all of the fun times that they shared together and the activities that they participated in with their friends and families. In addition, the young married couple was taken back to their wonderful times at Nelly's Breakfast Diner and Mission Beach in San Diego. The two of them also had flashbacks to their visit to the Sea Trench Aquarium in San Diego and The Sea Anemone Aquarium in Atlantic City, New Jersey. They were also taken on a flashback trip down memory lane of going to Mountain-High Amusement Park, especially when Ben won the stuffed dolphin for Sophia. The two of them also remembered the ride on the Ferris wheel and their conversation there. The young married couple was also taken back to their fantastic visits to the San Diego Zoo and SeaWorld. Finally, Ben and Sophia had flashbacks of their wonderful and amazing wedding, marriage anniversaries, Valentine's Days, and birthday celebrations. In addition, the times that the two of them watched *Smallville*, *Star Wars* movies, and *The Count of Monte Cristo* together flashed through their minds.

"You know that we won't be married in heaven, right?" Ben asked his wife in a quieter, more private voice between the two of them. They were still doing their slow dance.

"Yes, I know," Sophia responded in a similar voice near Ben's right ear while still lovingly resting her head next to the right side of his neck. "I'm totally good with that. We, along with the other Christians in heaven, will be and are the bride and wife of Christ, which is the church. It will be absolutely amazing. Plus, you and I will still know and interact with each other in addition to remembering all of what we did in our marriage on this Earth. What do you think about collectively being the bride and wife of Christ?"

"I agree," Ben wholeheartedly and genuinely said. "It will be absolutely amazing to be the collective bride and wife of Christ and to be in His presence forever, in addition to remembering our marriage and being with each other in heaven."

"Amen," Sophia enthusiastically agreed in that quieter and more private voice.

"Amen," Ben responded in agreement as the time came to 1:49 p.m.

The next five minutes, starting at 1:50 p.m., would be the most intense five minutes of everyone's lives since Ben and Sophia got shot on January 11th, 2003. The young married couple's friends and families and Harold and Esther didn't even see Rajim Nemas approaching them. They were too enraptured with watching the young married couple dance with each other for the last time on Earth. He also blended in well with a growing crowd of people who had come to Crystal Park almost a half hour ago. Rajim was a fit, six-foot-five-inch, forty-year-old Middle Eastern/American man. In addition, Rajim had semi-disheveled mid-neck length dark brown hair, a somewhat messy three-quarter-inch length beard of the same color, and brown eyes. Anger was written all over his face and in his eyes. He was wearing a red and black patterned short-sleeved shirt, black jeans, and black shoes. Rajim was concealing a black pistol underneath the back of his jeans.

Rajim shoved his way past Diego, Vanessa, Dave, and Sam and walked a few feet inside the wooden building. Nobody among Ben and Sophia's friends and families, including Harold and Esther, dared to attempt to stop Rajim because of the words Harold said. They all knew Rajim's name, but they didn't know why he was doing what he was doing. The large group just gasped as the Middle Eastern/American man forced his way into the wooden building. Buster was barking at Rajim, but he didn't care. Ben and Sophia stopped dancing once they saw Rajim. He had already taken out his pistol and aimed it at the young married couple, but he wanted to say some things first. Ben beat him to the punch by speaking first.

"I take it that you are Rajim Nemas," Ben calmly said as he looked face-to-face with Rajim. The twenty-one-year-old wanted to catch the Middle Eastern/American man off guard.

"How did..." Rajim began in a loud and frustrated voice before recognizing what Ben was doing. "I see what you are doing. It's not going to work. It doesn't matter how you know my name. You are Ben Lawson, correct? Answer me, or one or more of these people behind me die. I will instantly know if any one of them moves to try to stop me. If you do manage to escape, my uncle, Demar Reevas, and some other men I recruited will track you down and kill you. They are expert hiders and trackers. Some of them are hiding out in this very park, completely out of sight."

Josh had stirrings in his heart and spirit for a second after his brother spoke those words. The sixteen-year-old began to think that he was the only person who would be able to stop Rajim. Josh, who was standing on the left side of the large group of friends and families, looked at Harold, who was right next to him. The teen silently mouthed and asked Harold, "Is it me?" while pointing with his right index finger to himself. The prophet only gave a thumbs-up to Josh with his left hand. This was a signal that Josh, indeed, was the only person who would be able to stop Rajim and prevent Ben and Sophia from dying again. Josh gave himself a few seconds to pump himself up and prepare himself for what he was about to do.

"All right," Ben had responded in a scared and precautious tone while all of those things had happened to Josh. A lot of Ben and Sophia's friends and families screamed in fear as Rajim looked at the whole crowd out of the corner of his left eye. "I am Ben Lawson. Don't shoot my and my wife's friends and families."

"Oh, I see," Rajim had said with a grin on his face after he had heard that Sophia was Ben's wife. "I thought that she might be your girlfriend or wife because of the way you two were holding each other. Now I know. I used to have a wife...and a son. You ruined my family, though. I know that you used to work at American Burgers. I know this because your coworker, Daniel, told my twelve-year-old son about this God that you told Daniel about. My son, Haram, took to heart the teachings that Daniel taught him, and my son told them to his mother. Both my wife and son became Christians. We three were raised in the Muslim religion, so you and your wife can imagine what kind of pain my and my wife and son's conversion caused me. I forced my wife, Bera, and my son to tell me how they learned about this God and Christianity. I refused to convert to Christianity. So, after all of this was said and done, Bera took Haram and left Evart. Now, I am here to kill you and your wife because of the tremendous amount of pain that you caused me, Ben Lawson."

It was 1:54 p.m. when Rajim was done telling Ben his sad story. Josh had decided thirty seconds ago to quietly take three out of the six steps that it would take to reach Rajim. The teen knew that the Middle Eastern/American man would be distracted while talking about his wife and son. However, as soon as Josh was cautiously preparing to take the fourth step, which was when Rajim was done talking, the forty-year-old became keenly aware of the teen. Rajim tried to whip his gun around fast enough to shoot Josh, but it was too late. As soon as Josh saw Rajim's gun hand, the sixteen-year-old quickly sprang his right hand upward with a lot of force, grabbing Rajim's hand and gun. The forty-year-old fired aimlessly up into the air at an angle because of Josh's move. Rajim tried to regain control of his pistol, but the teen twisted his wrist, and the gun dropped onto the floor of the wooden building. Ben walked a few steps forward, stooped down, and took the gun. This move by the twenty-one-year-old caused Rajim to be momentarily distracted again. Josh took the opportunity and slammed the Middle Eastern/American man down onto the hard wooden floor with the force of all of his weight. Once Rajim hit the floor with a loud thud, he was knocked out. Ben placed the pistol on the wooden floor, just beside Rajim's unconscious body.

The time was now 1:55 p.m. in the afternoon after the brief fight ended. Ben, Sophia, and their friends and family heard sirens in the distance. Somebody else in Crystal Park must have heard the gunshot and called the police. Sophia and her husband only had five more minutes before they went back to heaven. The two of them knew that Rajim's uncle and men would not be phased by any of this. The group of men would secretly go to a different place and regroup for another chance to take out Ben and Sophia. As for now, the young married couple and their families and friends were starting to recompose themselves. Buster was still barking, but not as much.

"As scary as these turn of events have been," Dave Lawson began. "Ben and Sophia should continue to enjoy each other's company while dancing."

"Agreed," Diego said in a slightly shaken voice.

The rest of Ben and Sophia's friends and families agreed with Dave as well. They knew that the police would be here in four or five minutes, judging by the faint sound of the police sirens. That would be too late because Ben and Sophia would have already gone back to heaven by then. It was now 1:56 p.m.

"Yes," Ben agreed before switching his attention to Sophia. "I'm sorry that we had to experience that. Do you want to continue on what we left on?"

"Yes," Sophia answered without much hesitation. "We shouldn't let this ruin our last minutes on Earth."

"Absolutely," Ben responded before shifting his attention to Josh, who was still a few feet in front of him. The twenty-one-year-old walked up to his brother and continued to speak. "Bro, I want to express my deep gratitude and appreciation of what you did to save me and Sophia. That was very brave, and I know that you will find out what you are supposed to do next in your life really soon."

"You're very welcome, Bro," Josh responded before he and his brother hugged each other. "Thanks as well."

"You're welcome," Ben replied as he and Josh let go of each other.

"Definitely," Sophia said with profound gratitude in her voice as she came up to Josh. The two of them also hugged each other before Sophia continued to speak. "Thank you for saving us. You were so brave."

"You're welcome, Sophia," Josh kindly said as he and Sophia let go of each other. "You and Ben only have two minutes left. You two should cherish those minutes while dancing with each other."

"All right," Sophia responded before she and Ben addressed Josh and their friends and families one last time. "Ben and I just want to say this one last thing. God will always be with you all."

"Yes," Ben agreed while addressing the crowd as well. "He will always be with you all in the good times and the bad times."

"Amen," Ben and Sophia's friends and families said in chorus before the young married couple resumed their slow dance. Once again, everyone in the crowd was watching the two of them, savoring every last second of it all. Sophia and her husband only had several seconds over a minute left before they went back to heaven. Their bodies touched each other while they swayed away. The two of them passionately kissed each other for nearly twenty seconds before just enjoying each other's company while they danced and lovingly held each other in their arms. Then, when only twenty seconds were left before it was 2:00 p.m., Ben and Sophia stopped dancing and waved goodbye to their friends and families. The crowd waved, with several people in the crowd starting to tear up. Ten seconds remained, and Ben wanted to ask Sophia a question.

"So, are you ready, my love?" Ben lovingly and genuinely asked while staring into his wife's hazel-green eyes for one last time on Earth.

"Yes, my love," Sophia responded lovingly and genuinely. She and her husband shared one final kiss before the young married couple disappeared in an instant. The only things that remained of Ben and his wife in that wooden building at Crystal Park were their wedding rings, clothes, shoes, socks, and flip phones, in addition to Ben's prosthetic legs.

"You look great in the way you glow," Sophia complimented on the way that Ben glowed once the two of them got to heaven. They were standing in and on that same cloud-like atmosphere that each of them experienced when they first went to heaven. Sophia and Ben had let go of each other when the two of them had arrived. They knew that the two of them were not married anymore. The marriage law had passed away once Ben and Sophia got to heaven. Now, the two of them were staring at the pearly gate that was about twenty feet away. They also saw one of the angels who was guarding the open pearly gate. Ben and Sophia were dressed in long white shirts and pants. The two of them were barefoot, but they knew that their feet, in addition to the rest of their bodies, would never wear out or get bruised. Sophia began to speak again. "It is absolutely amazing here. I remember the first time that I was here."

"Same, it feels really great to be back here," Ben responded while looking at Sophia. "You look extremely beautiful with your glow."

"Thank you," Sophia said with appreciation in her voice before she finally noticed Ben's legs and feet under his long white pants. "Hey, you have your legs back. They look fantastic."

"You're welcome," Ben kindly responded. "Thank you as well."

"You're welcome," Sophia said in a similar tone.

Jesus walked up to the pearly gate and had the angel step to the right of the open gate. The Son of God continued to walk towards Sophia and Ben. The young redhead and the young black-haired man instantly recognized Jesus and quickly ran to Him. Jesus's straight, wavy, and somewhat curly shoulder-length brown hair and facial hair looked as great as ever.

"Well done, good and faithful servants," Jesus said to Ben and Sophia once the three of them got to each other. Then, Jesus hugged the two people. Sophia and Ben completely fell into the arms of Jesus and hugged Him back. The angel was watching all of this and was delighted by all of it. Jesus, Ben, and Sophia were so happy to see each other in heaven again. The Son of God let go of the two young people and began to speak again. "It is really great to see you two again. I take it that you two had a fun time while being married on Earth, in addition to telling My messages to everyone you two met."

"Definitely," Sophia responded as she, Jesus, and Ben turned around and began walking toward the pearly gate. Sophia was on the left, Jesus was in the middle, and Ben was on the right. The Son of God had both of His arms draped over Ben and Sophia's shoulders as the three of them walked together. "Ben and I had a great time with being married on Earth and telling Your messages to everyone we met."

"For sure," Ben agreed. "It was fantastic to be married to Sophia and to partner with her in telling Your messages of love, provision, protection, and the kingdom of God to everyone we met."

"I'm so glad to hear that, Ben and Sophia," Jesus warmly said to the two young people before changing the subject. He was going to have fun talking with Sophia and Ben about the subject that He was going to bring up. "Now, I know that you two were quite fond of a Clark Kent TV show on Earth called *Smallville*. I want to say that the show lasts for ten seasons. Would you two like to watch some of season five after saying hi to the angels and every other believer who is here? That season and the entirety of the series was edited here because of some bad things in them."

"No way!" Ben exclaimed in excitement as he, Jesus, and Sophia were several steps away from the pearly gate and the angel who was guarding it. "Yes, I'm up for all of those things!"

"Absolutely!" Sophia exclaimed in excitement as well. "All of that sounds amazing!"

"All right," Jesus responded as He laughed a bit in joy and appreciation. "It is really good to see and hear you two be excited, Ben and Sophia. Let's start out by saying hi to this amazing angel."

Ben and Sophia said hi to Samuel, the angel who was guarding the pearly gate in front of them. The two young people knew his name because they were given all knowledge in heaven, but they asked him his name anyway. Samuel had the appearance of a Jew, with thinly shaved dark brown hair and a neatly trimmed quarter-inch beard and mustache of the same color. He was six feet and four inches tall and was thirty-three years old. Samuel was really fit as well. He was wearing the same clothes as Ben, Jesus, and Sophia. Jesus, Ben, and Sophia walked onto the streets of gold after saying hi to Samuel. The two young people were simply awestruck at the streets of gold, the twelve-foundations wall, and the other things that were in heaven before they said hi to the rest of the angels and other believers with Jesus by their sides. Thus, Ben and Sophia's heavenly romance continued on for all eternity as a part of

Jesus's bride and wife, which is the whole church, and they knew that the church was all of the believers.

EPILOGUE:

Bittersweet Endings and New Beginnings

Approximately two months had passed in Evart since Ben and Sophia went back to heaven. The Lawsons' dog, Buster, had whimpered in sadness after the two young adults disappeared. Then, the police arrived at the wooden building at Crystal Park a minute after Sophia and Ben disappeared. Dave and Leslie made sure to hide Ben's prosthetic legs, clothes, and other items when the police arrived. Sam and Candace had followed suit by hiding Sophia's stuff. None of the four people had wanted there to be any confusion for the police. So, the Lawson and O'Donnell parents, in addition to the rest of Ben and Sophia's family members and friends, had made up a story about how Rajim Nemas wanted to kill Josh because of the fiasco with Rajim's wife and son and Daniel from American Burgers. All of what the group of friends and families had told the police was true, except for the people that Rajim wanted to kill. They knew that the police wouldn't believe that the Middle Eastern/American man wanted to shoot Ben because Ben was no longer on Earth. Now, on Saturday, July 9th, 2005, the Lawson and O'Donnell families were at Ben and Sophia's apartment, gathering up and distributing their possessions.

All of what Jesus and Harold Trenton had foretold about Rajim Nemas's uncle, Demar Reevas, and the other recruited men had begun to come to pass. Demar and his men attacked and robbed a lot of stores and restaurants five to seven times per month from May 14th to July 9th. These savage men even killed and injured ten to twenty people during that time period. They wanted to find Ben and Sophia and kill them in addition to freeing Rajim Nemas, who was put in a maximum security prison in Evart. Demar and his men wouldn't stop doing the horrific things that they were doing until they had Rajim and shot Ben and Sophia.

Sophia and Ben's friends and family had taken extra precautions to steer clear of the attacks and robberies until more help arrived. That help would have to wait to arrive because Demar and his men shot anyone who dared to stop them. Demar and the rest of the Middle Eastern/American men excelled at concealing their faces and hiding themselves, which made it extremely difficult for anyone to catch them. The violent men were also experts in combat and tracking people. The group of Ben and Sophia's families and friends knew that these attacks and robberies would go on until June 4th, 2006, just like Jesus said. The Lawson and O'Donnel families, in addition to everyone else in the group, were grateful that Ben and Sophia were spared from dying again, but they also deeply missed them.

As for the current moment, on July 9th at 3:00 p.m., Josh Lawson was in the living room area of his older brother and wife's apartment. Josh's girlfriend, Alicia O'Donnell, was right beside him, and the rest of the Lawson and O'Donnell family members were scattered around the apartment, taking all of Ben and Sophia's possessions, according to what the two of them had said that they could have. The two families hadn't wanted to visit the apartment before this day because of the emotion that it would bring up and also because of the attacks and robberies from Demar and his men. Luckily, the violent men hadn't robbed Ben and Sophia's former apartment during the past two months.

Josh and Alicia were just looking around at the apartment that their older siblings once lived in as a married couple. Alicia was wearing a solid pink shirt with light blue jean shorts and white and light blue patterned shoes. Her now shoulder-length light brown hair was in a straight fashion. Alicia's brown eyes were on the brink of spilling tears out of them. Josh had chosen to wear a plain dark green shirt in addition to black shorts and black shoes. His short blonde hair was neatly styled, and his greenish-blue eyes were not focusing on a single item for more than fifteen seconds. Josh emotionally sighed as he looked at the purple love seat. The teen couple remained in the living room area for ten more minutes.

Josh and Alicia slowly walked together into the bedroom while holding hands. They were mentally and emotionally preparing themselves for the framed pictures that they would see of Ben and Sophia. Going into the bedroom for Josh and Alicia felt strange and weird. The teen couple finally walked into Ben and Sophia's former bedroom and found their parents. Dave, Leslie, Sam, and Candace were gathered around the shelf that held the framed pictures of their firstborn children. Dave was also holding a leash that had Buster at the end of it. Alicia and Josh could feel the great emotion that their parents were feeling. The two teens said hi to and petted Buster for almost half a minute as the dog stood on his four legs beside Dave. Then, Josh and Alicia walked to the back of their parents and said that they would like to see the framed pictures of Ben and Sophia. Leslie and Candace were in between Dave and Sam. So, the two older women walked over to the other sides of their husbands with tears falling down their faces. Dave and Sam were sniffling a bit as they looked at the pictures of Sophia and Ben.

Alicia and her boyfriend walked in between Dave and Sam. Then, Alicia began to cry as she saw the framed picture of Ben and Sophia, which was of the two of them at Mission Beach. Nothing could have really prepared her for what she was seeing. Josh sniffled as he also looked at that picture. He also reached out his left arm and lovingly held his girlfriend's shoulders to comfort her. Alicia greatly appreciated and totally accepted the gesture and laid her head in the crevice between her boyfriend's neck and left shoulder. Josh warmly accepted his girlfriend's gesture. He could both feel Alicia's love for him and the sadness she had in her heart about Sophia being gone along with Ben.

Several thoughts raced through Josh's mind as he and Alicia looked at all of the colorfully framed pictures of their older siblings: *If it weren't for Demar and his men, my brother and Sophia would still be with me, Alicia, and the rest of our friends and families. Surely, God would have let him and his wife experience more of their marriage together. God knows that those two could handle and get through any hardship together.* Then, Josh felt a stirring in his heart and mind, just like the ones that he had before he stopped Rajim Nemas from killing Ben and Sophia. This stirring was about the next thing he was going to do with his life. The teen was absolutely certain of the stirring that he was having. Josh decided that was going to join the army after he helped defeat the vile Demar and his band of violent men.

TO BE CONTINUED...

ABOUT THE AUTHOR

Jeffrey T. Bristol is a twenty-nine-year-old strong Christian. He believes in and credits God for giving him the idea to write this novel through the Holy Spirit. Jeffrey is also currently working hard on getting walking again after having two brain hemorrhages at the very early ages of two and a half and three and a half. He is very close to being able to walk again. Jeffrey is a tenacious, kind, compassionate, funny, hard-working, and godly young man who doesn't let his current disability define him and take away the enjoyable things in his life. He has traveled to a lot of states and has done several fun activities with his friends and family, which include snorkeling in Maui. The author currently lives in Tucson, Arizona.

Milton Keynes UK
Ingram Content Group UK Ltd.
UKHW050857081024
449372UK00010B/115

Cambridge University Press
www.cambridge.org/elt

Cambridge Assessment English
www.cambridgeenglish.org

Information on this title: www.cambridge.org/9781108565325

First published 2019

20 19 18 17 16 15 14 13 12 11 10 9 8 7 6 5 4 3 2 1

Printed in the United Kingdom by Latimer Trend

A catalogue record for this publication is available from the British Library

ISBN 978-1-108-56532-5 Student's Book without answers with Online Practice